THE SOCIETY

#StalkerProblems

IVY SMOAK

ISBN: 978-1-942381-51-8

2021 First Edition

To anyone who dares to join the Society.
You're invited...

Chapter 1
MY STALKER
Tuesday

I stared at the different smoothie flavors. The strawberry banana was calling to me. But I'd promised myself I'd try a new flavor every time I came here. I was kind of celebrating though. I'd officially signed my divorce papers this morning. Goodbye, Joe Dickson. And good riddance. I thought I might get emotional today, but I was feeling pretty freaking fantastic. Strawberry banana kind of fantastic. *Maybe…*

"Next," the barista called.

Oh no. I hadn't made a choice yet. I hated when this happened. Indecision was the worst when there was a line. And I'd rather drink anything than make someone else feel annoyed waiting.

"Any day now, sweetie," the barista said and put his hand on his hip.

I hated when he sassed me. So I blurted out the first flavor my eyes made contact with. "Could I please have A Date with Buckwheat Hemp?" *Ew, what?* The name was kind of cute, but the actual smoothie sounded freaking terrible. I didn't want buckwheat or hemp anywhere near my mouth. And the date part of the name made me shiver. I hated the taste of dates. And I hated all actual dates. I'd stopped going on them after…*the incident.*

The barista laughed. I wasn't sure if it was because of the name of the smoothie or the look of horror on my face.

It was probably my face. Which was fine. *Be scared of me, barista man.* I preferred my men at a safe distance anyway. That way I couldn't accidentally set them on fire. *Damn it!* I promised myself I'd never think of *the incident* ever again. But it just kept popping up. And now that I was thinking about it, I couldn't stop. It was like it was happening all over again. My heart started racing as I pictured Matthew Caldwell's dick catching fire. Because I'd set it on fire by accidentally knocking a candle into a saucer of oil and flinging it at his junk. The shriek of horror out of his perfectly kissable mouth haunted my dreams. It was the worst thing that had ever happened to me…and I hadn't even been the one in flames. God, if I ever saw Matthew Caldwell again, I'd just die.

"That'll be $9.25," said the barista.

I tried to shake the image of Matthew Caldwell out of my head. "$9.25?" The strawberry banana one was only $7.

He shook his head and pointed to the sign behind him.

All the sass. Why did something so gross cost so much? I pulled out my card and swiped it through the reader, trying not to wince. *Please let me have $9.25 left in my account.* My card cleared and I breathed a sigh of relief. Being unemployed really sucked. My now-official-ex-husband taking all our assets in the divorce sucked even more. And if I didn't figure out something soon, I'd end up like the homeless guy in my apartment. I mean, he didn't live in my apartment. If he did he wouldn't be homeless. But he broke in all the time and liked to lick my freshly delivered pizzas. Homeless Rutherford and I were not on good terms.

I stepped to the side as I waited for my smoothie to be made. I'd had an interview today for my dream job. And I thought it went pretty well. But I'd had to pee the whole time and was too nervous to ask where the restroom was, so I'd almost peed my pants. They probably thought there was something seriously wrong with me as I'd sprinted out of the room. Why had my bladder failed me at the worst time? *Almost.* Almost failed me. I hadn't actually peed my pants.

The barista was still looking at me weirdly as he placed my smoothie down on the counter. *Jokes on you, buddy. I'm not interested in dating you.* Besides, I was almost positive he was gay.

"Smoothie for Ass."

"It's Ash! Not Ass. How many times are we going to have this discussion?"

He just shrugged.

I grabbed my smoothie. There was only one man I was actually interested in anyway. And I was about to go stalk him. Er…view him from a safe distance where I couldn't accidentally set him on fire. If anything, *he* was stalking *me.* But I kind of loved having a stalker. The way he stared at me…

My phone started buzzing in my purse.

I jumped, causing some of my smoothie to splash out onto my pants. *Gross. Does hemp buckwheat stain?*

I fumbled with my phone as I pulled it out. I didn't recognize the number. What kind of psychopath calls someone's phone? Had they not heard of texting? Or email? I debated not answering because they were basic, but it was ringing and everyone in the smoothie shop was staring at me. "Hello," I whispered, trying not to disturb anyone.

"Hi, it sounds like you're breaking up. Is this a bad time?"

Yes this is a bad time! There's millions of people staring at me! "Who is this?" Apparently I'd forgotten how to have a normal conversation. Not that I'd ever known how. I tried to huddle in the corner of the shop so everyone would leave me alone.

There was laughter on the other end. "It's Bee. From…"

"Bee Inspired Media Group." I held my breath. She was the woman I'd interviewed with earlier today. The same interview that I'd sprinted out of because of my bladder. My dream job.

"That's the one," she said. "We loved your ideas. We really think you'd be a perfect addition to the team. If you could start next Wednesday…"

"Yes!" I screamed into the phone and somehow managed to spill some of my smoothie onto my shirt now too. Now everyone really was staring at me.

"That's wonderful," Bee said. "We're so excited to have you. I'll see you at 9 am next Wednesday morning."

"It's a date." *Oh my fucking God, what did I just say?!* Did I just ask my married new female boss out on a date? *Why? Really…why?*

Bee laughed. "See you Wednesday, Ash."

I squealed when she hung up. At least, I hoped she'd hung up. Because I really didn't want to break my new boss' eardrum. "I got a new job!" I yelled to the sassy barista.

"Cool," he said.

How was he not excited for me? Oh, he didn't know why else I was so happy. "And I'm officially divorced!" This was the best day of my life!

"Shocker."

Rude. I needed to start going to a different smoothie place. If only there was another one so close to my stalker's residence and my spin class… But alas, there wasn't. So I was stuck with this rude boy.

"We're closing," the barista said. "So you need to leave."

Shit. I looked down at my phone. It was almost 8 o'clock. I was going to be late! I ran out of the smoothie shop and sprinted as fast as I could. My best friend always made fun of me for wearing sneakers…but in this case, they came in handy.

I realized about halfway to my stalker's apartment building that I had smoothie stains all over my shirt and pants. I started blotting at them as I ran, somehow spilling more of the pungent smoothie everywhere. Did buckwheat have some kind of weird magical attraction to clothing?

I skidded to a stop in the middle of the sidewalk when I saw someone come out of my stalker's building. He lived in One57. It was the most prestigious apartment building in the city. I couldn't even fathom what someone did for a living to afford a place in there. But I didn't have time to daydream about his profession today. Because it wasn't my stalker that had just walked out onto the sidewalk.

No.

No, no, no.

Matthew. Freaking. Caldwell. The man whose penis I'd set on fire.

I couldn't face him. I'd seen him once after the flaming pants incident and I'd jumped into a lake to avoid him. It hadn't worked. I'd wished I'd drowned.

I ducked into an alleyway before he could spot me. There was an open dumpster calling to me. It was overflowing with bags of trash. It would be the perfect place to hide. But I was deathly afraid of germs. It was like at the top of my list of greatest fears. Right under being late. This was what I got for being late for my stalker's stalking. *God. What do I do?*

I started fanning myself because I was breaking out in a sweat. There wasn't really a choice here. *Screw my life.* The dumpster was the only option. I was just about to fling myself into it when I thought I should probably at least check to see if Matt was coming this way.

I peered around the corner toward One57. And...Matt was nowhere to be seen. I breathed a huge sigh of relief. He must have been going the opposite direction. Or maybe I'd just imagined him. I often dreamt of running into him again and having to hurl myself into oncoming traffic. *Phew.* Today really was my lucky day!

I debated emerging from my hiding spot. On Tuesdays and Thursdays at exactly 8 o'clock, I always sat on the bench across the street from One57. For my stalker's optimal viewing pleasure. But today I had stains all over myself. And I was sure my face was flushed from running and almost having to dumpster dive. So it was probably better to keep hiding. This was why I always brought binoculars with me. Just in case.

They weren't creepy stalker binoculars. Because I wasn't a stalker. He was. These were like fancy opera watching binoculars. Or ones you'd use to watch the Kentucky Derby. I wasn't doing anything weird. I pulled them out just in time.

My stalker emerged from One57. God, he was so handsome.

I audibly sighed. The only reason I put up with his stalkery tendencies was because he was gorgeous. His expensive tailored suit stretched perfectly across his broad shoulders. His jaw looked like it had been chiseled by a sculptor. What I would do to lick it...

And his smile. *God.* He smiled down at his driver, a little man in a butler's uniform that always seemed to be bowing and scurrying about. Honestly it was hard not to laugh at his driver in his little costume. But my stalker didn't laugh at him. I liked that he treated his employees like the humans they were. He was kind and warm and compassionate. I assumed.

But it was his confidence that really made him intriguing. His suits were always colorful. Today the fabric was crimson with black polka dots. The sides of his head were shaved, with the top kept long and pulled into a man bun. *Who the hell is confident enough to dress like that?* God knows I wasn't. And I think that was why I was so attracted to him. Er...I mean, that's why I didn't report him to the cops for being a stalker. Because he dressed, walked, and probably talked with so much confidence.

I had no idea what his name was. Even though I assumed he knew mine. I didn't even know what he did for a living. But if he lived in One57, he was definitely filthy rich. Was he a powerful CEO? No, a CEO wouldn't dress the way he did, or have a man bun. He was unique. Danger oozed off of him. Maybe he was in the mafia. Or maybe he was the owner of a club. It was easy to picture him sitting in the VIP section, a cigar in his mouth and each arm draped around a beautiful model. *Ew, no.* Scratch the models. I amended my vision to include a few bouncers keeping the hordes of club girls away from him. Except me. If I were there, we'd lock eyes, and he'd tell the bouncers to let me approach.

I watched as his eyes darted toward the bench I usually sat on.

He scowled.

Oh my God, he scowled! He was sad that I wasn't there. *He really is stalking me!* I'll be honest, for a few months there, I'd been a little worried I was the stalker.

I adjusted my binoculars. This wasn't all in my head. Sometimes I wondered if I just imagined us making eye contact every Tuesday and Thursday evening. But this proved that I wasn't just daydreaming. My stalker really did stare intently into my eyes twice a week. The only explanation I could think of was that he was stalking me. I didn't condone stalking. But I really liked the way he stared at me. He made me feel...beautiful.

And honestly, this was the only kind of relationship I trusted myself to be in these days. I got to ogle him from a safe distance so that I'd never repeat *the incident.* And he...I don't know what was in it for him. I was pretty sure he was just madly in love with me. *Such a stalker.*

I watched as his driver opened the door of his black Rolls Royce Phantom limousine. My stalker glanced once more toward the empty bench.

God, I could watch him like this all day. I took a sip of my smoothie, forgetting for a moment that I'd ordered one with hemp and buckwheat. I started gagging. Why did I keep trying superfoods? Superfoods were the freaking worst.

When I looked back at my stalker, he was staring at me. Holding my binoculars. With smoothie dribbling down my chin. I'd been caught looking every bit the stalker in this situation.

Kill me now.

Chapter 2

STRANGER DANGER

Tuesday

I swore my stalker laughed at me. But it happened so fast, I couldn't be sure. The next thing I knew he'd climbed into the back seat and his driver had sped off. The limousine drove past me, license plate number B783... Just kidding. I totally didn't have his license plate memorized or anything. Because that would be crazy. And I wasn't crazy. He was. The guy was nuts.

Such a stalker.

I stared at the car disappearing into traffic as I took another sip of my smoothie. I immediately gagged again, somehow forgetting the disgusting flavors from a few seconds ago. *Gross.* Trying new things sucked. I threw the smoothie into the dumpster. The sight of it made me shiver. *Did I really almost jump in there?*

That would have been crazy.

As soon as my stalker's limo was out of sight, I emerged from my hiding spot. That was a close call. Yes, he'd seen me spying on him. But I'd seen him looking for me. I was already in a good mood. But him missing me? That was the icing on the cake. I smiled to myself. I wanted to dance and jump and sing in the middle of the sidewalk. But if I didn't hurry, I'd be late for my spin class.

My ex-husband had royally screwed me in the divorce. The stupid cheating asshole had blackmailed me with a sex tape I'd made for him a few years ago. He had only left me with two things in the divorce: enough money to pay three months' rent in the dingy old apartment we'd gotten when we first moved to New York, and a membership to this stupid spin class right in the center of Manhattan. He'd given it to me two years ago for Christmas. I'd taken it as an insult and never gone. So of course he left it to me as one final jab at my self-confidence.

The joke was on him, though, because I'd been coming here for months, focusing on getting the best damned revenge body in the history of revenge bodies. And I was confident-AF. Most days. I also didn't mind that coming here gave me an excuse to lurk outside One57 at 8 pm on Tuesdays and Thursdays so that my stalker could get me out of his system. Did I say lurk? I meant casually lounge on a bench. Those biweekly encounters were probably the only thing keeping my stalker sane and preventing him from showing up at my house with a knife or something crazy. That was a scary thought.

Hopefully my stalker was of the sweet variety. Although, I bet he was a beast in the bedroom. He had that look about him. *Rawr*. I bet he rawred in the bedroom. I pictured him stalking me like a lion on the prowl. Pouncing on me and tangling us up in the sheets. I couldn't wait to run my fingers through his hair. And feel the scruff on his jaw line. And ask him a million questions about his personal life.

I walked into the locker room. It always felt like I'd accidentally wandered backstage at an Odegaard fashion show. Seriously. Joe had definitely picked out this place specifically to torture me. But I wasn't phased. After all, none of these women had the most gorgeous stalker on earth. I did.

I opened my locker and started to change. I ignored the way my jeans tried to rip off my underwear with them because they were so tight. I pretended I didn't have stretch marks on my ass that grew too fast in college because of the all-you-can-eat buffets. Spoiler alert, I could eat a lot. Because food without hemp was delicious. Luckily for me, a lot of the food went straight to my boobs too.

I snuck a sideways glance at the girl next to me. She had stripped down to her $500 lingerie and was literally measuring her waist. She had a tape measure in one hand as she jotted down the measurements with her other. I shouldn't have looked. But I couldn't help myself. Twenty-two inches. Twenty-two! How was that even possible?

Fine, maybe it bothered me a little to be surrounded by all these supermodels. I pulled my red hair into a messy bun. It wasn't worth comparing myself to these women though. They were stunning, yes. And me? I just had a smattering of freckles across my nose and a face that made me look like I was forever in high school. But my stalker stared at me like I was sexy. Not cute. Hopefully he'd never accidentally stroll into this room. Because I couldn't deal with my stalker stalking anyone else.

Maybe he preferred cute little redheads to wine, dine, and cut up into little pieces. *God, why am I suddenly picturing my stalker as a serial killer?* I needed to stop with my overactive imagination. He just likes to wine and dine and have magnificent sex with redheads. No murder necessary. But what man really preferred redheads?

I was pretty sure the answer was none. Because gingers are weird and people think we don't have souls. For the record, we do. But I did understand why guys preferred blondes with tanned skin. All the ones I knew were always smiling. It truly seemed like they did have more fun. And there was no doubt about the existence of their souls.

"Hey girl," said someone behind me. A normal person would have turned around and said hi. But I wasn't normal. The thought of a stranger talking to me made my heart rate double. Small talk felt like being waterboarded, and it was only amplified by the fact that small talk at this spin class was mostly about how Yvonne had taken three whole weeks to get back into Instagram shape after having her baby. What a lazy slut, huh?

Please don't be talking to me. Please don't be talking to me, I thought as I buried my head in my locker. I tried to look busy by moving my bag around.

"Ash," said the person.

Not necessarily me. There could be plenty of Ashleys here.

And then they tapped on my shoulder.

Screw my life. I didn't want to talk about Yvonne's weight loss when technically I'd been gaining weight over the past few months instead of losing it. I didn't know how that was happening. I was pretty sure it was because I was gaining muscle. And maybe a little because I refused to stop eating ice cream. What kind of monster gives up ice cream? Although, talking to one of the members of my spin class might be helpful. Because I was really wondering if I should be eating protein before or after my workout. I'd been getting these protein smoothies before coming here and now I was just worried that was exactly what I shouldn't be doing. Hmm…

"Ash!"

Oh God, I can't stall anymore. I slowly turned to see which of the supermodels deigned to speak to me. But it wasn't one of them. It was my best friend, Chastity.

"What are you doing here?" I asked. I didn't wait for her to respond before I threw my arms around her. I was just so relieved I didn't have to talk to a stranger today. My best-day-ever streak was continuing.

Chastity laughed. Then she pulled back and gave me a devious smile. "I wanted to come see what drags you all the way out here to midtown twice a week. I have to admit, I'm disappointed so far. I was expecting there to be a pizza and ice-cream buffet. Or at least some hot guys."

Oh God, does she somehow know about my stalker? I kind of liked having this one thing all to myself. Although if he were a serial killer, it would be good to give Chastity a heads up. I bit the inside of my lip. Telling her could wait. He hadn't even done anything dangerous yet. Just those sultry looks. Mmm. "Sorry to disappoint."

"So what am I missing? Is it the instructor? Is he #gorg or..."

That was definitely not it. But if I admitted there were no hot guys here, she'd leave. And I was super happy she was here. I slammed my locker closed. "Come on, class is about to start." I grabbed her arm to pull her through the sea of models.

Chastity shook her head. "Spin classes are so 2010. If you really want a good workout, you should come to my nude yogalates class sometime."

Never.

"But for now, we should go back to my place, get some takeout, and watch whatever show you want. Burgers on me."

That was such a tempting offer. Especially because today had been amazing and I had so much to celebrate. But I needed this. After my separation from Joe, I'd resolved to focus on finding myself. And I wasn't going to find myself at my favorite burger joint. "But you haven't even seen the hot instructor yet." I raised both my eyebrows. He wasn't actually hot. But Chastity didn't need to know that yet. Hopefully once she was in there, she'd just finish the class with me. Although I never really knew what to expect with Chastity. She'd probably flirt her way out of the class somehow.

"I knew it," she hissed. "Look at you, you can't stop smiling. I knew you came down here all the time to ogle some hottie. I'll be your wing girl and try to get his number for you."

I was smiling because I was finally divorced. And I'd confirmed that my stalker was stalking me. And I'd gotten my freaking dream job! Oh, I badly wanted to tell Chastity that I got the job. After all...she'd hooked me up with the interview. We'd been talking about getting to work together ever since graduating from college. It was going to be so much fun. But if I told her right now, she'd definitely pull me out of here and say we needed drinks to celebrate. And I wanted to get my spin on. I'd tell her right after we were done.

"This is perfect," Chastity said. "I keep telling you, you're going to feel so much better after you get laid."

I laughed. She was going to be wildly unimpressed by my spin class instructor. If only she could somehow get the number of the guy I was stalking. I shook my head. *He* was stalking *me*. And I didn't need a wing woman when it came to my stalker. I needed a restraining order. The guy was clearly obsessed with me. In a really good way.

I knew what I needed to do. And it had nothing to do with getting a restraining order. I needed to be my own wing woman. On Thursday at 8 o'clock I'd walk right up to my stalker and introduce myself. I just needed to figure out the particulars. And do some research to see if I could fit a fire extinguisher in my purse just in case I accidentally recreated the events of *the incident. And maybe do some light stalking of my own to make sure he's not a serial killer.*

Chapter 3

UNDER ARREST

Tuesday

One thing I'd learned since Joe and I separated was that I actually liked exercising. Well, maybe not the act of exercising. It felt like slow torture. But I liked the results. I liked that it made me look younger and more toned. Yeah, I wasn't a supermodel like these women. But I felt really good about myself now after years of Joe putting me down. And each time I came to spin class, the workout got easier. I could actually feel the corners of my mouth tick up as I started spinning faster.

I wanted to believe I was doing this completely for me. But my stalker was in the back of my mind all the time. Did he notice my transformation? Did he like it? I tried to shake away the thought, but it was impossible. It was like I was living in a constant daydream. *He stares at me too.*

The instructor yelled profanities at us for motivation and I spun faster.

I didn't care at all that the instructor wasn't a hot dude. But apparently Chastity did. Because we only made it about two minutes into the class before Chastity screamed bloody murder and jumped off her bike.

"I don't know her," I muttered as all my fellow spinners turned to look at us. But as Chastity rolled and flopped around like a soccer player who had just received a fake life-threatening injury, I began to get concerned. More about her mental health than her ankle, but still concerned. *What the hell was she doing?* I got off my bike and knelt by her side while the entire class watched. "You okay?" I asked. I hated everyone's eyes on us. I was never going to live this down. Now I'd have to sell my membership...

Chastity winced and grabbed at her knee. "My ankle," she cried. "I think it's broken." She looked down and grimaced. “Definitely broken.”

"You're holding your knee."

She quickly repositioned her hands. "Can you take me home?"

"Is she okay?" asked the instructor, even though it was pretty clear that Chastity was faking her injury. She knew I hated when people made a scene. Why was she doing this to me? *Oh right…I'd lied to her about the instructor being hot.* Payback was a bitch.

"She'll be fine," I said. Together, the instructor and I pulled Chastity to her feet and helped her back into the locker room. Then we got an Uber back to her apartment. She stayed true to her story that her ankle was broken throughout the ride, but to me she seemed much more concerned with touching up her makeup and texting. I craned my neck to try to see who she was talking to, but she was quick to block my view.

"You're being weird," I said.

"You'd be weird too if you had a broken ankle. This shit hurts." She puckered her lips and stared into her handheld mirror as she checked out her freshly applied lipstick.

We were just going to her apartment. Why was she putting on lipstick? “Then shouldn't we be going to the hospital?”

“What kind of insurance do you think I have? No. I just need some ice. Oh, ice!” She started texting again.

Yeah, she was definitely being weird. “Should we stop and get some?” I asked.

“What?” She finally looked up from her phone.

“Some ice.”

“No, I've got it covered.”

Okay…

She went back to texting.

When our Uber arrived at her building, she requested I help her up. She put her arm around me and hopped on one leg…which was the same leg she had supposedly broken. If the spin class had been too intense for her, she should have just pretended to get an urgent text or something. This ankle thing was way over the top. And I was kind of annoyed that she'd made me miss the rest of my workout. Maybe I could go for a run later. I almost laughed out loud. A run? I was divorced. I hadn't lost my mind. I bit the inside of my lip. Or maybe I loved running and I just didn't know it yet? I'd add it to my list of things to try.

"Here," Chastity said, handing me the key to her apartment as she tossed her long blonde hair over her shoulder and popped her hip like she was posing for an Instagram picture.

"What are you doing?"

"Huh?" She looked down at her pose. "Nothing. Stop being weird."

"I'm not being weird. You're being weird."

She shrugged and held up her phone like she was about to take a picture of me.

Yeah, she was definitely being weird. Which was saying something. Because I had quite a bit of experience in that department. I unlocked the door and turned to help her in. I closed the door behind us and tried to find the lights.

"Someone's been naughty," a deep voice said from somewhere in the dark apartment.

I screamed at the top of my lungs.

Chastity flipped the light switch on.

And standing in the middle of the apartment was a very well-built police officer. He flashed us his badge and then lifted up a pair of handcuffs.

"You're under arrest, Ashley Cooper."

No. I hadn't done anything wrong. I wasn't going down like this!

"Turn around slowly," he said.

Fuck that. I did the first thing I could think of and sprinted toward the fire escape.

"You're going to regret resisting arrest!" the officer yelled behind me.

Shit! Was I breaking the law by running? It was too late now - I was already climbing down the fire escape. How many years in prison would I get for this? And what had I done to get arrested in the first place? I never broke any laws. Going to jail was on my list of greatest fears!

"Ash!" Chastity yelled from behind me.

Sorry, Chastity. It was every woman for herself. And it didn't sound like he was there to arrest her. He'd said my name. I was the one running from the law. I was going to have to change my name. Again. *Damn it!* I'd just changed my last name back to my maiden name earlier today. God, I hated going to the DMV. Not that I could go to the DMV now. I was a wanted woman.

The stairs clanged beneath me as I picked up my pace. I needed to get out of the city. Could I make it to the docks before getting caught?

"Ash, stop!" Chastity yelled again.

I was pretty sure I heard a chorus of people yelling "surprise" too. But I wasn't sure. And I didn't have any time to think about it because I hopped onto the landing wrong and fell off the side of the fire escape. And right into an open dumpster.

I screamed at the top of my lungs as my ass collided with a bag of foul-smelling trash, popping it and making it seep all over me. I'd known I was doomed to end up in a dumpster today as soon as I saw Matthew Caldwell. Fate, you filthy mistress.

"Ash!" Chastity yelled from somewhere not in the dumpster. "What are you doing in there? He's just a stripper!"

Say what? I peered over the side of the dumpster, cringing when my hand made contact with the metal. "What are you talking about? Did he follow me?"

"I hired a stripper for you. To celebrate signing the papers. Happy Divorce Day!"

"That's not a thing!" I knew she'd been faking her injury. I should have suspected that she was luring me to a party I didn't want to attend.

She laughed. "I got you so good."

"You know my rule about strippers!" I wanted to laugh too. Because this wasn't the first time this kind of thing had happened to me. For my bachelorette party, a stripper had shown up yelling about a fire he needed to put out. I'd thought the building was burning down so I fled down the fire escape. I'd legit run barefoot for three blocks before I realized he was a stripper rather than a real fireman. The fact that I saw no flames or smoke tipped me off. I'd made a no stripper rule after that for a reason. And rules were not meant to be broken.

"You're single again, Ash. Which means Single Girl Rules are back in effect! So your no stripper rule is trumped by Single Girl Rule #10: All celebrations of important life events must involve strippers."

"No Single Girl Rules!" The only good thing about being with Joe was that I got out of all Chastity's crazy Single Girl Rules. They were not normal girl code rules. They were fucking nuts. Just like her.

"Come on, let's get you back inside. All the guests are waiting..."

"All the guests?! Chastity, I'm covered in garbage!" I tried not to gag.

"But...there's food and presents..."

I did love food and presents.

"And your whole extended family..."

"What? Chastity, why is my whole family here?" And why would she invite a stripper to a family affair?

"You know Aunt Carol tags along everywhere with your parents."

Aunt Carol was technically my great aunt. And she couldn't be trusted to be left alone, so my parents always brought her to events like this. Well...not like *this*. I had no idea what the hell this was. Divorce Day parties weren't a thing.

"I need a shower and some alone time," I said. "Not a party."

Chastity sighed. "I'll make a deal with you. I'll let you have a shower. But how about we still have a girls' night?"

"A very small girls' night."

"Exactly."

I didn't really believe her. But I wanted out of this dumpster as soon as possible. "Fine. Help me out of here and then get rid of everyone. Including the stripper."

"You're #lame. But fine."

***

I pulled on a pair of Chastity's sweatpants and a tank top she'd let me borrow. I'd scrubbed myself raw until the water turned cold. And I still felt dirty. And not in a good way like my stalker made me feel.

I peered out of the bathroom to see if Chastity had kept her promise. I spotted all my friends through the sea of balloons. And when I say, "all my friends," I mean Chastity and two other girls my age, one that I liked and one that I really didn't but had to pretend to because my other friends maybe kind of liked her. Chastity had kept her word. It was just a very small girls' night.

"Finally," Chastity said. "Come join us.

"Your mom made that zucchini bread you love. And I made one too." She pointed to a raw zucchini on a plate with a dinner roll on each side, resembling a penis.

"That does not classify as zucchini bread," I said. "Chastity, why on earth did you invite a stripper to a party that my parents were attending?"

Chastity laughed. "They didn't care. And Aunt Carol seemed particularly pleased by the fake police officer. She couldn't look away."

"She can barely see." I plopped down on the couch next to Madison, the other friend I actually liked. I didn't bother to say hi to Liz because she was probably already asleep. Really…why did my friends keep inviting her to things? She wasn't even conscious.

I lifted up a slice of pizza. At least there was the promised food. And presents. My eyes landed on the pile of presents next to the couch. "Can I open those?" If I'd known that getting divorced meant I'd be getting a pile of presents, maybe I would have dumped Joe a long time ago. Way before I found out he was cheating on me with an instamodel.

"I thought you'd never ask." Chastity tossed me the first present.

It was a self-help book titled "You Are Not Worthless" from Madison. *Um, I know that.* Why did people assume I was depressed because I got divorced? I was happy. Next up was a definitely re-gifted bread maker. Followed by three sets of wine glasses, two pieces of divorce-themed wall art, and a bunch of stuff from Hallmark. There was a set of lacy black lingerie that I assumed was from Chastity. "Thanks, Chastity."

She shook her head. "That wasn't from me. I got you the stripper."

Right. I turned over the card. It said it was from Aunt Carol. *Ew.* I felt dirty again. Almost as dirty as when my body was in the dumpster.

I quickly lifted up the last present. It was a six-month subscription to Match.com. *Great.* Whoever gave me this must not have realized that I couldn't be trusted around men and fire.

"Perfect," Chastity said and snatched it out of my hand. "Let's get you signed up tonight!"

"What? No way."

"Why not?"

"You know I can't date right now. Not after..." I looked both ways like someone that didn't know about it would overhear. But they all knew... "*The incident.*"

"Would you stop whispering that?" said Chastity. "It's not a big deal. You set some guy's dick on fire one time. That's not a reason to give up dating!"

"It was more than just that. I stripped in the public restroom and he caught me nearly naked drying my shirt under the hand dryer."

"And on your next date you're not going to do either of those things."

"I was also late." The worst of all the things. I poured myself a glass of wine to distract myself. I didn't want to relive that date right now. *Don't think about it. Don't think about it.* I gulped down a huge sip.

"If you go on time to a date you look desperate. Come on guys, help me out here."

Liz snored.

"I think it's great that Ash is taking some time off from the dating scene," Madison said. "She needs time for just us girls right now. We don't need men to be happy."

I laughed. Madison had always thought Joe was an ass, and he always thought that she had a big lesbian crush on me - his words, not mine. The fact that she loved watching the Yankees and talking about the players' hot little butts did not influence his opinion of her. Because she'd never had a boyfriend. And she had a penchant for making penis mutilation jokes. Either way, she was my friend. She had been since before I ever met Joe. And now I needed everything pre-Joe more than ever.

"You're seriously not going to sign up?" Chastity asked.

I shook my head. I didn't need to date right now. I had my stalker. The last thing I needed was for him to get jealous. He was probably crazy, after all.

"Well there goes that plan. I was definitely going to have you sign up for a dating app tonight. But fine. Onto more important matters. Let's discuss the Single Girl Rules instead, because there have been a few modifications since the last time you were single."

"We're 28 years old. We're not following those silly rules anymore." God, the things she'd tried to make me do in college with those damned rules. I'd even almost gotten arrested one time thanks to her.

"Here's your official membership card." She handed me a little credit card that said SINGLE GIRL RULES at the top and then had dozens of rules broken into various sections. First were the 10 commandments:

1. Boys are replaceable. Friends are forever.
2. Girls' night is every Friday. No exceptions.
3. Never let a friend go into a bathroom alone.
4. You can never have too many shoes.
5. Have wine in your purse at all times.

I stopped reading at #5. "Chastity, how many times do I have to tell you that you have to get rid of rule #5? Having a flask of wine in my purse almost got me arrested!"

"I didn't make up the rules."

I laughed. "Of course you did."

"Nope. They're well-known sacred laws of single ladies all over the world. Ask any single girl."

"I'd never heard of them before meeting you," said Madison.

See. But I didn't have time to protest anymore because there was a loud knock on the door. I threw myself onto the ground. "Not more strippers!" I hissed.

Chastity laughed. "If it is strippers…I didn't order them. Must have been Madison."

"I'd never degrade someone like that," Madison said. "Even if it is a man."

I rolled my eyes. Was it really degrading someone if they were getting paid? Wait…that didn't make sense.

"You should answer it," Chastity said. "It's probably for you. It is your Divorce Day party, after all."

Oh God… I got up off the floor and hesitantly peered out the peephole. There were no strippers. Just an empty hallway. *Weird.* I opened the door and looked down the hall just in time to catch the sight of a well-built FedEx man stepping onto the elevator. He hadn't left any packages - just a little black envelope about the size of an iPhone.

"Who was it?" asked Chastity.

"FedEx guy. He left this." I held up the envelope for them to see. It felt more like silk than paper, complete with black lace detailing and gold trim. The back was sealed with a runic symbol pressed into gold wax. "Well this is fancy," I muttered. *Please be cash. Please be cash.* I knew I was starting my new job next week, but I could really use the money before my first paycheck came in.

"Open it!" yelled Chastity.

I broke the seal and pulled out the contents - a single piece of thick white parchment. I read the message out loud:

THE SOCIETY

Congratulations! You have been nominated to become a member of the Society. To join, please fill out this form in its entirety and mail it to PO Box 157.

Below that, there was only one question:

What is your first wish?

The Society? *What the heck is this?*

Chastity gasped. "No. Freaking. Way."

Chapter 4
THE INVITATION
Tuesday

I stared at her. "Um…what?"

She looked like she was in shock. Or maybe she was pretending like she had with her broken ankle. But playing along with that had led to me falling into a dumpster. I wasn't falling for her tricks again.

"Really, what is this?" I held up the invitation.

"I've heard rumors about the Society." Chastity shook her head as she eyed the invite. "I can't believe it's actually real."

She was really milking this. "So what is it? A club of some sort?"

"A sex club," Liz said.

I jumped. I hadn't realized she'd woken up.

"The most exclusive sex club in the city. Or at least, that's what my students say about it."

A sex club? I laughed. *Good one.* But Chastity actually looked genuinely surprised now. Maybe she hadn't sent this invitation. But then…who the hell had? Chastity had invited lots of people to this party tonight apparently. Most of whom I probably didn't know because my only friends were still sitting on the couch. *Which weirdo gave me this invitation?* Whoever it was must have spent hours designing and handcrafting the silky envelope and figuring out how to seal it with wax. Of the people I actually knew, my first guess was Aunt Carol, but she'd already given me lingerie. *Gag.* That left Liz as my top suspect. She was always doing weird artsy shit with her boyfriend when they weren't too busy shopping for antiques or dressing up as furries. And she hadn't given me a present. Although, she never gave me presents.

Not even at my wedding. What kind of monster showed up to a wedding empty-handed? And she'd heard the rumors about the Society too…

"Did you give me this?" I asked her.

Liz shook her head. "No, I didn't bring any gifts."

No surprise there.

"This is a big deal," Chastity said. "It's more exclusive than any other sex club in town."

She seemed to know more than she was letting on. Because I'd never heard of the Society…or any sex club for that matter. I changed my mind. It was definitely from her.

"What are you going to wish for?" she asked.

The invitation wasn't real, so my answer didn't really matter. "I think I'm going to wish for this girls' night to end before more strippers arrive."

"Well that would be a waste of a wish. I only hired the one."

I laughed. Maybe I should wish for my new job to go well. I was really starting to get nervous. Yes, I loved marketing and it was a dream come true to be working for one of the top firms in New York. But I didn't love the idea of having to interact with other humans from 9 to 5 every day. Or having to wear pants. I preferred only dressing up on Tuesdays and Thursdays for my stalker. Why was I even thinking about this? The invitation was clearly a joke. *Right?* But that did remind me… "I got the job. At BIMG."

"Ah!" Chastity screamed. "That's awesome. But back to the Society invitation real quick. You should wish for a new man."

Wow, I thought she'd be a little happier about the fact that I'd be working with her. Madison worked there too. I turned to her. She'd congratulate me for acing the interview.

"Oh!" said Madison. "You should wish that Joe gets his dick torn off in a meat grinder!"

I laughed. "I'm not going to wish for that." I couldn't believe that even Madison was more excited about the invitation than my new job. But now I had no choice but to humor them and play along. "I guess revenge on Joe would be pretty sweet."

"Well of course you're going to get revenge." Chastity pointed to my single girl membership card. "Rule #37: The best way to break up with a guy is to fuck his best friend."

"But that would violate Rule #21: No kissing uggos." Yes, I knew the rules by heart. And I was pretty sure this was the first time one of them had actually come in handy.

"Let's just beat him up instead," suggested Madison.

"Hmm…" I said. "Maybe we should leave the specifics up to the Society. Or Santa Claus. Or whichever one of you gave me this weird letter." I grabbed a pen and wrote on the parchment, "I wish for revenge on my stupid cheating husband." I probably should have written ex-husband, but whatever. They'd get the point.

As soon as I wrote it down though, I regretted it. There was only one thing I really wanted. *The man at One57. My stalker.* But I couldn't say that out loud. No one would understand. I was worried that as soon as I told someone they'd make me feel weird about it. What we had wasn't orthodox. But it worked for us. And honestly, I'd kind of been living for Tuesday and Thursday nights. I mean…he'd been living for those nights. Since *he* was stalking *me.*

"While you're at it, you should also wish for shoes," said Chastity.

"Okay, shoes too then." I grabbed the paper and added, "And some free shoes, please." Technically it was two wishes. But none of that mattered, since nothing I wrote down would come true. Wishes? Yeah right. If wishes came true I wouldn't accidentally set men on fire on blind dates and I'd be happily married to my stalker. I held up the paper for everyone to see. "There, my wish has been made. Now it's cake time." *And then it's time for me to go home.* I needed to take at least three more showers before I'd feel truly clean again.

We had some cake, and then I left. I debated taking my wish so that I could mail it later. A fake wish for a fake invitation-only sex club wasn't worth the postage when I was drowning in debt. *If only wishes really came true.* I slid the paper with my wishes back into the envelope and left it on the coffee table. And even though I didn't believe in wishes, I wished that my stalker would talk to me on Thursday.

***

PO Box 157. I hadn't thought anything of it when I first read that I was supposed to mail my wish there. But now, as I lay sleeplessly in my bed at 3 in the morning, it was all I could think about.

Was it a coincidence that the letter was supposed to be mailed to PO Box 157 and my stalker happened to live in One57? Maybe. But then factor in that the FedEx man who delivered it had been about the same height and build as my stalker, and it suddenly seemed less like a coincidence. Had my stalker delivered that letter? If only I had gotten a better look at that FedEx man…

Not that any of it mattered. Because I'd left the invitation at Chastity's apartment. It was all a joke anyway. Secret societies didn't exist. Well maybe they did. But not for people like me.

I rolled over and tried to find a colder spot on my pillow. I almost apologized to Joe for being "so wiggly" (as he had frequently called me), but then I snapped back to the reality where Joe had cheated on me with Sierra the Instagram model. Was he sleeping with her right now? *Gross.*

I grabbed my phone off the nightstand and checked Sierra's Instagram. Nothing new since I had last checked. Which had been right before I'd climbed into bed. I had a ritual. Wash my face, brush my teeth, check my Instagram to see what Joe and Sierra were up to, and then go to bed.

Yes, I knew I had a problem. I bit the inside of my lip as I started scrolling through all her pictures again. She looked perfect. According to GQ.com, she was the hottest redhead in New York. Which was total bullshit. Because she didn't even have *real* red hair. It was clearly dyed. Was she trying to be me to steal my husband?

Ha. She wished she could be like me. Then she could be stalked by my stalker instead of spending time with Joe. Joe and Sierra were both total losers. They belonged together.

I didn't check their Instagram accounts before bed because I was sad or jealous or anything crazy like that. I just liked to know what was going on with people who used to be in my life. It was normal. *Oh God, I really am a stalker.* I pushed the thought aside. *Am not.*

I needed something to distract myself, so I forced myself to get up and do something productive. I stared down at my list of new things to try now that I was single. The only things on the list were finding my favorite smoothie flavor and my new addition from this evening – go for a run. I wasn't trying to get mugged, so running was off the table in the middle of the night. Getting blackout drunk wasn't on my list. But it was something I'd never done before. And I'd just gotten some shiny new wine glasses at my party. I wrote it down so I could cross it out later, and then climbed out of bed and filled up one of the glasses with vodka instead of wine. *Cheers to me.*

Fine. Maybe I was a teensy little bit sad. But it was my divorce day. I was happy to have finalized the divorce. Truly. And I was thrilled about my new job. And that my stalker was being extra stalkery.

I just…I really hated Joe and Sierra. So much. I was only a little sad because I'd wanted my marriage to work. Not that I wanted it to work out with Joe. Commitment was a big deal for me. I never expected to make such a terrible choice.

Happy divorce day. I took a big sip of vodka. *And cheers to blacking out for the first time ever.* I loved crossing things off my list.

Chapter 5

A MILLION DOLLARS?!

Wednesday

Ow. I put a fresh ice pack on my head and sat back down on the couch. I hadn't blacked out like I'd planned. I remembered everything about last night. Checking Sierra's Instagram a dozen more times, trying to google my protein predicament to no success, and researching rich people in NYC in an attempt to find my stalker. Spoiler alert – I couldn't find him. I also took two more showers because…dumpster. I hadn't even blacked out a little bit. Which meant I couldn't cross anything off my list.

And apparently now that I was almost 30, I couldn't drink vodka out of a wine glass at 3 in the morning and expect to feel okay when I woke up. *Getting old sucks.*

Now I was nursing the worst hangover in the history of hangovers, while also stressing out about my new job. I adjusted the ice on my forehead. I didn't know how to act at work. Or with coworkers. Or what to talk about at a watercooler, if those were even still a thing. I hadn't had a real job since my freshman year of college when I worked at Sears. Ever since then, I'd put every working hour into saving Joe's family cupcake business. Until he divorced me and took 100% of the business.

Stressing out probably made my headache worse. It was like a never-ending cycle from hell.

I pulled my laptop onto my lap and squinted at the bright screen. I needed a new wardrobe of work-appropriate clothing. Even though I didn't know how to behave at an office, I could at least look good trying. Maybe a nice pair of slacks could be a conversation starter. I wanted to vomit at that thought. Slacks and conversations both sucked balls.

And now I was starting to get sweaty just thinking about socializing.

I was officially spiraling. I slapped the side of my face. *Focus, Ash. Work-appropriate clothing.* I googled it. Yep, I didn't have anything appropriate. It wasn't that all of my clothes were too slutty or anything, they just weren't fancy enough for a major marketing firm. Yoga pants and T-shirts were my thing. I was a workout aficionado now. And yoga pants were also really comfortable for curling up on the couch while nursing a vicious hangover.

My head hurt too much to sift through Amazon and determine what was actually legit and what would arrive at my doorstep three months from now looking like a twelve-year-old Thai girl had sewn arms onto a trash bag and called it a "Women's Fashion Blazer." I'd try again tomorrow. I curled up in a ball with my ice pack and promised myself I'd never drink vodka ever again.

***

I was staring at my screen again the next morning, still trying to determine what would come in time. And honestly…I had no idea. I just needed to make a decision. But decisions were really hard to make sometimes when you didn't have a sounding board.

I eyed my phone. Chastity would love to help me with this. But I also didn't always trust Chastity's fashion advice. She erred on the side of promiscuous. I was pretty sure she was sleeping with someone at BIMG and that was the only reason I'd gotten the job. You know, since I'd almost peed my pants at the interview. I hadn't even been smooth about it.

This was a choice I'd have to make for myself. God, I'd rather die than wear a blazer. But I still hit the "proceed to checkout" button on Amazon. I'd be able to pay all this back as soon as I got my first paycheck. I cringed as my mouse hovered over the "place your order" button. I couldn't procrastinate this huge decision any longer.

Wait. *Wait.* What if I went out to a work function at a fancy restaurant like the one I went to with Matthew Caldwell and the unthinkable happened? I couldn't risk ever causing a second *incident.* And I couldn't afford to lose this job, because I was about to order a bunch of stupid clothes I didn't want. And Amazon was easy to order from, but it was very hard to return things thanks to their insistence on using UPS for returns. I only ever saw FedEx men for some reason. Maybe it was because they wore bright colors. Either way, I wouldn't be able to return anything I got because it seemed too complicated. Which meant I couldn't set any dicks on fire anytime soon.

I quickly searched for mini fire extinguishers. *Oh. My. God. Yes!* They had a portable one about the size of a can of Lysol. It even looked like a spray can. Which was good, because I technically had no idea how to use a fire extinguisher and this looked easy. I'd have to start carrying around a huge purse to accommodate it. But I'd rather have back problems than light another man's junk on fire. *Add to cart.* Having something I actually wanted in my cart made the whole process of actually clicking "place your order" a lot easier.

Phew. I immediately felt the stress of indecision melt off my shoulders. Maybe all the clothes would look terrible. But that was a problem for another day. Besides, as a last resort I could go to a physical store with actual humans in it. I laughed at the thought. *Never.* That's what the internet was for.

My stomach growled. God, how long had I been sitting here? It felt like I hadn't eaten in years. And I definitely deserved some kind of culinary reward after nursing a hangover for two days and online shopping for stupid grown-up clothes. I put on my pants - shut up, you'd shop pantsless too if you lived alone - and walked out of my apartment and down the rickety stairs. The Panera across the street was calling to me.

I checked my mail on the way out. A money mailer, a Viagra advertisement for the old dude who'd lived in my apartments years ago, some circulars, an electric bill... There was a reason why I didn't check my mail more often. None of it was ever exciting. My mom occasionally sent me a greeting card and $10, but that was as good as it got. I was about to close my mailbox when I noticed that I had missed something: a little black envelope, just like the one at the party.

Come on, Liz. Yup, I'd decided that Liz was the mastermind behind the envelope. It fit her MO perfectly. Not only was it weird and artsy, but it was also a clever way for her cheap ass to avoid actually buying me anything. Sending a second envelope was just overdoing it, though. I would have much preferred if she had just like...I dunno, moved to California or something. Now *that* would have been a gift worth getting excited about.

No matter how much Liz sucked, I was still curious to see what weird shit she had come up with now. I assumed it would be a super lame play on my wish, something like a drawing of shoes and an article about how sinners burn in hell.

But what if this wasn't Liz's work after all? What if this had been Madison's gift? In that case, the envelope would probably contain Joe's severed penis. No…it was too flat for that. Joe was small, but not *that* small.

I tore through the golden wax seal and opened the envelope. Just like the first one, it contained a single sheet of parchment. I unfolded it and read:

Welcome to the Society! Your wish has been received and is being processed.

The Society thanks you for your security deposit of $1,000,000. This deposit will be returned in full upon you leaving the Society, as per clause 6 of our terms and conditions.

Your first complimentary spa session will be Thursday, April 6 at 3 p.m. at the Shifting Sands Spa.

That's today. More importantly, what the hell did I just read?

I definitely had not sent them a million dollars. Nor had I even mailed my wish in the first place. *But Chastity probably did.* I rubbed my forehead. I'd left the invitation at her apartment, right? It was hard to remember. I was pretty sure I was still hungover from all that vodka that hadn't *quite* gotten me blackout drunk.

I took out my phone and called her. Twenty minutes later, we slid into a booth together at Panera.

"Of course I mailed in your wish," said Chastity. "You think I'd let you pass up the opportunity to join the Society? I mean…I'm assuming that wasn't a real invitation. But what if it was?!"

"I feel like you know more about the Society than you're telling me."

"Not a ton. I just know it's the most exclusive club in the city. Only the top 1% of 1% get invited. I've heard it costs a million dollars to join."

I rolled my eyes. "Very funny. And do they also give their members free spa sessions?" I pushed the letter across the table so she could read it, even though I was now quite certain that she was the one who had written it in the first place. How else would she have known about the astronomical security deposit?

"Holy shit! They really sent you this? Where did you get the million dollars to pay the entrance fee?"

I just stared at her. "I didn't. I have zero money. You know this."

"Weird. Maybe that's how they get girls to join. Lure them in with the promise of a million-dollar payout at the end… It's actually quite clever."

"Why would such a prestigious club need to *lure* women into joining?"

"Uh..." Her cheeks actually turned rosy. I'd never seen anything that made Chastity blush.

This is bad. Really, really bad. "Spill it."

She waved me off. "It's probably not true. It's better if you go in without any preconceived notions."

"Yeah. I don't want to get my hopes up when this whole thing is clearly just a charade you set up to trick me into getting some sort of erotic massage." I put *massage* in air quotes. Because I was pretty sure she was trying to get me to do something illegal.

Chastity narrowed her eyes. "Wait, you really think I sent these letters?"

"I mean...you kind of gave it away when you knew about the million-dollar buy-in."

"I didn't realize that was for real. It's just what I've heard."

"You swear it wasn't you that made these letters?"

"Cross my heart and hope to die. I think you should just accept that it's real. Haven't you ever seen those Hallmark movies where a girl makes a wish and it comes true? Or the one where the two dudes pee into the fountain and switch bodies? Maybe joining the Society is your pee fountain!"

"First, don't ever use the words 'pee fountain' again." I shivered just thinking about almost peeing in a conference room at BIMG. "Second, those are movies. Wishes don't just magically come true in real life. And broke divorcées don't get invited to secret clubs." This wasn't real. It couldn't be.

Chastity took a loud sip of her chai latte.

"So what do you think?" I asked. "Is Liz behind this?"

Chastity sighed like I was exhausting her and pointed to the logo on the broken wax seal. "I think you just need to accept that it's from a handsome suitor with a magic lamp."

My stalker! I shook my head. In a city of millions, the chances were slim to none. "Or a Nigerian Prince trying to scam me out of a million dollars. And what makes you think that's a magic lamp? It looks more like…" I stared down at the strange symbol.

It could really have been anything. "A bird? An ancient Norse rune? Two people banging?"

"It's definitely a genie lamp," said Chastity.

"I don't know. That feels like a bit of a stretch." I squinted and tilted my head. "Ohhh, if you tilt it, it kind of looks like a dude in a wheelchair with a really big foot."

"So let me get this right. You think that the Society - a super-secret club that grants its members wishes - made their logo be a dude in a wheelchair rather than a genie lamp?"

"You make a convincing argument. I'm still more concerned about who invited me." *And if it was my stalker.*

"There's really only one way to find out," said Chastity.

"Go to the FBI and let them dust these letters for fingerprints?"

"No!" She shoved the letter in front of me. "You have to go to that spa appointment, Ash."

"I'd prefer not to get raped and murdered today, so I think I'll pass on that." Not to mention that the thought of getting naked and being massaged by a stranger was horrifying. I'd never been to a massage parlor before, but it sounded like a place that perverts would like to frequent.

"Fine." Chastity snatched the letter off the table. "If you don't go, then I will."

"And get murdered? No." What would I do without her? She was literally the last person in my life that truly knew me.

"I'm sure the spa is perfectly legit. Here…look at the Yelp reviews."

She handed me her phone and I scrolled through the reviews. There were quite a few five-stars, but also some one-stars.

"Okay," I said. "The general consensus is that the ambiance is lovely, they'll try to up-sell us on bath salts, we won't understand a word they say, and a certain masseur by the name of Hassan will go to town on our asses, whether we want him to or not." *Perverts.*

"Oh, I like the sound of this Hassan." Chastity put her elbows on the table and leaned in. "Does it have a picture of him? And when you say go to town...do you mean massage? Or...?"

"I feel like the Hassan reviews were meant to be more cautionary than enticing."

"So are you going to come, or am I going alone?" asked Chastity. "I'll tell you what. If Hassan is there, I'll sacrifice myself to his wandering hands."

"How noble of you."

We went back and forth for a while longer about the pros and cons of going to the spa. Being the huge pushover that I was, I eventually caved and agreed to go with her. What was I supposed to do when I grew up as the middle child of four siblings? My older sister and brother were much more vocal than me, and Rosalie had been the adorable baby. Which meant no one ever cared what I wanted. It was annoying, yes. But it wasn't all bad. I had always been terrible at making decisions, so it worked out well that I never had to.

In this case, though, maybe I wasn't totally being a pushover. I needed to keep Chastity safe. And fine, maybe a little part of me may have been intrigued by the thought of some stranger grabbing my ass. But not really, because...germs. Who knew where Hassan's hands had been?

Oh God. Am I really going to do this?

I spent the next couple hours showing Chastity pictures of all the clothes I'd ordered on Amazon, which she pretended to like, and then at 2:30 we set out in search of the Shifting Sands Spa. Google Maps said it was only ten minutes from my apartment, but I *hated* being late. If I had to make a list of my greatest fears, being late would be at the top. Or maybe centipedes. Or germs. No, definitely public speaking. Whatever, you get the point. Being late was not an option.

Chapter 6

HANDSY HASSAN

Thursday

It was a good thing we left early, because this spa was not easy to find. As we got closer, all the store signs changed from English to...I don't really know what. Korean? Swahili? Arabic? Probably all three of those with ten others mixed in. Street vendors held up various cooked meats and shouted things at us. I wasn't sure if the yelling or the combination of smells was more disturbing. It reminded me of that time I tried to cook curry without a recipe and nearly burnt my kitchen down. I'd never been to this part of town before. And I was glad Chastity was with me.

Eventually we looked up a street view on our phones and tried to match it to what we were seeing. The door that Google Maps pointed us to was wedged between a Middle Eastern restaurant and some eye doctor's office. The only marking on the door was a small yellow sign with Arabic writing.

"Are you sure you want to go in there?" I asked. I was all into trying new things. But getting murdered wasn't on my list. And I didn't care what the Yelp reviews said. This whole place was sketchy, not just Hassan.

Chastity didn't answer. She just opened the door and walked in.

She owes me big time for this one, I thought as I followed her through the door and up a flight of stairs. I didn't have my fire extinguisher yet, but I did have mace. I rummaged around in my purse. *Got it.* We pushed through a curtain of beads and suddenly it felt like we had been transported to Morocco.

"Welcome to the Shifting Sands Spa," said an attractive middle-aged woman standing behind the counter. At least, I thought that was what she said. As promised in the Yelp reviews, her accent was so thick that it was nearly impossible to understand. And based on the abundance of bath salts displayed on the wall behind her, the bit about upselling us had been true as well.

I just stared at the woman. Talking to strangers wasn't my strong suit. My mom had done too good of a job teaching me about stranger danger. But the woman didn't seem dangerous. I dropped the mace back into my purse.

"Hi," said Chastity. "We're here for our 3 o'clock massages."

The lady said something I didn't understand. I zoned out during the rest of their conversation. Something about the sweet smell of cinnamon in the air was very distracting. And soothing. God, I couldn't remember the last time I'd felt so relaxed. Eventually, Chastity reached into my purse and fished out the black envelope. That got things moving in the right direction, and a second later I had a clipboard in my hands with a release form.

"Fill this out," said Chastity.

"No. Only you," said the woman, pointing at Chastity.

Finally something I can understand. But why only Chastity? I needed a form too. I wanted to tell them all about my Penicillin allergy and my strong aversion to Hassan pounding my ass for 90 minutes.

"Why don't I get one of those?" I asked.

"No idea," said Chastity.

"Follow me," said the woman.

I looked to Chastity for help.

"Go ahead," she said. "I'll be right here the whole time. Well, not *exactly* right here. I'll be in a room with Hassan. Apparently he had a last-minute cancellation!" Her face lit up.

"I wonder why." I would have said more, but the woman grabbed my arm and pulled me through an archway into a tiled hallway. The rooms we passed were all small but well decorated. The thought of having a stranger massage my naked body in one of them made me sweat a moderate amount, which was less than the buckets of sweat I would have expected my armpits to be expelling in such a situation. Who could say why...maybe it was the cinnamon in the air. Or my clinical strength antiperspirant. *Ha, I wish.* I didn't have clinical strength antiperspirant. I'd always wanted it, but it was too expensive, so I'd never taken the plunge.

I forgot all about my sweaty pits when we got to my room, though. Because instead of being one of those tiny murder rooms, it was a massive indoor pool surrounded by brightly colored arches.

Oh God. Are they going to make me get naked in a public bath? That hit all my fears. Germs, public nudity (which was like public speaking only even more mortifying)...there were probably even centipedes crawling around the edges. And there were no clocks, so I could easily end up being late for the next part of my appointment. See? All the fears. Kind of like all the feels, only awful.

The woman started speaking again. I tried my best to listen, but it was still unintelligible. After she left I decided that she had told me to get naked, lie on the massage bed off to the side of the pool, and put a towel over my ass. But who really knew. She could have just as easily told me to definitely not get naked. Which would lead to a rather awkward encounter with the masseuse. Or masseur. *Oh God, what if Hassan sneaks in here and grabs my ass?*

Before I could change my mind, I stripped off my clothes, lay on the massage table, and hid my entire body under the towel. Then I thought twice and folded it down so that it only covered my ass. And then I rethought everything and decided I had lost my mind and needed to get dressed immediately. But I'd waited too long to back out now. The masseuse would be here any minute, so if I stood up and tried to get dressed, they might walk in on me fully nude. I bit the inside of my lip. I just needed to pretend getting a massage was on my list. Then I could cross it off and move on with my life. A life that would not involve any public nudity or bad parts of town.

It was a good thing I stayed put, because a second later the masseuse walked in. She had olive skin and long, thick dark hair. *God, I wish my hair was that thick.* For whatever reason, my crazy red hair was also the thinnest in the world. Even though it reached all the way down my back, when I put it up in a bun it practically disappeared into a marble. Okay, maybe not that small. More like a really big marble. Or half a full-grown gerbil.

"Good afternoon, I'm Amira," she said. Her accent wasn't as extreme as the receptionist's. "I'll be taking care of you this afternoon. If you need anything at all, just ask."

"Hi, I'm Ash." I reached out to shake her hand, but immediately realized that doing so exposed both of my breasts. *Fuck my life.* I pulled back and lay flat on my stomach. "Sorry, didn't mean to be rude. Or show you my boobs. I was just going to shake your hand and then I realized I was flashing you so I stopped." I gave an awkward laugh.

Mercifully, she ignored my awkwardness. "Today we'll be starting with a facial, so I need you to turn over. You can cover yourself with the towel if you'd like."

If I'd like? Do some people that come here just lie here completely naked during a facial? What the hell is wrong with society? Or…*the* Society. Did only people from the Society come here?

Amira turned away while I rolled over, pulling the towel up to my neck for good measure.

"Okay, ready," I said when I was all covered.

"Just lean back and relax." She put fresh cucumbers on my eyes and dribbled some oil on my shoulders. Then she started massaging. At first her touch made me tense, but little by little, the tension melted away... God, I was so sleepy. Vodka hangovers made it hard to sleep. But now I was finally vodka-free. I yawned. I could actually get used to getting massages. They were so relaxing…

Suddenly, I woke up to searing pain right above my vagina. "What the fuck?!" I screamed. My eyes shot open and I tossed the cucumbers on the floor. Amira was still massaging my neck while two other women dressed in masseuse clothes stood by my legs. One of them was holding a strip of cloth covered in little red hairs. I was completely naked, and the pain was them waxing my freaking vagina. The pain was worse than the embarrassment though, and that was saying something. *Ow.*

Amira pressed behind my ears to try to relax me. "It's okay," she said. "That was the most painful part. The rest is not as bad."

I covered my breasts with one hand and my vagina with the other. "Who said you could wax me?" *Oh God, how do I get out of this? Where had my towel gone? It hurts so fucking bad!*

"Part of the Society Special. Just sit back and relax."

That was easier said than done, especially when I was bare-ass naked while two women yanked the hair off my privates with hot wax. *If this was Liz's idea, this is fucking weird.* And totally out of character for her. A massage would have been expensive enough, but a waxing during a facial? That must have been at least like $200. Liz would never splurge for that. Maybe it was...

"Ow!" I yelled again as they pulled off two more strips of hair. I did a quick calculation to decide what would be less awkward. My options were to either lie there completely naked while two strangers waxed my privates or jump off the massage table and run out of the place screaming with some kind of strange half waxed hoo-ha. Somehow, lying there naked was the lesser of those two evils. And anyway, I was already in too deep. They were already half done. I decided to at least use the experience to try to get more info about the mysterious letters. I kept my hands on my breasts, even though any sense of modesty was way out the window. "Do you have a copy of the charges for today? I want to make sure my billing address is correct."

"Sorry, I do not understand," said Amira. Her accent suddenly sounded thicker.

"What can you tell me about the Society?"

Amira just stared at me blankly.

Maybe I'm dreaming, I thought. Yes, that was it. I had to be dreaming. Because no spa would put a customer to sleep and then start waxing their vag without permission. This was all just a bad dream. *That explains everything.*

Yes, it was a weird dream. But whatever. There was probably a perfectly normal explanation for it. Was getting a Hollywood wax subconsciously my deepest desire? If it was, I blamed it on the trophy wives at my spin class. They were always perfectly smooth - not a stray hair to be found in that locker room.

I didn't think that was it, though. It was more likely that the wax was just preparing me for my real deepest desire: my stalker. Any minute now he'd walk through the door and we'd bathe together in the pool. And it would definitely be germ and centipede free. And I'd straddle him under that water and…

"Turn over please," said Amira.

I opened my eyes and looked down. My vag was all smooth. Well, kind of. It looked the way I imagined a chicken would look if it was freshly plucked and very sunburnt. *Thank God the wax is over.*

I flipped over and eagerly awaited the arrival of my stalker in my dreamlike state. Instead, I got hot wax slathered all up in my ass. It surprisingly didn't hurt very much when they tore the strips away.

"All done," said Amira. "See, not so bad." The women all left the room.

Is this when my Stalker appears? Or maybe Hassan. *Oh God. Not Hassan.* My dream was quickly turning into a nightmare. I hopped off the table and pulled on my clothes. I'd had enough. Dream or not, I was getting the hell out of here. I needed to give this place a zero-star review. At least they never got a chance to upsell me on bath salts, because I couldn't afford anything in this place.

Chastity was waiting for me in the reception area.

"How was it?" she asked, her face flushed with excitement. "If yours was half as good as mine..."

"Let's get out of here," I said. *Apparently it wasn't a dream.*

"That bad, huh? Next time you'll have to get Hassan. Hey, what happened to your arm?"

"My arm?"

"Yeah." Chastity pointed at my arm. There was a Band-Aid on the inside of my elbow with a little dot of blood right in the center. It looked like I had gotten a shot. Or given blood.

What the hell did they do to me while I was asleep?

Chapter 7
LITERALLY DYING
Thursday

"Okay, weirdo, let's say they did inject you with something. What are your symptoms?" asked Chastity.

I lay back on my couch and put a pillow over my eyes. I was too young to die. There were still so many smoothie flavors I had to try. "My head hurts. And my teeth. I think I have a cavity."

"Which tooth?"

I pushed my tongue against my front teeth. "My front ones."

"What?" Chastity pulled the pillow away from my face. "How would you even get a cavity in your front teeth?"

"I don't know. Maybe that's a side effect of being injected with embalming fluid."

"They definitely did not do that." Chastity plopped onto the couch next to me as she scrolled through more articles on WebMD. "You'd be dead."

"I wish I was dead. It would be better than suffering through this slow, painful torture. What else would cause head and tooth aches?"

"I don't know. You look it up." She tossed me her phone.

I bobbled it like a hot potato and sent it flying back at her. "I can't."

She just stared at me. "It's pretty simple. You just go to the symptom checker..."

"Oh no, I definitely know how. I'm just not allowed."

"Says who?"

"My mom. Sophomore year I had a mole on my head. I looked it up on WebMD. The next day I had scheduled appointments with a dermatologist, oncologist, gynecologist, and podiatrist."

"Podiatrist?" asked Chastity, sounding more shocked than I'd expected. "Aren't those people that molest children?"

No. That's a pedophile. "I guess if a kid with a foot fetish went to one it could get a little sketchy, but generally, no. Anyway, who knows what would have happened if my mom hadn't stepped in. I think I would have just made them amputate."

"Your head?"

I shrugged. "I was convinced it was the only option." *And it still might need to be done.* My hand wandered up to the little bump on the back of my head. The dermatologist had assured me it was just a normal mole, but I had a feeling she was lying. It was definitely skin cancer. And it had been haunting me for years.

"Alrighty then," said Chastity. "Maybe it's best if we log out of WebMD for a bit and attack this from a different angle. What possible reason could they have had for injecting you with something?"

"To murder me. God, I should have listened to my gut. Creepy letters that keep showing up unexpectedly have *serial killer* written all over them." My stalker was definitely involved in this. I hadn't been in my normal spot on Tuesday, so he must have freaked out and gone full serial killer on me. I knew he was nuts.

"Okay, that's one option. What else?"

"To kidnap me. Redheads are probably a hot commodity in the human slave trade in Casablanca."

Chastity shook her head. "Unlikely. Highly unlikely. With over 14 million Berbers in Morocco, redheads are actually quite common there. I'd put my money on natural blondes being worth the most."

"Since when do you know about the demographics of Morocco?"

"I mean, it's kind of impossible to fully grasp the geopolitical climate of Northern Africa without studying the Berbers."

Where the hell is this coming from?

"And I've heard the Berbers have really big dicks."

I nodded. *Now it all makes sense.* "Back to the topic of my impending death. What if they're using me as a guinea pig for some new drug? Any minute now it'll probably kick in and I'll suddenly think I'm an orange and start peeling myself." *Actually, now that I think about it...I kind of do feel like an orange.* I pulled on a strand of my hair and looked at it. *Orange!* I let go and blew it out of my face.

"If you were their lab rat, they'd need some way of following up. As far as I can tell, they have no way of getting you to ever come back. Especially now that you're pissed at them for injecting you."

"Maybe they just didn't think it all the way through."

"So they didn't consider basic things like that, but they took the time to make elaborate letters and envelopes? That doesn't make sense."

"Okay then, genius," I said. "What do you propose they injected me with?"

"Maybe it was some sort of relaxing serum. For all we know that's a perfectly normal part of a Moroccan massage."

"Shouldn't you know that, Miss Berber Facts?"

Chastity rolled her eyes. "Berbers are nomads, not wax techs."

"Okay, then you'll have to trust me. Injections are definitely not part of a Moroccan massage. They lured me there for a reason..."

Chastity snapped her fingers. "That's it!"

"What?"

"The letters. The Society. It all goes back to that. If we can find information on the Society, then we'll know what they're up to."

That was actually a good idea. I ran over to my laptop and googled *the Society*.

The first result was for something called *The Society International*, which the website claimed was a brotherhood created by a New York Times bestselling author. The site was fairly vague, so at first I thought it might be it, but then I noticed that the branding didn't match the letters. The font wasn't the same, and there was no sign of the logo that had been pressed into the wax. And there was nothing about injecting innocent women with random drugs.

The next link went to the homepage for a branch of the Church of England.

"I think that's them!" said Chastity.

"The Church of England?"

"Yeah. They lured you to the spa so they could molest you. Those filthy podiatrists."

I stifled a laugh. "First, that's Catholics. Second, podiatrists deal with feet."

Chastity scrunched up her nose. "Ew. I knew they molested little boys, but I didn't realize they were foot freaks. That's just sick. Jesus would not approve."

"It's good to know that Jesus draws the line at foot fetishism. Moving on..." I clicked back to Google and went to the third result, which brought me to the website for some hoity-toity NYC modeling agency. Forcing women to get bikini waxes was most certainly something they did, but I doubted it would be performed in a seedy Moroccan spa. Their models probably got waxed while sipping on Mimosas in a penthouse. More importantly, I was me. I was awkward, short, and had a big ass. Not exactly model material, even if I did believe I could rock it on the runway in my yoga pants and sneakers.

I scrolled through a few more pages of results and then kicked my chair back from my desk. "It really would have been helpful if they'd picked a more specific name than *the Society*."

Chastity tossed her phone on the couch. "Yeah, I didn't find anything either. I think that's kind of what they were hoping for."

"What else do you know about the Society?"

"I've just heard rumors. Some say that it's a secret sex club at the top of a skyscraper."

"One57?"

Chastity shrugged. "Other people claim that the Society rents out places to have wild sex parties. And some people even claim it's an international organization. Really, the only thing that's clear is that it's super exclusive and super secretive."

A lot of help that is. "I need to call my doctor." I *hated* doctors. But the situation was dire. They could have given me Ebola. Blood could start pouring out of my orifices at any moment. *Do people ever confuse Ebola with having their periods?* I felt like I was going to be sick.

"Are you okay?" asked Chastity. "Oh no, do you think you're an orange? Whatever you do, *do not* peel yourself." She jumped up and grabbed a coat out of the closet. "Where's the duct tape?"

"Why do you need duct tape?"

"I'm making an emergency straitjacket. Just sit tight..."

If I hadn't been freaking out about the Ebola coursing through my veins, I would have giggled at her unintentional pun. "I'm not going to peel myself. I was just thinking about Ebola and periods."

"Oh thank God. I mean, that's a horrible comparison. But I'm glad you're not going to peel yourself."

"Right. Back to doctor calling." I looked down at my phone and was about to scroll through the contacts when I saw the time. *7:30.* "Shit!"

"What's wrong now?" asked Chastity. She had found the duct tape and looked to be about halfway through making a definitely-not-functional straitjacket with my winter coat. "I promise your front teeth can't get cavities."

"I'm going to miss my stalk...spin class."

"Did you say stalk? Oh no. You think your *Jack and the Bean Stalk* fantasy is finally coming true. It's not. I repeat: do not climb out the window. There is no magic beanstalk." She frantically taped the second sleeve shut.

"Chastity, I appreciate your concern, but I'm fine. Some spinning is just what I need to clear my head." *Really I need my stalker. I bet he would know exactly how to handle this situation.* Especially since he was probably the one behind the injection. Dirty stalker. He was probably waiting for me to appear tonight at 8 o'clock so he could kidnap me. And the injection was some kind of slow-release sedative. God, he was seriously deranged. He was definitely going to cut me up into little pieces as soon as he got me back to his lair.

No. Bad fantasy. I tried again, convincing myself he could help me instead of hurt me. He probably had a private doctor at his beck and call. Or maybe he had a fancy medical pod like in those sci-fi movies. He'd just tell me to lie down in the pod and it would scan my body and know exactly what was wrong.

There was no time to daydream about that, though. I was going to be late! Just the thought of it made my front-tooth cavity flare-up.

I ran into my room and grabbed my gym bag. As I sprinted back towards the door, Chastity popped out from behind the sofa and tried to bag me like a nematode, but instead of a microfiber blanket like one would use in a traditional nematode bagging, she used her makeshift straitjacket. We rolled around on the ground. Somehow she managed to get both my arms into the sleeves. I laughed to myself, knowing that the tape wouldn't hold up against any amount of force. But my amusement came to an abrupt end when I tried to burst free and found that I was wrapped up tighter than Jason Momoa in size-small Spanx.

"Let me out!" I yelled.

"Can't do that," said Chastity as she wrapped more duct tape around me. "You'll thank me later."

I tensed my whole body and tried to get free. All it did was make me sweat.

"Oh no, you're turning all red. How do you feel?"

"Trapped."

Chastity grabbed her phone. It was still open to WebMD. "When you say trapped...do you mean tightness in your chest? That coupled with your excessive sweating might signal that you're having a heart attack."

"Or it might mean my best friend duct-taped me into a winter coat. And let's cool it with calling it 'excessive.' This is a perfectly normal amount of sweat." I glanced at the time on my DVR. 7:35. *Shit shit shit! Triple shit!* There was only one way I was going to make it on time. "Have I told you about the hot guy I always pass on the way to spin class?"

Chastity's eyes lit up.

Gotcha, bitch. "He walks out of One57 every Tuesday and Thursday at 8 pm on the dot. If we leave now, we can still catch him."

"How hot are we talking? Like a classic New York ten, or...?"

"Picture if Zac Efron and Chris Hemsworth had a baby. I mean, don't picture the actual birth. Or the gay sex. Just picture the full-grown male result of their DNA combining."

"Say no more." Chastity jumped on me and tore into the duct tape with the strength of an adrenaline-filled mama bear lifting a Ford F150 off her child.

Twenty minutes later, we were standing outside One57 just in time for my biweekly viewing of my stalker. My heart was pounding out of my chest. I just needed to see him. Seeing him staring at me would make me feel so much better.

"Is that him?" asked Chastity, pointing to some schlup in normal slacks with an average haircut.

"Does that look like the lovechild of Zac and Chris?"

"No."

"Then it's not him. Believe me, you'll know him when you see him." *But you better keep your hands off him. Oh God...was it a mistake bringing her here?* A horrible thought took hold of me. What if he stared at Chastity instead of me? I pulled out my phone and adjusted my hair in my mirror app. I still looked like a sweaty mess. *Crap.*

Suddenly I didn't want him to come at all. I looked longingly at the alleyway with the dumpster. I didn't want to dumpster dive twice in one week. *Please don't come,* I wished.

And…he didn't.

We waited a few minutes past 8, but neither he nor his Rolls Royce or little butler man made an appearance. I was relieved that he didn't get to see me in my messy state. But I couldn't seem to make myself move. It was 8 o'clock. He was supposed to be stalking me right now. Where was he?

Was he upset that he caught me with binoculars the other day? Or just the fact that I hadn't been on my viewing bench? Had he met someone new? Was he lurking in my apartment right this second waiting to finish the deed?

"I should have known you were lying just to get out of that straitjacket," said Chastity. She sounded crestfallen.

"I really wasn't. Let's just give him...wait! There he is!" I pointed at the next guy to walk out of One57. He was about 5'8, half bald, and had a rockin' dad bod. He was most definitely *not* my stalker. At the closest, he was my stalker's accountant. Not even the head accountant though. More like some sort of junior accountant. Or an accountant's assistant. Or the dude who polishes their transparent green visors after hours.

Chastity blinked and tilted her head. "Just to be clear, you said he's the combination of Chris Hemsworth and Zac Efron, right? Because that dude looks like Seth Rogen after an unfortunate accident involving his hair and an industrial meat grinder."

I shrugged. It was actually better if Chastity thought this was the guy I was obsessed with. That way she couldn't win over my stalker for herself. "Potato, potahto."

"Uh, no. I don't need WebMD to tell me that whatever they injected you with has ruined your vision."

"Nope. Don't think so. That's definitely him. God, I'd love to run my hands through his thinning afro." *Gag.*

On the way to spin class, I wondered if my wish had actually worked. For months, my stalker had been appearing like clockwork. And then I wished that he wouldn't appear, and he didn't. It seemed like too much of a coincidence to dismiss. *Did they inject me with some sort of magic powers?* The Society's logo *was* a genie lamp, after all. Maybe. That was still up in the air.

I shook away the thought. There was no time to dwell on magic powers. The elevator was about to take us up to our spin class, so I had to mentally prepare myself to deal with the trauma of being surrounded by thirty women who were all taller and skinner than me. *Strut your stuff, Ash. You're confident AF and mastering the perfect revenge body.*

Chastity and I got onto the elevator and hit the button for floor 3. Just as the elevator doors closed, I thought I saw a glimpse of an electric blue suit flash by.

"That was him!" I said, trying to wedge my hands between the doors before they shut completely. But it was too late. They slammed shut and the elevator lurched upwards.

"What about that other guy?" asked Chastity.

"No really, it was him this time." *It definitely was.* "I was just lying about that other guy."

"You can't back-track now. I know that you secretly love ugly dudes. I mean, I should have known after you married Joe…"

"That's a fair point. But in my defense, I thought I was going to die single and be eaten by my cats, so at the time Joe felt like a pretty good option. In hindsight, I can see that death by cats would have been preferable." *And it would still probably be my fate.*

Chastity kept making fun of me for my love of uggos, but all I could think about was my stalker. *Had it really been him? What was he doing here?* My imagination started to run wild. I looked around at the trophy wives in the locker room. Was one of them his wife? *Could be.* A beautiful man like him deserved a beautiful woman.

No! No, no, no! I hated that idea so much. I wanted him to be all mine. I *needed* him to be all mine. The thought of him stalking me was the one thing in life that kept me going. Otherwise I'd spiral into constantly thinking about setting Matthew Caldwell on fire. Reliving that incident every day would drive me crazy. And I wasn't crazy.

I took a deep breath. He *was* my stalker, so the most reasonable conclusion was that he had been here to stalk me.

"Did you leave that there?" asked Chastity.

"Huh?" I snapped back to reality. She was pointing at a little black envelope sitting at the bottom of my locker.

"Uh, no. I haven't been here since before the party on Tuesday." How did that get in there? I looked both ways, but everyone around me looked innocent enough.

"Then open it!"

"Shh," I said. I didn't want her to draw any attention to us. Not because I didn't want people to know about the envelopes. I just didn't want anyone to remember the scene Chastity had caused at my last spin class. I was hoping everyone could just forget about it and move on. If anyone mentioned it today, I for sure would never show my face here again.

Before I could reach for the envelope, Chastity had already snatched it up and broken the gold wax seal. She pulled out the single piece of parchment contained within.

We hope you enjoyed your first spa session. To check your results and accept our terms of service, please log in to the Society app.

Username: Raven

Password: 8JTY79

"Results?" asked Chastity.

"App?" I added. "Every one of these letters gets more confusing." And who the hell was Raven?

The last girl to leave the locker room gave us a judgy look on her way out. Usually I would have been annoyed, but now I was just happy we were alone so we could freely discuss what the hell this letter was talking about.

I pulled out my phone and searched the Google Play Store for the Society's app, but that was as useless as our earlier Google search. "There's no app called that."

"Are you sure?" Chastity searched too, and her face looked more crestfallen by the minute. "Damn."

Oh well. I was done with the Society and their creepy letters. The only thing that concerned me was scheduling a doctor's appointment to figure out what those Moroccan assholes had injected into my arm. Or at least...that should have been the only thing that concerned me.

Instead, I found myself wondering if my stalker had been the one to deliver that letter.

Chapter 8

TAX CODES

Friday

Usually having to wait an entire day for a doctor's appointment would have been impossible, but the mystery of the Society, my stalker, and that damned app made the time pass in a flash. I searched everywhere for clues about any of it, but my searches were completely and utterly fruitless. Probably because the letters had been for some chick named Raven. It did kind of all make sense now. I was just getting them by mistake. And now I kind of wished I was this Raven person. Because her life was probably super glamorous. And her name was super cool. Raven. She sounded so badass.

I'd dreamt of my stalker again last night. He'd appeared and saved me from my injection. And then he locked me up and kept me all to himself. It should have been a terrifying dream. But he made being tied up quite enjoyable.

Not even reminiscing about my dream could help me out of this hell though. I was sitting in the doctor's waiting room, holding my breath. There were so many kids everywhere. If I breathed, I was worried I'd catch something.

"Ms. Cooper," called the nurse. "We'll see you now."

Thank God. I kept holding my breath until I was safely in the exam room.

The nurse took my vitals. I was 5'2 and 119 pounds, which felt horrifying. The trophy wives in my spin class were probably the same weight, but it was spread out over their 6-foot frames. I really needed to ask them about all the protein muscle weight. I was definitely doing something wrong. Then she took my pulse. And then she took it again.

"Take a few deep breaths," she said as she pressed her fingers across my wrist.

That's not how this works. My normal heart rate, if it was taken at home and not after I nearly contracted the plague from Timmy in the waiting room, was fine. Probably 65 or 70 beats per minute. But my heart rate at the doctor's office had always been off the charts. I guessed she was probably clocking me at over 150 beats per minute.

She scribbled some notes on a clipboard and then took my blood pressure. Then she told me to sit tight and that the doctor would be with me shortly.

I waited patiently for the first 10 minutes, but then I got worried that I was doing something wrong. Was I supposed to be putting on a gown? There was one hanging on the door.

No, that would be weird. It was like the Moroccan spa all over again. Why did I always end up in situations where I wasn't sure if I was supposed to get naked or not?

I started reading all the posters and signs to help pass the time. There was a chart of the gastrointestinal system on one wall and a biohazard warning on a waste bin in the corner. But what really caught my attention was the ad for GenieMD taped to one of the cabinets. It boasted the secure storage of personal health records, educational material, and even video visits. *Video visits!* That meant no more germ-filled waiting rooms. I was sold. I immediately pulled out my phone and downloaded the app.

I tried memorizing all the parts of the gastrointestinal system while it finished downloading. Then I navigated to my apps page, and I was about to click on GenieMD when I noticed something odd. Bitmoji had always been last on my list of apps, but now there were *two* new apps after it. One was GenieMD, but the other was something called Tax Codes. *Tax Codes? What the hell is that?* I clicked on it and my screen turned black with two text boxes in the center. One was labeled *Username.* The other was *Password.*

Did Chastity put another password-protected porn folder on my phone? She had done that a few months ago to try to help me through the divorce, so it wouldn't be unheard of.

Then it hit me. *Of course!* This was the Society's app. They must have taken my phone at the spa and loaded it on there. I remembered my username was Raven. Or well…Raven's username was Raven. But I couldn't recall the password. I rummaged around in my purse until my hand closed on the folded-up letter.

Was it wrong to log in to this app when I wasn't the person it was meant for? They had already sent me all these invitations. So didn't that kind of make them mine? And the mistake was on them, not me. Besides, I was too curious to care. When I entered my username and password, a loading screen with the Society's genie lamp logo popped up, and then it was replaced by the home screen:

Welcome, Raven Black!
Wishes Completed - 0
Last Spa Visit - April 6
Last STD Test - April 6, Clean

STD Test? So that's what the needle mark was for! That was good news, but I wasn't out of the woods yet. They still could have injected me with stuff. Or used an unclean needle. In a few minutes the doctor would come give me the bad news, but for now, I wanted to explore the app and get some answers.

Below the bit about the STD test, the words "Action Required - Sign Contract" were written in bold red letters. I was about to click it when the door to the exam room swung open.

Dr. Wozniak hadn't been able to see me on such short notice, but she'd said that the pediatrician in her office had an opening. She hadn't, however, warned me that he was super hot.

His muscular arms threatened to rip out of his lab coat, and his short blonde hair effortlessly stuck up and to the left in a stylish yet very heterosexual way. He looked more like a doctor from a porno than from an actual doctor's office. Not that I've watched a ton of doctor-themed porn or anything. Okay, fine. Maybe I watched a few clips from Chastity's folder. Don't judge me. Divorces are lonely. And then I wasn't allowed to go on any dates because of *the incident.*

He put his clipboard down and looked up at me with his beautiful baby-blue eyes.

"Good afternoon, Ms. Cooper," he said. "I'm Dr. Lyons."

"Hi," I said, but it came out all squeaky and weird.

"So it says here that you were worried about STDs, blood poisoning, and overdosing on just about every illegal drug I've ever heard of. Is that a mistake, or...?"

"Nope, that's correct," I said. "I'm concerned about all of those things." God, I didn't want to have this conversation with him. I wanted my old lady doctor with the glasses. Not this handsome imposter that was making me sweat more by the second.

"Oh. Well then." He narrowed his eyes. "Do you mind telling me how you think you contracted all that?"

"I don't want to talk about it."

"Do you need a rape kit? As a pediatrician that isn't really my specialty, but..."

"No, I don't think so."

"You don't think?" He nodded. His blue eyes were filled with concern. "I guess the bit about the drug overdoses makes more sense now. If you need help with drug addiction, I can refer you to a specialist."

"I'm not a crackhead." Oh God, I'd definitely said that in a super defensive way that made it seem like I was a crackhead.

He nodded and jotted something down on my file.

"Hey. What are you writing?" I craned my neck to see, but he turned to block my view. "Are you writing that I'm a crackhead? Because I said I'm not."

He gave me a sympathetic smile. He had definitely added "crackhead" to my file.

"Can you just tell me about my blood work?"

"Of course." He flipped the page. "It looks to me like you're fine. The preliminary drug test is clean, although we won't have the full results until next week. And you definitely don't have blood poisoning." He paused. "You may have diabetes, though."

"They gave me diabetes?!"

He looked at me like I was crazy. "Did you fast for 12 hours before your blood test this morning?"

"Yes," I said. But it came out as more of a question.

"Are you lying to me?"

"Okay, fine. You caught me. I had two donuts right before the test. I get all barfy if I don't have carbs in the morning. And I really don't like getting my blood taken so I was nervous. And I like to eat when I'm nervous."

Dr. Lyons smiled, his eyes twinkling with amusement. "Okay, no diabetes then." He flipped the page again. "Hmmm, the STD report is missing. Excuse me for a moment."

I let out a sigh that I'd been holding ever since I left the Shifting Sands Spa. They hadn't pumped me full of meth. They hadn't poisoned me. And if the app was to be trusted, I was STD-free.

I pulled out my phone and texted Chastity: "Got the blood work back. No drugs, no STDs." Then I went back to the Society's app and clicked on *CONTRACT*. Maybe that would finally give me a clue about what this crazy society was all about.

Chapter 9
YES, DOCTOR
Friday

The Society contract popped up on my screen. I figured I had a while until Dr. Lyons returned, so I started reading:

TERMS AND CONDITIONS

MISSION STATEMENT

The Society provides a safe space for the fulfillment of our members' wildest fantasies.

To ensure a positive experience, all members must agree to the terms and conditions included herewithin.

NON-DISCLOSURE

1) The Member will **never** speak of the Society to anyone.

MEMBERSHIP

2) The Member begins as an initiate (bronze).

2.1) Novus (silver) membership is obtained automatically upon the completion of the Member's three wishes.

3) The Member must be single and under 40 years of age.

3.1) The Society may grant exceptions to this rule on a case-by-case basis.

4) The Society reserves the right to refuse membership as they see fit.

5) The Member will pay a $1,000,000 security deposit.

6) The Member may end her affiliation with the Society at any time via the app. At that time, her security deposit will be refunded in full so long as:

6a) The Member has graduated to at least novus (silver) membership.

6b) The Member is not being terminated as set forth in Clause 49.

7) Once the Member reaches the level of novus, she will be eligible to nominate new members for consideration by the Society.

8) The Member must never speak to a nominee about the Society or ask if the nominee was accepted.

WISHES

9) Wishes refer to all Society-sanctioned events.

10) The Member will begin with three wishes.

10.1) More wishes can be earned as set forth in Clause 39.

11) The Society will fulfill all wishes to the best of its ability. However, the satisfaction that the Member garners will be dependent upon the clarity with which the wish is worded and the performance of other members.

11.1) For specific instructions on wish formation, see Appendix A - Wish Formation.

AVAILABILITY

12) The Member will be assumed to be available on the following days:

12a) Tuesdays, 8:30 pm to midnight

12b) Thursdays, 8:30 pm to midnight

13) If the Member will not be available on days listed in clause 12, she will note it on her calendar via the app.

14) Wish invitations will be delivered via discreet black envelopes. Once an envelope is received, the Member will accept or decline the invitation via the app. Please note that participation in some wishes is mandatory. For those, there will be no option to decline.

WARDROBE

15) The Member will arrive in appropriate clothing for all wishes.

16) The Member will maintain a wardrobe of the following categories:

16a) Casual
16b) Activewear
16c) Lingerie
16d) Business
16e) Formal

17) If costumes or props are required, the Society will provide them to the Member.

EXPECTED BEHAVIORS

18) The Member will be ready and willing to engage in:

18a) Role-playing
18b) Kissing
18c) Fellatio
18d) Receiving cunnilingus
18e) Voyeurism
18f) Unprotected sex
18g) Public Sex - only in front of other members
18h) Group sex

What the actual hell? Voyeurism? Unprotected sex? Public sex? What kind of crazy sex club had I accidentally been signed up for? My heart was pounding. This was all a joke. *Right?*

I backed out of the app and sent Chastity another text: "I found the Society's app. The contract is rather enlightening."

Chastity immediately called me.

"Tell me everything!" she said.

"Okay, okay." I brought her up to speed on how I suspected that someone at the Shifting Sands Spa had installed the app on my phone and how my tests had come back clean. I read her the mission statement and then skipped to the expected behaviors.

"Please find a way to let me join," said Chastity.

"Well, according to clause 7, I can nominate you as a member as soon as I've obtained novus membership."

"And how do you do that?"

"By getting raped three times. Sorry, I meant to say completing three wishes."

Chastity sighed. "Now you're just being dramatic. Getting raped wasn't listed as an expected behavior."

"True, but I've only read half the contract."

"Rape isn't even allowed in the seediest sex clubs. And the Society is pure class. Search for it...I'll wait."

I did a quick search function for the word rape. The only place it appeared was clause 49, which was a list of behaviors that would result in immediate termination. "Okay, fine. Rape isn't allowed." I heard footsteps in the hall. "Hold on, I think my doctor might be back." I listened for a second, but it turned out to just be someone else walking by. "False alarm. Wasn't him."

"Him?" asked Chastity. "I thought your doctor was some old polish lady?"

"She couldn't see me today, but the pediatrician in her office was nice enough to squeeze me in."

Chastity gasped. "Oh no. Another child molesting foot freak?"

I was going to explain that he was neither a podiatrist nor a pedophile, but it wasn't worth it. "No, just a children's doctor."

"Is he hot?"

Of course she'd ask that. "Depends. Are you into tall blonde guys with dreamy blue eyes?"

"How tall?"

"Six feet. Maybe six one?"

"Um, yes please. Can you send me a picture?"

"No."

"Boo. You're lame." Chastity sounded heartbroken. But then she made an excited squeal. "Oh my God. What if this is your first wish?"

"What?"

"Think about it. When else have you gone to a doctor that's super-hot?"

Huh. "Never."

"And what's like...the number one fantasy for women? Doctors!"

"Actually, that's fourth on my list." *Right behind my Jack and the Bean Stalk fantasy.* "And anyway, that's not what I wished for. I wished for free shoes and revenge on Joe. This has nothing to do with either of those things. Although I guess the contract did make it seem like I would be participating in wishes other than my own."

"Aha! I knew it!"

I glanced over at the GenieMD poster. Was that a sign that this was sanctioned by the Society? It didn't have their logo anywhere, but it was still related to genies and wishes. I wasn't ready for this. I hadn't even finished reading the contract yet. Oh God, was that why my doctor was taking so long to return? So that I'd have time to be prepared for whatever weird wish this was? "Shit, I gotta get out of here."

"Are you crazy? You're about to get to play doctor with a gorgeous man. That's like every girl's fantasy."

"Fantasy is the operative word there. As in, imaginary. Not real."

"What was the mission statement again?" asked Chastity.

"The Society provides a safe space for the fulfillment of our members' wildest fantasies."

"Boom. You're definitely experiencing a fantasy right now."

"I don't know. Sex in a doctor's office seems cool in my head, but now that I'm here...eh. Getting probed on this awkward exam table feels more like a nightmare."

"Well that's because you're thinking of it as getting probed. Instead, think of it as getting ravished. Or devoured."

"Now I'm picturing him as a cannibal." I scrolled up to double-check that cannibalism was not on the list of expected behaviors.

"You just have to relax and have fun with it."

"You do know who you're talking to, right? I can hardly have a conversation with a stranger, much less seduce one."

"Well, you don't have a choice, Ash. I'm invoking Single Girl Rule #8."

"No."

"You said he was tall and handsome. I bet he has 8 abs and 8 inches…"

"Stop it."

"And if a man has 8 abs and 8 inches, he can't be refused."

Fuck my life. I hated these damned rules. But also…it had been a really long time since I'd had sex. "My fire extinguisher hasn't come in yet."

"Would you stop it with the flaming pants incident? You can't set him on fire in a doctor's office. You're completely safe. All you have to do is play along with the doctor fantasy and everyone will come out unscathed."

"But I don't know him."

"Exactly. Isn't that the whole point of your list? To try new things? To figure out what you truly like? To freaking live your life? It's exactly what you're trying to do."

I never should have told her about my list. "Chastity…"

"This is your chance to get to know someone new. With your body."

"Ew, no. I don't do one-night stands."

"Because you married the first guy you ever dated. Taking a few men for a test drive sounds like just what you need. It's not like the next man you find will think you're a virgin. And anyway, guys don't care about that. Most guys would be super freaked out if a 28-year-old woman was a virgin."

"I guess."

"Then what could it hurt?"

"The cleanliness of my…mouth." It came out as more of a question than a statement. Because I had no idea what this wish would entail.

"If he's in the Society then he must have had the same STD tests as you."

"There are germs other than STDs." Visions of viruses and bacteria multiplied in my brain.

Chastity sighed dramatically. "You're impossible. The Society is serving you up a hot guy and your fourth biggest fantasy and you're going to pass it up because you're worried about germs and being awkward?"

"Harsh."

"It is. But it's the truth. Ash, I can't just sit back and watch you be single for the rest of your life. You're too pretty and smart and wonderful for that. You deserve love. Or at the very least, a very good bang."

"Maybe you're right." Had I just said that out loud? I was officially losing my mind. Not having sex for over a year really did something to a girl's soul. Something filthy.

"I am. Shit, my food is here. Good luck! I hope you enjoy having your throat swabbed. Or maybe he'll give you some mouth to mouth. Or..."

I hung up before it got too gross. A million questions were swirling in my head. First there was the issue of whether or not the Society even existed. My original hypothesis that it was the work of Liz was clearly wrong. She wouldn't have spent all that money on the spa treatment, and she had no idea how to make an app. Which meant the Society was in fact real. So who invited me? Or Raven? Or did someone think my name was Raven? Was it really possible that my stalker had paid my million-dollar security deposit?

There was no way it was him. If it was, wouldn't he be the fake doctor in the lab coat? I shook my head. It was way more likely that one of the girls at my spin class had taken pity on me after my divorce. They all probably had the money. Or at least, their husbands did.

The final and most pressing question was whether or not this doctor's appointment was a Society event. The Society had proven to be ninja-like with their delivery of envelopes, and they certainly had a lot of money if all their members made million-dollar security deposits, so maybe they had set this up. And Chastity was right...doctors that looked like Dr. Lyons were a rare breed.

The only way to tell for sure would be to play along and see how things went. The rational part of my brain told me to run away. If I stayed and tried to act out some sexy doctor fantasy, I'd probably just be awkward and mess it up. Or get his germs. *No!* screamed the other half of my brain - the irrational part, the part that fantasized about my stalker. It told me that Chastity was right. That trying new things was actually a way to grow as a human. I had to let go of my fears if I wanted to experience something new.

So I did.

I let my mind wander to thoughts of Dr. Lyons. He didn't need a back story like most people I saw on the streets. He already had one. He was a pediatrician who dedicated his life to healing children. If that wasn't sexy, I didn't know what was. I wondered what he was doing at that very moment. Going over lines for his role-play as a doctor? Slipping into a sexy doctor's outfit? An image of him in a tight little white dress with red crosses over his nips popped into my head. *Ew.* I shook my head and switched the image to him shirtless with a stethoscope around his neck. *Much better.*

"You can do this," I whispered to myself. I looked in the mirror and adjusted my breasts. Just then, Dr. Lyons walked in. *Did he see me? Oh God, he definitely saw me.* My face started to turn red. *No! Be confident!*

He cleared his throat. "Sorry that I took so…long," he said in a very suggestive voice.

I turned around and saw that he was dressed just as I had hoped. The stethoscope dangled over his naked pecs.

This is really happening. I couldn't believe it.

"Good news: you're STD-free. According to the blood work, that is. I'd still like to do a few...additional tests. Just to be sure." He raised one eyebrow ever so slightly.

"What kind of tests?" I asked in my sexiest voice.

"You'll see." His eyes undressed me as he snapped on two latex gloves.

I turned away from him and pulled my shirt over my head. Then I looked back and locked eyes with him as I unhooked my bra and let it fall to the ground. His Adam's apple rose and fell as he watched me. I bit my lip slightly as I slipped out of my jeans and thong in one silky movement.

"Get on the exam table and spread your legs," he growled. It wasn't a request. It was a demand.

God this is so hot. "Yes, doctor," I said. I hopped up and opened my legs wide. The exam table paper crunched under my bare ass.

He stood still for a second. His eyes took in every inch of me. The anticipation just made me want him even more. And based on the growing bulge in his scrubs, I knew he felt the same way.

Slowly, torturously slowly, he approached me. His gloved hands traced down my thighs as he gazed into my eyes. "Try to relax, Ms. Cooper."

Relax? How could I relax at a time like this? My heart was racing a million beats per minute. If the nurse took my pulse now, she'd be horrified. I pictured her awkwardly taking my pulse as the doctor inched farther up my thighs. Was she going to walk in? I tried to see if the door was locked, but my view was blocked by Dr. Lyons' broad shoulders. Based on the expected behaviors listed in the contract, the nurse walking in wouldn't be that surprising. Public sex and voyeurism *were* on the list. But rather than being horrified, I found the idea somewhat exhilarating. Or maybe it was just the fact that Dr. Lyons' fingers were now only inches away from giving me the pleasure I wanted. The pleasure I *needed.*

Just before he got there, the door opened and I crashed out of my fantasy.

My heart was pounding in my chest like I'd just been caught doing something terribly dirty. Even though it had all been in my head. I hoped I wasn't blushing when I turned to see Dr. Lyons entering the room. Much to my dismay, he was fully clothed. No stethoscope over naked man chest...yet. But for the first time, I thought I could actually do this. That I actually *wanted* to do this. I knew how to be sexy. And ultimately, it was his fantasy I assumed. So he'd be leading the way. *I can do this. I can experience new things. This is my chance.*

"I found the final page of the tests," he said. "It looks like you're STD free. At least, you don't have any of the serious ones that get in your blood."

"What about the others?" I asked.

"A quick examination should tell us everything we need to know. If you wouldn't mind pulling your pants down to your knees, we'll get this over with and then you can be on your way with a clean bill of health."

Shit! What do I do? Thanks to my fantasy, I was soaking wet. I couldn't let him poke around down there. But also…I wanted to. Or else I wouldn't have just daydreamed about it. I took a deep breath and silently promised myself that I was going to seduce the shit out of Dr. Lyons. Just like in my fantasy.

"You think it's that easy to get into my pants?" I asked, jumping onto the exam table.

"I uh..." He was totally flustered.

Dude, step up your role-playing game. I leaned back and stuck my breasts out. "How about we start with a breast exam." It sounded more awkward than I'd hoped, so I added, "To get to know each other."

"I'm not sure that's necessary."

"But Doctor," I said in a super high-pitched voice. "I think I felt a lump the other day." I bit my lower lip and stared into his blue eyes.

"Oh, okay then." He put on a glove, not even bothering to sexily snap it, and then poked my breast hard with two fingers.

Ow. What kind of amateur hour is this? "Would it help if I take my bra off?" I asked.

He cleared his throat. "That really won't be necessary. Good news, though. I don't feel any lumps."

"You must not be doing it right, then. You have to really squeeze them. Like this." I reached up and massaged my left breast.

"If you're feeling discomfort in your breasts, it may be due to hormonal changes caused by your menstrual cycle."

Now he's talking about my period? Either he was really bad at role-playing, or he was into some seriously kinky shit. *You want kinky? I'll give you kinky.*

"Time to examine my pussy," I said. "I bet you'll like it more than grabbing little boy's balls and making them cough all day, you filthy pervert." *Wow, what?* I wanted to take it back as soon as I said it. In my head it had sounded sexy and playful. In reality, it was the exact opposite.

"Excuse me?"

I forced a laugh. This was quickly falling apart. I thought back to my flawless fantasy. What had I done to seduce him then? *That's right!* The shirtless version of him had loved my striptease.

I hopped off the exam table and turned away from him. I tried to unhook my bra, but the clasp was stuck. *Damned $10 JCPenney bra.*

"What are you doing?" he asked.

I turned to look at him over my shoulder. "Wait and see," I said with a wink. Finally I got my bra undone and pulled my shirt off. I was about to slip my jeans off, but I started to panic. *My big ass. What if he hates the stretch marks? And my vagina!* The freshly waxed skin kind of looked like an alien.

Focus! I told myself. Why was I suddenly feeling so self-conscious? I hadn't felt this way at all when the fantasy was all in my head. I needed to be more like my imaginary self. She wouldn't be self-conscious of her hoo-ha. She would own that shit. *Guys love vaginas.* Even though Joe hadn't. In fact, he had seemed pretty scared of her.

I arched my back and started to slide my jeans and thong off all sexy, but I couldn't get them over my big ass. When I wiggled to help move things along, I lost my footing and started to fall.

Dr. Lyons caught me in his strong arms. "Are you okay?" he asked.

Finally we're getting somewhere! "Now I am," I said as I leaned in for the kiss. One of my hands gripped his broad shoulders while the other wandered to his crotch. I grabbed his huge, erect... Nope. He was flaccid. Not even half-mast. Completely and utterly limp. Like he was ice-fishing naked in January.

"Whoa!" he yelled, dropping me on the ground. The linoleum was hard and cold against my half-naked ass. "Okay, no. This is totally inappropriate. This appointment is over."

He stormed out of the room and slammed the door shut.

My tail bone ached, but I hardly noticed. I was too busy thinking about how much I had just embarrassed myself. My worst nightmare had just come true. I would never be able to show my face in this office again. Possibly even in public.

"Well that could have gone better," I muttered.

In all fairness to me, though, I had tried. He was the one who wasn't into me. What kind of wish was that?

And then it hit me. *No.* It wasn't a wish at all. It had nothing to do with the Society. The GenieMD poster had just been a coincidence. *Oh my God, what the fuck did I just do?!* This had just been a normal doctor's visit. Well, normal until I had forced him to fondle my breasts and then called him a filthy pervert.

Fuck my life.

I was an embarrassment to the world. I could never leave my apartment again.

Chapter 10
HOMELESS RUTHERFORD STRIKES AGAIN

Friday

My night of hermitting was everything I'd ever wanted. I'd snuggled up on my couch with my kindle and some boxed wine and gotten lost in a world where an awkward college girl seduces her professor. I even lit a candle that smelled like fresh apple pie. For a few hours, I was able to pretend like I hadn't practically raped Dr. Lyons.

But then I started to get hungry. I looked in the fridge, but I was pretty much out of everything. *Damn it!* Going to the grocery store would involve me leaving my apartment, so that was out. I wasn't about to break my vow of reclusivity. Really there was only one viable option: order some 'za.

I opened the website for Nico's Pizza and was all ready to check out when a horrible thought occurred to me. *I'm going to have to interact with the pizza guy.* That was a problem. After my experience at the doctor's office, it was clear that I couldn't be trusted around other humans. I'd probably panic and answer the door completely naked. I'd probably make weird innuendos about extra sausage and drop to my knees instead of just signing the stupid receipt.

How awful would that be? And what if it wasn't even the pizza boy at the door? What if it was a SWAT team coming to take me in on rape charges? In that case, answering the door nude would basically be a signed confession. They wouldn't even give me a trial. They'd just send me straight to sex rehab. Maybe that was where I belonged.

I couldn't risk flashing the pizza boy, but I also needed some pizza. So I left a comment in the delivery instructions: "Please knock and leave the pizza on the welcome mat."

I had only just gotten back under my blanket and turned on my kindle when there was a knock. It had only been like...a minute since I ordered the pizza. That would have even been fast for the Chinese takeout place down the street. I was still working out how they delivered so quickly, but ninjas were definitely involved.

"Leave it on the mat!" I yelled. *How long should I wait to go get it?* If I went too soon, I risked compulsively molesting the pizza boy. But if I waited too long, I risked Homeless Rutherford stealing it. Or worse...he might just lick all the hot cheese and then leave it there as a germ-trap. This wouldn't be the first time. He was a monster.

There was another knock.

"I said leave it on the mat!" I yelled even louder.

"Ash!" he yelled. But he sounded very feminine. Maybe it was actually just a woman. "Let us in!"

Shit! The SWAT team is here! And they even sent female officers so that I wouldn't try to rape anyone. *Clever...*

"We're coming in!" yelled the officer.

I dove behind the couch to avoid getting hit by splinters when they rammed the door. But instead they just used some sort of skeleton key and opened the door the old-fashioned way.

"Ash?" she said.

"Ash isn't here," I said as robotically as possible. I reached up and pulled a blanket over myself.

"I think she's hiding behind the couch," said another female voice.

"She's definitely not," I replied.

I braced myself as they tugged the blanket off me. But instead of staring at a SWAT team, I found myself staring at Chastity and Madison. And Liz. *Damn it.* Getting arrested and taken to sex rehab would have been better than having to hang out with Liz.

Madison gave me a quizzical look. "Why are you hiding under a blanket? And why aren't you answering your phone?"

"I took a vow of reclusivity. And hid my phone in my desk."

"But it's Friday. We always hang out on Fridays."

"Not anymore. I'm never leaving this apartment again."

"It went that bad, huh?" asked Chastity.

I gave her a stern look. "I really don't want to talk about it."

"Talk about what?" asked Madison.

"I..." I started, but Chastity held up her freshly manicured hand to stop me.

"She got food poisoning from some Indian place," said Chastity. "Had explosive diarrhea earlier. It was truly awful. You know how that goes with curry."

What? I appreciated her lying for me, but there was no reason for her to make it so graphic. She was probably just pissed that I didn't call her immediately after my doctor's appointment. I almost had, but then I decided that it was better for the story of Dr. Lyons to never be told. Or rather…*incident #2*. God, I hated that I'd experienced two unspeakable incidents.

Liz plopped down in my favorite spot on the couch. "Explosive diarrhea? Ew."

"Yeah, it was pretty bad." I walked over towards the door. "Well, thanks for stopping by. But you guys should probably just hang out without me tonight."

"No way," said Madison. "If you're not feeling well, we'll just stay here."

"You really don't have to..."

"Best friends don't leave each other alone."

I really wish you would. "Aw, that's so sweet."

"And Single Girl Rule #2…" Chastity said.

I sighed. "Yeah, yeah. I know the rule. Girls' night is every Friday. No exceptions." *Damn it, those crazy rules!*

"And if you're not feeling well, that means more cookies and drinks for the rest of us," said Madison, protectively cradling her Oreos and six-pack of wine coolers.

"I'm actually pretty hungry. Here, let's get those in the fridge." I pried the bottles out of her death-grip and took them into the kitchen. I cracked one open for myself, offered one to Chastity, and then hid a few in the back of the fridge. No one had ever taught Madison's cheap ass that it's polite to leave whatever's left of the food you bring to a party, so I had taken to hiding half of whatever she brought. At least she brought something, though. Liz always arrived with nothing more than a bad attitude and a penchant for falling asleep before 9.

Once we were all settled on the couch, Madison asked what was new with everyone. Chastity told us about her latest Tinder match. Liz shrugged and said nothing. Then they looked at me.

I took a sip of my wine cooler to buy some time to think of an answer that wasn't horribly shameful. "Mainly just getting ready for my first day of work."

"I can't wait for you to come work with us!" said Madison. "It'll be like we're back in high school. This is so exciting!"

"Yeah," I said with mock enthusiasm. "It's gonna be so much fun waking up at 6 am every morning and having to put on pants."

"Pants are a great choice," said Madison. "I don't know if they've done any studies on it, but I have a suspicion that women who wear pants are more likely to make *almost* as much as men doing the same jobs. It's one small way to trick the patriarchy..."

Chastity shook her head. "I respectfully disagree. You gotta go skirts all the way. The shorter the better. How do you think I got you this job at BIMG?"

I knew it.

Madison glared at her and took a huge swig of alcohol. "Please tell me you're joking. That's the sort of thing that's ruining..."

"Hey," I said, cutting her off before this conversation really got out of hand. "How about we watch a movie or something?"

"Good idea," agreed Chastity. "I think Spaceboy is performing on the Night Show tonight and I've been secretly dying waiting for you to say it was okay to turn on the TV. Ah! They're on!"

Madison snatched the remote from her. "What are you doing? Ash doesn't want to watch that."

I don't?

"Why not?" asked Chastity.

"She used to love listening to Spaceboy with...*him*," said Madison.

She can't even say Joe's name? "You can say his name, you know," I said. "Joe, Joe, Joe. It's not a big deal. I'm over it. And yes, I did used to listen to Spaceboy with him. And yes, one or two of their songs still remind me of him. But their new stuff is amazing."

"And don't forget about how hot they are," said Chastity.

"Amen to that." I took a sip of my wine cooler and then lifted my wine glass in my free hand. Who knew the combination of wine and wine coolers was so scrumptious?

"They're okay," said Madison.

Chastity stared at her in disbelief. "Uh, are you blind? Look at them!" She pointed to the screen as it zoomed up on DJ Spaceboy's perfect face. Or what we could see of it. As always, most of his face was covered by a futuristic visor. But his soft lips and magnificent jawline were left exposed. "The things I'd let him do to me with those lips…"

"Wait," I said, turning to her. "I thought he was dead to you?" I actually remembered perfectly, because that meant DJ Spaceboy was all mine.

"He was. But I've forgiven him. I thought about it more, and I realized that it was my fault that he ignored me. I mean…I flashed him in like, the most boring way possible. Pulling up my t-shirt and just letting my boobs flop out works on most guys, but DJ Spaceboy is a freaking rock star. He probably sees like twenty boobs a day. Maybe even twenty pairs. If I want to get a backstage pass, I'm gonna need to step up my flashing game."

"How exactly does one step up their flashing game?" I asked.

Chastity put her drink down and scooched forward on the couch as if she was about to share something really important. "Well, first off, I'm not going to flash DJ Spaceboy. He gets all the attention, but his crew deserves attention too. So I'm going to dress up just like them - full space helmet, clingy body suit - and then slowly unzip it. I'm still toying with the idea of wearing nipple tassels underneath. Yes, it's a little 1920s burlesque, but it would help get their attention. And it creates some mystery. Like…hey, I've got great tits, but if you wanna see the nips, you have to give me a backstage pass."

"Why debase yourself just for a backstage pass?" asked Madison.

Chastity hit pause and walked over to the TV screen. "Exhibit A and B," she said, pointing to the dancers' crotches. Their clingy body suits did little to hide the rather large outline of their dicks as they thrust at the air. "Ash, back me up here. What would you do with these beautiful men if you got a backstage pass?"

Um… Sweat profusely? Try to unmask them to see if one of them was my stalker? *Wait!* Was DJ Spaceboy my stalker? I squinted and tried to picture my stalker with DJ Spaceboy's visor on. Did they have the same chin? *No.* But that didn't mean he wasn't one of the two dancers. Their faces were completely covered. And they were both about the same height as my stalker… I pictured myself backstage, grabbing his huge cock through his spacesuit. Just like I'd done to Dr. Lyons. *Oh God. Not that.* If it was anything like that, he'd be limp. And then he'd toss me out and call security.

I reached for my bottle, but it was empty. My wine glass was empty too. *Have my friends noticed that I'm double-fisting alcohol?* Whatever. After today, I needed it. I ran into the kitchen and grabbed another one of Madison's non-hidden bottles. As I passed the window on my way back, I glanced outside to see if the pizza guy had pulled up yet. Sure enough, the Nico's delivery car was parked outside. I expected to see the pizza guy get out with my steaming hot 'za, but instead the car pulled away.

"Hey guys," I said. "Want some pizza?"

"Sure," said Chastity.

Liz woke up and wiped some drool off her face. "Pizza? Yes please."

"If you want," said Madison. "Just hurry up and order it. I'm starving."

"Alright, watch this." I snapped my fingers and then opened the front door.

My friends all looked shocked when they saw the pizza sitting on my welcome mat. As I leaned into the hallway to grab it, I saw Homeless Rutherford sashaying down the hall. *Oh no.* I had a horrible feeling that the cheese on my pizza had just been licked. *Damn it, pizza boy! Why didn't you knock like you were supposed to?*

"How much do we owe you?" asked Liz.

"It was like $20." Is she really going to chip in?

She opened her purse and pulled out a crumpled-up bill. "This should cover it." She tossed it on the table and grabbed a slice.

I was about to stop her from eating the cheese that Rutherford had definitely just licked, but then I noticed that she had given me a single dollar. Not a single *bill.* A single dollar. As in, a George Washington. One hundred cents. "That's perfect," I said. I choked back a gag as she bit into her slice.

Madison handed me a five. "How'd you summon this pizza?"

"Yeah," said Chastity. "It almost seemed like you *wished* for it and it just appeared."

"That reminds me of that weird letter that you got at your divorce party," said Madison.

"Ha, yeah," I said. "I forgot about that." *Please let's not talk about it.* I polished off my second wine cooler and then poured myself another glass of wine. I was so hungry, but I wasn't about to touch that infected pizza. A few Oreos would have to suffice.

"What do you guys think?" asked Chastity? She was holding a ruler up to the screen and scribbling numbers in a notebook with her other hand. "Is DJ Spaceboy 6'2? If you account for his distance from the camera…" She shifted her ruler to the paused image of the dancer's junk. Her eyes got wide. "Wow, the dancer's cocks are even bigger than I thought."

I swirled the wine around in my glass. It was almost empty. "No wonder Joe got so mad when I told him that Spaceboy was my celebrity hall pass."

Chastity spun around. "Whoa, whoa, whoa. Hold everything. You guys had celebrity hall passes? And by Spaceboy…do you mean DJ Spaceboy only? Or all three of them? Because that's a pretty baller move to try to get a gangbang out of your celebrity hall pass."

"I never specified. But it wasn't real." Well, I mean…I fantasized about it. But that was beside the point. "I just said it to piss him off. He had come home late the night before and I was getting a little suspicious that he was cheating. Guess I was right."

"God, I hate that asshole," muttered Madison.

"Fuck Joe," said Chastity.

"Yeah. Fuck Joe!" I drained my glass.

Chastity and Madison raised their glasses and drank them down. Liz would have too, but she had fallen asleep again. Or maybe Rutherford's germs had killed her. *Oh well.*

Madison slammed her empty bottle down on my coffee table. "We should take a selfie of us having fun to make *him* jealous."

Was it really necessary for her to ruin my coffee table? God, I hated house guests. "Jealous of what? Not being here? I don't think he hated anything more than getting stuck participating in girls' night."

"You have a better idea?" asked Madison.

"How about a picture of Ash on a sexy date?" suggested Chastity as she poured us all more wine.

I nodded. "It's a good idea, but such a picture would only exist if I had actually gone on a date. And you all know that I don't date after *the incident.*" And incident #2. Which no one needed to know about.

Chastity stared at me. It felt like her eyes were boring into my soul. Did she somehow know about what I'd done to Dr. Lyons? I could mentally hear her saying, "Single Girl Rule #6: Always kiss and tell."

Oh God, she knows! "Okay, fine!" I yelled. "I admit it. I'm a rapist."

Chapter 11
THE CONTRACT
Friday

Madison spit her wine into her cup. "What now?"

"I raped a man today."

"That's not possible," said Chastity. "Girls can't be rapists. You can't fuck a limp dick."

"Sure you can. You just have to fold up the dick and balls and shove it all up there."

"Uh..."

"I tried it with Joe once when he couldn't get hard. It was just as unpleasant as it sounds. Although in a way it does kind of serve as a nice metaphor for our relationship. Being with him was like trying to fit a round peg in a square hole. Only in this case, the round peg is his limp dick and balls all folded up like origami and the square hole is my vagina."

Madison made a gagging noise. "I think I just threw up in my mouth."

"Anyway," I said. "I guess you guys are right. I didn't rape anyone. It was more of a sexual assault, if you want to be technical about it."

"Now that just sounds fun," said Chastity. "The doctor, I assume?"

I nodded. "Oh God, it was horrifying. I called him a filthy pervert and then fell over while trying to take my pants off." Saying it out loud made me want to crawl under the couch and never come out.

Chastity laughed and muted the TV. "Whole story. Now."

The alcohol pumping through my blood made it easy to tell the whole story. By the end I was even laughing about it. *God, had I actually done all that?* It felt like a strange dream.

"Wow," said Chastity. "You really misread that situation."

“Because of you!”

She laughed.

"Don't feel too bad," said Madison. "He's probably raped plenty of girls before. He had it coming."

"Well I didn't do it all on my own," I said. "Chastity was the one that convinced me it was part of the Society."

"I just thought you'd flirt with him a little and maybe get his number. How was I to know that sweet innocent Ash was suddenly going to turn into a huge slut?"

"Hey!" I crumpled up some paper and threw it at her.

Chastity swatted the paper away. "I mean...you tried to fuck your doctor. I'm not sure how to sugarcoat that."

"You told me to! And the terms and conditions were very ambiguous. They should have been more clear about how to identify if I was in a wish."

Madison looked back and forth between us. "The Society? Terms and conditions? I think you two have had too much to drink."

"Oh yeah, I didn't tell you? I joined a sex club." The alcohol had won. My filter was completely gone.

"It's true," said Chastity.

Madison shook her head. "Stop messing with me."

"We're not." I went and got my phone out of its hiding spot. I clicked through the ten missed call alerts from Madison and logged in to the Society's app. "Here are the terms and conditions." I tossed her my phone.

She looked horrified as she scrolled down. Chastity read over her shoulder.

"Whoa, hold on." Chastity snatched the phone from her. "Clause 14. Wish invitations will be delivered via discreet black envelopes. Once an envelope is received, the Member will accept or decline the invitation via the app."

"Yeah," I said. "That's how it works apparently. So what?"

"Did you ever receive an envelope telling you to seduce Dr. Lyons?"

"No."

"And was it on a Tuesday or Thursday after 8:30 pm?"

"No..."

"Then why the hell did you think it was a wish?"

I threw my hands in the air. "I don't know. There was a stupid GenieMD poster. And you were very convincing." *And I haven't had sex in ages!*

"You know what I think it was?" asked Chastity.

"What?"

"I think you just really wanted to bang Dr. Lyons."

I was going to protest, but maybe she had a point. The fantasy I'd envisioned in my head was hot. The contract itself was kind of hot. Everything about the Society seemed wrong but oh so right. I swallowed hard.

"Honestly, I'm not sure you read these terms and conditions at all," Chastity said. "Even mentioning the Society is a blatant violation of the very first rule. Much less letting all of us see the app."

"You're right. Give me my phone back. I won't tell you anything else about it. Mainly because there won't be anything else to tell. After that train wreck, there's no way I'm going on another date. Or wish. Or whatever it's called." Besides, I'd broken the rules. Surely I was going to be kicked out.

I reached for my phone, but Chastity tossed it to Madison. It was a classic game of drunken monkey in the middle. And there was no way I was going to win. "Okay, I give up. I'll let you keep reading, but you have to let me read too. I've only read up to the part about expected behaviors."

They agreed, and we huddled around my phone. Madison set the ground rules: we'd read each section, and then we'd discuss.

EXPECTED BEHAVIORS

18) The Member will be ready and willing to engage in:

18a) Role-playing

18b) Kissing

18c) Fellatio

18d) Receiving cunnilingus

18e) Voyeurism

18f) Unprotected sex

18g) Public Sex - only in front of other members

18h) Group sex

19) The Member will receive a description of the role she is expected to play in each wish.

20) The Member will stay in character at all times during wishes.

21) If the Member is expected to make a sexual advance, it will be clear in her role description.

22) The Member should not expect to engage in sexual intercourse during every wish. Often times she will be an extra in the fulfillment of another member's wish.

"This whole thing is horrifying," said Madison, "but I am impressed that they went out of their way to mention that you'll likely receive cunnilingus. I thought for sure the men in this group would just be using you without returning the favor. The use of the feminine pronoun is also a nice touch."

"I've always wondered what public sex would be like," said Chastity wistfully.

"I'd prefer the group sex," said Madison. She immediately clasped her hand over her mouth and giggled.

She's definitely drunk. As far as I was concerned, both sounded hot. *Wait, what?* I meant horrifying. I tried to think about where they would rank on my list of fears, but I couldn't seem to remember. I just kept thinking about the fact that it was pretty obvious my doctor's visit was 100% not a wish. *I'm a sexual deviant.*

HARD LIMITS

23) The Member will respect all of the following hard limits:

23a) No acts involving fisting

23b) No acts involving human waste

23c) No acts involving extreme choking

23d) No acts involving burning

23e) No acts involving electrocution

23f) No acts involving cutting

23g) No acts that leave a permanent mark

23h) No acts of pedophilia

23i) No acts of bestiality

23j) No acts of necrophilia

24) The Member will not use or accept payments in real currency while interacting with other members during a wish.

24.1) If the Member makes payments to other members during wishes, she will do so using Society-issued credit cards or monopoly money.

I giggled. "Monopoly money. If I'm gonna be a whore, I hope I'll at least be worth more than a hotel stay on Park Place." I pictured my stalker all dressed up like Uncle Pennybags, complete with the top hat and mustache. Somehow It wasn't an awful look for him.

"And you won't even have to fuck any horses or dead bodies," added Madison. "This is sounding better by the minute."

PRIVACY

25) Many wishes involve voyeurism and public sex. To facilitate these wishes, the Society often rents public spaces. The Member will stay within the confines of the wish to avoid disturbing the public.

26) During wishes, the Member will wear something black on her left wrist. It can be anything - a watch, a leather

bracelet, a delicate chain - as long as it is black and worn on the left wrist.

"Damn it," I said. "Why didn't I read this before I raped Dr. Lyons? He definitely wasn't wearing anything on his wrists."

"Shhhh," Madison hissed. "I'm not done reading yet."

27) If police are part of a wish, they will always show up with both a black wristband and a special badge with the Society logo in the center.

28) If real police show up, the Member will cooperate with their instructions but not give them any information.

28.1) Under those circumstances, the Society guarantees that the Member will be free to go within an hour with no permanent record.

29) It is possible that the Member may encounter other members during her wishes that she knows outside of the Society. In such a situation, both members will stay in character. The encounter will never be spoken of outside of Society functions.

30) During wishes, the Member's cell phone will automatically switch to "Society Mode." This mode will:

30a) Block most apps.

30b) Change the Member's contacts list as necessary (i.e. add the plumber's number).

30c) Allow the Member to dial 555 for fake emergencies. 911 will still work as usual.

30d) Save all media to a secure cloud.

"Can we talk now?" asked Chastity.

Madison nodded.

Chastity took a big gulp of wine and giggled drunkenly. "I forgot what I was going to say. Let's just keep reading."

PREFERENCES

31) The Member will fill out a form with her preferences for potential sexual partners, including:

31a) Height

31b) Hair color

31c) Build

31d) Penis size

31e) Race

"Ooooh!" said Chastity. "I wish I could order men like this." She turned to an imaginary person next to her. "Yes, waiter, for my entrée I'd like a 6'2 muscular Berber with dark hair."

"Berber?" asked Madison.

I shook my head. "Long story."

"And for my dessert I'll take a ten-inch cock." Chastity handed her imaginary waiter her menu. "Oh, wait." She snatched it back. "Make him blonde. I like my meat rare."

I reached for the imaginary menu. "I'll take a number One57."

"What's that?" asked Chastity.

"Basically a mix of Zac Efron and Chris Hemsworth. With a man bun."

Chastity's eyes lit up. "Oooh. I get it! What about you, Madison?"

She pretended to take the menu. "I can't decide. I guess I'll just share with you guys."

"Ew, no," I said. "Order your own!"

"Okay, okay. Fine. I'll take the biggest, blackest man you have."

Wow. Where did that come from? I was loving that for her.

Chastity whistled. "Now we're talking! Oh! We should order Spaceboy!" At this point, she was basically screaming with excitement. My neighbors must have been so confused.

"Let's keep reading," I suggested. "There might be more juicy details."

32) The Society will try to match the Member based on her preferences. However, the Member should keep an open mind - members often report higher levels of satisfaction when they step outside of their comfort zone.

33) Priority will be given to the preferences of the member whose wish is being fulfilled.

34) The Member may update her preferences at any time via the Society app.

POST-WISH EVALUATIONS

35) After each wish, the Member will log in to the app and submit her post-wish evaluations within 48 hours.

36) The Member will rate her satisfaction from 1 to 10, 10 being the best.

37) If the Member engages in sexual intercourse (anything beyond kissing), she will evaluate her partner on:

37a) Overall Experience
37b) Hygiene
37c) Attractiveness
37d) Role-playing
37e) Sexual Prowess
37f) Wardrobe

38) The Member may also give accolades to or report violations by any members present.

39) The Society will award highly rated members with extra wishes as they see fit.

40) If the Member receives poor ratings, they will risk discipline as set forth in Clauses 48 and 49.

"Discipline? Ow ow!" yelled Chastity.

"I don’t think it's sexy discipline. I feel like it's more about getting evicted from the group. Which is funny, because that's what's going to happen to me with this apartment if you don't keep your voice down." Although somehow Liz had slept through all of this.

Chastity frowned. "Party pooper."

PERSONAL UPKEEP

41) Once a week, the Member will attend a spa session at a Society-approved spa.

42) At the spa, the Member will receive:

42a) Massages

42b) Waxing

42c) STD tests

42d) Birth Control (if not already obtained through a gynecologist)

42e) Fitness evaluations

43) The Member will stay in excellent physical condition and arrive to all wishes with impeccable hygiene.

44) To prevent STDs, the Member will not engage in any sexual relationship outside of the Society.

45) If an STD test comes back positive, the Member will be notified. All operations will be suspended until all members have been retested.

DISCIPLINE

46) If the Member misses a spa appointment, she will be suspended until the appointment has been rescheduled and completed.

47) If the Member fails a fitness evaluation, she will be suspended until her next spa appointment.

48) If the Member's approval rating drops below 50%, she will be suspended for a minimum of one week. Reinstatement will occur at the discretion of the Society. Prior to reinstatement, a written or in-person evaluation may be required.

49) The following will result in immediate termination of membership:

49a) Violation of clause 1 (nondisclosure).

49b) Violation of clause 24 (payment in real currency).

49c) Rape.

49d) Gross misconduct, as determined by the Society.

49e) Three suspensions of any kind.

49f) Two suspensions due to low approval ratings within any 6-month period.

Oh no, I've already done two of those things!

AMENDMENTS

50) The Society reserves the right to make amendments to these terms and conditions at any time.

51) When amendments are made, the Member must accept the amendments before participating in any more wishes.

52) If the Member does not accept the new terms, she may end her affiliation with the Society. Even if she is still an initiate, she will receive a full refund of her security deposit.

LIABILITY

53) By participating in a wish, the Member hereby releases the Society from liability for all claims, including but not limited to personal injury or death.

54) If the Member becomes pregnant during her affiliation with the society, she agrees that the father (if a member) and the Society are not liable.

Madison started to say something, probably about how shitty it was that the father wouldn't be liable, but I wasn't really listening. And I wasn't entirely sure what happened next. Because I was pretty sure I was finally experiencing something on my list. *Blackout time. Check.*

***

The next morning, I woke up on my couch, still wearing the same clothes as last night. It felt like I'd been run over by a truck. My head ached, and I was pretty sure the contents of my stomach were about to end up on the couch. I ran into the kitchen and forced myself to eat a few Ritz crackers. Like I told Dr. Lyons: if I didn't eat carbs in the morning, I always got all barfy. Mixing two wine coolers with God knows how many glasses of wine on an empty stomach the night before certainly hadn't helped.

I was about to open the microwave to make some tea when I noticed something horrifying in the glass reflection. A woman with long black hair and no face lurked behind me. I threw my mug of water - luckily not yet boiling - in the air and grabbed a chef's knife out of the butcher block as I spun around. I was ready to cut a bitch. Or zombie. Or whatever it was.

It turned out to be neither a bitch nor a zombie. It was just a black wig sitting on a wooden mannequin head. The rest of the table was covered with open boxes of monopoly games. There were at least three dozen of them. The pieces were strewn everywhere, except for the money. It was all organized and wrapped in currency straps.

"What the hell did we do?" I mumbled. It looked like we had robbed Uncle Pennybags himself. *That's it! Monopoly!* I thought back to the part in the contract about monopoly money being used in wishes. In our drunken stupor, we must have visited every 24-hour store in Hell's Kitchen and bought all their copies of Monopoly. Apparently we had concluded that in-wish purchasing power was of the utmost importance.

As for the wig, I had no idea.

I opened the Society's app to search the terms and conditions for a mention of wigs, but the bold red letters about action required were missing. Instead, it just said: *Contract Signed - April 12.*

No. There was no way I would have signed something. Besides, I wasn't Raven Black. It had been fun reading the terms and conditions, but I was not going to participate in the Society. I wasn't even going to leave the house. I couldn't break my vow of reclusivity. *But I already have.* Otherwise, I wouldn't have spent $1314 on monopoly games. I hadn't found a receipt for the wig, but it looked expensive. *Please have generous return policies.*

I clicked on the line about the signed contract. It took me to the bottom of the terms and conditions:

CONTRACT

On this 7th day of April 2023, the Society and the Member enter into this binding contract.

As set forth in the above terms and conditions and all associated appendices, the Society agrees to fulfill three wishes for the Member.

This contract will stay in effect in perpetuity until either party chooses to terminate the relationship, as per Clause 6.

At the bottom was my signature and yesterday's date.

What have I done?

Chapter 12

HERMIT WEEKEND

Tuesday

I *hated* when things were up in the air. And right now, it felt like everything was.

I was nervous about my new job starting tomorrow.

I was worried the police would come arrest me for the rape of Dr. Lyons.

But most of all, I was torn up about the Society.

My good sense told me to terminate the contract and never think of it again. They had taken my blood without my consent. There was something shady going on with the million dollars that they seemed to think I'd paid. And they expected me to have unprotected sex with strange men. That felt like three strikes, and those were just the first three things that came to mind. And yet...when the prompt on the app asked me, "Are you sure you want to terminate your contract?" I couldn't bring myself to press YES.

Terminate it, said my twelve-year-old self, the one that went to religious education classes every Wednesday and mass with my dad every Sunday. The one that prayed every night and tried to follow every rule to a T. I had always been susceptible to peer pressure, so when that pressure was coming from priests and those priests were telling me that I'd go to hell if I disobeyed God, I listened. My faith, or rather, my fear, was the reason why I didn't drink until I was 21. And why I didn't have sex until my wedding night. When I was a kid, the priests would get mad at me because I'd usually say that I hadn't done anything to confess during confession. They'd badger me about it until I finally gave up and made up some lie about punching my brother. And lying to them gave me something real for my next confession. It was a terrible cycle that I still felt bad about. Despite that, I still played by their rules.

Until my divorce.

In the eyes of the church, my soul was damaged goods. The door to heaven was closed to me. Just because Joe was an asshole. The priest told me I could try to get an annulment so that I could marry again without offending God. The next day he was arrested for molesting four altar boys. That was when I realized that my entire religious upbringing had been a sham.

Screw you, twelve-year-old self and your pious bullshit.

Was my spitefulness the only thing keeping me from listening to reason? I didn't think so. Chastity thought wishes from the Society could count toward my list of new things to try. Which was true. And it was also peer pressure.

The letters from the Society added even more pressure. It didn't have a face, but it felt like there was this group of people expecting me to fulfill the contract I had signed. Or…they expected Raven Black to do it. Gah, I was an imposter! That was a good reason to terminate the contract. But…they had sent it to me.

Besides, I was too far in. I would die of curiosity if I didn't go to at least one event. Or die of horniness. Whatever label you want to give it, the fact remained that it was drawing me in. What if I really could fill out a form about my perfect man and the Society would deliver him to my doorstep, wrapped in whatever fantasy I desired? What if I could really complete my three wishes and then terminate the contract and get a check for a million dollars? What if I could really find love? *With my stalker.* It wasn't lost on me that I saw my stalker leaving his apartment every Tuesday and Thursday at 8 pm and wishes were scheduled to occur at 8:30 on those same days. A half-hour would have been plenty of time for him to get to wherever the wishes were taking place.

I lifted up my list of new things to try. I'd tasted 32 new smoothie flavors and still preferred strawberry banana. And

I'd blacked out. That was pretty much it. Trying gross smoothies wasn't living. Having sex with strangers was! *Gah, no. Gah, yes! Just…gah!*

To terminate or not to terminate. There were pros and cons for both. And the decision was paralyzing. I couldn't bring myself to terminate the contract, but I also couldn't promise myself that I'd accept the first wish. Hell, I didn't even know *when* the first wish would be. Would the next black envelope arrive tonight? Tomorrow? Three months from now? It was just one more thing up in the air. And it was driving me freaking nuts.

Instead of enjoying my weekend of reclusivity, I'd spent most of it stress cleaning and compulsively checking Joe and Sierra's Instagrams to see if they were officially together yet. I didn't know why I tortured myself with it. It didn't matter if they were together. I would never take him back. Actually, it did matter if they didn't work out. I wanted nothing more than to see that she had cheated on him the way he cheated on me. Like I said, I was spiteful.

By Tuesday morning I had cleaned pretty much everything in my apartment. Twice. Okay, okay. I'm lying. It was three times. The only thing left to do was try on my new clothes and pick out an outfit for my first day of work tomorrow.

I was halfway through the fifth box of clothes when I heard a knock at the door. *Weird.* I was pretty sure all of my clothes had already been delivered. I counted the boxes again just to be sure. Yup, all nine boxes had arrived. For twelve outfits. All shipped from Amazon Prime. And all the boxes were at least five times too big for their contents. Why didn't they ever just ship everything together?

There was another knock, this time accompanied by Chastity's voice yelling something about food. *That tricky bastard.*

"Why is it so clean in here?" asked Chastity as she pushed past me into my apartment. I wouldn't have even opened the door if not for the Red Robin take-out bag in her arms.

"There better be a cheeseburger in there. And fries. If you Trojan Horsed your way in here..." The cheesy, greasy aroma wafting up from the bag stopped me mid-sentence. In a second, my apartment went from smelling like a 900 square foot container of Febreze - the original scent, not that stupid new odorless one - to smelling like a fast-food kitchen.

My mouth was watering almost as much as it had been when my stalker dropped his pants during that filthy delivery boy dream I'd had last night. *Yeah, that's right.* After hermitting all weekend, I had started having fantasies about my stalker coming to my door dressed as a FedEx man. The night before that he'd been a pizza boy hell-bent on giving me sausage with my pizza whether I ordered it or not. And the night before that I'd just dreamt that Amazon had a sale on cleaning supplies. My vow of reclusivity wasn't working. I was definitely still a pervert.

"Come on, I wouldn't do that to you." Chastity pulled two Styrofoam boxes out of the bag and put them on the coffee table.

"Thank you, you're amazing and I love you." I plopped down next to her on the couch and took a huge bite of my burger. I knew it was terrible for me, but I didn't care. Red Robin was the one unhealthy thing I still enjoyed. And pizza. And maybe ice cream…

She laughed. "Love you too. So what have you been up to?"

"Oh, you know. Watching some TV, cleaning a little…"

"A little? This place is immaculate. It looks like a serial killer just sanitized it to destroy the evidence of his latest kill."

"Thank you." I bet my stalker's apartment was this clean too.

"The only thing out of place is...that." She nodded towards the kitchen table. It was still covered with monopoly games and the creepy black wig. I had started to clean it up, but I couldn't even. Having to do one return was bad enough, but we had gotten them from like twenty different stores. And I hated people.

"I think I'm just going to keep them," I said.

"Didn't you say they cost $1300?"

"$1314 to be precise, and that's just the monopoly games. Don't even ask me how much the wig was."

"I still can't figure out why we bought that thing," said Chastity. We had texted about it multiple times throughout the weekend, but neither one of us had any recollection of why we'd purchased it. I'd read the contract front to back looking for any mention of a wig. No such mention existed.

There was only one explanation. "It was probably Liz's idea."

"That makes sense. Really, how much was it?"

"Oh, only $1500."

Chastity nearly choked on a French fry. "Holy shit. Ash, you have to return everything."

I casually took a bite of my burger to appear like I didn't care. "It's not worth it." But I did care. I cared so much. Wasting money made my skin feel like it was melting off. The prospect of my fake security deposit getting returned at the end of three wishes softened the blow a bit, but it seemed too good to be true. They'd probably realize their error and refuse to pay me. Or just pay me in monopoly money. *God knows I already have enough of that.*

"What if I help?"

"You'd really go with me?" That was good. Having her there would make it less awkward. If I was tricky enough, I thought I might even be able to get her to do most of the talking.

"You don't even have to come if you don't want to. I don't want to disturb your vow of reclusivity." At first I thought she was being the best friend ever, but then I noticed the twinkle of mischief in her eyes.

"What's the catch?"

She pretended to look hurt. "Why do you think there's a catch?"

"First you're eating burgers with me and it's not even your cheat day. And now you're offering to run around town returning all that crap. There's no way there's not a catch."

"That depends. Do you consider making you go out tonight a catch?"

"Definitely."

"Then I guess there is a catch."

"Forget it. I'll keep all of it. Maybe Monopoly will go out of print and they'll suddenly be worth millions on eBay."

"Oh come on. I found this awesome little speakeasy where famous actors like to hang out."

"Tempting, but no thanks."

"Why not? You have to go to work tomorrow anyway. You're just going to be more nervous than usual if you haven't reintroduced yourself into the wild yet."

"Into the wild? What am I? A zoo animal?"

"Speaking of zoo animals...what do you think the odds are that the guy at One57 will be wearing a leopard print suit tonight?"

I shook my head. "Unlikely. He never wears the same suit twice, and he wore leopard print five Thursdays ago."

"Okay, stalker."

"What? I was kidding." I laughed awkwardly. "I don't remember his suits." *Besides, he's the stalker, not me.* And having a good memory didn't make me a criminal.

"Sure you don't. Well, either way. I bet he's going to look super hot. Oh no, and you're staying here so you can't see him. Do you want me to try to take a selfie with him so you can see?"

Damn it, damn it, damn it! Why had I ever told her about my stalker? I should have known she would use it against me. At least I didn't actually tell her that I thought he was stalking me. She never would have believed it, even though it was 100% true. "Okay, here's the deal. You return all that shit we bought, and I'll go to spin class tonight, no speak-easy though."

"Deal."

We finished our burgers and then attempted to make it look like none of the boxes of Monopoly had been opened.

It took us at least 10 trips to carry all the games down to Chastity's car.

And it was going to take us just as many trips to carry them all back up since all the stores rejected the returns. Well, not all. Chastity said one store in a particularly sketchy part of the city took back three of them for store credit. But the rest could tell that they'd already been opened. Eight stores in, the cashier at a CVS told Chastity that they weren't accepting returns of any monopoly games because it had been flagged as organized retail crime.

"And the wig place?" I asked.

"Apparently Amy just started working there."

"Huh, I haven't talked to her in a while. I should reach out." She and her husband had been best couple friends with Joe and me. But I hadn't really heard from them since the divorce.

Chastity looked away. "Maybe don't?"

"Why?"

"Let's just say I think Joe got her and Bill in the divorce."

"Why?" I asked again. I needed details.

"Did you guys have a fight? She told me I shouldn't hang out with you. I think the words *homewrecker* and *dumb slut* were used. Did you sleep with Bill?"

"What the hell? No! Joe must be telling people that the divorce is my fault." *And thanks to the blackmail, I can't do a damned thing about it.* I clenched my fists. I wanted nothing more than to punch Joe right in his stupid lying face.

"Wow. What an asshole."

"Whatever, he's dead to me." The divorce was the last thing on my mind right now. I was a little preoccupied with all the Monopoly games Chastity couldn't offload.

"Well...anyway, she wouldn't accept the return. Apparently they have a NO RETURNS policy. Although I have a sneaking suspicion that it only applies to us." Chastity tossed me the bag with the wig and then loaded me up with four monopoly boxes.

"We have to find a different way then. Maybe I can sell them two for $50, kind of like that homeless dude with the Oreos." It had happened a few months ago, but it was so strange that I could still picture it perfectly. Chastity, Madison, and I had been walking to get some Thai food when this guy holding two boxes of Oreos had approached us and said, "Two for $3." We respectfully declined his offer. "I always wondered how he had been able to offer us such a good deal," I said. "Now we know. He must have signed up for a sex club that uses Oreos as currency, drunkenly bought a million boxes of them, and then had buyer's remorse."

Chastity laughed. "At least someone can eat two boxes of Oreos. Two boxes of Monopoly, on the other hand, are completely useless."

"Maybe we can convince someone that it's good to always have a back-up."

"Oh yeah, that'll totally work."

"Do you have any better..." As we walked into my apartment, my left foot slid out from underneath me. I tossed the four Monopoly boxes in the air and ended up on my ass. "What the hell?" I muttered. I had just cleaned everything. What could I possibly have slipped on?

"Looks like the Society paid us a little visit while we were downstairs." Chastity bent down and picked up the lacy black envelope that I had just slipped on.

Chapter 13

#HORSEFACTS

Tuesday

Seeing the envelope made my stomach churn with a combination of nerves and excitement. Or maybe that cheeseburger was just coming back to haunt me. Greasy food didn't always agree with me.

Chastity opened the envelope and read, "Ms. Black, I've found a few places that might be just what you're looking for. If you're free tonight at 8:30, I'd love to show them to you. Signed Frankie Underwood of Frankie Underwood Realty." She passed me the envelope. "What do you think it means?"

"It sounds like this Frankie fellow is going to take me to some grimy apartment and try to get in my pants."

"Ohhh, hot. He'll probably offer you a few months' rent if you blow him. #WorthIt."

"I won't need to. Not when I walk in armed with a suitcase full of Monopoly money. The joke's on him."

Chastity gave me an exaggerated frown. "Boo. Where's the fun in that?"

"Don't blame me. The Society should have paid more attention in Econ 101. Currency must be scarce."

"In their defense, they probably didn't think anyone would be crazy enough to buy this many copies of Monopoly. What are you gonna wear?"

"Nothing."

"Wow, bold move."

I laughed. "I didn't mean I'm going nude. I meant I'm not going at all."

"What? Why?"

"So many reasons." I held up a finger. "One, my vow of reclusivity." I held up another. "Two, getting raped by Frankie does not appeal to me. Or worse, I might rape him." I shivered at the thought of what I had done to Dr. Lyons. I held up a third finger. "And finally, I have my first day of work tomorrow. I'll go to spin class with you, but I'm coming home immediately after." I still wasn't entirely convinced that I would terminate my contract, but I definitely couldn't go tonight. Not the night before my first day of work.

"Why do you need to be home early? You hardly ever sleep."

"Who said anything about sleep? I was just planning on sitting here all night mentally preparing myself to interact with humans. And to wear pants. And a bra." *Going back to work is going to be the worst.*

"And that's exactly why you need to go meet Frankie. It'll get your mind off things. You're going to make yourself sick if you sit here all night stressing."

Sick?! Being sick in general was terrifying. Being sick on a workday was even worse. But being sick and missing the *first* day of work? I couldn't even fathom it. I had kept a perfect attendance record throughout all of high school. Well, almost. One time I felt awful but went to school anyway. Before the first bell rang, my homeroom teacher sent me to the nurses because I looked so pale. I made it about ten steps into the hallway before I barfed into my hands and all over the floor. Needless to say, I was not allowed to stay.

"You look like you're actually considering my point."

"I was. But I decided you're wrong. I'll be nervous all night, but I won't actually be sick. No bacteria or viruses can get me in here. But if I go out tonight..."

"What happened to the enthusiasm you had for the Society when you tried to seduce Dr. Lyons?"

"That's kind of the point. What if I try to seduce Frankie too?" I still had no idea what had come over me. Dr. Lyons was just a poor innocent bystander. "I've already proven I can't control myself." I was a menace to society.

"Yes you can. But the wonderful thing is that you won't have to. Frankie is clearly a part of the Society. You've read through all the rules. You know how it works now. The black envelope came, just like it was supposed to. This is definitely a wish."

"Yeah, it came. And I slipped on it. I can't even receive mail without making a fool of myself. If I'm not careful, I'm going to be known as the clumsy redheaded rapist. Now, would you help me off my ass?"

Chastity grabbed my arm and helped me up, but halfway through her face lit up and she dropped me. "That's it!" she said.

Ow. "I have no idea what you're about to say, but I don't think I'm going to like it."

"I remember everything."

"What?"

"I must not have blacked out completely. Maybe I grayed out. Either way, I remember everything about Raven Black now."

Oh wow. "We found her?" I really was a good stalker. Crap, did this mean I had to hand over my membership to her? Because now that I could be part of the Society I for sure wanted to be. Damn reverse psychology!

"No, silly," said Chastity. "It's you. You're Raven Black. Right before you signed the contract there was this little paragraph about what you wanted to be called. You could go with your real name, stick with the randomly assigned name Raven Black, or choose a new one. You went with Raven Black and decided to wear a disguise."

"Really?" I definitely didn't remember that. "So the invitation really was for me?"

"Yeah. Oh! The wig! We must have gotten it as a disguise. It's perfect. By day, you'll be innocent little redheaded Ashley Cooper. But by night, you'll be Raven Black, the raven-haired seductress."

Interesting. If I wore the wig, I'd be unrecognizable. I could do whatever I wanted and not get in trouble.

Well…not everything. I'd still have to learn how to stop inappropriately touching men. "Somehow I actually don't hate that idea." Raven Black really did have a nice ring to it. And whatever awkward things I did as her wouldn't matter. Because no one would know it was me. I started smiling. This was the perfect situation for me. Incident #1 and #2 started to fade away. Raven Black hadn't done those things. She wasn't awkward. She was so smooth.

"It'll be like Clark Kent and Superman," said Chastity. "Only in this case, Superman *really* loves dick. #NotHis-Kryptonite."

"And now you're making it weird."

"Okay, okay. Fine. Superman is only moderately interested in dick. And thanks to the rape protection in his contract with the sex club, he doesn't have to get any dick he doesn't want."

Every word that came out of her mouth made me less interested. But she did have a point. While the terms and conditions encouraged sexual contact, clause 49c did explicitly ban rape. "I'll consider it if you promise to never talk about Superman wanting dick again."

"Works for me. Where's your phone? You need to accept the invitation before Frankie gets booked for someone else."

I got up and grabbed my phone off the coffee table. Then I logged into the app. Not to necessarily accept the invitation, but I at least wanted to see if there was more information. The home screen popped up. There were two buttons at the bottom: View Preferences, and RSVP.

I was about to click on RSVP when Chastity said, "Oh! Let's fill out your preferences real quick."

"That's probably not necessary..."

She reached over and clicked the *View Preferences* button. The preferences form popped up with all the answers filled in.

"Weird. It looks like it comes pre-filled." My voice cracked halfway through.

"Oh my God. You already filled it out!"

"Did not." *How did she know?!* It was like she could read my lying soul.

She stared at me.

"It probably just prefilled with the most common features of their members. I guess Frankie is going to be a white 6'2 male with brown hair, an athletic build, and a nine-inch penis."

"Do you know what percent of the population is white, 6'2, with brown hair and an athletic build?"

"Half?" I suggested.

"Definitely less than one percent. Finding a single guy like that is like finding a unicorn. And finding such a man with a nine-inch dick? That's like finding a unicorn with a nine-inch dick."

"Wow, vivid imagery there. But I feel like nine inches might actually be fairly common for an animal in the Equus genus. Maybe even a bit small. #HorseFacts."

Chastity laughed. "You never use hashtags right. They're for sass. Not horse facts. But fair point. Anyway, that perfect specimen of a man you just described is super rare. There's no way that's what the Society's average member looks like. Not even Berbers are that well hung, much less white New Yorkers." She stared at me expectantly.

Really, how did she always know I was lying? I must not have had a good poker face. Or maybe it was because I always got all fidgety when I was lying. I scratched under my chin like a weirdo. Damn it, I was doing it right now! "Fine! I filled it out. Is that so wrong? What did you expect me to do when I was here all weekend having sex dreams about FedEx men? You would have filled it out too."

"Sex dreams about FedEx men? Ow, ow! We'll circle back to that later, but first I want to talk about how you want a nine-inch dick. I'm impressed. And a little surprised. That's a lot of meat for such a little girl."

I could feel my face turning bright red. "I didn't think you could say anything grosser than your gay Superman metaphor, but that takes the cake. Well done."

"Seriously...what made you say nine inches? Was Joe packing way more than you let on? I thought you said..." Chastity held up her pinky finger and wiggled it around.

"That's about right. And I dunno why I said nine. It just felt like a nice round number."

"Do you have any idea how big that is?"

I pressed my lips together. I mean, I had a pretty good idea. That was why I'd selected it. And I was very excited about my decision. "Normal sized?"

Chastity walked over and grabbed my can of ginger ale. "Picture this as a penis."

"Ew. Why is it so short and thick?"

"Because it's only half the penis." She grabbed another can and stacked it on top. "That's more like it."

"It's still so thick."

"The proper term is girthy. And yes, that's what happens. As they get longer, they also get girthier."

There's no way that would fit in me. Oh God, what have I done? "I think I made a mistake." I quickly changed my penis size preference to two inches.

"Only two?" she said through her laughter. "You overcorrected a bit. How about we settle somewhere in the middle. Try six or seven."

"What beverage would that be comparable to? A water bottle? Or...?"

"It's normal. Just say six. You'll like that. That's nice and average."

Average? How boring. I wanted above average. I typed in seven and clicked back to the home screen before she could see. Then I went to RSVP:

Realty Meeting
Tuesday, April 11, 8:30 p.m.
Frankie Underwood Realty

One57, Suite 212
New York, NY 10019

One57? I almost squealed. That's where my stalker lived. *I think*. I didn't know for sure because he was really hard to stalk.

Below were two options. Accept or Decline. I prepared myself to swat Chastity's hand away when she inevitably tried to click "Accept" without my permission. But she didn't.

"What are you gonna do?" she asked.

"You mean you aren't going to force me to go?"

"No. I'm kind of hoping that you don't."

"Why?" I eyed her suspiciously. What was her end game here? I tried to think of what Single Girl Rule would make me deny an invitation to go on a date at an illicit sex club. But my mind was coming up empty. Really denying it would go against the general principle of the rules.

"Because if you don't go, then I'm going in your place."

Ah. That makes sense. I looked back at the address. It was tempting to just give her my phone and call it a day. I was really out of my element here. But…*One57*. I'd been spying on that building for months. And now I had an opportunity to get in and explore/stalk. How could I pass that up? If slipping on the envelope had been a sign that I shouldn't go, this felt like a sign that I should. More importantly, what if Frankie Underwood *was* my stalker. I'd never forgive myself for letting Chastity go in my place. Before I could change my mind, I clicked "Accept." My stomach immediately started twisting in knots.

"Was that for me or for you?" asked Chastity. She sounded hopeful.

"I'm not sure yet." Images of some creepy dude named Frankie trying to bang me in a cheap apartment made my skin crawl. And it got even worse when I thought about the expected behaviors listed in the contract. He wouldn't just bang me. He'd bang me without protection. While other people watched. Maybe some would even join in. And thanks to my preferences, Frankie would probably have a humungous double-soda-can dong. God, what had I been thinking? "How about we both get ready, and then if I chicken out, you can go in my place?"

"Good enough for me," agreed Chastity.

We spent the next half hour going through all my clothes. The first outfit was too formal. And the next was something Chastity thought her grandma would wear. I tried to up the sexiness factor by putting on my best heels. They were white with a little bow on top. I had worn them for my wedding. And my college graduation. And prom. Actually, they were my only heels.

Chastity laughed in my face when she saw them. "Those are like two inches tall. Where are your other shoes?"

I pointed to a shoe rack in the corner of my room.

"No, I meant your heels."

"This is it."

"Come on, stop messing with me."

"I'm being serious. Have you ever seen me wear any other heels?"

"No, but what about when we go shoe shopping? You always love the craziest heels. I just assumed you came back later and bought them so I wouldn't know that you wore them to seduce Joe."

"Nope. Looking at shoes is my guilty pleasure, but I know I could never pull them off like you do."

"Says who?"

Good question. The first thing that came to mind was my fear that I'd break my ankle if I wore shoes that tall. My Mom had planted that idea in my head. Or maybe it was because she called them hooker heels whenever my little sister wore them. Actually, no. I knew the real answer. "Joe. He always said they were a waste of money. And that they looked bad on me."

Chastity shook her head. "You know he just didn't want you to be taller than him, right?"

Oh my God. She was right. "That little asshole!" How had I not seen it sooner? I couldn't believe I had been missing out on fun shoes just because of Joe's stupid insecurities.

"Good thing you wished for revenge on Joe and free shoes. Speaking of which, how do you think those wishes fit into the whole real estate thing?"

"Maybe I'll break a heel walking between apartments and my muscular realtor will come to my rescue."

Well, you're certainly not going to break one of those two-inch heels. Here, try these on." Chastity unbuckled her strappy, floral print heels and tossed them to me.

I dodged to the side and the six-inch stiletto stuck in the wall behind me. "Jesus. Be careful with those things. You could have punctured my liver." *My greatest fear.* Sometimes it felt like public speaking, germs, or being late was at the top of my list of greatest fears. But that was just in the moment. When I was calm and not about to jump in a dumpster it was easy to think clearly. My greatest fear was definitely the punctured liver thing. God, that was truly terrifying. "Anyway, I think those are a few sizes too big."

"Sorry." She pried it loose from the wall. "Do we have time to swing by Fifth Avenue before 8:30? I feel like Raven Black is going to be the kind of girl who rocks heels."

Yasss! "She definitely is. But no, we don't." Then I remembered something. Hadn't there been a clause about getting a role description before each wish?

I grabbed my phone and went to the app. Sure enough, a *Wish Details* button had appeared in place of *RSVP.* It had the same address and time as before, but there was a new paragraph at the bottom. I read it aloud. "Raven Black. You recently got divorced and are seeking a fresh start in a new apartment." *Damn.* I had been hoping they were going to make me something cool. Like a secret agent looking for an apartment that shared a wall with an international drug lord. The truth wasn't nearly as fun.

"So basically you're just you," said Chastity.

"I guess so. At least the role-playing won't take much effort."

"What's in here?" asked Chastity as she pulled a bag out of the back of my closet.

"Don't…" I started, but it was too late. She'd already untied it and pulled out one of my little sister's dresses.

"Damn, this is hot. Is this what you and Joe were into?"

"No." I bit the inside of my lip so I wouldn't burst into tears. "Those were Rosalie's clothes."

"Oh." Chastity looked away.

Rosalie was my little sister. She'd been my very best friend in the whole wide world. Three years ago, she'd vanished. And a little piece of my heart had vanished with her.

Chastity folded the dress up and shoved it back in the bag. "Sorry."

"It's okay," I said, holding back the tears. It was pathetic, but even after three years it was still hard to be reminded of her. I still hoped she would come back. And then it hit me. *Of course.* I don't know how I didn't realize it sooner. "Chastity. What if she's the one behind these envelopes?"

Chastity put her hand on mine. "Don't do this again."

"Do what?"

"You know what."

I pressed my lips together. I knew what. After Rosalie had disappeared, I kept seeing signs from her everywhere. But none of them turned out to be real. As my therapist helped me realize, it was all just wishful thinking. Just like this was now. *She's gone. She's not coming back.* I took a deep breath, but tears still threatened to spill from my eyes. "Can you give me a few minutes?"

Chastity nodded and left me alone in my room.

I knew I shouldn't have done it, but I grabbed the bag and looked through Rosalie's clothes. They still smelled like her oil paints. I hadn't touched anything in this bag since I'd packed up Rosalie's life. I remembered shoving her belongings in the back of my closet, hating the fact that everything she owned fit into a few bags.

It wasn't right. Rosalie's presence had been greater than life. She'd filled up every room with her laughter. Honestly, she was the opposite of me. I sat down next to the bag that Chastity had opened. Rosalie had been fearless. I lifted another dress from the bag. It was even more inappropriate than the first. Part of me wanted to put it on. Maybe being a little like Rosalie while I pretended to be Raven Black was exactly what I needed. But just holding the fabric in my hands made me cry. I wasn't ready. And despite what Chastity and my therapist thought...I didn't think I'd ever be able to admit that she was really gone. Everyone else had given up on her. I couldn't do that. And I'd keep her things here with me until she came back and needed them.

I placed the dress back in the bag and shoved it back in the corner of my closet. I took a deep breath to clear my head. Rosalie would have wanted me to put myself out there. She'd want me to keep living my life. I opened one of my drawers and picked out something that was more me. I wasn't going to pretend to be a different person just because I had a fake Society name. If I'd learned anything from Rosalie, it was that our time to live was limited. I wasn't going to waste any more of mine.

A few outfit changes later I settled on a fitted T-shirt with a panda graphic, my favorite jeans, and some neon green flats with a pattern that looked like bamboo. When I came back out of my closet, Chastity smiled. A fake one.

She clearly hated my outfit, but to her credit, she held her tongue. Instead she focused all her energy on covering my face in way too much makeup and figuring out how to get my black wig to stay.

When she finally let me look in the mirror, I hardly recognized myself. From the neck up, I looked more like the spin class trophy wives than I ever had before. Well, kind of. I was wearing as much makeup as they did. And my hair was dark and shiny and voluminous. For a few weeks there after the divorce, I'd been pretty down on myself. I would have seen a plain girl that no makeup could fix. But now? I smiled. I was me with an awesome wig. I was already comfortable in my skin when I wasn't setting men on fire. But being Raven Black gave me an extra boost.

"So what black jewelry do you have to wear on your wrist?" asked Chastity.

"Eek, I forgot about that. I don't think I have any."

"No bangles or anything?"

"Nope." I wouldn't be caught dead in loud, annoying bangles. My red hair was loud enough by itself. "I do, however, have a sharpie, white paper, and a glue stick."

"Classy. What about watches? Didn't you say you used to love wearing watches?"

She was right. When I was a kid, I thought watches were the ultimate accessory. Sexy *and* functional? Yes please. Thanks to my watches, I had never been late for a single class.

I opened my jewelry box and rummaged through my watch collection. My first instinct was to go for the one where the face looked like a panda, but it was green instead of black. *Damn.* It would have gone so perfectly with my outfit. Instead, I grabbed a sporty black one...*SHIT!* The time read 7:45. How had I lost track of time so badly?

Yes, it was plenty of time to get there before the 8:30 appointment. But I wanted to get there at 8 so I could see my stalker. Him staring at me would be just the confidence booster that I needed before my date. God, I really loved the way he stared at me. I crossed my fingers and made a silent wish that he'd be Frankie.

"That's perfect," Chastity said. "There's just one more thing."

I strapped the watch on. "I have to get going, or I'll be late." There was a good chance that I'd lost my mind, because for some reason I was actually thinking about going through with this. And I knew that I'd chicken out if I stopped for even a second. I tried to step around her, but she blocked my path.

"We need to talk about this." She held up my list of new things to try. "Tasting 32 random smoothies with gross names was not what I meant by living."

I knew I should have hidden that. Telling her about the list was one thing. But her actually seeing the lame things on it? I snatched the list out of her hands. She'd added, "Participate in my three wishes to gain silver membership and then nominate Chastity to the Society." It seemed like more of a bullet point that would benefit her more than me.

"Real talk," she said. "I know you keep saying you're fine about the divorce. And I get it. We both know you're better off without Joe. But…it's scary to start over."

It was scary to start over.

"I know you don't think you know who you are without him. But this is your chance to find out."

I knew she was right. And despite how nervous I was, I was pretty sure this was the feeling I was chasing by guzzling gross smoothies. For the first time in years I was actually excited about something. I swallowed hard. "I'm going to get you that invite to the Society," I said. Actually, Raven Black probably said it. Because Ashley Cooper was nervous AF.

"Atta girl. Now go bang Frankie and come back and tell me all about his nine-inch penis. And don't forget Single Girl Rule #7: Pics or it didn't happen."

Yeah, I'd definitely lost my mind.

Chapter 14
BLUEBERRY PIE
Tuesday

For the third time ever, I hoped I *wouldn't* encounter my stalker. At least, not at the entrance to One57. Because I wanted him to be Frankie Underwood, waiting patiently for me in Suite 212. I could so easily picture our first real meeting. Definitely a love at first sight scenario. We'd smile at each other as I got on the elevator. We'd act all nonchalant about it, but then we'd get off at the same floor and laugh. And then when we walked to the same suite…we'd realize we were always meant to finally meet like this. We'd laugh about how he caught me with binoculars. But he'd confess that he was the one stalking me the whole time. And then he'd make love to me against a wall in his real estate office. Because we both couldn't wait to make it to a bed. Too much pent-up sexual tension after all our eye fucking for the past few months.

I smiled. Yep, that was how it was going to go down. And his black Rolls Royce limo wasn't parked out front, so that gave me some small hope that this could all actually happen.

I pulled out my phone to check my appearance. I almost screamed when I looked into the mirror app and saw the dark-haired woman staring back at me. *Oh, right. That's me. Raven Black, the seductress of the night.* Or something like that. I had hoped that the wig would give me newfound confidence since I could leave *the incidents* behind me. But it didn't. If anything, it just made me feel like people were staring at me. And wearing it gave me a brand-new fear: my wig flying off. I still hadn't decided where it ranked on my list, but my preliminary assessment was that it would be similar to having a centipede crawl up my leg, but not quite as bad as being late for an appointment.

Speaking of being late...it was 8:01, and my stalker still hadn't made an appearance. I knew I said I hoped he wouldn't appear, but I didn't actually believe it would happen. I interacted with my stalker in fantasies. In dreams. But not in real life. If my stalker was Frankie Underwood, I couldn't even imagine how weird I would act. I'd probably jump up on a sofa Tom-Cruise-style and yell that I was in love. Or get my wig caught in the door. If that happened, I would literally flood his office with the gallons of sweat that would pour out of my armpits.

Coming here was a mistake. I should have let Chastity take my place. She belonged in the Society. Not me. Whoever nominated me had messed up. They'd probably meant for her to open that envelope at my divorce party. After all, we had been at her apartment.

I waited for twenty minutes, but there was still no sign of my stalker. And then I couldn't wait any longer. I was already flirting with lateness. I ended my stakeout and entered One57. The lobby was just as sleek as the glass exterior. Every surface was polished to a mirror-like finish, including the hair of the man at the front desk. He was the human equivalent of a marble floor. The only thing amiss was the cluster of fancy old people crowding around the elevators. I had never seen so much fur in a single place.

If I had been a chinchilla, I would have run away screaming. But luckily I was a human woman. So I didn't have to scream until later when Frankie Underwood would inevitably lure me to a sex dungeon and make a coat out of my skin. The ancient Aztecs used to do that. They would sacrifice virgins and then male priests would turn them into skin cocoons and wear them all over town. I shuddered.

I had worse problems than Aztec skin cocoons, though. The chinchilla killers were hardly moving. After sitting there for a few minutes, I realized that only one elevator was working. Which meant there was no way I'd be able to get to suite 212 in time for my meeting. Unless I took the stairs.

I checked my watch. 8:28. *No!* Where were the damned stairs? It took me a second to find them, and as soon as I did, I took off in a dead sprint. I didn't even slow down for the door. I just burst right into the stairwell.

Or at least, I tried to. I only got the door half open before it hit something, or rather, someone. All at once, papers flew into the air and I heard a thud, a grunt, and a sickening squish. *Oh God. Did I just puncture someone's liver with the doorknob?* I looked up to see my victim.

He must have been carrying a pie when I hit him, because an aluminum pie dish was stuck to his face. Blueberry filling dripped down onto his shiny black suit slashed with neon blue zigzags. There was only one man who would have been wearing such a wild suit. *My stalker.*

Oh no. No, no, no! For just a second I was frozen in fear. I could have reacted in a million different ways. A normal person would have helped him clean up his papers. Or found him a towel to wipe the pie off his face. Or at least apologized. But this was my stalker. And I couldn't have this be our first real encounter ever. So I just did the first thing I could think of - I laughed. Right in his pie-covered face. And then I ran upstairs as fast as I could.

Why the hell did I laugh at him?! This had incident #3 written all over it. *God, what was wrong with me?* But wait…had he seen me? I didn't think so. The pie would have blocked his vision. At least the squishing noise was a pie to his face rather than his liver being flattened. It was possible that I was in the clear. Raven Black didn't experience *incidents. Hopefully.*

The whole thing could have been so easily avoided if he had just been paying more attention. And what was he doing in the stairwell anyway? *Oh, right.* The elevators were down. That would also explain why he had been so late. I pictured him painstakingly carrying that pie down sixty stories only to have me throw it in his face. *God, I was such a monster.* I guess it could have been worse, though. At least I didn't kick him in the nuts and tell him to watch where he was going. That would have added insult to injury. Or I guess injury to insult.

Really, he should have known I was coming. He was stalking me after all. Maybe he wanted me to hit him with the door. No. It was an accident. All of it was a terrible, hopefully anonymous accident. *Please don't have seen me.*

I exited the stairwell into the second-floor hallway and pressed my back against the wall. It felt like my heart was beating out of my chest. Why did I have to be me? If Chastity had run into him like that, she would have known just what to say. She would have apologized and seductively licked the pie off his face or taken off her shirt and used it to clean up the mess. And then they would have gone back to his place for a change of clothes. And fallen in love. It could have been the perfect meet-cute, but I had ruined it. I'd even laughed in his face. Why in God's name had I done that?

Maybe it's not too late! I could still go back and apologize. I could play it off like I had run away to find him a towel. I looked around for a cleaning cart. Those things were always stocked with fresh towels. But there were no carts to be found. The hallway was empty except for a statuesque blonde in a stylish maroon pantsuit approaching.

I sized her up. There was no way I was going to ruin my beautiful panda shirt with blueberry filling, but if I could trick her into giving me her blazer...

No, that wouldn't work. I could hardly talk to strangers, much less convince them to give me their clothes. The only option was to sacrifice my own. I looked down at my favorite panda shirt. It would be a crime to get blueberry filling on such a finely crafted garment. And it would also literally be a crime for me to strip down to my bra in the stairwell. If the police weren't already hot on my trail after the Dr. Lyons incident, stripping in One57 would lead them right to me.

"Raven Black?" asked the woman.

"It wasn't me!" I screamed. She was either an FBI agent coming to arrest me on rape charges, or she was a member of my stalker's personal security detail. Either way, I was screwed.

"You're not Raven Black?" she asked.

I looked to either side for an escape route. "That depends. Who are you?"

"Frankie. Frankie Underwood." She gave me a huge smile and offered me her hand.

"Ha. No way. Frankie Underwood is supposed to be a big strong man with a nine-inch penis. I'm not into girls." Was being a lesbian on the list of expected behaviors? *No.* It definitely was not. Oh my God, had I just said all that out loud? Had hitting my stalker with a door made me lose my mind?

"I'm not really into girls either. But I am into helping girls find new apartments."

I eyed her skeptically. "I feel like this is a trick." She was definitely FBI. I was wanted on so many charges at this point.

"If you think I'm trying to trick you into finding a place you'll love, then you're right. This is a trick."

Hmmm...maybe she is telling the truth.

I studied her a bit more closely. She had a black bracelet on, which meant she was part of the Society. It looked like she had made it herself out of beads…just like Rosalie used to do. Suddenly my mind flashed back twenty years. Rosalie and I were sitting cross-legged on the family room carpet. I had a piece of bread stuffed in my mouth (my way of circumventing the "no food in the family room" rule) while we threaded plastic beads onto string. I tried to shake away the memory. The last thing I needed was to burst out in tears in front of this FBI agent. Or…normal person? Actually, the fact that she was wearing a beaded bracelet made me feel a little less nervous. How dangerous could she be if she made homemade bracelets?

"Ready to find your dream home?" asked Frankie.

It didn't seem like there was a way out of this. And I didn't want to go back in the stairwell and run into my stalker. It was better if he never knew I was here. *Let's go hide out in a random apartment to avoid him.* "Yeah, sure."

"Wonderful."

I glanced down at Frankie's blazer. She even had a laminated nametag with her picture, name, and the logo for Frankie Underwood Realty. This wish had nothing to do with free shoes or my husband, so it wasn't one of my wishes. Which I guess meant it was one of hers. Had she wished to be a successful real estate agent? It wasn't the kinkiest fantasy, but whatever. Maybe selling houses really got her excited. In a way, that was close to my Jack and the Bean Stalk fantasy. Only in that scenario, the buyer was a giant, and the real estate was a sky castle. Or maybe the buyer was a giant's penis and the real estate was my vagina. You know what...just forget it. It made more sense in my head.

"So we're really just going house hunting tonight?" I asked. *You're not going to turn me into a skin cocoon?*

"Yup. That's the plan. But first let's duck in here and go over a few of your preferences." She walked over to Suite 212.

"Okay, sure. I'll be right there. I just need to uh, use the bathroom real quick. I think I saw one in the lobby." *What am I doing?* I thought as the words came out of my mouth. Was I running away from this lesbo FBI agent in disguise? Did I really have to pee? Was I going back to see my stalker? Maybe it was a combination of all three. "I need your blazer. I mean, can I borrow it?"

She gave me a weird look. "Are you going to pee on it?"

"What? Ha. No way. I'll return it to you completely clean. Unless there's a horrible blueberry accident in the stairwell. You know, I've heard that's a real issue around these parts. I'm just cold. Brrr." I tried to rub my arms to look cold, but I only succeeded at jiggling my boobs. And then I realized that I was entirely too awkward to talk to my stalker. It was a blessing that he'd taken a pie in the face and not seen me. I needed to learn to interact with other humans and then I could try again. "Actually, just forget it. I suddenly don't need to pee anymore."

She glanced at my crotch.

"I didn't pee my pants, if that's what you're thinking. I just have a weird bladder thing. Spastic bladder is what they call it." I cleared my throat to try to stop the awkwardness coming out of my mouth. "So…you were going to help me find an apartment?" I walked past her and into the office.

"Yup!" she said, mercifully ignoring the whole spastic bladder thing. "I just have a few questions and then we can head out and look at some places." She pulled out a chair for me and opened her laptop. "Okay, let's see... First things first. Are you looking to rent or buy?"

I don't know. I wasn't actually in the market for real estate. My financial situation could not exactly be described as healthy. If Chastity hadn't hooked me up with my new job, I would have been homeless soon. Joe had taken everything from me. And I couldn't do anything about it. Not unless I was cool with him releasing that sex tape he had of me. And I definitely was not cool with that. Thus…I was left with nothing. *Asshole.*

So yeah…no new real estate for me. Especially not after my thousand-dollar Monopoly shopping spree. *Monopoly!* If my count had been right, I had over $750,000 in monopoly money. Could I use that to buy an apartment from the Society? I decided to pretend like I could. "I'm up for renting or buying. If you find me the right place for under 750K, I can pay in cash."

"That's a good strategy. It's hard to say if you'll want to rent or buy until you see the place. Me? I'm renting a few different places with the option to buy once I decide which one I like the best."

"You can do that?" I asked. I'd heard of that with car leases, but not with houses. This was so fancy.

"Sure. I have my landlords wrapped around my finger."

Of course she did. She was exactly what you'd expect from a member of a sex club. Long blonde hair. Legs for days. Dimples. Somehow even the bullring in her nose wasn't totally repulsive, which was shocking. Because those things were freaking disgusting. No matter how well she cleaned it every night, it would never be enough to get rid of her nose germs. *Thank God I'd talked Rosalie out of getting one of those back in college.* Unless Frankie's landlord was a total germaphobe like me, then the poor guy would probably give her the entire apartment building for free.

Frankie scrolled to the next question. "Do you care if your house has had more than three previous owners?"

"What? Why would I care about that?"

"Well, you know. Sometimes people are picky about that sort of thing. They want everything to be brand new. And sometimes lots of previous owners in a short time means that there's something wrong with the place. Or at least, that's what my therapist told me to look out for."

Therapist? For house hunting tips? Weird. "Now that you mention it, I guess I would prefer for it to be brand new." *Nice and germ-free.* Unlike her nose ring. *Gag.*

"Would you like it to be pet-friendly?"

"No pets. I want the opposite of pet-friendly. I'm pet-hostile."

"But puppies are so cute." She reached for her phone. "Look at this picture of my friend's adorable little Pomeranian..."

What now? I was about to smack a bitch. The only thing good about a little dog was how easy it would be to punt it out a window. "Have you seen an air filter from a house with dogs? Or looked at a dog owner under a black light? I did once. All that slobber lit them up like a Christmas tree." Oh God, that reminded me of when I'd lit Matthew Caldwell's pants up like a Christmas tree. *Stop it.* "Dogs are the offspring of Satan and Stalin."

"Wow, okay. No pets. Let's move on. How important is it to you that your apartment is reliable?"

What does that even mean? "Are you talking about stuff breaking a lot? Yeah, I'd love for shit to break all the time."

"Got it. You want something that makes you work a little," she said as she typed it into her laptop.

"What? No. Don't write that down. I was being sarcastic. Of course I want it to be reliable. Who would want a place that they have to constantly fix?"

"Me, apparently." She laughed and asked me a bunch more questions, but none of the usual stuff. She didn't really say anything else about my budget, and she didn't ask about how many bedrooms or bathrooms I wanted. The answer to that, for the record, would have been two of each. Or at least two bathrooms. That was the key. Otherwise I'd never be able to have anyone over. A single bathroom was a pants-pissing incident waiting to happen.

"Just one final question and then we can start looking at some places," said Frankie. "Do you care if it's carpeted, or do you want it to be completely smooth?"

Completely smooth? Who talks about a floor that way? I was suddenly feeling like I wasn't the most awkward person in the room, if that was possible. "Carpets are okay in some rooms, but I don't want those little germ nests anywhere near kitchens or bathrooms."

Frankie nodded as she made a few more notes and then closed her laptop. "Okay, let's go look at some apartments!"

As we went down the stairs, I tried to hide behind Frankie in case my stalker was still there, but he was gone. The only trace of him was some blueberry filling splattered on the floor.

Had I missed my only chance to meet my stalker? I sure hoped not. And I really, really hoped he hadn't seen me.

Chapter 15

SMOOTH FLOORS?

Tuesday

"Drive or walk?" asked Frankie.

"How far is it?"

"Just down the street. At the Caldwell Hotel."

Hearing the name Caldwell made me shudder. It was like no matter how hard I tried not to think of *the incident*…it kept popping up. *Curse you, Matthew freaking Caldwell.* I tried not to think about it as the hotel came into view. *Wow.* I didn't know if my 750,000 monopoly dollars would even make a dent in the down payment for a place at the Caldwell Hotel. I'd never been inside, but I knew that Chastity's boss and Matthew's older brother, Mason Caldwell, owned the building. He'd bought the Manhattan a few years ago and totally rebuilt it. Now it was one of the most expensive hotels in the city. And it showed.

Every bit of the building oozed class. Gold trim, polished marble…even the doorman's forest-green suit looked like it had been handcrafted by some name-brand designer.

"I thought this was a hotel?" I asked as Frankie led me to the elevators.

"Only the bottom 20 floors or so. The rest is residential." The elevator dinged open and a liftman held the doors open for us. Unlike the doorman who had been well over 60, the liftman was around my age. And *damn* was he handsome. Was he part of the Society? I was so busy checking him out that I nearly tripped. I tried to play it off like it was no big deal.

"41st floor, please," said Frankie.

"My pleasure." The liftman pressed the button and up we went.

On the ride up, Frankie explained that all the apartments had access to all the amenities of the hotel, including a heated indoor pool, a fully equipped gym, room service from the restaurant downstairs, a la carte bath butler services, and daily maid service.

"This first apartment is the base model here. Two bedrooms, one and a half baths. Pretty standard. Nothing too fancy, but it's a good solid apartment. You really can't go wrong with it."

"Sounds boring," I said. If I was going to splash almost a million fake dollars, I didn't want the base model. I wanted something freaking amaze-balls.

"Noted. Just try to keep an open mind and afterward we can discuss what you liked and what you didn't."

Maybe if she'd asked me better questions than if I wanted a "completely smooth" floor she'd have known that I didn't want something #Lame, as Chastity would say. Score! I'd finally used a hashtag right! I couldn't wait to tell Chastity all about it. But right now I needed to focus.

Frankie swiped a keycard through the lock and the door clicked open. I went immediately to the kitchen. That was always my favorite thing to see on all those HGTV shows. Well, that and the master bathrooms. This kitchen was okay. Not amazing, but definitely better than mine. I was looking at the stack of listing flyers when a man said, "Hello."

Holy shit! I threw the entire stack of papers in the air and nearly fell over.

"Sorry, didn't mean to startle you," he said.

"Are you the owner? I'm so sorry. I just assumed Frankie had arranged for us to be here. We'll leave right away."

"I'm the listing agent. John." He stuck his hand out for me to shake. "Nice to meet you."

I shook it, but I didn't reach in far enough, so he just ended up wiggling my fingers like wet noodles. "Cool," I said.

"Cool," he agreed. "Just let me know if you have any questions." He gave me a friendly smile. I know that you're probably thinking he was super hot and that I was going to rape him or something. But that wasn't the case. Other than his smile, the rest of him wasn't really worth describing. Actually, I don't really remember what he looked like. I think he was average height with an average build, probably dressed in a standard realtor outfit of a white button-down and some slacks.

It only took me a few minutes to tour the entire apartment. According to the listing flyers I had thrown all over the kitchen, it was only 730 square feet. Most importantly, I didn't once try to get naked or rape John during the entire tour. I was very proud of myself. My reintroduction into the wild was going quite well, other than the whole pie thing with my stalker. And the more time I spent out in the wild, the more I realized that had totally been my stalker's fault. What kind of stalker didn't know where his stalkee was at all times? I just taught him a lesson to step up his game. He'd thank me later.

Frankie was waiting for me in the foyer. "So what'd you think?" she asked.

"I think we should keep looking."

John looked disappointed. Maybe he was really in need of that commission check of monopoly money. "Well, thanks for considering it. Good luck finding an apartment."

"You too." *Damn it.* I always said shit like that. Especially at restaurants when the waiter would tell me to enjoy my meal. Or when people wished me happy birthday. The worst was one time when I said it to some girl who had the same birthday as me. I immediately took it back, and then I really looked like an asshole. *You too. Actually, don't have a nice birthday, bitch!* Rather than try to awkwardly backtrack with John I just walked out and hoped he hadn't noticed.

"So what turned you off about this one?" asked Frankie when we were alone in the hallway.

"It was okay. It was just so...boring."

"I get that. But what specifically didn't you like? The more you give me, the better I'll do with the next one."

"Well I definitely didn't like how John surprised me in the kitchen. Why was he there? Was he having an open house?" If he was, he did a terrible job advertising it. There hadn't been a single sign anywhere on the way up. And there weren't any glasses of complimentary champagne. In all the fancy showings on TV, there was always champagne. Poor, simple John. He wasn't going to sell that place in a million years.

"For apartments this expensive, the listing agent usually likes to be there to answer any questions."

"Ah, gotcha." *Crazy rich people.*

"So what else didn't you like?"

Where do I even begin? "I didn't like all the walls. I'm looking for more of an open concept. And the kitchen was just so...blah. I want a big island. And granite countertops. And a sexy backsplash. Oh! Definitely a gas stove with one of those fancy hoods over it."

"So you're looking for something with a little more flair?"

"Yeah, I guess you could say that." I hadn't been in the housing market for a while, but it sure seemed like she was using some strange lingo. It didn't really matter though. There was no way the Society would actually let me buy a place here using Monopoly money. I decided to just have some fun and pretend like I was on *My Lottery Dream Home.* "You know what, I can get more than $750,000 for a down payment. Just show me the most extra place you've got."

"Now that's what I like to hear." Frankie clicked a few buttons on her phone. "I have just what you're looking for."

We took the elevator up to the 58th floor. If the elevator buttons were to be trusted, that was only a few floors away from being the top of the tower. *Fancy indeed.* In fact, it was so fancy that there wasn't even really a hallway. Just a little foyer with two doors labeled 58A and 58B. 58B was our destination. And it was freaking awesome.

"Hello, gorgeous," said the realtor, shutting his Cosmo magazine and setting it aside. "Pink Ocelot, at your service." He bowed and kissed my hand. Usually I would have been grossed out by such a gesture, but he was so well groomed that I wasn't even sure his lips had any germs on them. Seriously. I'd never seen a man so impeccably groomed. His skin was flawless, his fuchsia dress shirt had clearly been pressed, and his hair was…huge.

I probably should have said hi, but instead I just stared at him. I had so many questions. *How much gel did it take for him to pull off that hairstyle? And what the hell kind of name is Pink Ocelot?*

"We can start the tour in a minute," he said. "But I have to ask…who did your hair? It's divine." Ocelot ran his hands through the ends of my black wig. "Paul Mitchell called, he needs his model back."

Am I the model? Or does my wig have a model number or something? Shit! Is it that obvious that it's a wig?

"Ocelot, please!" said Frankie. "Try not to touch my clients."

"How can I keep my hands off perfection?" He growled like a tiger. Or did Ocelots growl? Either way, he growled.

"I'm sure you'll find a way. How about you show us around?"

"What would you like to see first?"

I didn't answer. I just started wandering around trying to imagine how much this all must cost.

The ceilings were all at least ten feet high, the whole living space was open, and every surface was sparkling white. It looked like the Property Brothers had just been there and worked their magic. Every room had unique details that brought the whole place to life. I wasn't sure if my favorite part was the black and white zigzag accent wall in the master bedroom or the flamboyant marble statue of Dionysus in the dining room.

Then we got to the bathroom.

It was modern and sleek, with lots of glass. There was even a fireplace in the corner for no apparent reason other than to be extra. But two things caught me off guard. First, there was a bidet - the world's most disgusting invention. And second, the shower wasn't nearly as big as I would have wanted for such a sick bathroom.

"So what do you think?" asked Ocelot. "Fabulous, right?"

"Yes. But why is the shower so small?"

"I wouldn't call it small. More like slightly above average. Most importantly, though, this shower knows how to hit you in all the right spots at just the right time. Not just any old shower can you do that, you know."

Is that what all those buttons are for? "Hmmm…I don't know. It really seems small to me."

He looked insulted for a moment, but then he smoothed his shirt and regained his composure. "My dear girl, don't get me wrong. Big showers are amazing. In fact, I've looked at real estate all over the world in search of the biggest shower. But big showers are best as a sometimes thing. A special treat, if you will."

What the hell is he talking about? "I have to disagree. I want the biggest shower ever, right in my house. It's actually at the very top of my must-have list. Oh! How about a double shower head? I've always…"

Ocelot put his finger to my lips. "Shush. Say no more, my dear. I could never fault a girl for wanting a bigger shower. And I've always thought that double showerheads just make sense."

"Is the small shower a deal-breaker?" asked Frankie.

"Slightly above average," corrected Ocelot.

"Yeah, I think so." *And this place must cost a bajillion dollars that I don't have.* It was better to bow out gracefully because of the shower than to embarrass myself by letting them find out I was broke.

"Alright then," said Frankie. "Onto the next place." She looped her arm through mine and guided me out while Ocelot bowed deeply.

"That guy was so weird," I said when we were back in the hall. "But I kind of loved it. I've always thought it would be so fun to have a gay best friend."

"Ocelot isn't gay," said Frankie.

"Say what now? Was he not just reading *Cosmo* when we walked in? And did you see that freshly pressed shirt?"

"I actually think it's hot how well he takes care of himself. If more men were like Ocelot, the world would be a better place."

I couldn't argue with that. Even if he was gay - which I was quite certain he was - he still would have been an infinitely better husband than Joe.

"You know," said Frankie as we waited for the elevator. "For a second I thought you had found your dream home. That you loved it. Or were in love with it, as Ocelot likes to say." She laughed to herself.

I felt like I was missing the joke. "Nope. I need that giant double shower. Non-negotiable."

"Any other notes about Ocelot's place?"

"Well…I always thought I wanted white walls. But now I'm not so sure. It was elegant, yes, but also a little clinical. How about a little color?"

"Black walls?"

"Whoa, no. Aren't black walls supposed to make everything look smaller?"

Frankie looked at me like I was crazy. "Not in my experience. But I understand. Black walls can be an acquired taste."

"How about like…light walls with lots of splashes of color?"

"Let's see what's available." Frankie scrolled through her phone and then let out an excited squeal. "On a scale of one to ten, how excited are you to meet your future home?"

"Ten?"

"Good answer. Because I just found exactly what you're looking for. You, Raven, are in for a real treat."

The next place was a few floors down. I had to blink when I walked it. My brain knew I was in an NYC skyscraper, but my senses told me I was in a Spanish villa. The terra cotta floors, the rustic wood, the colorful accent tiles… It was incredible. It even smelled like freshly baked churros. I would know, because I spent a semester in Barcelona. Just kidding. I never did that. But my 10th-grade Spanish teacher brought us churros one time, so that was basically the same thing. Either way, the smell was intoxicating.

"What do you think?" asked Frankie.

"I think I'm in heaven. I've always wanted to go to Spain."

"So this is the one?" She sounded so excited.

"It just might be. How tall are these ceilings?!" They were so high that they made Ocelot's place seem cramped in comparison.

"At least 12 feet. And look at how perfectly smooth these floors are."

I looked down. The tile floors were nice and all. But that didn't really feel like a big selling point. *And why does she keep talking about smooth floors?* I really needed to study my real estate lingo. "Where's the kitchen? Actually, scratch that. I wanna see the master bath."

"Good choice. I think you're going to be *very* impressed."

I followed her up the spiral staircase. If the amazing detail on the wrought iron railing was any indication, then Frankie was absolutely correct. *I really hope they take my Monopoly money.*

The bathroom wasn't exactly what I'd imagined. I'd always pictured something very modern. But this was even better.

"O.M.G. This shower is huge! No, that's an understatement. It's ginormous."

"Double nozzles, just like you wanted. So you can get it from both sides at once." She wiggled her eyebrows at me.

Naughty Frankie! Speaking of naughty…for an evening facilitated by a sex club, things had been extremely tame. Were they trying to get me comfortable with a tame first date so that I'd walk straight into a gangbang on my next date? If so, then it was totally working. *Well played, Society. Well played.*

"Have you ever tried a double shower before?" asked Frankie. "Or is it just a lifelong fantasy of yours?"

"Lifelong fantasy." I ran my hand along the columns on each side of the shower. *God, this is amazing.* "Actually, that's not accurate. I don't think I even realized it was a thing until high school. But ever since I realized it was an option, I've been obsessed."

"Wanna give it a try?" She gestured to the shower handle.

"Sure." I reached in and turned on both nozzles. They were a little further away from each other than I'd expected. I'd been hoping to be able to stand in the middle and get sprayed on my front and back at the same time, but this seemed like more of a setup for a couple showering together. It would have been perfect for Joe and me. Whenever we'd showered together, he'd always been a jerk and hogged all the water while I stood in the back freezing my naked ass off hoping that a sprinkle or two of hot water would reach me.

"Impressive, huh?" asked Frankie.

"Yeah, it's... Holy penises!" *Where did these two naked men come from?!*

Chapter 16

DOUBLE, DOUBLE, SHOWER TROUBLE

Tuesday

I stared in shock at the naked men. Their tattoo-covered, completely hairless torsos were like big sexy arrows pointing downward directly to their humungous erections. Chastity hadn't been kidding about stacked soda cans.

One of them raised a seductive eyebrow. "Like what you see?"

"What?" *What the hell is happening?!* "Why are you naked?! And who the hell are you?!" My eyes gravitated down to his penis again and then snapped back to his face.

"I'm Angel," said the shorter one.

"And I'm Diablo," said the other. "And we're naked because you said you wanted to try us out." He took a step towards me as he stroked his thick cock.

"I wanted to try the *shower*!" *So much for this being a tame evening.*

"Don't worry," said Angel, pushing his longish hair out of his eye. "I promise we'll be gentle."

"At first," added Diablo.

Holy shit. Am I about to get raped? I glanced down again. *Hot damn.* How would that huge monster feel inside of me? *What the actual fuck am I thinking?* They were just. So. Big. *Stop staring at their huge penises!*

Diablo took another step toward me.

Nope. Not happening. That thing would never fit in me. Before the two men could get any closer, I screamed "RAPE!" and ran out of the bathroom. Oh God, were they following me? Was this how I died? I didn't stop running until I was safe in the elevator.

"Where to?" asked the liftman.

Holy shit. I ignored him and frantically jammed the LOBBY button. The doors were taking forever to close. *Come on. Come on!* I slammed my fist against the LOBBY button again. Was this how Dr. Lyons had felt when I sexually assaulted him? Maybe this was karma. All rapists eventually got raped themselves.

"Can't you make the doors close?!" I practically shouted at him.

"Is everything okay?" he asked.

"No!" I was going to elaborate when the doors finally started to slide shut. My overactive imagination pictured a hand reaching between them at the last second. Or what if it was something else? What if Diablo stuck his gigantic penis between the doors? Would it get chopped off? Joe's would have. No question about it. But Diablo's? That thing was like a third arm. If anything, it would probably end up damaging the elevator door, not the other way around.

The doors were *almost* closed when something really did stop them. But it wasn't a penis, or a big rapey hand. It was a feminine hand with lots of rings.

The doors slowly reopened. "You okay?" asked Frankie.

"No I'm not okay! I almost got raped!"

The liftman somehow didn't react to that.

"They weren't going to rape you. They just thought you were asking for it."

I was asking for it? "Oh yeah, this panda shirt makes me look like such a whore."

"Not what I meant. I meant you said you wanted to try the shower..."

"Exactly!" This girl was out of her damned mind. "I wanted to see how the shower worked. Not be double-teamed by two strangers. Unless shower is suddenly a code word for penis, I don't see how those two things could possibly be confused..." And then it hit me. *Oh my God.* Shower *was* a code word for penis. I wasn't house shopping. I was man shopping, and all the weird house lingo corresponded to attributes about the "realtors". That was why Frankie had referred to the floors as being completely smooth. And why asking for colorful walls with a double shower had brought me to an apartment with two tanned and heavily tattooed men. I suddenly felt kinda bad about repeatedly telling Ocelot how small his shower was. "Oooh," I said. "I get it."

"I'm sure Angel and Diablo are still willing to entertain an offer if you think that's the apartment for you."

"Are you sure about that?" *Did they actually want me?* The thought was actually a little…exhilarating. What would two beautiful men like that want with a weirdo like me? Was it my fancy wig?

"Yeah, I'm sure. You saw how hard they were, right?"

"How could I *not* have seen?" They'd been hard. Really, really hard.

Frankie laughed. "Good point. So what's the verdict? Are we moving on to the next place? Or do you want to sign a lease with Angel and Diablo?"

"If I do go back in…what would happen? Could I ask them to do whatever I wanted?" *What am I saying?* I'd officially lost my mind.

"Of course you could," said Frankie. "Although I should warn you…Angel and Diablo do have a bit of a reputation. If you walk back in there, you better be prepared to get double-teamed."

Holy shit. I pressed my legs together. A devil's threesome had always been a fantasy of mine, but only in theory. I never thought it was actually a thing that could happen. "Can I look at the listing again before I decide?"

"Sure." Frankie clicked a few buttons and handed me her phone.

A picture of the foyer was front and center. The Spanish architecture really was beautiful, but that wasn't what I'd been curious about. I scrolled down until I got to a picture of the listing agents. They were even more beautiful than I remembered. On the left was Angel with his pouty lips and longish hair that swept in front of his capitating pale gray eyes. And on the right was Diablo. I'd been so distracted by his uh…jawline that I hadn't noticed it in the bathroom, but he had a cross tattooed under his left eye.

"Does Diablo really have a face tat?" I asked.

"He does," said Frankie. "It's so hot, isn't it?"

On anyone else it would have looked trashy, but the rest of his look was so polished that it somehow worked. His tan skin and chiseled jawline didn't hurt. *Am I seriously considering this?!* My brain told me to run home. But the rest of me wanted to run back into that apartment and make all of my wildest fantasies come true. I mean it *was* a threesome. With two super hot guys. That sounded kind of amazing.

No. I couldn't. I didn't even know them. But that could be fixed…

"So what do you know about Angel and Diablo?" I asked.

"Not much. They're brothers, and they do everything together. Including fucking. Most people say Angel is the nice one, but I'm not so sure. I knew a girl who spent a night with them, and she said that they're equally devilish between the sheets. She also said it was the best sex of her life."

Chastity would never forgive me for passing up this opportunity. It went directly against Single Girl Rule #8 about 8 inches and 8 abs. And I was curious... I bit my lip as I stared down at the picture of them. What was I even thinking? I couldn't do this. Frankie's story about her friend reminded me of one very important fact: these guys probably had a million diseases.

And even if they didn't, I was way too awkward of a person for a threesome. I'd probably end up trying to make their penises talk to each other like sock puppets and totally kill the mood.

I shook my head. I needed to put a stop to this before I did something insane. Like actually have a threesome with two strangers. This was what happened when you let a sexual deviant out of her hermit cave. I needed to be locked up for good. "I think I'm done for the night."

"Oh come on!" said Frankie. "I still think I can find you the perfect home. I take it you don't want a double shower after all?"

"Single would be preferable."

"What about the size of that shower? Too big?"

No way. I needed that in my life. "Not necessarily. But a bit smaller would be acceptable."

"Good. Because those are just about the biggest showers we've got. Smooth floors?"

"Uh, I'd like the upstairs to be carpeted. Downstairs can be either. Not like a shag carpet though." *Hopefully that's the right lingo. Wait...why am I answering these questions?* I didn't want her to find me some random dude to bang. The only random dude I wanted was my stalker. Which gave me a wonderful idea. "Actually, can you find me a place where the upstairs has a long carpet? Preferably brown. And crazy colored walls. No, not walls." Crazy-colored walls would have meant the realtor was some neon-skinned sex alien. "White walls. But crazy colored art." *No, that's tattoos.* "Not permanent art though. Removable art."

Frankie smiled. "I've got just the place."

I had no idea if anything I'd just said made sense. So I held my breath as we entered the next apartment. Was it going to be my stalker? Nope. No such luck. Instead it was some long-haired bro in bright orange workout shorts doing squats with skinny girls in slutty workout gear.

"This place is only available for rent," said Frankie. "And you'd be sharing it with some roommates."

"Gross." I quickly backed out of the apartment before anyone noticed me. Apparently my stalker wasn't an option. Because of course he wasn't. What were the odds that my stalker would have been part of the Society? "I really do need to get going," I said. "I'm starting a new job tomorrow so I shouldn't stay out too late."

Frankie frowned. "But we've only tried a few. The average homebuyer visits 8 to 10 apartments before they find the one. Not to mention that I'm the best realtor in town. What are you going to do…use an app? Every place I show you has been thoroughly vetted. You think Zillow cares about the accuracy of their listings?"

Translation: you'll get AIDS if you hook up with some dude on Tinder. Which was probably accurate. Besides, Chastity had used an app to set me up on the blind date from hell with Matthew Caldwell. So yeah…I didn't want to use any dating apps. They were dead to me. Which meant my two options were to be alone forever or play along with Frankie's little real estate game. If I didn't do this, Chastity would never let me live it down. And…I was really curious. What could a few more places hurt? As horrifying as tonight had been, it had also made me laugh. I was having fun. I took a deep breath. I was living. And if I figured out Frankie's lingo, I might be able to order up the perfect man.

So what was my ideal man? *My stalker.* But I couldn't have him. Mainly because if I ever saw him again, I'd be so embarrassed about the pie incident that I'd probably scream and hide. Or just laugh in his face again. I didn't think he'd seen me, but there was a slim possibility. And that was enough to make me never want to show my face near One57 again. Damn, I was really going to miss seeing him twice a week. But not as much as he was going to miss seeing me…since he was the stalker in this scenario.

"Sometimes it's hard to know exactly what you want until you see it," said Frankie. "But that's where I come in. Just trust me and I promise I'll find you the perfect place."

"Okay, let's do it." It was better that way. When I'd tried to describe my stalker with man-house metaphors, I'd almost ended up being some gym bro's sidepiece.

Her first try was okay. He was handsome. He was friendly. He had a nice smile. But I just didn't get the right vibes from him. And he was like seven feet tall.

"All these high ceilings are making me dizzy," I said. "Can we go a little shorter?"

"How short?"

"Surprise me."

And she did. Because the realtor at the next place was a dwarf. The ceilings in the apartment may have been short, but the realtor assured me that the shower was *huge.*

No thanks.

Frankie tried a few more times. One realtor was an earthy cowboy playing a guitar, but the excessive taxidermy on the walls was a pretty big turn-off. The next was a polished wall street type with slicked-back hair and a five o'clock shadow. He was like Joe, only a million times better looking. But he was still like Joe. *Hard pass.*

The more apartments we visited, the more I wondered about the Society. How did they have such a wide variety of men sitting around waiting for me? And how did they afford all these apartments?

"I think I might not be ready for a new apartment yet," I said after I had rejected five more men. Or rather, after I rejected four men and got kicked out of the fifth's apartment for making a particularly distasteful comment comparing the smell of Indian food to a cow's rear-end. In my defense, I hadn't seen that the realtor was Indian when I made the comment. "I'm gonna get going."

"I just have one more," she said. "And I think it might be everything you're looking for."

"Oh yeah?" That was hard to believe. I'd decided that Frankie was terrible at her job. She had no idea what she was doing. She was an idiot person.

"Yeah. It's a gorgeous place that just recently went on the market. The molding is all custom. There's a gourmet kitchen. The ceilings are nice and tall. The realtor will probably even be baking something to make it feel homey."

Hmm. "Sounds perfect."

"As your realtor, though, I feel compelled to advise you against making an offer. It may look beautiful on the outside, but it's all just a façade. Behind all the paint and granite and trim, the foundation is a mess. Bad wiring, rusty pipes. It wouldn't surprise me if there's even asbestos or some lead paint."

It sounded like this guy was a hot mess. Which if I was being honest with myself was actually right up my alley. I was pretty sure my foundation was a mess too. And I didn't really have anything to lose. "He sounds perfect."

She stared at me, because she'd literally just said he wasn't. "Did you hear anything I just said?"

I shrugged. "Something about rusty pipes. Let's do this."

Chapter 17

JUMP!

Tuesday

The elevator opened directly into the penthouse of the Caldwell Hotel. And *damn* was it nice.

"Like what you see?" asked Frankie.

I took it back. Frankie wasn't an idiot person. She was amazing. "Why was this not the very first place you showed me?"

"Have you already forgotten my warning?"

Screw her warning. This was the apartment for me. I just knew it. The only question was…who was the realtor? The walls were white, which meant he had white skin. What did the glass walls mean, though? Did he wear lots of mesh tank tops? Or was he so pale that his skin was practically translucent?

"Come on," said Frankie with a tug on my arm. "You haven't even seen the best part."

She led me towards the kitchen, which was part of a two-story great room. I was kind of obsessed. Not to mention the wall art. In a normal house the bright colors and geometric patterns would have been too much, but against the white walls and paired with the sleek modern furniture, they were kind of perfect. They also meant that the realtor probably wore bright clothing…

"Good evening," said a deep voice behind us.

I turned around and found myself staring directly into my stalker's beautiful brown eyes. There were still speckles of blueberry on his shirt. *Oh. No.* I immediately ducked behind the nearest piece of furniture. *Shit! Shit shit shit!* Had he seen me? Yes, I'd wanted to meet him. But now that it was happening, it kind of felt like my entire body was going to explode. Or melt. Wait, was I already melting? Or was I just sweating *that* profusely? I closed my eyes. If I couldn't see him, he couldn't see me. That was how things worked.

"Are you hiding?" he asked.

I stayed still. Maybe he was talking to someone else. I just wanted to disappear.

"You know I can see you through that glass table, right?"

I snuck a glance back at him. Sure enough, I could see him clear as day through the top of the glass table I'd ducked behind. *Damned modern furniture.* I stayed still for a second, hoping he'd just walk away and pretend this hadn't happened.

Instead, the corner of his gorgeous mouth ticked up.

"I'm not hiding," I said way too defensively. "I was just…tying my shoes."

"Tying your flats?" His voice was filled with amusement. "They don't have laces."

"Don't be rude to your guest," said Frankie.

"You're right, I'm sorry," said my stalker. "I'm just having one of those days. You wouldn't believe what happened to me on my way over."

Please don't recognize me from the pie incident.

"Anyway, I'm Ryder. Pleasure to meet you." He stuck his hand out for me to shake.

By some miracle it seemed like he hadn't seen me hit him with the pie. I breathed a sigh of relief. God, he was so beautiful up close. And his name was Ryder? That was a super hot name. And it suited him. I bet he could ride me all night. "I'm meeting to pleasure you."

He raised an eyebrow. "Well that's rather forward of you."

What? Then I realized I had jumbled my words all around. *Fuck my life.* "Er…it's a pleasure to meet you."

"I kind of liked your other greeting better."

Kill me now.

"Raven here was just telling me how much she loves this apartment," said Frankie. "We've visited a bunch, but this seems to be the only one she's interested in."

My stalker…er, Ryder…nodded. "Then she has good taste." He turned and locked eyes with me. "What other places did you look at?"

"Uh…" How could I phrase this? For all I knew, all those guys were his friends. "Before I answer that, I have a question for you."

"Ask away."

"Are you good friends with a gay man or two rapey Spanish men?" *Shit!* That had seemed a lot less offensive in my head.

Ryder laughed. "I take it you met Ocelot and the brothers?"

"Maybe."

He turned to Frankie. "What in the world made you think she'd like those apartments?"

Frankie put her hands up. "Don't blame me. She asked for the biggest double shower I could find."

"Really?" asked Ryder. His eyes locked with mine again. "I never would have guessed."

I could feel my face turning red. "I didn't fully understand what I was asking for," I said. "But yes, I did technically request that."

Ryder raised an eyebrow. "And it wasn't what you wanted?"

"Not at all." I shook my head. "Especially when I didn't even have time to prepare myself. Prepare mentally. For the shock of it. Not like…prepare with lube. Although I imagine a lot of lube would be necessary…" *What the hell am I saying?!* I cleared my throat to try to distract my stalker from the pure awkwardness that had just left my mouth. "So…how about you show me around this place?"

"Got it." Ryder pulled out a little notebook and jotted something down.

"What are you writing?" I asked.

"Nothing." He tucked the notebook back into his jacket pocket. "So where shall we begin with our tour? The master bedchamber?"

"Sure." *Who the hell calls it a bedchamber?* I thought I was the only one who said weird stuff like that.

He led me up the stairs and into a ridiculously awesome bedroom, complete with a four-poster bed. He kicked something into a closet and slammed it shut.

"Was that a Croc?"

"What?" asked Ryder with a laugh. "Why would there be a crocodile in the penthouse? That sounds like the title of a children's book."

Okay... There was no time to dwell on that, though. Because my eyes went straight to the silk neckties tied securely to two of the bedposts. "What are those for?" I asked.

Ryder stared at me. "Would you like to find out?"

I gulped. Was my stalker about to tie me to his bed? I'd had this fantasy before. But it usually ended with him cutting me up in little tiny pieces. Luckily Frankie would never let that happen though. "That depends. Have you used them before?"

"Oh definitely. But they've been thoroughly cleaned since then." He took a step towards me. But then he stopped when his cellphone started ringing. "Hold that thought." He answered his phone. "Talk to me."

I tried to listen. Was he getting a call from the last girl he'd tied to this bed?

I couldn't make out much, but I thought I heard a guy saying something about agents coming.

"You're sure?" asked Ryder. "Okay. Thanks for the heads up."

"What was that about?" I asked.

For a second Ryder's confident smile faltered. "Nothing important. Want to see the balcony?" He put his hand gently on my back and guided me through a maze of rooms and out onto the balcony.

And then the wind blew through my hair and the familiar sounds of honking taxis and squealing brakes filled my ears. For the first time since I'd stepped foot in NYC, I felt like I was able to get a breath of fresh air. And the view… God, the view was everything.

"Not a bad view, huh?" asked Ryder.

"It's amazing." *Is this even real life right now?* I had no idea how I had gotten so lucky to end up on this balcony with my super sexy stalker. Who apparently wanted to tie me to his bed and do unspeakable things to me. Trying new things was working out pretty damned well for me.

And it was about to get even better.

My stalker leaned down towards me. *Is he going to kiss me? Oh my God!* I closed my eyes and got ready for it. I wasn't even scared of whatever germs he had. I just wanted to taste him. But instead I felt his breath on my neck.

"Stay calm," he whispered into my ear. "And don't look back. There are some agents after us. Frankie might be one of them."

My eyes flew open. "Agents? Like…FBI agents?"

Ryder nodded. "Yup. Exactly. FBI agents."

What? "Quit messing with me." God, why did it always seem like the FBI was after me?

"I wish I was." He looked dead serious. "But an acquaintance of mine in NYC was recently taken, and I think I'm next. I'm sorry, I never meant to tangle you up in this."

Taken? What?

"Where'd you guys go?" called Frankie from inside.

"We'll just be out here another second," yelled Ryder. "Why don't you go ahead and draw up a rental agreement?"

"That's up to my client. Is this the one, Raven?"

Ryder nudged me.

"Uh, yeah," I called to Frankie. "Yup. Sure is." My voice cracked as I talked. Playing it cool was definitely not my strong suit. Ryder wasn't serious, was he? All the FBI talk had to be nonsense. This secret sex society was completely legal. *Oh wait…*

Frankie squealed with excitement. *Excitement to send me to prison forever for dirty sex things.* But I hadn't even done anything bad yet! If anything she should be arresting Angel and Diablo for trying to rape me in the bathroom. I'd tell the judge everything and ask for leniency.

I looked back at Ryder. "Do we have to kill her? I can't go to prison. I'm not made for it."

His perfect smile reappeared for a second. "We could do that. But I'd rather jump."

"JUMP?!" My stalker was out of his mind. Which also made sense. Because he was a freaking stalker!

"Shhh!" He pressed his hand over my mouth. It smelled like blueberry pie. I kind of wanted to lick it, but this was no time for such things. Wait…since when did I want to lick someone's hands? That was super gross. But licking his hand kind of seemed appealing? *Weird.*

"Seriously, what are we gonna do?" I could feel the sweat pooling in my pits.

"Jump. Well, zipline, to be precise." A zipline handle had appeared in his hands.

"Where did you get that?"

"From uh…under that plant." He pointed to a potted shrub that definitely didn't look like it had been hiding a zipline. And then he secured the handle to a thick metal cable that ran from his balcony all the way to an adjacent building. Above six lanes of traffic. Hundreds of feet in the air.

I was definitely going to die.

Chapter 18

THE ESCAPE

Tuesday

I shook my head. "Hell. No. I'm not riding that thing."

"You'd rather kill Frankie?" asked Ryder.

"Than go splat on the pavement? Yes," I hissed.

"Good luck with that. And the SWAT team."

"I thought it was the FBI?"

"Right…them." He checked his watch. "They should be here any minute." He adjusted his grip on the zipline and took a few steps back.

Then I heard it. The door breaking. The officers yelling, "FBI!"

Holy shit. My heart felt like it was about to explode out of my chest. I couldn't get enough air. All I could picture was myself in prison and splattered in the middle of traffic. Somehow at the same time. I couldn't move.

"Raven, look at me," said Ryder. He grabbed my chin and forced me to meet his gaze. "I won't drop you. I'll keep you safe. I promise." The sincerity in his voice. The look in his eyes. I knew he was telling the truth. And most of all…his hands on me made me whole body feel like it was on fire. In a good way. Not in a Matthew Caldwell flaming penis way. And in that moment, I knew I had to go with him. Because I didn't want him to stop touching me. And I certainly wasn't safe here. I'd joined an apparently illegal sex club. I'd tried to rape Dr. Lyons. I was wanted on so many levels.

"Fine. But if you drop me, I'll kill you."

For a second he paused, like he was going to leave me behind.

"I'm kidding. Please don't leave me." I jumped into his arms and he laughed.

"Hold on tight," he said.

I wrapped my arms around his muscular torso and hooked my legs behind him. I felt so small wrapped around him. And so safe. Even though we were about to jump off a freaking building.

"Three, two..." As he said, "one," he jumped off the roof. I hung on for dear life with my face buried in his chest. The wind whipped my hair everywhere. *My wig!* Was my wig going to fly off? Or did it already? What if it flew off back on the balcony? It would have my DNA all over it. The police would have my identity.

Before I could totally freak out - both about the wig and the cars below us - we slammed into a mattress and fell onto another. And there we were...two fugitives tangled up in each other after making an epic escape from the FBI. I breathed in the scent of blueberry pie mixed with sweat. It was intoxicating.

"Are you sniffing me?" He smiled down at me.

"What? No." I rolled away from him. "I think a uh, bug flew in my nose." I coughed and turned away.

"I didn't mind. I was just wondering. I probably smell like blueberries."

"And sweat."

"I thought you weren't smelling me?" he asked.

"Well not intentionally," I said. "But how could I not when you're all up in my business?"

"You mean preventing you from falling to your death?"

"Something like that. We were lucky there was a mattress propped on the wall like that to break our fall." I looked down at the mattress we were on. The owner must have gotten a new one and forgotten how hard it is to get rid of an old one.

"Lucky. Right. Well, we're not out of the woods yet. They'll see the zipline. We need to disappear. Follow me."

Ryder grabbed my hand and tugged me through some glass doors into an apartment.

"Whose place is this?"

"No idea, but I hope they have some clothes that fit us." He started opening dressers and rummaging through the clothes.

"Now we're robbing someone?" I was going to end up in prison for sure.

He pulled out his wallet and tossed a wad of money onto the bed. "That should cover it. Try this on." He tossed me a slinky red dress.

"Turn around," I said. "I'm not just going to undress in front of some guy I just met."

"Okay. But you better not peek at me either, then."

I turned around and pulled my shirt over my head. I had my pants halfway unbuttoned when the sound of Ryder's pants unzipping called to me. I snuck a look over my shoulder. *Damn.* I had pictured him out of his suits a thousand times…er, once or twice…but I had never imagined he'd look *this* good. I wondered how many times he'd pictured me naked. The dirty stalker.

And then he caught me.

"Hey!" I screamed. "You promised not to look."

He laughed. "So did you." His eyes traveled to my bra.

I put my arm over my chest. "I was just checking to make sure you weren't looking!"

"So was I."

I narrowed my eyes at him. "Fine."

"Fine." He couldn't even hide the smile from his lips.

We both turned back around and got back to dressing. The red dress was *just* stretchy enough to fit over my big ass. But when I pulled it up around my chest, I realized that I had entirely the wrong bra for it. T-shirt bras and cocktail dresses were generally not compatible, especially dresses with necklines as deep as this one. *Guess I have to let the girls free.*

I checked to make sure Ryder wasn't peaking again and then unhooked my bra. His head started to turn at the sound of it, but he was a gentleman and stayed true to his word. He also looked fantastic in his tight boxer briefs…which I shouldn't have been looking at.

"All done?" he asked a few seconds later.

"Yup. You?"

"Mhm."

We both turned around. He gave me the up-down, which I guess in this case was okay since he was checking to see if the dress fit. Fine, it would have been okay either way. I wanted him to look at me.

"It looks perfect," he said. "But it's missing something."

Yeah, a bra. Were my nipples everywhere? They probably were. They always acted up at the worst times.

Instead of a bra, he tossed me a pair of strappy black heels.

"Are you sure these are the best shoes for an escape?" I asked.

"Would you rather wear sneakers with that dress?"

"I'm not sure I'll even be able to walk in these." They were at least five inches tall…exactly the kind of shoes that Joe would have hated me wearing because he was a short loser. Which made me think: is this my first wish coming true? I had wished for shoes. And revenge on Joe. Half of that had now been fulfilled.

"You'll figure it out," Ryder said. "Just don't step on any grates. And avoid sand. Or anything soft."

I started to strap them on. "I didn't realize you were such an expert at walking in heels. Do you do it often?"

"No, I design…" he started coughing. Or fake coughing. For the first time, my stalker was the one who was tongue-tied. But he recovered quickly. "My calves would look amazing in heels. Don't be jealous."

I couldn't help but laugh. He was right. They would. But he'd also look super gay. I much preferred the shiny black dress shoes he had just laced up. Add in the tuxedo he'd stolen from whoever owned this apartment, and he looked amazing. I didn't know where our escape was headed, but part of me wanted to take it right onto the king-sized bed.

"Let's go," he said, grabbing my hand and pulling me into the hallway.

So much for taking it to the bed.

My heart was pounding as the elevator opened. I kind of expected us to be immediately swarmed by FBI agents. But instead it was empty. Ryder held the door for me.

"So what's the plan?" I asked.

"Get a taxi. Go get some dinner far away from here. Wait for things to cool down. And then go back to our normal lives and forget any of this ever happened."

Dinner with my stalker sounded perfect. But forgetting about him forever? No way. Was that really what he wanted?

Ryder hailed the first taxi we saw. And it stopped! *What the hell, taxi drivers?* It always took me like twenty tries to get them to notice me. But when a man like Ryder waved them down, they didn't think twice. Maybe all taxi drivers were gay and couldn't resist chauffeuring hot men around all day. *Figures.*

We switched cabs a few times before arriving at our destination: Trilogy. It was a super fancy restaurant that had just opened a few months ago. Chastity couldn't stop talking about how much she wanted some hunk to take her here. And by *take her here*, I mean get freaky with her in the bathroom.

I was too busy looking around at all the crystal chandeliers to listen to what Ryder said to get the hostess to give us a table, but whatever he said, it worked. He probably flirted with her. I glared at the little two-cent trollop as she showed us to our table. *Stay away from my stalker!*

"So are we safe?" I asked.

He nodded. "I believe so. Which means we get to sit back and enjoy our dinner."

How was he so relaxed right now? The freaking FBI was after us and he was calmly perusing the menu like it was a normal night. But he also probably hadn't tried to rape a doctor recently.

"What are you gonna order?" I asked.

He laughed like I'd just made a joke. "That's a good one. Which course are you most excited for?"

I looked back at the menu. It was just a list of the seven courses we would be eating, whether we wanted to or not. I thought I'd learned a lot about food while completely reinventing the recipes for Dickson & Son's Sugarcakes (yes…that was really the name of Joe's family bakery), but this menu was beyond me. I didn't understand a word of what was on it.

"What in the world is a balut?"

"Wow, it's been years since I've had a balut. Takes me back to my days in Cambodia." He pulled out his notebook and jotted something down. Looked around the restaurant. And made another note.

Takes him back? He didn't look that old. And hadn't he left that notebook in his other suit? "Did you grow up there?"

"What?" He shifted uncomfortably. "Oh, uh. No. Just visited. Anyway, you were asking about baluts? They're boiled fertilized eggs. Absolutely delectable."

I gagged a little.

"They're also our fourth course, apparently," added Ryder. "Well, I guess for me it'll be my fifth course."

"Huh?" I asked.

A smile played on the corner of his mouth. "Yeah, my first course was that blueberry pie you tossed in my face."

My eyes got wide. *Oh God, he does remember.* It was too late to duck under the table. He'd already seen me since we'd been hanging out for a while now. *What the hell do I do?* Where was a dumpster or a lake when I needed it? Maybe there was a lobster tank somewhere around here…

"Did you really think I didn't see you? You know there was a window in the door, right?"

I could feel the heat rushing to my face. There was no escaping this awkward conversation. "I'm *so* sorry."

"I know. I could feel your remorse. Especially when you laughed and ran away."

Was he mad? Shit, he was mad. "I'm so so sorry."

"It's okay. It was actually kind of cute."

Cute? I didn't want him to think I was cute. I wanted him to think I was a sex goddess. Raven Black the seductress. "You can throw a pie in my face if it makes you feel better." Great, that was super sexy. Not.

He laughed.

"I'll just stand there and take it, I swear."

"Oh, I know you will, baby." He leaned forward slightly. "But it's not going to involve a blueberry pie."

Holy shit. I crossed my legs under the table. He was staring at me so intently. What did he mean by that? Was he going to take me back to a sex dungeon? Was he going to bend me right over this table in front of all these people? Maybe they were Society members. The guy at the table next to us was wearing a black watch. But no one else was. And the Society had just been shut down by the FBI. Or maybe he just meant the pie would be lemon meringue instead of blueberry.

"Don't turn around," said Ryder. His playful smile was gone. "But a Gestapo agent just walked in."

"Gestapo?!" I whispered yelled. "Now Nazis are chasing us too? I thought it was just the FBI?"

"Right. I meant FBI. I always get those two mixed up."

Was that some sort of weird political commentary about the FBI being a bunch of Nazis? If so, I might have finally met someone as strange as me. I started to turn around to get a look.

He grabbed my hand. "I said don't look."

Oops. But it was really hard not to look when he specifically told me I couldn't. I wanted to see what he thought a Nazi looked like. Probably bald and fat. Or would they have Hitler-staches?!

"I'm going to pretend to go to the bathroom. In twenty seconds, calmly put your napkin on the table and meet me at the kitchen doors. Just do as I say and everything will be fine."

Fine? "Don't leave me out here."

"I'm not leaving you. I promise." His thumb slowly ran down my palm as he stood up. "I'll be waiting for you."

Of course he thought everything would be fine! He was leaving me as bait!

Chapter 19

HOLY MEATY GOODNESS

Tuesday

I'd hardly processed Ryder's escape instructions when he calmly walked away.

Oh my God, he left me. Why hadn't he let me disappear first like a freaking gentleman? I counted down from twenty, trying not to completely freak out. But I panicked and jumped from ten to one and threw my napkin on the table. I rushed to the kitchen, not doing anything calmly at all. And I was both relieved and a little surprised that Ryder was standing there waiting for me. He hadn't left me as bait for the FBI. We were in this craziness together.

Ryder grabbed my arm and pulled me through the swinging doors. We nearly knocked a platter out of a waiter's hand.

"May I help you?" asked the waiter with more than a hint of sass in his voice. God, he was just like that rude barista at the smoothie shop I hated. To clarify, I'm saying that I hated both the barista and the smoothie shop. The barista for the sass and always writing "Ass" on my cup. And the smoothie shop itself for selling disgusting smoothie flavors.

Ryder ignored him and pushed past another waiter. Then he shoved a cook out of the way and knocked over a rack of pastries to block anyone from following us.

"Hey!" shouted someone. "You can't be back here!"

This was probably where we'd get arrested. But I was pleased that Ryder was the one making the mess instead of me. Usually I was the one knocking things over. And even though Ryder was doing it on purpose…it was still his fault not mine. I needed to take this man with me everywhere.

"Run," said Ryder.

I heard more commotion from the front of the kitchen, where the FBI agents had probably just come in. *Run. Okay.* That was a good plan. Plus running was on my list of new things to try. *I'm fucking outta here.* I kicked my shoes off and ran through the kitchen. A busboy narrowly avoided being turned into a pancake by Ryder. We burst into a stairwell. Ryder grabbed me and pushed me up against the wall.

"Shouldn't we keep running…" my voice trailed off as he leaned in to kiss me. But he stopped a fraction of an inch before his lips met mine. *What is he doing?* Was I supposed to lean in? Were we still supposed to be running? I breathed in his exhales as my heart threatened to beat out of my chest. Was he waiting for my permission? *You have it, sir.*

As it turned out, he wasn't waiting for my permission. He was just waiting for an FBI agent to pass. Because as soon as we were alone, he pulled back.

"Phew, that was close," he said, completely ignoring the fact that we'd almost kissed. And that I was so turned on that I was practically panting.

Seriously…why did the combination of almost getting arrested and being pressed up against a wall by a stranger have me all hot and bothered? Probably because my stalker was hardly a stranger. We'd known each other through silent stares for months. And his lips had looked so utterly kissable for just as long. My gaze dropped back down to his mouth.

"Are you hungry?" he asked. "All this running has me famished. Come on, I know the perfect place."

"Oh. Um…" I looked down at my bare feet. But before I could protest, he scooped me up in his arms and carried me out to the street where he was able to hail another taxi on his first try. The cab stopped near the Caldwell hotel, which I thought was way too close to where the original FBI raid had happened.

"Shouldn't we go somewhere far away from here?" I asked.

Ryder shrugged. "Only an amateur would come back to the scene of the crime. They'd never expect that from me. And hence…it's the perfect place to go."

So he wasn't an amateur…what? Murderer? Burglar? Stalker? An amateur what?! I was tempted to tell the driver to step on it when Ryder climbed out of the car. But…how could I walk away now? If we'd really somehow avoided the FBI, this was my one chance to really get to know my stalker. And I'd been dying for this moment for months.

Before I could decide what to do, Ryder nonchalantly picked me up out of the taxi and carried me over to a food cart. It didn't have a name. The sign just said GYROS in big bold Greek-looking letters.

"You're going to show my underwear to everyone!" I said, pulling on the hem of my dress.

"Lucky them," he replied. "You know, I've been wondering. How many kinds of foot fungus are on the average New York City sidewalk?"

I suppressed a gag. But I was also kind of impressed. I don't think any other guy I had ever met would have been aware of sidewalk foot fungus. Or would have been willing to carry me around like a sack of potatoes to keep my bare feet away from said fungus. "If you drop me, I'll kill you." Why did I keep threatening to murder him?

For a second he looked at the ground like he was actually going to drop me.

"I'm joking! Please don't put me down."

There was that smile again.

"I wasn't planning on it," he said.

And he stayed true to his word. He carried me all the way to the front of the line and held me while the guy made our gyros.

I couldn't help but notice how strong he must have been. I wasn't one of those spin class Odegaard models. I had a little meat on my bones, and he just carried me around like I weighed nothing. I tried my best not to nuzzle against his strong chest. Because that would have been weird…right? *Maybe if I just…*

"These are the best gyros in town," he said.

Good, he'd distracted me from doing something awkward. I couldn't nuzzle his chest. I wasn't a cat. "Is that how it's pronounced? I always thought it was jie-roes."

The vendor gave me a dirty look.

"Have you never had a gyro?" asked Ryder.

"Nope." I'd also never been carried around NYC before, and I was loving that. I was down for trying something else new tonight.

Ryder's cellphone rang and he somehow answered it without dropping me. He listened to whoever was on the other end.

I leaned in a little closer, doing my best not to nuzzle as I eavesdropped. But the only thing I overheard was "safe."

Ryder breathed a sigh of relief. "Thanks, Marty. That was a close call. I really thought…" He looked down at me like he'd suddenly forgotten I was in his arms. "I gotta go. Keep me updated." He hung up and cleared his throat. "So you've really never had a gyro, huh?" he asked, like his phone conversation hadn't even happened.

"No." *What was all that about a close call?*

"Well that's good news for me. Because you're going to be so blown away by how delicious it is that you won't even be mad when I tell you that the FBI wasn't actually the…well…I just made up the whole thing." He shrugged.

"What?! I'm going to kill you!" I hit his chest, but instead of repeating the action, my fingers splayed across his muscles. I'd never touched something so perfect before. I was pretty sure my jaw dropped. *Oh, I should have been nuzzling this whole time.* I needed those muscles against my face. God, I really was a pervert. The real FBI would be after me soon enough.

"You've threatened that a lot tonight. So much so that if you actually were planning on killing me it would be suspicious. So I don't believe it for a second. Here, taste this." He shoved a gyro in my open mouth.

I reluctantly took a big bite. Holy meaty goodness, he was right. "Well that's amazing. But I'm still going to kill you." I hit his arm and immediately squeezed his bicep. *God, stop being a pervert!* I let go of his arm. "I can't believe you lied to me." I'd been moments away from a heart attack all night. And it was all a lie for…what? Why was he a dirty liar?

"How else could I have convinced you to take a zipline across the street and get you to change into this sexy little dress?"

"So this was all a punishment for me not dressing up enough? Frankie was right to warn me about you."

"She warned you, did she? What'd she say?"

"That your penis doesn't work and your bones are made of asbestos. Or something like that."

Ryder smiled. "I can prove she's lying about one of those things very easily." He force-fed me more gyro, like he was trying to distract me.

I took another bite to placate him. Only because it was so good.

His eyes locked with mine. "I like how receptive you are to me shoving things in your mouth."

I almost choked on the gyro. "Only delicious things."

He smiled down at me. "Thank you."

"I didn't mean your dick is delicious." *Cocky, arrogant…gorgeous jerk.* He could put whatever he wanted in my mouth. I sighed as I looked up at his beautiful face.

"So you *were* thinking about putting my dick in your mouth?"

"Ew, no." *Maybe. Yes. Yes, I 100% was.*

"I don't mind if you were. I just think we should get to know each other a little first. We have quite a bit we need to discuss. Want to come back to my place so we can talk?" He didn't wait for me to answer. He just turned and carried me toward the Caldwell Hotel.

"I never said yes. This is kidnapping." But I didn't even bother to squirm in his arms. I never wanted him to let me go. Honestly, I'd known he was a stalker all along. Kidnapping made sense. And I was here for it.

"I'll put you down any time you want. Just say the word." He stared at me, daring me to ask for an uncurable foot fungus. I stayed silent, so he continued to carry me into the building and onto the elevator. Then he plopped me down on the ridiculous comfy sofa in his two-story great room.

"Is it okay to eat in here?" I asked. Eating on the couch in my apartment was my jam, but doing it on his super expensive couch felt like an accident waiting to happen.

"Why wouldn't it be?" He sat down next to me.

"I dunno. Some people have rules against that sorta thing. When I was little my parents had a rule that I couldn't eat in the family room. So I used to just ball up a slice of bread and put the whole thing in my mouth so that I could slowly eat it while I watched TV."

"That's actually the rule here too."

I sized up the gyro. I had already eaten about half of it on the way over here, so there wasn't *that* much left. If I really balled it up good I could probably fit it. I unwrapped it and was about to roll it up when Ryder started laughing.

"I was kidding," he said. "I do plan to see how much meat you can fit in your mouth, but it's not going to be the gyro." His eyes dropped to my lips.

I swallowed hard and my throat made a weird squeaking noise. *Ah, stop it!* Ashley Cooper got nervous around handsome men. Raven Black did not. "You are, are you? You know, I'm starting to think you're all talk. First you said you'd punish me for the blueberry pie incident, and now you're threatening to put your meat in my mouth. But when you were an inch away from my lips in that stairwell, you didn't have the balls to kiss me." *Damn, Raven Black, you saucy mistress.*

"Like I said, I wanted to get to know you first." It was like his eyes were boring into mine. Like he could somehow read my mind.

"Well what do you want to know exactly?"

"Why are you here?"

"Because some asshole kidnapped me."

He laughed. "I meant why did you join the Society?"

"Are we allowed to talk about that? I thought the first rule of the Society was that you don't talk about the Society."

"That's fight club. Which happens to be an excellent movie."

"I know, right? So good."

"Top three movies of all time: go."

"Uh…" I hated trying to rank movies. I spent about half my time watching Netflix, so I had a lot to choose from. "How to Lose a Guy in Ten Days, Across the Universe. Geez, um. Frozen. No! Tangled. Or maybe Wedding Crashers. That movie is freaking epic."

"Wedding Crashers is the best. Maybe for our next date we can crash a wedding."

"Who said there's going to be a second date?" But if it were up to me, there definitely would be. Because he was so yummy. I didn't even care that he had almost killed me with that zipline thing.

"There will be." He sounded so sure of himself. It was kind of annoying how cocky he was, but also super hot. I remember when I had first started dating Joe back in college. It was all games and uncertainty. But with Ryder? He knew I wanted him, and he was making it clear he wanted me too.

"We'll see," I said and pulled my feet up onto the couch. It depends on what your three favorite movies are."

"Recent or all-time favorites?"

"Recent." Honestly I barely remembered what I'd eaten for breakfast. I wanted to make sure I knew what he was talking about so we could have good banter. Good banter was very important for a relationship. Not that we were in a relationship. *Yet.*

"The Thief of Bagdad, Shoulder Arms, and The Mark of Zorro."

"Um…what?" I'd never heard of any of those. Wait, maybe I'd heard of the Zorro one. But that couldn't be right. Because the one I was thinking of came out in the 1920s. "Those all came out recently?"

"Oh." He laughed. "It depends on your version of recent. In the grand scheme of things, aren't all movies recent? Since it's a fairly recent technological development?"

I'd consider recent anything after the year 2000. But that was just me.

"But what I meant to say was…uh…Old School, A Knight's Tale, and Billy Madison. Boom. Easy."

"I've never seen Billy Madison." But at least I recognized the name. Really…what were those other movies? I'd have to google them later.

"You're a bad person," he said completely seriously.

I started laughing.

"But don't worry," he said. "We'll fix that. You never answered my question, though. What made you join the Society?"

"Are you sure I'm allowed to answer that?"

"Technically, no. But I won't tell anyone if you don't. It can be our little secret." He gave me a wink.

I liked having a secret with him. Not that my answer was very exciting. "I got an invitation."

"Well yeah, that's generally how things work in an invitation-only club. Why did you accept?"

To meet you. Because you're stalking me. I shrugged. "My friend made me."

"So you told your friend about it? Now I definitely have to report you." He pulled out his phone.

"Wait! No!" *Shit!*

Chapter 20

"TRUE LOVE"

Tuesday

Ryder laughed and put his phone away. "You're adorable when you're angry."

"Shut up." I punched his arm again, but his bicep was so hard that it kind of hurt my hand. "Ow."

"See. Adorable."

I narrowed my eyes at him. "Don't be rude, Mr. Biceps of Steel." I hated being called adorable. I wanted him to think I was sexy and alluring and…not cute.

"Let's take a selfie."

"Okay…" This guy was not good at segues.

He handed me his phone.

"What, you don't know how to take a selfie?" I asked. I tried to hand his phone back to him.

"Girls usually have a certain angle they want to take it at."

Girls? Jealousy shot through me. I pictured him doing this with a thousand girls before me. Frankie's warning rang through my head. *It's all just a façade. Bad wiring, rusty pipes.* And FBI lies, apparently. I pushed the thoughts away and held the phone out.

Ryder slid his arm around my shoulder. "Put it a little higher."

I did, even though I wasn't sure why he no longer trusted my expertise.

"Higher."

"My arm isn't that long. If you're gonna be a diva about the angle, maybe you should take it."

"No, that's fine. Go ahead."

"Three, two, one…" I snapped the photo. And then I realized that my nipple had slipped out of my dress. Because I had reached so far. *Shit!* I dropped the phone and pulled my dress back into place.

Ryder grabbed the phone. "Looks like I've found my new background picture."

"Don't you dare." I tried to snatch the phone out of his hand, but he held it over his head. Which meant it was way out of my reach.

"Or maybe it would make some nice wall art. I've been looking for something new over the fireplace."

"Delete it." I barely knew him. He wasn't allowed to have pictures of my left breast on his phone. *Yet.*

"No way. I'm not going to delete our first photo together."

I jumped to try to get the phone, but all that did was make my boob pop out again. *Damn dress.* "It's going to be our last photo too if you don't hand it over this second."

"You're a bad liar. But you're welcome to keep trying to get it from me. I'm rather enjoying this."

Instead of jumping for it and flashing him again, I took a different approach. A tickle attack. And I wasn't messing around. I went straight for the armpit of his outstretched arm.

But it didn't work. He just stood there like a brick wall.

"Now we're doing a tickle war, huh? It's on." His free hand shot out and he started to tickle me real good. Like he was some sort of expert tickler.

"No!" I screamed, wiggling away and running for the stairs.

He pocketed the phone and chased after me. It didn't take long for him to catch me. He effortlessly picked me up and flung me over his shoulder.

"Put me down!" I punched his shoulder, injuring my hand again. "Damn it. Why is your body so hard?"

He tossed me on the couch and was on me in an instant. My heart felt like it stopped beating. I was sure he was going to kiss me. But…nope. He just tickled me until I could barely breathe. "Give up?"

"I give up! I give up," I gasped. "You win." But I kind of won too. Because I loved the way we were cuddled up on his couch. His blueberry sweat smell filled my lungs. I stared into his eyes. His face was only a few inches away from mine. *This is it! I'm going to kiss my stalker!* I started to lean in, but he cleared his throat.

"So you were telling me about why you accepted the invitation," he said.

What was up with this guy? One minute he looked freaked out and was fleeing from fake FBI agents. The next he was tickling me and looking like he wanted to devour every inch of me. And the next he was asking about the Society? He was so freaking weird. I smiled to myself. He was just as weird as me. And there was something very comforting about being with someone as weird as you. For the first time in my life, I didn't feel like I needed to double think everything I said before I said it.

"Right." I pulled back. "I may have accidentally gotten drunk and signed the contract. And then I was worried that I'd be in trouble if I backed out." *And I might get a million dollars when I leave.*

"You made the right choice. The Society definitely would have sued you."

"Really?"

"Absolutely. I'm sure there's strong legal precedent for a secret sex club forcing their members to participate."

I laughed. "You're messing with me again."

"You catch on fast."

"Asshole," I said with a smile.

"So adorable."

He kept saying that like it was a good thing. I tried to strike a sexier pose on the couch. "Why'd *you* join?"

"Because I believe in true love."

"Of course. I'm sure every guy in the Society does. They couldn't possibly have some other reason to join a club where they can bang models with no strings attached."

"Who said anything about no strings attached?"

"It's a sex club." Did he really not realize that? Men could be so dense sometimes.

"It's not actually a sex club. It's an organization to help people find true love."

"Ew." I frowned at him.

"Ew? Why is that gross?"

"Because it's not true. If you want to bang hot girls, just be upfront about it. But don't go around pretending to be some hopeless romantic." I shifted back a bit on the couch to put more space between us.

"What'd he do to you?" He suddenly looked sad.

"Who?"

"Your ex-husband."

What did Joe have to do with this conversation? And more importantly… "How'd you know I had a husband?"

"Um. Uh…" He pointed at my ring finger. "Your tan lines."

Psssh. My pasty ginger skin didn't have any tan lines. He was lying. I *knew* he was a dirty stalker! And now I had my proof.

"You don't have to tell me if you're not ready to talk about it," said Ryder.

"Oh, I'll talk about it. I walked in on my husband fucking some instamodel that he'd known for two seconds."

"He's an asshole."

"He's a man," I said.

Ryder shook his head. "Not all men are assholes."

"Prove it."

He flashed me his cocky smile. "I will. And now that we're on the topic of things that people shouldn't be doing…are you stalking me?"

"*What?!* No." That sounded way guiltier than I'd meant for it to. But he'd caught me completely off guard. With both the question and how such an accusatory question sound so sexy. It sounded like he'd just said "get naked so I can fuck you" instead. And he was still super bad at segues! "*You're* stalking *me*!"

"Stalking you?" he asked.

"Yes. Stalking me. That's how you knew I had a husband. And I see you staring at me every Tuesday and Thursday at 8 o'clock when you leave One57. And what are you doing there twice a week anyway if you live here?"

"Hmmm…sounds like you're the one stalking me."

I yawned. Running around all night had been exhausting. "No way. You, sir, are the stalker." I adjusted the pillow behind me to get more comfortable.

"You watch me with binoculars."

"That was one time!"

He narrowed his eyes at me.

Fine. It wasn't the only time I'd watched him with binoculars. I just hadn't thought he'd noticed. But the fact that he had noticed proved that *he* was stalking *me*. "You're definitely stalking me, buddy."

"Whatever you have to tell yourself to sleep at night. Speaking of sleep…I'm going to go slip into something a little more comfortable."

"Ow ow," I called as he took the stairs two at a time. What was he going to do? I was torn between him putting whipped cream on his junk or just coming back fully nude. Either way, something sexy was definitely about to go down. *Finally*. He had been teasing me all night. Didn't he know that was no way to treat a girl who hadn't had sex in months? I tried to get into a sexy pose, but nothing felt right. *Whatever*. I eventually gave up and just pushed my boobs together.

Don't rape him, don't rape him, I repeated to myself as his footsteps came closer. I did not need a repeat of the Dr. Lyons incident. And that incident reminded me of the original *incident*. I looked around for any lit candles. Luckily the coast was clear. I wouldn't be setting my stalker on fire tonight. And yes, despite what he said, *he* was stalking *me.*

I looked over my shoulder. Above the railing I could see his bare chest. *Yes!* God, he was so hot. But he wasn't naked like I expected. He was wearing gray sweatpants. *Yum.* What was it about guys in gray sweatpants? I wanted to devour him. And yet…I also wanted him to take them off. I held out hope for a striptease until he sat down next to me on the couch.

"Ah, that's so much better. Anyway, where were we? I think you were confessing to stalking me?"

"In your dreams."

His Adam's apple rose and then fell as his eyes lingered on my lips again.

Had he been dreaming of me too? I wondered if his dreams were as sexy as mine always were. Or if they were just murdery.

"You're stalking me so hard that I bet you even know the license plate number of my red Rolls Royce."

"Huh? I thought it was black?" I immediately clapped my hand over my mouth.

"That was entirely too easy."

"It's been a long day," I protested.

"It has. Want some wine?"

Another weird segue. I kind of liked that my stalker was a little awkward like me. My first instinct was yes, because wine also loosened me up. But then I realized I didn't even need it. Looking into my stalker's brown eyes put me at ease. Or maybe it was his pecs. Or his abs. *Yum.* And I didn't want anything to dull my senses tonight. I wanted to remember every minute of this night perfectly. I shook my head.

"Want to watch Billy Madison?"

I shook my head again and scooched towards him. "I told you how and why I joined the Society. Now it's your turn."

"I told you. True love."

"That answers the why, even if I'm still 90% sure it's bullshit. But how'd you get invited?"

"It's a long story."

"I've got time." I scooched even closer and before I could chicken out, I rested my head on his chest. His pecs were as hard as his biceps. I pressed my lips together so I wouldn't drool on him. I really liked being Raven Black. She was freaking fearless.

He put his arm around me and squeezed my shoulders. "It was years ago."

"Then why haven't you found anyone yet, Mr. True Love?"

His fingers gently brushed through my hair. "Just because I believe in true love doesn't mean I'm destined to find it."

"Did you hear that?" I asked.

"Hear what?"

"I think it's the world's smallest violin playing."

He laughed. God, I really liked his laugh. And the way his chest rumbled beneath me.

"What's the craziest thing you've ever done in the Society?" I asked. "Does all that stuff in the agreement really happen?"

"A gentleman doesn't kiss and tell."

I guess Single Boy Rules were different than Single Girl Rules. Because that directly violated Single Girl Rule #6: Always kiss and tell. I reluctantly lifted my head from his chest so I could see him. "Then why aren't *you* telling me?" I was such a sass queen tonight!

"Because I'm a gentleman. A lady, on the other hand, can kiss and tell all she wants. So what's the craziest thing *you've* ever done?"

Oh, so he does know the Single Girl Rules. And his question was easy. *Made a solo sex tape for Joe.* "Well, this one time I went on a date with a huge jerk. He lied about everything. And even though I had only just met him, I went back to his apartment. I'm pretty sure he was stalking me."

"You're telling me this date is the craziest thing you've ever done?" He eyed me skeptically.

"I mean…we did zipline across six lanes of traffic with no safety harness." Was this not the wildest night of his life too?

"Fair point. What's the craziest thing you want to do?"

A million different things came to mind, none of which were appropriate for a lady to say to a half-naked man on their first date. Even if he was decidedly not a gentleman. "Wouldn't you like to know."

"I would." He tucked a loose strand of hair behind my ear. "That's why I asked it."

"Maybe I'll tell you someday. But I don't even know your last name."

"Storm. Ryder Storm."

Storm. Of course it was something super sexy.

"And yours?"

Oh, right. Ryder Storm is just his Society name. Maybe. Unless he was confident enough to use his real name. He certainly seemed like he was. But for now…I'd just stick with my sassy alter ego. I needed my Superman powers. "Raven Black."

"So…Raven Black." He lay back on the couch and pulled me with him.

I laughed as I snuggled up into his arms.

"Is the Society the only secret society you're a part of?" He was staring into my eyes so intently it was hard to look away.

"Yes. Why? Are there others?"

He stared at me instead of answering.

"Ryder?"

"Sorry. I just…I'm usually really good at reading people. And I'm having a hard time knowing if you're telling the truth."

I laughed. "It's because you're making me nervous."

The corner of his mouth ticked up. "I make you nervous?" He started running his fingers through my hair again.

God that felt good. It had been a really long time since I'd been touched. And I'd let this man touch me anywhere. *Anywhere.* I tried to dare him to do it with my eyes. And then I realized I probably just looked like a crazy person, so I put my head back on his chest to hide. "So nervous." The sound of his heartbeat was so soothing. "Tell me more about yourself so I know you won't cut me up in little pieces tonight."

He chuckled. "Well, I promise not to do that. As long as you promise not to do it to me."

I laughed.

"You didn't promise."

Was he seriously scared I was the murderer in this situation? I wasn't stalking him! "I swear I'm not going to hurt you or harm you in any way."

I heard his sigh of relief. "Okay then."

"Now, tell me everything," I said.

"Where to even begin? I didn't grow up in the states..."

We kept talking for hours, but the time passed in a flash. He was full of insane stories from all over the world. He had lived such a rich, exciting life. And yet he seemed most interested in hearing *my* stories. Especially about high school. Apparently he'd grown up overseas and never really had a classic high school experience. I wanted the night to last forever, but before I knew it, the warmth of his body and the steady pound of his heartbeat put me right to sleep.

Chapter 21

THE ELEVATOR INCIDENT

Wednesday

What. A. Night.

I didn't want to get out of bed. Or couch. Or wherever I had fallen asleep in Ryder's arms. I was afraid that opening my eyes would take me out of whatever fairy tale I had been a part of last night. And my dreams? They'd been oh so naughty. I'd dreamt of him walking up to me and asking in that sexy voice of his, "Are you stalking me?" And then ravishing me on the bench outside One57. Because he liked that I was a kinky stalker like that.

I reached out to try to find Ryder, but my hands came up empty. I reached a little further and fell straight off the couch.

Ow.

I opened my eyes. The morning sun pouring through the two-story window of the great room was blinding.

"Ryder?"

No answer.

"Ryder?" I called a little louder.

Still nothing.

Where did he go? I got up to look around the apartment. He was probably just being a jerk and trying to make himself look all pretty so he could make fun of me for having sloppy hair and morning breath. I put my hand up to my mouth and breathed into it. *Rank. Shoot.*

There was no sign of him in the kitchen. And the fridge was completely empty, which was weird. Who keeps nothing in their fridge? There was no sign of him in the bedroom either. Or the other bedroom. Or the next one. *How many bedrooms does this place have?* And he wasn't in the bathroom either.

Oh well. I could wait for him to get back from wherever he went. Maybe he'd gone to get me breakfast! How romantic! Or maybe he was at work…

SHIT!

Today was my first day of work. What time was it?

I pulled out my phone. My heart nearly stopped when I saw the time. 8:42. And work started at 9. I was going to be late. *Late!* On my first day! That was like…the worst thing ever. I would literally rather die than be late to work ever, much less on my first day. I felt completely paralyzed.

Should I just not show up? Should I borrow Ryder's toothbrush to brush my dirty whore mouth? I could move across the country and never show my face in NYC again. Or maybe I should just kill myself. Yeah, that would be best.

My phone buzzing pulled me out of my suicide spiral. It was a text from Chastity: "Hey girl, can't wait for your first day!"

I started to type out a text, but there was no time. This was serious. For the first time in my life, I understood why phones still had the ability to call people.

Chastity answered on the first ring. "What's wrong?"

She sounded as hysterical as I felt, because I literally never called anyone. Out of principle. Out of the fact that I was a normal millennial. "Everything is wrong!"

"I'm going to need you to be a little more specific. And also stop screaming."

"I slept over at my stalker's place."

"Stalker? What? Who's stalking you? And wait, you did what?!" she shrieked. "Ah! I need all the deets!"

Oh God. I'd told her about the handsome guy that walked out of One57 every Tuesday and Thursday at 8 pm on the dot. We'd even tried to run into him together. But I never actually told her he was stalking me. And I didn't have time to go into this right now. "I'm not going to make it to work. Just tell them I died."

"No way. You're not going to screw me on this. Do you know how annoying the guy was that I had to blow to get you this job?"

"You blew someone to get me the job? You promised you wouldn't do that!" God, she blew someone! Not showing up would be a crime to humanity and a crime to her lips.

"Yell at me later. For now, tell me what I need to do to get your ass to BIMG in the next fifteen minutes."

I looked down at my red dress and lack of shoes. None of it was work-appropriate. Including my face. And there was no way I was going to get sidewalk foot fungus. "Go to my apartment and get the outfit I laid out on the bed."

"No time. I'll have to bring you some of my clothes."

"And shoes," I added.

"Done. Anything else?"

"Makeup."

"You think I'd ever leave home without makeup?" She sounded horrified.

"Fair point."

"Call an Uber," she said. "Now." *Click.*

I did. Luckily the Society app had switched off and I had access to all my normal apps. The Uber was two minutes away. Which meant I had just enough time to go find some of Ryder's shoes to steal.

I sprinted up the stairs and opened his closet. It was filled with…nothing. Well, not nothing. It was completely empty except for a pair of…Crocs? *What the hell?* Why were there no clothes? And more importantly…why were there only Crocs? In any other situation I would have taken appropriate action and burned the entire closet to the ground, but there was no time for that. Somehow, walking around in size thirteen Crocs was less horrifying to me than being late to work while simultaneously contracting a deadly foot fungus. Unless Ryder had foot fungus. And Crocs would totally fit that vibe. *Screw me.* I slid the hideous plasticky things onto my fungus-free feet.

I sprinted to the bathroom just to see if there was time to brush my teeth. But…there was no toothbrush. Or toothpaste. I pulled open another drawer. Everything was empty. What kind of maniac was Ryder? Who lived like this? *Fuck everything.*

I kept my black wig on to save whatever ounce of self-respect I still had left as I stumbled out of the Caldwell Hotel in my clown shoes and whore dress.

I expected people to point and laugh while I waited for my Uber, but no one did. In fact, no one even looked at me. *Ah, the beauty of New York City.* Only the liftman and doorman paid me any attention, and they had mercifully ignored my general appearance.

The Uber driver, however, definitely noticed. I was for sure going to get a one-star review, but I didn't care.

I watched the seconds tick by on my phone as my Uber wove between angry cab drivers. 8:54. *Shit shit shit! Drive faster!*

Three minutes later, we arrived at the BIMG building. I didn't bother to thank him. There was no point in trying to salvage my rating. I was Uber doomed. I'd never ride again in this town.

"Oh God," was all Chastity could say as I got out of the car. She handed me a pile of clothes and we took off into the building.

"Where's the bathroom?" I asked.

"No time." She dragged me across the lobby and onto the elevator. As soon as the doors closed, she turned to the five people crammed in there with us and snapped her fingers. "You all, turn around. My friend needs to change."

Here?! Now? What? Why! Whatever. There was no time. I kicked the Crocs into the corner while Chastity literally tore my dress off. Then she yanked off my wig and started to fix my hair.

"Now tell me about this stalker," Chastity said as she tried to get a comb through my hair. *There's no time for that!*

She pulled it harder when I didn't answer.

Ow. "The guy we tried to find outside One57 the other day."

"You mean the guy you're stalking?"

"I'm not stalking him! *He's* stalking *me.*"

"You creep outside his building every Tuesday and Thursday. You're the stalker in this situation."

"I am not." God, now everyone in the elevator thought I was a psycho. "I'm not," I said more determinedly. I was halfway into my skirt when the elevator dinged. The doors opened and I made direct eye contact with the guy waiting to get on. I had never seen a look of such pure and utter confusion. And...seduction? *Nope.* Just confusion. As if it wasn't already awkward enough - me with my tits out, Chastity holding my wig, and the five other occupants standing in the corner facing the wall like naughty little children who had been sent to time out - I had to go and say, "Top of the morning, good sir." I curtsied with my skirt bunched around my knees. *What the hell is wrong with me?*

After that, he and I stayed completely still, staring into each other's horrified souls, while we waited for what felt like three hours for the elevator doors to close. Of course he didn't get on. Because who in their right mind would hop onto this train wreck? I promised myself right then and there that I would immediately kill myself if I ever saw that man again. Death. No questions asked. He'd understand.

There was no time to dwell on it though. We were only three floors away from our destination and I was still half-naked surrounded by a bunch of strangers. Chastity zipped my skirt while I pulled on my blouse and buttoned the middle button. Then I slipped some heels on and ran my fingers through my knotted hair. And that was it. The elevator dinged again and the doors opened. And I prayed that I looked at least a little presentable.

"Good morning," said Bee. She was wearing a fancy suit and looked so perfectly chic. Especially in comparison to me. God, I never should have shown up. I backed up and ran right into Chastity.

"Hey, Bee," said Chastity as she pushed me out of the elevator

Bee smiled. "I see you already know our small business strategist. Ash, it's so nice to have you aboard. I promise I'm not usually a monster, but this is gonna be one heck of a first day. Because Rhodes VC just called and asked if we could have a presentation ready this afternoon."

"This *afternoon*?" asked Chastity.

"Is that bad?" I whispered. "That sounds bad."

Chastity nodded. "Uh, yes. That's bad. We usually have weeks to prepare a pitch."

"I'm sorry," Bee said. "But he insisted it had to be today. And if we land Rhodes, it'll double our business. And your Christmas bonuses."

Well, that sounded amazing.

"Plus he's a friend. We've been trying to get him to come in for ages. But now that he's finally coming…I doubt he'll be taking his business elsewhere. You still need to give him a great pitch though. Just let me know if you have any questions," Bee said. "See you two this afternoon."

Chastity and Madison introduced me to the rest of the marketing team and then we worked our asses off for three hours straight. We made graphics for the slides, tweaked the copy, and went over the notecards for the presentation. With my help - that's right, I'm awesome - we finished with an hour to spare.

"So who is this client that we just busted our asses for?" I asked.

"Oh, only one of the richest men in the city," said Chastity. "Tanner Rhodes. I'm pretty sure he's a billionaire."

I pulled out my phone to look him up, but I got distracted by a notification from the Society app. I clicked on it.

"RATE YOUR EXPERIENCE" popped up on the screen with a picture of Ocelot, the possibly gay realtor. Sorry, I mean the metrosexual.

"What's that?" asked Chastity, craning her neck to see my screen.

"The Society," I whispered. "I'm supposed to rate the guys I met."

"Ah! I need to hear all about it. Let's go in the conference room and pretend to set up."

Chastity, Madison, and I snuck off to a conference room with the biggest glass table I'd ever seen. It looked like the sort of table I'd try to stupidly hide behind. Chastity pulled the blinds closed and locked the door. "Tell us everything. And don't you dare leave out any details. Single Girl Rule #9: If you hear about a well-hung man, share the news."

I told them every detail of my evening, rating the men on the app as I described each apartment. Chastity agreed Ocelot looked gay, and Madison made some comment reminding us that it was totally okay to be gay. The rest of the guys were a mixed bag. The gym bro was good-looking, but as soon as I described how douchey he was, their opinions of him quickly changed. Chastity was particularly interested in the two well-endowed men that almost double-teamed me.

Anyway, I didn't really care about all that. I couldn't wait to show them my stalker.

"So that part of the date was okay," I said, "but the last part was amazing. I met my stalker!"

"And this was the same guy who you threw the pie at?" asked Chastity. "The one that you're stalking."

How many times did we need to go over this? "I'm not stalking him. And I didn't throw it at him. I accidentally nudged it onto him. But yes, him. His apartment was everything. I wish you could have seen it." I started describing the furniture and the kitchen and the great room. And then I told them about the FBI raid and the zipline and the gyros. And how the FBI was fake and that Ryder was really bad at segues but how we kept almost kissing and he liked weird movies and gah! It had been the perfect night.

"So wait…you didn't bang him?" asked Chastity when I was finished.

"Really?" I asked. "I tell you that I ziplined through the middle of the city and all you can ask is if I slept with him? I'm barely alive right now."

Chastity shrugged. "I mean, clearly you survived so it couldn't have been that eventful. You didn't answer my question, though."

"No, I didn't bang him. He was a perfect gentleman. Well, except when he took that selfie of me with my boob out."

"Can I see?" asked Madison.

"You want to see her boob selfie?" asked Chastity.

"What? No. I want to see the picture of him."

Suuure. "It was on his phone. But here's a pic of him." I hit submit on my very unfavorable ratings of the rude Indian guy and waited for Ryder's picture to pop up. But it didn't. The app just went to a black screen that said, "Thank you for your ratings!" in big white letters. "What the hell? Why wasn't I asked to rate Ryder?"

Chapter 22

TANNER RHODES

Wednesday

I stared at my phone in disbelief. Ryder's picture should have popped up. Where the hell was it?!

Chastity and Madison both gave me a skeptical look.

"I swear I met him," I said. "It must just be a weird glitch." *He is real, right? Or had all the stress about my new job made me hallucinate meeting my stalker?* I had certainly imagined meeting him before, but it had never felt real like this.

"Honestly, your whole description of the date sounded really weird," said Chastity. "And not sexually weird. Just plain weird. You made it all up, didn't you? I mean, Single Girl Rule #7: Pics or it didn't happen. And I see no pics."

"But…" I was going to plead my case further when someone knocked on the door.

Chastity unlocked it and let the rest of the team in.

"All set for the presentation?" asked Bee.

Chastity nodded. "We are."

"I knew you could do it. Good job." She took a seat near the front of the room.

Her husband, Mason Caldwell, walked in a moment later. Yes, Caldwell. He was Matthew Caldwell's older brother. And he looked so much like his younger brother. It gave me the heebie-jeebies. Not because he was ugly. In fact, he was scorching. But him looking so similar to Matthew reminded me of *the incident.* Luckily for me, though, I'd never set Mason's dick on fire. *Oh my God, don't think about the incident at a time like this!*

Mason gave us a nod and then pecked Bee on the cheek before sitting down beside her.

I began to wonder if Matt had told Mason what had happened. Hell, he might have even told Bee. How many people knew about *the incident*?! I stared at the glass windows that encircled the whole conference room. I should just fling myself out of one…

But then Mr. Rhodes and his posse arrived. A fit woman in a pencil skirt came in first, then a few guys. And then someone who could only be Tanner Rhodes took a seat at the head of the table. Chastity was right. He was super-hot with his glasses and five o'clock shadow and longish hair pushed to one side with the sides buzzed. He was almost as hot as my stalker. In fact, he looked a lot like my stalker. Like…a lot a lot. *Wait a second.* I blinked and it felt like my throat was closing up. He *was* my stalker. I immediately ducked to hide behind the table. The glass table. Again. *Fuck my life.* Why was I even hiding? It wasn't like I had just thrown a blueberry pie in his face.

I tossed my pen on the ground and pretended like I was crouching down to pick it up. I snuck a glance at him through the glass table. Had he noticed me yet?

As I stood up, I accidentally bumped my head on the table. No, bumped wasn't the right word. Slammed. Because everything went black.

I woke up a second later with the most handsome man in the world cradling my head. His deep brown eyes stared at me through his glasses.

"Are you okay?" he asked.

"I…" *What the hell just happened?*

He looked at one of his assistants. "We need an ice pack." Then he turned back to me. "Do you remember your name?"

"Ash. Ashley Cooper."

"It's a pleasure to meet you, Ashley. You hit your head against the table and knocked yourself out."

Then it all came flooding back to me. My new job. The presentation. My stalker walking in pretending to be named Tanner Rhodes instead of Ryder Storm. Me hiding behind

ANOTHER glass table and then knocking myself out like a total idiot. *God, why did I always have to be so embarrassing?* I could feel my face turning red. Everyone in the room was gathered around staring at me. I laughed awkwardly. "I'm fine. I meant to do that."

"You meant to knock yourself out?" asked Tanner. He looked confused. And very concerned.

I nodded. Then, just loud enough for him to hear, I whispered, "I wanted to snuggle with you again. Last night ended too soon." I added a saucy wink for good measure.

And he gave me the most puzzled look in the world. It was like I was speaking another language. *Oh no.* Had I started talking in German? One time I read about an Italian guy who hit his head and then only knew how to talk in French. Or was that a weird sex dream I had? I mean…it is kind of sexy to think about. An Italian stallion with a French accent? Yes please.

Tanner handed me the bag of frozen peas that his assistant had fetched. "Here, this should help. You should still probably see a doctor, though."

"Am I going to die?"

He laughed. "No, but you may have a nasty bruise."

Chastity knelt down next to me. "Don't worry, Mr. Rhodes. I'll look after her tonight." She brushed his arm and gave him her best seductive smile.

Hey, slut! That's my man! I needed to separate them ASAP. "You know what? I feel all better. Let's just get on with the presentation." *So that everyone can stop staring at me.*

"Are you sure?" asked Tanner. "We can always postpone it for another day."

"Really, I'm fine." I pulled myself to my feet and plopped unceremoniously into my chair before I fell over. The room was the thing spinning, not me. Or was it me? *Am I spinning right now?*

Chastity began the presentation as the room settled around me. I kept sneaking glances at my stalker, but he seemed to be focused on the presentation. Or maybe he was just focused on Chastity. As always, she looked amazing. I had never competed with Chastity for a man before, but I hated the thought of it. There was no way I stood a chance against her showstopping beauty and world-class flirting skills. After the presentation I'd tell her that Tanner Rhodes was actually my stalker and that I'd called dibs. And thanks to Single Girl Rule #31 (A girl who calls dibs has 2 weeks to close the deal), she'd be forced to back off. I snuck another glance at him. *Mine!*

Something didn't feel right, though. Why was he dressed so differently than usual? When he stalked me, he was always wearing colorful suits and had his hair up in a bun type thing. But today he was dressed in a crisp black suit and his hair was pushed to one side. And he was wearing glasses. I could easily explain away the glasses by telling myself that he wore contacts during stalking because stalking was difficult work and no one needed their glasses falling off their face while they were perched in a tree outside your window.

But the change in suit preference hardly made sense. He was a freaking billionaire. He could wear whatever the hell he wanted and no one would say a word. He could have shown up to the meeting in a pair of his stupid Crocs and a man thong and no one would have flinched. He'd be able to pull that combo off way better than Brett Favre had in that sext. I pictured it in my head. My stalker, not Brett Favre. I couldn't decide if it was a good look or not. I mean, on one hand, his package looked amazing. It was like someone had stuffed an anaconda into a spandex sock. Sorry, bad analogy. But you get the point. His junk looked great. The Crocs were kind of throwing me off though. I mean, why was he wearing them? Was he an old lady gardening or a little boy on the beach?

Someone shook me.

"Ash?" asked Chastity.

I snapped my head around to pretend like I hadn't been staring directly at my stalker for the past five minutes. "Huh? What? Sorry, still a little dazed from hitting my head." *Please don't make me talk in front of all these people.* What the hell was she thinking? She knew public speaking was my 5th biggest fear.

"I was hoping you could elaborate on this slide about our Facebook ad strategy?"

"I uh, sure." I stood up and started stumbling through the slide.

Tanner chimed in halfway through. "I've heard enough."

Shit. Was me talking for two seconds really bad enough to blow the whole deal?

"I think BIMG would be a great fit for us. We're happy to sign the deal." Tanner stood up to shake hands with Bee and Mason.

I let out a sigh of relief. I didn't blow it after all. I took a step toward Tanner as he disengaged from Mason. Not only had we had the perfect night together, but now he'd saved me from public speaking. I was in love. I waited for him to come congratulate me and whisper something sexy in my ear about meeting up later that night, but instead he just turned and left the conference room.

What the hell?

"Ah!" squealed Chastity. "We did it!"

"Well done," said Bee. "I hate to ask this of you, but can you have copy and graphics for the Mills Winery campaign done by the end of the week? I really want to show Mr. Rhodes that he's making the right choice."

We agreed. Then Madison rushed over to me. She brushed her hand against where I hit my head. "Are you okay?"

"Yeah, yeah," I said. "I'm fine."

"I didn't know you had so much game," said Chastity. "Pretending to hurt yourself so that Tanner would get all worried about you. Clever."

"That wasn't what I was doing. I was hiding. He's my stalker."

Chastity shook her head. "Say what now? You can't just get dibs on Tanner by claiming that he's your stalker."

"No, really. He is."

"But you said your stalker wore colorful suits and had a man bun. Tanner only wears black suits. And I don't even know if his hair is long enough to put up in a bun."

"It's definitely him."

"And I thought you said his name was Ryder Storm?"

I knew what was going on here. Duh. "That's his Society name. Kind of like how I'm Raven Black. He must want anonymity in the Society because he's so well known. It's him. It has to be him. It has to be. Why else would he have spared me from doing part of the presentation?"

"Uh…because I had already done such a kickass job?" suggested Chastity.

"Or maybe he felt bad for you because you just hit your head," added Madison.

No. No! It had to be him. Otherwise… *Oh God.* Why did I have to go and whisper that thing about last night and snuggling? And had I winked at him? Saucily? Why did I keep acting so saucy recently? I was out of control. Now Tanner's look of utter confusion was seared in my brain. It was so clear that he had no idea what I was saying. Despite that, though…I still kind of thought it was him. Just like I knew my stalker had been stalking me. I had a sixth sense about these things.

Oh! "Maybe he didn't recognize me with my red hair. I was wearing a black wig last night."

"Well," said Chastity. "We need to sort this out immediately. Because if it is your stalker, that means you have dibs on him. But if he's not, then we'll have to find a different way to settle it."

"And how do we figure it out?" I asked.

Chastity gave me a mischievous grin. "We stalk your stalker. Just like you've been doing for the past several months."

I pressed my lips together. *He's* stalking *me*. But the particulars didn't really matter right now. I needed dibs on Tanner Rhodes. So if I had to stoop to his stalking levels, so be it. Besides, I already knew a ton about him from my observations while I watched him stalk me. And he'd told me a lot about himself last night too. This was going to be so freaking easy. *Move over, Chastity. He's mine. Time to get my stalk on.*

Chapter 23

TWO RUDE SURPRISES

Wednesday

We went straight from work back to my apartment to stalk my stalker. I didn't even bother to change out of Chastity's slutty clothes before plopping onto the couch with my laptop. I couldn't wait another second to learn everything about my stalker.

I started by googling Tanner Rhodes.

The first result was a Wikipedia article. *Fancy.* I clicked on it. There was no picture and only one sentence:

"Tanner Rhodes is an American billionaire businessman from New York City."

I read it again. *Billionaire. With a B.* I couldn't even imagine that much money. Chastity had said he was a billionaire, but I didn't realize she meant he was for-realsies a billionaire. I thought she was just throwing out the highest number she could think of and had forgotten the word bajillion.

Just to confirm, I went back and clicked on the second link, Tanner's profile on Forbes:

#413 Tanner Rhodes

Net Worth: $4.3B

- Tanner Rhodes is the founder and chairman of Rhodes Venture Capital, a private investment firm based in New York City.

- Rhodes VC is most notable for being an early investor in Tesla and Shopify, which is where the bulk of Rhodes' net worth is derived.

STATS:

Age - 28 (estimated)

Source of Wealth - Rhodes Venture Capital, Self-Made

Residence - New York, New York
Citizenship - United States
Marital Status - Unknown
Children - Unknown
Education - Unknown

Unknown, unknown, unknown. Gah! What kind of shoddy operation were they running over at Forbes? Their whole purpose in life was to know about rich people, and they didn't even know where Tanner went to college? Hell, they weren't even sure about his age. No wonder the owner of Forbes wasn't even a billionaire…he sucked at his job. They needed to hire better stalkers. Or journalists. Or whatever politically correct term they were going by these days. I did a quick Google search to make sure that the owner of Forbes really wasn't a billionaire. *Boom.* Steve Forbes' net worth was only $430 million. Million! What a complete and utter loser. The small sum in my bank account started to wander into my thoughts but I kicked it back where it belonged. In the toilet. Because all the money I had would literally fit in a toilet.

Anyway, back to Tanner. The only thing of real value in the whole article was the picture of him. But it was kind of blurry. Classic Forbes. So incompetent.

"Booyah, found a picture of him," I said.

"For real?" asked Chastity. "I've been looking for weeks now and haven't been able to find a thing. The guy is a ghost on social media."

"It was on the second search result."

"Oh, the Forbes one? I never look at that. That website is trash."

"I know, right?"

We both laughed.

"Send me that real quick," said Madison. A minute later she turned her laptop for us to see. She'd transferred the picture into MS Paint and sketched a man bun onto him. "Does that look more like Ryder?"

I shook my head. "Uh, not really."

Chastity lit up. "Boom. That's proof that Tanner's not the same person as Ryder. The sex muffin billionaire is mine!"

"I mean…she used MS Paint to draw that," I said. "Cool your loins, woman."

"Well right now that's about the only evidence we have to go on."

"Then let me get back to work." I tuned her out and went back to searching. All real estate transactions were public records, so all it took was a few quick searches on the NYC Department of Finance website and I had the names of every person who owned an apartment in One57. Er…kind of. It was more like a list of LLCs that owned apartments in One57. Apparently billionaires weren't fond of their addresses being publicly available. Steve Forbes, on the other hand, probably didn't even know what an LLC was. Stupid millionaire. Such a basic bitch.

I almost gave up on the real estate angle, but then I realized that as the official marketers of Rhodes VC, we had just gained access to lots of private files. Including a list of all the businesses they owned. I cross-referenced that list with the list of One57 owners.

"Got him!" I yelled.

"Bullshit," said Chastity.

"Tanner Rhodes is the proud owner of apartment 89 at One57. Which means he's my stalker."

"Or it means that they're twins and Tanner's been kind enough to buy his little brother a baller-ass apartment."

"That's a solid theory," agreed Madison.

"What? No it isn't. And why is Ryder his little brother? I thought they were twins in this scenario."

"One still has to come out first," said Chastity. "And it was definitely Tanner."

"Maybe this will help to clear it up," said Madison. She pointed to an Instagram picture on her laptop of some beautiful model posing at a party.

"Uh…how will that help us?" I asked. "Is that an escort we can hire to get all his secrets?"

"No," said Madison. "And way to judge her just because of her looks. Evie Martin's not a prostitute. She's a successful businesswoman."

"And that helps us how, exactly?"

Madison rolled her eyes. "She's Tanner's personal assistant. You literally met her like four hours ago."

I did? I guess there had been a girl by Tanner's side, but I didn't remember her looking like *that.* Because she'd been dressed professionally, unlike me. I looked down at my outfit and cringed.

"If you'd stop slut-shaming her for two seconds and opened your eyes, you'd see that Tanner is in the background of lots of her photos. Single Girl Rule #26: Slut-shaming a fellow single girl is unforgivable."

That was the only Single Girl Rule Madison ever quoted. I was trying to get Chastity to dump that rule, but she always insisted she hadn't made them up. *Lies.* I squinted and got closer to the screen. It was hard to be sure, but a guy in the background did kind of look like Tanner.

"What's he doing going to parties with his PA?" I asked. Images of Joe banging Sierra flashed through my mind. And then they morphed into Tanner and Evie. "They're probably having sex. I hate Tanner. He's dead to me. He's basically just like Joe."

"Well that seems a bit extreme," said Chastity. "Tanner is nothing like Joe."

Madison made a gross noise with her throat. "All men are the worst."

Chastity zoomed up on Evie's hand in the picture. "Well she's not wearing a ring. So even if they are banging, he hasn't proposed yet."

Madison stood up. "Now that you guys are over Tanner, what should we do?"

"Uh, did you miss the part about him being a billionaire?" asked Chastity.

"So what?" asked Madison. "We don't need to rely on men for money. We're all strong, beautiful, independent women."

"Psssh," scoffed Chastity. "You don't know what you're missing. Having Daddy's credit card was the best thing ever."

Was. Chastity grew up rich, but her dad lost all his money in bad real estate. Her fancy apartment, fancy clothes, and fancy lifestyle had gone poof overnight. I knew she missed it. But she was being a trooper. I didn't even believe her whenever she talked about marrying a man just for his money. She was just joking. *I think.*

"And Daddy's working on a new real estate deal, did I tell you guys? I think it's going to be big."

Gross. "How many times do I have to tell you that a grown woman should never use the word Daddy? Unless it's like a weird sexy roleplaying thing. Actually, scratch that. Doing it as part of sex just makes it worse. Especially if they're having sex with their real daddy."

Chastity shrugged. "I can't help it. I'm a daddy's girl."

Madison and Chastity continued to debate the ethical implications of having a sugar daddy while I went back to my computer. Now that I'd thought about Sierra, I couldn't stop myself from checking all her social media accounts. Yeah, I knew it wasn't healthy. But what can I say? I had a sickness.

I typed "Sierra Vega" into Facebook and clicked on her. And *WHAT THE ACTUAL FUCK?!* Her relationship status had changed to IN A RELATIONSHIP WITH JOE DICKSON. I'd already thought they were together, but now it was Facebook official. That was next level. And it was soul-crushing. Like it actually felt like a brick had fallen from the ceiling right onto my chest.

I was over Joe. I didn't want him back. I didn't want to ever see him again. But I hated that he was so happy with her and her big stupid eyes and perfect bone structure and huge boobs. Why did he deserve happiness? He was the one that cheated on me. And then blackmailed me with my freaking sex tape. I should have been the one to find happiness while Joe got molested by a homeless dude.

"You okay, Ash?" asked Madison. "You look really pale."

I barely heard her through the cloud of depression that surrounded me. "Huh? I uh…" A knock on the door saved me from having to answer. "That must be the pizza." I wandered over to the door, still in a daze. It barely even registered when I opened the door and the guy standing there didn't have a pizza. Not that I had even ordered one. Wait, no, I had. But this wasn't it.

"Hey," said Dr. Lyons.

"Fuck me!" I yelled involuntarily as I slammed the door in his face. *Oh God, oh God, oh God. What is he doing here?! God, did I just ask him to fuck me? Stupid whore mouth!*

"Did you just ask the pizza guy to fuck you?" called Chastity from across the room.

I took a deep breath and opened the door again. "Dr. Lyons," I said calmly in a weirdly low professional voice. *Stop being weird.* "What brings you to my humble abode this evening?" *What? Why am I talking like this? Don't try to rape him this time!*

"I wanted to talk. Is this a good time?"

"What for? To serve with me a lawsuit? Fine. Just get it over with." I put my wrists out for him to slap the cuffs on me. Which made no sense because that's not how lawsuits worked. Well, maybe in pornos. But if this was a porno he'd definitely be wearing a super sexy cop uniform. And he wasn't.

"What? No. I wanted to apologize. I was totally unprofessional. I know it's not an excuse, but I don't really have much experience with women." He coughed. "Er, with examining women's bodies. As patients. Not in a sexual way. Because I'm a pediatrician."

I laughed and he looked super relieved.

"Ash!" called Chastity. "What the hell is taking so long? Hurry up so we can decide which of us gets to bang your stalker!"

Dr. Lyons blinked a few times. "Um, should I come back another time?"

Damn it, Chastity! She made it sound like we had a stalker tied up and we were deciding which of us would rape him. Which probably made sense to Dr. Lyons given his prior experience with me. "Ignore her." I stepped into the hallway and shut the door behind me. "She just likes to mess with people. You should see her when the mailman comes. She always has to play the penis game."

Dr. Lyons stared at me, completely confused.

"You know. Everyone takes turns yelling 'penis' and whoever yells it loudest wins."

He laughed. "Right. I have friends like that. Anyway, I'll cut to the chase. I wanted to tell you that I can't be your doctor anymore."

"You came all the way here to tell me that? Just to rub in how awkward I was?"

He lowered his eyebrows instead of responding. Which basically meant, "Hell yeah, Ash, you're awkward AF and I want nothing to do with you."

I was already feeling pretty low from my stalker not remembering me. And seeing Sierra's relationship status. I didn't need this right now. I cleared my throat. "I guess…thanks for not arresting me?" *Asshole.* I turned to go back inside just as Chastity opened the door.

"Where's my pizza?" she asked. Then she smiled at Dr. Lyons and looked him up and down. "Who's this hunky gentleman and why haven't you invited him inside?"

"This is Dr. Lyons."

"*The* Dr. Lyons?" She winked at me. "You said he was hot, but not this hot."

Usually I would have been mortified, but Dr. Lyons was such an asshole that I didn't really care. "Well, he just came here to tell me that he didn't want to be my doctor anymore because I'm the most awkward human being on the face of the earth. If you want him, he's all yours."

Dr. Lyons cleared his throat. "I was actually coming by to ask you out to dinner. That's why I can't be your doctor anymore."

Now he was just messing with me. "No thank you," I said. Because even if he was serious, I could still barely look at him after my attempted rape. Besides, he would just cheat on me with an instamodel or a secretary or something. Did pediatricians have secretaries? No. They had nurses. And that was just as bad. Maybe worse.

"What she meant to say," said Chastity, "is that she can't tonight because we're in the middle of a super awesome girls' night. How about Saturday at 8?"

Dr. Lyons grinned from ear to ear. "Done." He turned to me. "I'll pick you up at 8."

"I don't…" I started, but Chastity pulled me inside and slammed the door.

"Ah!" she squealed. "You have a date! And he's ridiculously hot. No wonder you tried to rape him."

"Why did you do that? I can't go on a date with him. Like you just said, I tried to rape him. I can't be trusted around strangers. You know this."

"Guess he liked it."

Huh. Maybe he did. The annoyance of seeing Sierra's relationship status coupled with the sheer embarrassment of seeing Dr. Lyons had clouded my judgment. It was just now sinking in that he stopped by because he had a crush on me. I couldn't prevent the smile that spread over my face.

"Congrats on your new boyfriend," said Chastity. "Now that you have him you won't be needing Tanner or that Society membership. I'll be happy to take both off your hands."

"He's not my boyfriend yet."

"Who's not?" asked Madison.

"My doc…" I stopped mid-sentence when I saw what Madison was wearing. She had changed into a floral pantsuit, pulled her hair into a tight bun, and drawn a beard on herself with a marker.

She struck a manly power pose.

"What the hell am I looking at?" asked Chastity.

"I'm ready to take one for the team and cut my hair to see how short it can get before you can no longer put it in a bun."

"So why the suit and beard?" I asked.

"I had to get in character."

"Did you though?"

"Well I have good news," said Chastity. "Ash has a date with her doctor, so now Tanner is all mine."

"Whoa whoa whoa. No way. If Tanner is my stalker then I still have dibs. No way I'm giving up a billionaire for a pervy doctor." Not that he was the pervy one. That was clearly all me. And he was pretty hot…

Chastity pouted. "Not fair."

"What's not fair is that Joe and Sierra are officially an item." I pulled out my cellphone to show them. I cringed as the two of them stared down at my worst nightmare. Joe moving on with his life. While I just stalked people and acted rude to nice handsome doctors.

Chastity gave me a big hug. "I'm sorry. The good news is that there's no way it will last."

"Why do you say that?" I wasn't sure why that made me so hopeful. But I just so badly wanted Joe to be more miserable than me.

"Come on…why would a girl who looks like Sierra be with Joe? Clearly she just wants his money."

"You think so?" I asked. Wait, was that a burn on me?

Chastity nodded. "I know so. You're definitely going to find love, Ash. You deserve it."

"So I can have Tanner?" I asked.

"Ha, nice try. Tell you what…tomorrow is Thursday."

"So?"

"So that's when you always see your stalker. And when the Society dates are. So either you'll have a date with him, or we'll kidnap him outside One57 and make him tell us everything."

"Or maybe just approach him and ask him nicely?"

Chastity shrugged. "Not quite as fun, but okay."

My heart started beating faster. I had been so distracted trying to figure out if Tanner and Ryder were the same person that I'd forgotten all about going on another Society date tomorrow. When would the card appear? What would the date be? And most importantly…would Ryder be there?

Chapter 24

CLAUSE FOURTEEN

Thursday

My second day of work got off to a better start than the first. I didn't flash anyone on the elevator, and I was wearing normal clothes. But the actual work part was unbearable because I couldn't seem to focus.

Every five minutes I kept checking my phone for a Society invitation. And then I'd look over my shoulder to see if Tanner had arrived. And then I'd hop on Facebook to see if Joe and Sierra had switched their Facebook statuses back to SINGLE (spoiler alert - they hadn't). And then I'd check again for a Society invitation. And then…well, you get the idea.

Before I knew it, it was already lunchtime.

"So what's the plan for tonight?" asked Chastity as she tore into some Chinese takeout.

I shrugged and took a bite of orange chicken. "No invitations yet."

"How do you know? You've been at your desk all day."

"I've been checking the app."

Chastity shook her head. "That's not how invitations come. Clause 14. Wish invitations will be delivered via discreet black envelopes. Once an envelope is received, the Member will accept or decline the invitation via the app."

"Do you have the entire contract memorized?"

She shrugged. "What? It seemed important."

"Uh, guys," said Madison. Her marker-beard hadn't come off very well, so she was sporting what looked like five o'clock shadow. "I think this might be what you're waiting for." She pulled a black and gold envelope out of the takeout bag.

"Those sneaky little dildos," said Chastity as she snatched it out of Madison's hand.

We gathered around as Chastity opened it.

"Hey girl," she read. "Get ready for a night out on the town. XOXO Frankie. P.S. Wear something that's easy to take off."

"Well that wasn't really what I was hoping for." I drowned my disappointment with a huge bite of eggroll. I just wanted to see Ryder again. Or Tanner. Or whatever name he was going by today. Why did they keep making me hang out with Frankie? At least she wasn't actually in the FBI.

"Frankie was a woman, right?" asked Chastity.

I nodded.

"It seems like she's into you."

Madison shrugged. "Maybe you should give her a try."

"Yeah," agreed Chastity. "At least she wouldn't cheat on you with an instamodel. Or her secretary."

Madison shot her a look. "Why do you say that? Women are every bit as capable as men at harassing their secretaries."

"Female secretaries?" asked Chastity. "Or male secretaries? Because if it's male secretaries, then I'm all for it." She bit her lip. "The things I'd love to do with a photocopier and a pair of handcuffs…"

"What do handcuffs have to do with a secretary fantasy?" I asked. "You know what, I don't want to know." *I'm already rapey enough without Chastity's crazy ideas.* "I feel like we're getting off-topic. We need to figure out what this date card means." Because if it was a girl date, that wasn't my cup of tea. I wanted a tall glass of Ryder.

Chastity smoothed her skirt and tried to regain her composure. "Right. I think the card is obvious. You and Frankie are definitely gonna go clubbing."

"And get naked?"

"Maybe. It *is* the Society that we're talking about. But no, I think the part about wearing something easy to take off is probably just because she's gonna find you a hot man at the end of the night."

"I don't want just *any* hot man. I want Ryder." I pulled out my phone and opened the Society app. RSVP was now an option. *How did they know I got the invitation?* Chastity was right - they really were sneaky little dildos. I clicked RSVP:

Night Out
Thursday, April 18, 8:30 p.m.
11th and W 51st
New York, NY 10019

"Hey, that's my address!" I said.

"Not much of a night out if it's happening at your apartment," scoffed Madison.

"It actually sounds perfect. Maybe they're just going to deliver Ryder right to my front door." *Hopefully Homeless Rutherford doesn't lick him before I get a chance to.*

"Can't you get more details once you accept?" asked Chastity. Her encyclopedic knowledge of the Society contract and app was impressive. And suspicious. Was she secretly a member?

I clicked "Accept" and then navigated to the wish details. I read it aloud: "Raven Black. You recently got divorced and you're seeking a fresh start."

"So you're just you again," said Madison.

"Yup. Looks like it."

"Whatever," said Chastity. "What matters is how we're going to use this date to determine that Tanner and Ryder are two different people. #ThatBoyIsMine."

"Or that they're the same person," I suggested.

"Yeah, whatever. Here's what I propose. Ash, you go on the date and see if Ryder's part of it. Madison, you wait outside One57 to see if he walks out and gets into his Rolls Royce. And I'll go to Tanner's office to keep tabs on him. If we catch them in two places at once, then it'll prove they're two different people."

I tried to think of a plan that wouldn't involve Chastity possibly flirting with Tanner, but I came up blank. "Alright, let's do it."

Chapter 25
ODEGAARD GANGBANG
Thursday

I glanced down at my phone. 7:55. Almost go time. But the plan was not off to a great start.

Tanner had been in meetings all day, so Chastity had been forced to just wait in the Rhodes VC lobby. Then when he left his office around 6, she failed miserably at following. So now she was camped outside of One57 with Madison. I was terrified that she would walk up to him and confront him. Or seduce him. I cringed at the thought. Ryder was mine!

Or at least, I wanted him to be. I just didn't know how to make it happen. Our date had been wonderful and it felt like he was into me, but why would he like *me?* I wasn't like those models at spin class. Or his slutty secretary. I pulled her picture up on my phone. Yeah, I had saved it. Don't judge me. She was tall and had impossibly big boobs for her impossibly skinny waist. I couldn't compete with that. Maybe that was why he hadn't kissed me the other night. He had kept calling me *cute.* I needed to spice it up.

I rummaged through my drawers. None of my clothes seemed right for the occasion. What was good for clubbing and also easy to take off? I pulled my tightest dress over my head. It was a sexy little red number that I'd bought for my first Valentine's Day with Joe. And somehow it still fit. Kind of.

I got it over my shoulders, but then it got stuck around my boobs thanks to the mega-pushup bra I was wearing. For a second I couldn't breathe. My life flashed before my eyes. I pictured the police showing up and finding me on the ground half-naked. But before that all happened, the dress tore in half. *Son of a bitch!* It must have been made of the cheapest fabric in the world.

"Eh, it would have been too hard to get off anyway," I said to no one in particular. Really I was just trying to make myself feel better about literally tearing a dress in half. It was the damn muscle weight. I still hadn't figured out if the protein before a workout was a good idea. Maybe I just had to give up protein completely…*God no.* That sounded terrible. I'd take the splitting dresses over no protein any day.

I eventually settled on a flared skirt and a tank top. I finished it off with the pair of white heels that I'd worn to my high school graduation. The two-inch heel was soooo sexy. At least, it had felt that way when I bought them in freaking high school.

My phone buzzed. 8:01. I looked at the text from Madison. There were no words. Just a picture of Ryder ducking into his Rolls Royce.

Ah! It's happening! Tonight was the night. I was going to see Ryder again. Or maybe I should just not go. I *did* have a crap-ton of work to get done if we were going to finish those new ad campaigns by tomorrow afternoon. Missing a deadline was just as bad as being late, which was my second biggest fear.

No. I shook my head. *You got this, Ash.* I refused to let myself wallow in misery while Joe and Sierra lived happily ever after. I was going to get my happily ever after too, and I was going to get it with a billionaire. Besides, I only had to complete my three wishes before I got to cross it off my to-do list and nominate Chastity to be part of the Society. *Three chances to make Tanner fall in love with me. Or Ryder. Or whatever his name is.*

I put on my black wig, fastened a black bracelet to my wrist, and headed outside before I could change my mind.

A black Rolls Royce limo pulled up right at 8:30. *OMG! Ryder came to get me!* The driver got out and opened the door for me. My heart was beating out of my chest. What would I say to him? Would I act natural? Would I playfully be mad at him for leaving me alone after our first date and then pretending not to know who I was at the meeting?

Apparently I'd do neither, because Frankie was the only one in the back of the limo. I should have known because the driver wasn't the little man in the butler's outfit that usually drove Ryder around. *Crap.*

"Hey Raven!" she said, handing me a glass of champagne and giving me an awkward seated hug.

I took a big sip.

"How was your date with Ryder?"

"Kind of amazing. Did you know he was gonna pull that whole FBI thing?"

She looked confused. "I have no idea what FBI thing you're talking about, but I warned you he was dangerous."

That doesn't answer my question. "He didn't seem dangerous. He was actually quite a gentleman."

"But not in bed, I bet?" She winked.

I took another sip of champagne. "We actually didn't do that. We just talked."

"Right," said Frankie. "Of course."

She definitely did not believe me. "What can you tell me about him?"

"I don't really know him. I've just…heard things."

"Like?"

"It's not really my place to say. It wouldn't be fair to either of you for me to poison things with rumors."

"But you didn't mind poisoning things by telling me that he had rusty pipes and asbestos in his walls."

"Maybe I was just telling you what you wanted to hear. It seemed like you have a thing for bad boys."

"I guess I do. I mean, my ex-husband left me for a woman he barely knew." I downed the rest of my champagne. "And now they're Facebook-official."

"There's a difference between bad boys and bad people. And your ex sounds like the latter."

"Which one is Ryder?" I asked.

"I'm not sure. But I'll let you know if I find anything out. In the meantime…" She poured me another glass of champagne. "Get ready to have the night of your life."

"Doing what?"

"The best thing you can do when you've just suffered a bad breakup."

"Oh God." My heart started pounding. "I knew this was gonna be a gangbang."

Frankie spit out her champagne. "Wow. What? Is that how you usually get over breakups?"

I laughed awkwardly. "Ha. No. Of course not. I know that what we're really doing is…"

"Shopping!" she yelled, hoisting her glass into the air.

"Shopping!" I yelled too. I had never been much of a shopper, but her enthusiasm was contagious. "Oh, that's why my clothes needed to be easy to take off."

"Uh, yes. We have to get you a whole new wardrobe, and the boutique closes in three hours. Wait, did you seriously think you were going to a gangbang? Because my roommate and I went to one of those a few weeks ago and it was way more intense than I thought it would be. But if you really want one I'm sure I can get a few guys together…"

She got out her phone and started typing.

"No!" I swatted her phone out of her hand.

"Well, if you change your mind, just let me know." She sounded 100% serious. As if a gangbang was a totally normal thing.

The car came to a stop and the driver opened the door. We stepped out onto 5th Avenue. The fashion center of New York. And we were right in the middle of it, standing outside of the Odegaard boutique. I had never been there, but Chastity talked about it all the time. It was the store of her dreams. And it was the store of my nightmares. Every dress in there was worth more than my life.

"Ready to shop?" asked Frankie.

"Only if they take monopoly money." It was the only money I had plenty of. So much that it made that poor Forbes millionaire look like even more of a loser.

"They don't. But tonight, we have this." Frankie pulled a sleek black credit card out of her wallet.

"A Society card?"

She shrugged. "Close enough."

"Close enough? What does that mean?"

Frankie didn't answer. She just ushered me through the ten-foot-tall glass doors into the boutique. And that's where things got weird. Not like...sexually weird. Just unusual from a shopping perspective. First, the entrance to the store didn't seem like the entrance to a store at all. There wasn't a dress in sight. It looked more like the entrance to a five-star hotel, complete with marble walls and a massive chandelier. If this was a murder mystery, someone would definitely get crushed by it. But my life wasn't a murder mystery. It was a rom-com. Or erotic romance? *Oh God. What if I'm in a murder mystery and I just haven't realized it yet?* I imagined the chandelier squashing Frankie.

"Good evening, ladies," said a girl in a little black dress. Which raised two questions. First, was she a greeter? And if she was, why the hell did such an upscale store have greeters? I thought those were just a weird thing Walmart did to try to make people feel uncomfortable and never want to come back.

"Hi," said Frankie. "We have an appointment for 8:45."

The girl looked down at a tablet. "Raven Black?"

"That's me," I said.

"Great, follow me." She led us through another set of doors into a giant room that looked like it was straight out of *Say Yes to the Dress*, but instead of wedding dresses, the place was filled with clothes of all types. Well...not all types. There were no cheap clothes. There were also no other clients. All twelve of the changing areas were empty.

We wove through mannequins and clothes racks to the changing area on the far side of the store.

The girl clicked a few more buttons on her tablet and then looked up at us. "Your personal fashion consultant will be with you shortly. Can I get you anything while you wait?"

Personal fashion consultant? Were rich people too helpless to pick out their own clothes?

"We're fine, thanks," said Frankie. As soon as the girl disappeared, Frankie started browsing the racks. "Oh! You've gotta try these on." She was holding a pair of black leather leggings.

"Is that even allowed?" Being around so many expensive things was making me sweaty. Which meant I was going to get pit stains on all the clothes. And they'd have to cut the leather leggings off of me if I got too sweaty. The thought made me sweat even more. I didn't need to buy fancy clothes to get over Joe. I just needed Ryder.

"It's our appointment. We can do whatever we want. Now go try these on." She tossed the leggings at me.

I caught them and cradled them like a baby. I should have been more careful though. They were probably worth more than a baby. And somehow, they were about to be on my body. I went into the changing room and slipped them on. And by slipped, I mean jammed my ass into them like I was a sausage. But they actually looked really good. My spin classes were definitely working. I'd be crossing off revenge body in no time. "Damn, check out my ass," I said as I walked out of the changing room.

"Gladly," said a deep voice.

I looked up and saw Ryder standing there in all his glory, complete with his man bun, floral suit, and piercing eyes. Staring directly at my ass. Because I had just told him to.

Chapter 26

MY FASHIONISTA

Thursday

I put my hand on my hip and stared at Ryder. I tried to picture him with glasses and his hair down like Tanner Rhodes. They could be the same person. Or not. *Gah!*

"What are you doing here?" I asked.

"I'm your personal fashion consultant. And it's lovely to see you again, Miss Black."

"Miss Black?" I asked. "Why are you being weird?"

"I'm being professional."

"By staring at my ass?" I arched my back a little to make him stare more.

He shrugged. "One of the many perks of my job."

"What are the other perks?" I asked.

"You'll just have to wait and see."

I gulped way louder than I meant to. *What if I don't want to wait?*

"We should get down to business, though," continued Ryder. "How can I help you ladies this evening?"

Frankie looked back from one of the racks she'd been browsing. "Raven needs a complete wardrobe overhaul. She just got divorced and she's looking to meet some men." She winked at me.

Is that a gangbang reference? Oh God...

"I see," said Ryder. He looked disappointed. "I think we can arrange that. Wait here." He disappeared into the racks of clothes.

"What was that?" I asked Frankie. "I'm not trying to meet other men. I just want him."

"I know that. But you can't let *him* know it. Men want what they can't have. Especially men like Ryder."

I nodded. *Of course*. He was a billionaire. He could have anything he wanted. So if I made myself seem like the one thing he couldn't have, he'd be hooked.

Ryder returned a few minutes later with at least a dozen outfits slung over his arm. "I found some good stuff. Ready to try them on?" He started hanging the outfits up in the dressing room. And then he didn't leave. Instead he leaned against the doorjamb and smiled. "Are you stalking me?"

God, was that going to be the weird way he always greeted me now? We'd been over this. *He* was stalking *me*. And just because he asked the question in an incredibly sexy way, didn't make it any less rude. "You're the one that showed up here."

"I work here."

Yeah right, you're a secret billionaire. "We've already been over this. You're stalking me. And if you'll please excuse me…" I glanced at the dressing room door. I needed him to leave so I could figure out what the hell was happening.

"I was going to stay and help."

"How do I know you're not just trying to see me naked?"

He pretended to be shocked by my allegation. "That would be very unprofessional. And anyway…why would I need to do that when I already have a picture of your boob?"

"Hey! You said you were gonna delete that."

"I never agreed to that."

"Fine. If you don't delete that picture, I'll just tell the whole world that you wear Crocs."

"Do I? Because I'm pretty sure that's you." He pulled his phone out and showed me security footage of me leaving the Caldwell Hotel in Crocs.

I snatched for his phone, but he easily pulled it out of my reach. "I wouldn't have had to wear them if you hadn't left me there all alone. And why is there no stuff in your apartment?"

"I had to go work and I didn't want to wake you. Has anyone ever told you how adorable you are when you snore?"

Oh God. Please tell me I wasn't really snoring. And hey…he hadn't answered the second part of my question!

"Now, you should probably try these clothes on before we run out of time. Good luck with the blue one." He turned and walked out, closing the door behind him.

I stared in horror at the blue dress he had was referring to. Or was it a romper? I couldn't tell. But I was determined to get it on without his help. I pulled it off the rack and looked for a zipper. *What even is this thing?* Whatever. I'd get to that later. Instead I slipped on some yoga pants and a sports bra that only cost…$1700?! And it didn't cover enough of my stomach, so I tried on the next outfit. And then the next. It was like Chastity had designed all of these clothes, because they were more than skimpy enough to satisfy Single Girl Rule #16: Either your legs, cleavage, or stomach must be showing at all times. Preferably all three.

"You okay in there?" called Ryder.

"I'm just fine, thank you. Although I'd be even better if my personal fashionista was a little better at his job."

"It's personal fashion consultant. And I can only find you better garments if you come out and show us how they look."

"Fine." I finagled my way into a super awesome dress. It kind of reminded me of something a gladiator would wear. But all the clean lines and the expensive white fabric made it look super modern. Almost futuristic. I guess that made me a space gladiator?

I opened the door and walked out to the platform surrounded by mirrors.

"Damn," said Ryder and Frankie at the same time.

"You look amazing," added Frankie.

Ryder got up and walked around me, inspecting the fit on every inch of my body. "Guess I am good at my job after all."

"Is this even your real job?" I asked. *Or are you a billionaire investor?*

"You really think I would have been able to pick out a dress that fit you that well if this wasn't my real job?"

He made a good point. But I was still 90% sure he was the same person as Tanner. I just had to prove it. Which meant I had to get him into a pair of glasses and take his hair out of the man bun. "Do you have a hair tie? I feel like this dress would look so much cuter if my hair was up."

"I have one," said Frankie. She took one off her wrist and handed it to me.

Damn you! I wanted Ryder's hair tie! I shot it over a rack of clothes and tried to play it off like an accident. "Oops." I turned to Ryder. "Could I use yours?"

"Sure." He pulled back his colorful sleeve and took a hair tie off his wrist. "Here you go."

I fumbled with it for a second and then shot it across the room. "I'm so clumsy. Do you have another?"

"It really seems like you're trying to get the one out of my hair. Which kind of freaks me out. Are you trying to steal a strand of my hair so you can make a Polyjuice potion?"

"You're a Harry Potter fan?" I asked. *He really is my soulmate.*

"Uh, of course." He looked genuinely offended that I thought he might *not* be a Potterhead.

"What house are you?" I asked.

"What house do you think I am?" he shot back.

"Hufflepuff."

"Excuse me?!" Now he *really* looked offended.

"Hufflepuff are the humble ones. And since you're pretending to be a fashionista…"

"Personal fashion consultant," he corrected me.

"Whatever. Pretending to be that when you're secretly a billionaire is quite humble."

"Billionaire? I wish. And anyway, such a charade seems more like something a Slytherin would do."

I stared at him. I could never tell when he was lying. "What house do you think I am?"

"Definitely Ravenclaw," he said.

"And why is that?"

"They're the creative ones. And this fantasy that you've created about me being a billionaire is certainly creative. Also, they're the hot ones." His eyes scanned my body.

He thinks I'm hot?! My face started to blush. I ran back into the changing room before he could see. I was supposed to be playing hard to get, not melting the second he gave me a compliment. I got into the strappy blue dress and walked back out. "What do you think my date this weekend will think of this one?" I asked, fighting the urge to adjust the straps to make sure I wasn't showing any underboob.

"He'll love it," said Frankie.

Ryder stared at me. Was that a look of jealousy? Or was it a look of skepticism?

"It looks amazing," he said. "Because I picked it, so of course it does. But whether he likes it really depends on his level of taste. And the date. Where's he taking you?"

Shit! He's onto me! "I…he…Chuck E. Cheese." *What?* I could have literally said any other place and it would have been more believable.

Ryder raised an eyebrow. "Is your date a small child?"

"Jealousy doesn't suit you."

"I'm not jealous. I'm genuinely curious about what kind of man child would take you to Chuck E. Cheese."

"A really hot one," said Frankie.

"Yeah," I agreed. "The hottest. Ten feet of pure muscle."

Ryder laughed. "Ten feet? Well, tell Shaq that I hope he doesn't get stuck in any of the plastic tunnels."

"His name isn't Shaq. It's Dr. Lyons."

"You call him Dr. Lyons? That's creepy. That reminds me of this book I read where this girl was having sex with her teacher and kept calling him Professor Hunter."

"Ew," said Frankie. "I didn't realize they had sex with the teachers in Harry Potter."

Ryder and I didn't bother correcting her. Clearly she wasn't a Potterhead, and thus not worth talking to.

"Seriously though…do you really call him Dr. Lyons?" asked Ryder.

"No. I call him by his first name."

"Which is…?"

I have no idea. Which was weird. *I should probably find that out on the date.* Or was it too late to ask? Whatever. It didn't matter. I wasn't actually going to go on the date with him. Because by then I would be married to Ryder. Er…dating. Dating Ryder. Not married to. Because I had only known him for two days, and wanting to marry someone after two days would be super creepy. And I wasn't. And now Ryder was staring at me because I was just standing there awkwardly thinking about marrying him. I cleared my throat. "His name is none of your business. All you need to know is that he's super handsome."

"And ten feet tall. Which means you'll need a pair of heels." Ryder disappeared through some double doors on the other side of the store.

"How am I doing?" I asked Frankie.

"Amazing. But I do have a few notes…"

"So you mean I'm doing awful?"

"Don't bring that negative energy in here. But if you want some advice…maybe try making him a bit more jealous. Rather than making him think that you're into lanky pedophiles."

"*Handsome* lanky pedophiles," I corrected.

"That's not much better. Dr. Lyons isn't real, is he?."

"Oh, he's real. Well, kind of. I have a date with him this weekend. But he's not lanky or a pedophile, despite what my best friend thinks." I giggled to myself about Chastity's mix-up with pedophile and pediatrician.

Frankie gave me a weird look.

"Oh, no. My friend doesn't really think he's a pedophile."

"Well that's reassuring," said Ryder from behind me. "Otherwise I would have felt obligated to warn Chuck E. Cheese. Now try these on." He pushed a box into my arms. No, not any box. A white leather shoe box. With *Odegaard* written in blue script on the lid.

I wasn't really into fashion, but I knew that Odegaard was known for their shoes. It was the shoe brand of the rich and famous. It was impossible to scroll through Best Dressed lists without seeing the wild designs and signature blue bottoms. Chastity had one pair from before her family went bankrupt, and she never wore them. She just kept them in a locked glass case.

"This is too much," I said, pushing the box back to him.

"You didn't even look at them."

"I didn't have to. I can see that they're Odegaards."

"Well of course they are. We're at the Odegaard boutique..." Ryder opened the box. And I had to admit, the shoes were freaking awesome. But they weren't for me. I'd worn heels the other night, and it wasn't lost on me that Ryder had avoided kissing me at all costs. Because I looked bad in heels, just like Joe had always told me. That was probably why Ryder had picked out the most expensive shoes in the world. He thought putting $3000 shoes on me would help distract everyone from my weird knobbly knees. "Don't you have anything a little tamer? I don't look good in tall shoes."

"Says who?" Ryder asked.

"My husband. Er, ex-husband." It still felt weird to say that.

"The one who you walked in on shagging the instamodel?"

"That's the one."

Ryder frowned. "Was he blind?"

"Not that I know of."

"I wouldn't be so sure. Because the other night you looked amazing in those heels. At least try them on."

"If you don't, I will," said Frankie.

"Fine." I kicked off my lame shoes and put on the sky-high heels.

"What other lies did your ex tell you?" Ryder asked as I fumbled with the straps.

"Who knows. Until five seconds ago, I didn't even realize the shoe thing was a lie." Chastity had hinted at it, but for some reason the way Ryder looked at me made me actually believe him.

"If he was such a jerk, why'd you stay with him?" Ryder knelt to tighten one of the straps. "Was he some sort of sex god?"

I laughed. "Ha. Not even close."

"He never even gave her an orgasm," said Frankie.

What? How did she know that? And why is she saying it out loud? Gosh darn it, Frankie!

"But Dr. Lyons is going to fix that Saturday night in the ball pit," she added.

Sex in the ball pit? The thought made me want to throw up in my mouth. I could just picture flailing around and getting a used AIDS needle stuck in my ass. That sorta thing happens in ball pits, by the way. So don't have sex in them. Or go in them at all. Or let your kids in them. Really they should all just be burned.

"Have you really never had an orgasm?" asked Ryder.

My face started turning red again. "Of course I have."

Ryder shook his head. "You definitely haven't."

"Why do you think that?" I asked. I stared at my reflection in the mirror. My knees looked completely unknobbly. I looked...hot. But my face was still getting redder by the second talking about my sex life. Or lack of one.

"I can just tell."

"I think you're the one who's never had an orgasm." It was a terrible comeback, but it was the only thing I could think of. I needed to change the topic immediately. "Shut up and find me more clothes." I ran away and locked myself in the dressing room.

Ryder brought me tons more clothes. Dresses, yoga pants, slacks, bikinis. And I felt confident and beautiful in all of it. I could get used to shopping at fancy boutiques.

"Alright," said Ryder. "Your appointment is almost over, but we have time for one more thing." He tossed me some black lingerie. The blue dress from earlier had been complicated, but this was on an entirely different level. It was a mishmash of rings, straps, and fabric. Actually, there wasn't much fabric. It was just rings and straps.

"Ooh la la," I said. "I'm definitely gonna need help putting that on."

"I thought you might say that." His voice was dripping with desire. He totally thought he was gonna get to see me naked.

I turned and walked into the changing room. Ryder followed, but I put my hand on his chest - his very muscular chest - and stopped him at the door. "Nice try, but I think I'll have Frankie help me."

Frankie walked past him and closed the door in his face. "That was perfect!" she whispered.

"Really?"

"Yes. You've got him wrapped around your finger." She tried to organize the straps on the lingerie as I stripped down. A few days ago I would have been super uncomfortable with Frankie seeing me naked. I still kind of was. But changing in front of Frankie hardly seemed daunting after getting waxed, trying to rape Dr. Lyons, and that horrifying elevator incident that I really should not ever mention again. Crap, was that officially incident #3? Yes, yes it was. That poor bastard's face when we'd made eye contact was going to haunt my dreams.

Even so, I put the lingerie on as quickly as possible. It took Frankie like five minutes to get all the straps situated correctly.

"Damn you look hot," said Frankie. "Now put on the rest of your clothes and let's go."

"Isn't that shoplifting? Joe's best friend tried to steal a pair of tights from Sports Authority his senior year by hiding them under his other clothes. They caught him and he lost his scholarship because of it."

"Uh, cool. But we're gonna pay for it, so it's not a big deal."

"Right. Of course we are." I put on the skirt and top that I'd worn to the store. You could just barely see the top of the stockings under the hem of my skirt. It was super slutty. And my knees looked kind of weird in the stockings…

But then Frankie opened the door and Ryder's eyes devoured my body. "Wow," he muttered.

That's right. I look hot. And in that moment I realized that it wasn't the fancy clothes that were giving me confidence. It was the way Ryder looked at me. When his eyes were on me, I felt like the most beautiful girl in the world. It was a weird feeling, but I kind of liked it. *Lies. I freaking loved it.*

Chapter 27

CASH OR CREDIT

Thursday

"That'll be $34,700," said Ryder.

My eyes got big. That was an insane amount to pay for clothes. Good thing this was fake. *But what if it isn't? What if the Society bills me for all this stuff?*

"Cash or credit?" he asked.

Frankie smiled and handed him the credit card. "Courtesy of her husband."

My husband? It took me a second to work out what was happening. Then it hit me. They were just fulfilling my wish for free shoes and revenge on my husband. They gave me shoes, and now they were making it *seem* like my husband was footing the bill.

Ryder took the card and stuck it in the chip scanner. It beeped aggressively. He frowned and tried again. Same beep. Ryder narrowed his eyebrows. "I'm sorry, this card has been reported as stolen." He yanked it out of the reader and cut it in half.

Is this part of it? My mind started racing. What if the Society was a criminal organization and they'd really stolen Joe's credit card? We *had* just been approved for an AmEx black card. Right before he divorced me and took all our money.

"Her husband cheated on her," said Frankie. "Buying her a few new dresses is the least he can do."

"We should go," I said, glancing out the window. The flashing red and blue lights of a police car approached. *Oh God. They're coming for us.* I pictured them screeching up to the boutique and storming in to arrest me. But the squad car sped right past. I let out a huge sigh of relief.

"Did you bring any cash?" asked Ryder.

"Um, yeah." I rummaged through my purse and pulled out some monopoly money. I counted it as I put it on the counter. "$800."

"Great, that'll get you half a legging." He held up the awesome pair of leather leggings that Frankie had picked out and got ready to cut them in half like they were some sort of stolen credit card. "Actually…" said Ryder. "I don't usually do this, but everything looked so good on you. And we do need some new pictures for ads. How would you like to model in exchange for the clothes?"

"No thanks, perv," said Frankie.

"Suit yourself." Ryder grabbed all the bags of clothes off the counter. "But I'll need you to take off that lingerie."

I looked down at my amazing cleavage and super cool stockings. They were so pretty. And the way they had made Ryder look at me… "Wait. I'll do the modeling." I immediately wished I hadn't said it. I knew *nothing* about modeling. I could hardly make a decent duck face for a selfie, much less pose for a 5th Avenue billboard.

Ryder smiled at me like he had known I would do it all along. "Great. Follow me." He led us through a different set of doors into a showroom lined from floor to ceiling with shelves of Odegaards. Frankie plopped herself down on a white leather loveseat while Ryder put all my clothes next to a privacy screen in the corner.

"So what shoes do you want to model first?"

Shoe modeling? I suddenly wished I had waited to join the Society until after a few more months of spin classes. Odegaards deserved to be on some six-foot-tall angel with thighs the size of toothpicks. "Uh…" I looked at the shelves. Making a decision like this was my worst nightmare. There were strappy sandals, plain pumps, thigh-high boots with wild prints, and everything in between. The only thing they all had in common were the bright blue soles that matched the exact color of the carpet.

"How about these," suggested Ryder. He grabbed a pair of white 6" heels with tips that curled back in a way that would have put a civil war general's mustache to shame. *Sexy elf shoes?*

I must have given him a weird look, because he immediately put them back on the shelf. "Sorry," he said, clearing his throat. "Old habits die hard."

What? Did he used to have some sort of weird elf fetish?

"How about this instead?" He picked up a fairly normal pair of lacy black heels.

I shrugged. "It's your ad campaign."

"Oh! Those would look great with your new little black dress," suggested Frankie.

"I agree," said Ryder. He rummaged through my shopping bags and tossed the dress over the top of the privacy screen. That was my cue to change.

"Should I keep the lingerie on?" I called as I stripped off my lame, sub-$1000 clothes.

"For now," replied Ryder.

As in…he'll be tearing it off me later? Or did he just mean that I wouldn't wear it in some later shots? I gulped.

When I came out from behind the screen, Ryder had transformed the showroom into a photo studio complete with super-bright LEDs and those weird foil umbrellas on tripods. I sat down on a bench to start putting on the shoes, but Ryder put his hand on mine to stop me.

"Allow me," he said, taking the shoe out of my hand. He knelt in front of me. I pressed my thighs together to prevent him from seeing right up my dress as he cradled my foot in one hand and slipped the shoe onto me with the other. His gentle touch sent a jolt of desire up through my nylon-clad legs. I pressed my thighs together harder. But then he stood up and the moment was gone. He directed me to stand in front of one of the walls of shoes while he handed Frankie a box fan.

"Strike a pose," commanded Ryder.

I put one hand on my hip and smiled as hard as I could while the fan gently blew through my hair, giving the illusion of a romantic breeze.

Or at least, that was how I pictured it in my mind.

Ryder snapped a few shots and then clicked through the images on the camera's LCD display.

"How'd I do?" I asked.

"Uh…"

"Let me see." I snatched the camera from him so Frankie and I could see the pictures. Frankie immediately burst out laughing so hard that I thought she might pull a muscle. And I couldn't blame her. The picture was awful. My pose looked so forced and unnatural. And my smile…*oh God.* Every tendon in my neck was visible. It reminded me of the horrible 2nd-grade school portrait that my mom still had framed in her hallway. The fan didn't help, either. Rather than creating the illusion of a gentle breeze, it made for more of a reporter-in-a-category-4-hurricane sort of situation.

"Not a bad start," said Ryder mercifully. "A few notes though… Frankie, let's dial it back on the fan a bit. And Raven, try not to smile so hard."

I took a deep breath. I wanted him to think I was sexy instead of adorable. This was my chance to prove that I could be. *I've got this.* I went back to the wall and struck another pose. Ryder told me it looked great and then…proceeded to change literally everything about it.

Damn it.

"Both hands on your hips," he said. "Shoulders back. Neck out - no, not that far. Turn a bit. Good, good. Butt out. Suck in your stomach. Tits up. Shoulders back again. Pop that elbow a bit…"

"Am I modeling or trying out for Cirque du Soleil? What kind of contortionist do you think I am?" I was seconds away from falling over.

He ignored me and kept giving more instructions. Once every muscle in my body ached from pretzeling myself into the most unnatural position possible, Ryder finally snapped a few pictures.

"Damn," he muttered.

Frankie ran over and looked too. "You look hot." She turned the camera so I could see it.

Holy shit! I did look hot. "What kind of magic did you just use to make me look so skinny and my boobs look so big?"

He gave me a funny look as if I had just revealed his deepest secret. "None. No magic. I just put you into the right pose so that the camera would capture your true beauty. It's hard to make a 2D image look as good as the real thing."

Do I really look that good? Seeing that picture coupled with the way Ryder had looked at me earlier had given me a newfound confidence. I got back into position and got ready for more pictures.

"Okay, the last thing we need to work on is your face," said Ryder.

Well, crap. "What's wrong with my face?"

"It's beautiful, but you need it to tell a story."

"And what story should I tell?"

"Well…these shoes are supposed to be sexy. Fierce."

"Got it." I squinted to try to do sexy-eyes.

"Good, good," said Ryder as he snapped photos. "But I want more. Here, try saying *prune.*"

"What?"

"Just do it. Prune."

"Prune," I said. I felt ridiculous. But when Ryder showed me the picture of it, I almost fell over. My lips were perfectly puckered and my cheekbones looked better than ever. "How'd you get so good at this?"

Ryder shrugged. "I'm a man of many talents."

"And you're modest too," I said with a laugh as I struck another pose.

Click, click, click. More photos. "Prune," I said again as I lifted the hem of my skirt slightly and put my leg out.

"Yes, perfect," growled Ryder. The bulge in his pants caught my eye. Had that been there a minute ago? Was it growing? Because of me?

I leaned over and crossed my arms to give him the perfect cleavage shot as I bit my bottom lip.

Frankie cleared her throat. "I better go uh, take this call. You two have fun." She hurried out of the room.

Ryder and I hardly even noticed she left. We were in the zone. I was hitting pose after pose while Ryder zipped around the room finding all my best angles.

Each flash of the camera made me feel sexier and sexier.

"Lose the dress," he said.

I swallowed hard. "But…"

"I said lose the dress." His tone left no room for argument. And I didn't want to argue. Twenty minutes ago I would have been terrified to pose in lingerie, but Ryder made me feel like the most beautiful woman in the world. I had no doubt that his photos would be amazing.

I bit my lip and then reached back to unzip the dress. Slowly, ever so slowly, I unzipped it and let it fall to the floor, leaving me exposed in the strappy black lingerie. I was embracing every moment of this Society date. And even though I was nervous, I was so freaking proud of myself. I was standing in lingerie in front of the most handsome man I'd ever met. I snuck a glance at him.

Ryder's Adam's apple rose and fell. He snapped a few more pictures and then walked over to me. He grabbed one of the straps and untwisted it. His finger brushing against my exposed skin sent a chill down my spine. He kept his hand on my clavicle and my heart started beating double time.

"Are you supposed to touch your model?" I asked. My voice came out so airy. God, I wanted him to kiss me. I'd wanted him to kiss me since the first moment I saw him.

"I'll do whatever I want to my model."

The way he was looking at me made me feel alive. "Oh yeah?" I bit my lip again.

And then he was on me. His lips crashed against mine as his strong hand slid behind my neck and pulled me closer.

I melted into him. His tongue flicked against my lips. *Yes.* I parted my lips and let him in.

He grabbed my ass and lifted me into the air. I wrapped my legs around his waist as he deepened the kiss. He pushed me against the wall and some small part of me was vaguely aware of the shoes crashing to the ground. My ass slid perfectly onto the velvet-lined shelf while our tongues battled. The scruff of his five o'clock shadow rubbed my face raw. He was devouring me as if he had waited three hundred years for this kiss. His hands wandered to my hips, caressing every inch of flesh exposed between the straps of my lingerie. He squeezed my ass and pulled me against his erection.

"God yes," I moaned. I tore at the buttons of his shirt. The hard muscles underneath were begging me to let them free, but he grabbed both my hands and pinned them against the wall. The full weight of his body pressed against me.

And then the entire shelf snapped in half. Hundreds of thousands of dollars' worth of shoes went crashing to the floor. We fell too. I didn't have time to think about the destruction because he rolled on top of me. He flicked his tongue against mine before trailing kisses down my neck and along my clavicle. I sunk my fingers into his long hair. He was grinding against me now, rubbing my bare ass against the plush blue carpet.

"I need you," I said breathlessly. I reached down and felt his erection through the fabric of his slacks. *Yes.*

His body tensed and he pulled back. He ran his hand through his hair. "I'm sorry. I shouldn't have…" He shook his head and stood up so fast it was like my skin had burned him.

"Wait." It came out as a moan and I instantly felt embarrassed when he took another step back from me. Like he finally realized that I wasn't model-worthy. Like I disgusted him. "Ryder?" I hated that it sounded like I was begging him to stay. I felt as unworthy as he thought I was.

"I can't. I can't. I'm sorry, Raven. This was a mistake." And then he was gone.

Chapter 28

SPECIAL DELIVERY

Friday

I was ready for work an hour early, which still didn't feel early enough after my close encounter with lateness a few days ago. I had set my alarm for…

Okay, fine, I'm lying. I hadn't set an alarm. Because I hadn't slept a wink. I had just stayed up all night replaying my kiss with Ryder. And the way he'd left so suddenly. *What the hell had gone wrong?*

In the moment, I'd thought he just changed his mind. That he no longer thought I was sexy. But that didn't make any sense. How can you go from kissing someone one minute to being repulsed the next? I didn't want to believe it was true. So it had to be something else.

Had I freaked him out by grabbing his junk? If we had been in middle school maybe that would have been a possibility. But he was a grown-ass man.

Or maybe he was worried I was going to #MeToo him and sue him for billions. He was, after all, kind of my boss. Or at least, I thought he was. I still wasn't 100% sure that Ryder and Tanner were the same person. Maybe he ran from me because he realized I knew his true identity…

Gah! Thinking about all this made my brain hurt. I needed to see him again so I could get some answers. So it was a good thing we were giving him our marketing presentation for his wine company today at 3 o'clock. I still needed to concoct a plan to get him alone afterward. I'd think of something. Worst case scenario I could always run into the wall and knock myself out.

I had just finished straightening my hair when a knock sounded on the door.

Who would be here this early?

Probably Chastity. I had sent her the world's longest text last night all about my date, so I assumed she was showing up to get the full scoop. But it could also be the cops coming to ask about Joe's stolen credit card. Or how I had gotten thirty-grand worth of designer clothing in exchange for a few photos. Or how I had raped Dr. Lyons. Although that case seemed to be closed now that we had a date planned.

I looked through the peephole and found that both of my guesses were wrong. Instead it was a FedEx man. I opened the door.

"Raven Black?" he asked.

"That's me."

"Sign here."

I gave him my signature, and he gave me a package. I started to close the door, but he blocked it with his foot.

"Hold on. There's more." He disappeared into the hall.

More? All my amazon clothes had already arrived. Maybe Joe was sending me more of my stuff. Whatever. I didn't have time to deal with his crap right now. I tossed the package aside and went back to the bathroom to add a few finishing touches to my makeup. When I emerged a minute later...

Holy hell! Five FedEx guys were unloading carts of packages, and based on the floor-to-ceiling boxes that now occupied about 600 of the 800 square feet of my apartment, it must have been at least their third trip. Then it hit me. The FedEx guy had called me Raven Black. Not Ashley Cooper. Which meant this delivery was from the Society.

"Who sent this?" I asked.

The FedEx guy shrugged. "No idea. Have a great day."

I grabbed one of the packages and checked the label. No name was listed. The address was in NYC, but beyond that it didn't ring any bells. *What the hell is all this?* I used my keys to cut the tape on the closest box. Inside was a white leather box wrapped in blue crepe paper. *Odegaard* was scrawled on the side of the box.

Odegaards! Yes! They must be a gift from Ryder. Which meant he wasn't mad at me or repulsed by me. I couldn't contain the smile that spread across my face.

And then I remembered there were dozens more boxes. Were they all filled with Odegaards? No. They couldn't be. That would be like… I tried to estimate how many boxes there were and then multiplied it by $3000.

I tore into a few more boxes before it was time to leave for work. Sure enough, they were all filled with Odegaards. Including the pair of weird elf-style heels Ryder had wanted me to wear last night. I considered wearing them to the office, but I wasn't nearly confident enough to pull them off.

I can't believe he sent me all these. I didn't want to leave for work. I just wanted to keep opening box after box of Odegaards. You know how in first grade all your friends tell you Santa doesn't exist? Well they're full of shit. Because Santa does exist and his name is Ryder freaking Storm. I couldn't wait to see him today for our big presentation. Another kiss was definitely in my future.

I allowed myself to open one more box before I left. It was the one that the FedEx guy had delivered first. And it had a little black envelope in it. *Ah!* My fingers were shaking with excitement as I opened it.

Raven,
I'm so sorry about last night.
-Ryder

I flipped it over. *That's all?* Well, apology accepted. Really the note alone would have been sufficient, but the hundreds of thousands of dollars' worth of Odegaards was a nice addition. I hugged the note to my chest. Was this my first love letter? I think it was. The only time Joe had ever sent me a letter was when he served me with divorce papers.

And some guy in middle school had passed me a letter that said, "Will you be my girlfriend? Circle YES or NO." I had circled no because I was 100% sure he was gay, just like every other guy who had ever liked me in school. I was still trying to work out what that said about me.

Anyway…shoes. Tons of them. They were all mine. And so was Ryder. I bit back a squeal.

Before heading to work I triple-checked the lock on the door to make sure Homeless Rutherford wouldn't break in and lick all my beautiful shoes.

Chastity practically pounced on me the moment I got out of the elevator at work. "Tell me everything," she said. I had never seen her look so excited.

"Well, a limo picked me up, but only Frankie was in it."

"I don't care about that. Get to the good part. Did you find proof that Ryder and Tanner are different people?"

"They're definitely not different. After seeing him up-close again…yeah, I'm sure it's him."

"Damn it! Are you *sure*?"

"Who else besides a billionaire could afford to give me 74 pairs of Odegaards?"

"Say what now? Your text didn't mention those."

"That's because they arrived two seconds before I left for work. They came with a note." I took it out of my purse and showed it to her.

"Damn," said Chastity. "Even one pair of Odegaards would be an extravagant apology, but 74? That really makes it seem like he did something truly awful to you."

"Well he did leave immediately after I grabbed his penis. Which was rather rude of him." Thinking about it again made doubt to creep back into my mind. But Ryder definitely liked me. Or else why would he have sent me so many shoes? Or kissed me. Or started stalking me to begin with?

Chastity snapped her fingers. "Oh my God, that's it."

"What?"

"He came in his pants."

I laughed. "No way."

"Think about it. You were making out with him. You touched him. He came. And then he panicked and fled in shame."

"That's definitely what happened," added Madison from behind me. "He sounds like a real loser to me. I say you ditch him and never speak to him again."

"Guys, I really don't think that's what happened." *But maybe it is?* Could I really blame him? All that bumping and grinding and kissing had practically made me orgasm. Not that I knew what that felt like.

"So for the presentation…" started Madison but Chastity cut her off.

"Was he big?"

Of course she would ask that. "I think so?"

"How big?"

"I don't know." But maybe I'll find out after the meeting!

"I bet he's huge," said Chastity.

"Why?" asked Madison. "He's a billionaire, right? He's definitely compensating for something."

"So what's the plan for this afternoon?" asked Chastity.

I tried to process the change of topic. Which was super weird for Chastity since we had already been on her favorite subject. "Uh…let's start by mentioning the rebranding. If he's cool with it, then we'll show him all the logo mockups. And if he hates them I guess we better be ready to pivot…"

Chastity brushed my ideas aside. "No. Who cares about all that? You already sealed the deal on this contract last night when you made him cum in his pants. We could tell him that we were going to put swastikas all over his Facebook ads and he wouldn't care."

"We really shouldn't do that," added Madison.

"We're not going to. But we could. Anyway, I was asking what the plan was for *after the* meeting. As in, how we're going to get Ash alone with him."

"So you concede that Ryder and Tanner and the same person?" I asked. *Yes! I win!*

"For now. But if you find out that they're not…"

"Yeah, yeah. Tanner will be yours."

"Shhh," said Madison. She pointed to the elevator. Bee had just walked off. Even though she was probably the nicest boss in the world, it still wouldn't have been ideal for her to hear us discussing which of us would get to sleep with our new client. And Mason probably wouldn't like it either. Every time I saw him, all I could think about was Matt screaming as his pants caught fire. Chastity had assured me that Mason's little brother never came to the offices, but if he did show up, I was fully prepared to jump out the window. Actually, maybe it was time to activate my window-escape now, because Mason looked absolutely *pissed* about something. Oh my God, what if he'd just found out that they accidentally hired the girl that set his brother's dick on fire! He was about to fire me for sure.

Chastity and Madison both immediately started shuffling papers and pretending to work.

"What the *fuck* did you three do?" asked Mason. Smoke was practically come out of his ears.

My answer would have been, "Landed you your biggest client ever," but something told me that it was better to stay silent.

"Tanner shredded the contract. He's out."

"Out?" asked Chastity. "But we have a meeting with him at three about his winery."

"Not anymore. I've been trying to get him to come in for months. And he finally did. It was a sure thing. How the hell did you three mess this up? I knew I should have put Garrett on this instead."

"But…" started Chastity.

"But nothing. If he's not our client on Monday morning, then all three of you are fired." He turned and stormed off. Bee mouthed, "I'm sorry," and then followed Mason to the elevator.

"What were you saying about having this contract locked up?" asked Madison.

Chastity stared daggers at me. "What the hell, Ash?"

"Don't look at me. I did my best. Our first presentation was dynamite."

"Not the presentation. I mean what did you do last night? To Tanner. It sure seems like you did something awful. When you say you touched his penis...do you really mean that you kicked him square in the nuts?"

"I won't blame you if you did," added Madison. "He surely had it coming."

"No! We were having a super-hot kiss. We even broke a shelf in the heat of the moment." I paused and squeezed my legs together. Best first kiss ever? Yes. Although my only frame of reference was my first kiss with Joe. His Natty-Ice-scented breath and the stench of dirty laundry from his frat house still haunted my dreams.

"What exactly did he say when he stopped kissing you?" asked Chastity.

"He just uh...apologized I think. I don't know. It all happened so fast. But he's definitely not mad at me. Otherwise he wouldn't have sent me all those Odegaards this morning. And given me this note." I reached in my purse to grab the note. That was when I noticed the alert on my phone. From the Society app. Well, technically it was labeled *Tax Codes*, but that was just the disguise for the Society app. I pulled out my phone.

"That's not a note," said Chastity.

"I know. But I got something from the Society. Maybe it's about him."

"It's probably your post-date evaluation."

"Right." It still freaked me out that Chastity knew all the Society rules and procedures so well. I clicked on the notification and the screen turned black. The Society logo was at the top and then, in plain white text, it read:

Raven Black,

Your membership in the Society has been terminated for a violation of clause 49c.

Sincerely,
The Society

"What the hell?" I muttered. *What's clause 49c?*

"What?" asked Chastity and Madison.

I handed them my phone.

"Rape?!" yelled Chastity.

"Shhh," I hissed. Other people in the office were starting to look at us. Scratch that. They were full-on staring.

"Who raped someone?" asked Madison. "If Tanner raped you, I'll kill him."

"She raped *him*," said Chastity. "That's what clause 49c is. Immediate termination for rape."

I shook my head. "It was consensual. And it was just a kiss." I swallowed hard. Or was it? I'd tried to rape before. Oh God, what had I done?!

"Did you explicitly ask for consent?" asked Madison. "Or better yet, use a consent app? I'll send you a link to mine if you want."

"A what? No. We were two grown adults kissing each other." I was on the verge of tears. Why did I keep trying to rape people?!

"Well whatever you did must have really pissed him off. Because he definitely never wants to see your face again."

And then something snapped in me. Blood rushed to my fists. My whole body felt like it was on fire. My rage was usually contained in my fiery red hair, but sometimes it got out and spread to the rest of my body. This was one of those times. "If he never wants to see me again, then I hope he has good security. Because I'm going to his office. I'm not going to let this asshole get us fired for no reason."

Chapter 29
JERKFACE
Friday

Tanner's office was just a few blocks away from BIMG. I didn't even bother to get an Uber over. I thought walking might give me more time to compose myself. To think of a nice, calm way to approach him. It had the opposite effect. Walking in heels through the unseasonably warm weather coupled with the stench of trash day in the city just made my blood boil even more. All I managed to do was come up with curse words that I hadn't even known existed. All of them described Tanner perfectly.

The elevator dinged and I got off on Floor 18. I had thought that the BIMG offices were extravagant, but Tanner's office was on a different level. I don't even know the names of the rare stones the ultra-modern furniture was carved from, but it looked like some sort of bright blue granite veined with pure white. Was that even possible? Maybe the receptionist desk was just carved from the world's largest sapphire. And the woman behind it was effortlessly sophisticated. I could imagine her growing up in some Italian villa, splitting her time between tanning her perfect olive skin under the Tuscan sun and learning the minutia of fancy people etiquette.

Was Tanner banging her? That would explain why he had fled so quickly last night. I had probably broken some unwritten rule of the billionaires' make-out handbook. Was that a thing? If it was, I bet Steve Forbes didn't have a copy. #SickBurn. I was on fire with these hashtags recently.

Either way, it didn't matter if Tanner was banging Miss Roman Villa. Because I was freaking done with Tanner and his bullshit. I no longer took shit from any man. Ever. He was just playing some sick game that I wanted no part of. *Stupid dirty stalker.* I was just here to get him to sign that contract so that my friends didn't get fired.

"How may I help you?" asked the receptionist.

"I'm here to see Tanner."

"Is Mr. Rhodes expecting you?"

"He should be." *Biotch.*

She cocked her head to the side in a look of confusion. "Does that mean you have an appointment, or…?"

"Yup. I'll show myself back." I walked around the giant granite desk.

"You can't go back there without an appointment!" she called after me.

A few of his employees looked up at me as I snaked through the maze of cubicles. I had never been here before, but I knew that he'd be in the corner office. All fancy executives have fancy corner offices. Cookie-cutter lameazoids. Evie Martin - the blonde from all his pictures - tried to stop me at this door, but I ignored her and stormed into Tanner's office. "What the hell is your problem?" I demanded.

He was pacing by the window. He looked up when I came in. Surprise, or maybe fear, crossed his face for a second. He kicked off his shoes, which appeared to be elf-like Crocs, and then casually leaned on his desk as if he hadn't just done anything weird.

"I'm sorry, sir," said Evie. "I couldn't stop her. Should I call security?"

He waved her off. "That won't be necessary. Right…Amanda?"

"Amanda?" He was really pretending to not know my name now? Was he fucking kidding me? All those curse words I had crafted on the way over here leapt to the tip of my tongue. But I had more restraint than I realized, because I swallowed them back down. "So that's how you're going to play this? Like you don't know who I am?" *You asshattery!*

He snapped his fingers. "Oh, right. You're from BIMG. The one who bumped her head on the table."

"Ash. Not Amanda."

"Ah, my apologies Ash. Evie, please give us a few minutes."

She ducked out of his office.

"I know you're Ryder," I said the second the door was closed.

"Ryder?" he asked.

"Yes. Ryder Storm." I narrowed my eyes at him, hoping it would scare him into a confession. It did not.

"I don't know who that is, but it's not me."

I decided to take a different approach. "Why'd you kill the deal with BIMG?"

"Another firm gave us a more attractive offer," he said matter-of-factly.

"And why'd you send me all those shoes if you were just going to have me thrown out of the Society for rape?" I lowered my voice when I said "rape," but it still hung in the air awkwardly between us.

"Shoes? Society? Rape? Ashley, have you been drinking?"

"No I haven't been drinking!" *You stupid waffle stomper!* God, he was infuriating. I needed some way to prove that he was Ryder. The first thought that came to mind was to tear his glasses off, pull his hair into a bun, and force him to change into a colorful suit.

Or what if I was wrong? *Oh my God.* I had done it again. What was up with me thinking that every hot guy I met was part of the Society? First I'd raped Dr. Lyons, now I'd torpedoed my career. No, not just my career. Chastity's career. And Madison's.

"I'm so sorry," I muttered. "I must have you confused with someone else."

"Who is he? Is he part of this sex club you mentioned?"

"Yeah, he…wait a second! I never said the Society was a sex club."

For a second - the briefest of moments - his eyes grew wide with guilt. It was hardly noticeable. But I saw it. I was sure of it. I had caught him. "Sure you did," he said, glancing down at his phone to avoid looking me in the eye.

"No. I said that you had me thrown out of the Society for rape."

"Right. And everyone knows that the Society is a super exclusive sex club."

"Then why would rape get me thrown out? You sound like an idiot, you know." *Was that too harsh?* I cringed. At least I hadn't called him a shiteatery.

"Uh…you still aren't allowed to rape someone at a sex club. It all has to be consensual." He cleared his throat and set his phone back down. "So I've heard."

"Nope. I caught you. I knew it was you." And then I realized exactly how I could prove he was Ryder. I snatched his phone off his desk and opened his gallery.

"Stealing my phone isn't going to help anything."

"It will when I find that topless photo of me that you took."

"Topless photo, huh? Are you trying to trap me with some sort of sexual harassment lawsuit now?"

"No, I'm trying to prove…" I stopped talking and focused on scrolling through his gallery. But there wasn't much. Just scans of important-looking documents and photos of him shaking hands with fancy people in suits. There definitely weren't any pictures of me.

"Any luck finding that photo?" he asked. There was a hint of amusement in his voice.

"No. But I know it's on here somewhere. Probably hidden…" *Hidden!* Of course. I knew how to prove he was in the Society. I opened his apps and scrolled through until I found one labeled *Tax Codes*. I clicked it.

Welcome, Ryder Storm!
Last Spa Visit - April 13
Last STD Test - April 13, Clean

"Boom. You're Ryder Storm. Read it and weep, punk." I started to turn the phone so he could see it, but his hand closed around mine on the phone. His other caressed my jawline, tipping my face up towards his.

We locked eyes. I could feel his desire again. It was the same as it had been the previous night. He was ravenous. And he wanted to feast on me.

I went on my tiptoes as he bent down to kiss me. Our lips crashed together. I let out a gasp, but it was lost in his mouth. The phone in our hands was forgotten. One of us tossed it onto his desk and then his hand slid around my waist. I melted into him as his soft lips pressed against mine. And then I felt his tongue. It was the gentlest of flicks, sending a shiver all the way down to my toes. Or maybe only half the way…

Tanner lifted me off the ground with one arm and sat me on his desk, never breaking our kiss. My skirt rode up practically to my hips as my legs spread around him. I allowed my hands to wander to his muscular chest. God, he was so strong. Was it safe to unbutton his shirt? Or better yet, tear it off of him? I wanted to so badly. But I thought better of it. Touching him could have been what set him off on our last date. He, however, was not at all afraid to touch me. His fingers slid under the hem of my skirt, digging into my flesh. I moaned as our tongues fought for control. Even in our kiss we were still sparring. It was like he was furious with me, when really I was the one that was furious with him.

With one swing of his arm, he cleared his desk of everything. Papers, his phone, framed pictures, one of those little perpetual motion machines…it all crashed to the floor. He deepened the kiss and pinned me to the desk. I could feel his manhood pressing against me. "Yes," I moaned.

I reached for the buttons of his shirt, but his hands caught my wrists and slammed them back down. I was helpless against his strength. And I loved it. I bit at his bottom lip, stopping just before I might draw blood. I could hear him growl as he grew even harder.

And then a knock on his office door broke the spell. He pulled away and smoothed his suit jacket. I got up and yanked my skirt back into place (kind of…) just as his door swung open.

"Tanner, is everything…" Evie stopped mid-sentence and let out a gasp. "Good heavens! What happened in here?"

You cock blocked me!

"I think it was an earthquake," said Tanner with no hint of sarcasm. The lie rolled off his lips effortlessly. Which made sense given how much practice he had being a filthy rotten liar, always switching between being Tanner Rhodes and Ryder Storm.

"I didn't feel anything," said Evie.

"Weird." Tanner shrugged. "Anyway, we're fine in here. In fact, we were just about finished."

What? "Actually, we need a few more minutes," I said. He wasn't getting rid of me that fast again.

Evie looked to Tanner for approval.

"Give us two minutes," he conceded.

She disappeared.

I smiled at him with a smug grin on my face. I had won. I had gotten what I wanted. And he had all but admitted that he was Ryder. "So does this mean you're going to sign with BIMG after all, *Ryder*?"

"Shhh," he hissed. "What are you trying to do?" He glared at me.

"What am I trying to do? I don't know…have a relationship? After all, isn't the Society about true love? That's what you said."

He shook his head. "You're messing with things you don't understand."

"Then make me understand."

"I can't." His Adam's apple rose and fell as he stared at me. "You should go."

"Are you serious right now?" *What the actual fuck?*

"I never should have kissed you. I'm sorry." His eyes dropped to my lips. "I'm so sorry."

"What's your problem? Why do you keep kissing me and then pulling away? Am I really that repulsive?"

He looked hurt that I would even suggest that. "What? No. No. If anything it's the exact opposite."

"How so?"

"It's complicated. Like I said, you wouldn't understand."

"Try me."

"No." His voice was so firm that I almost backed off. *Almost.*

"Are you a born-again virgin or something?" I asked. "If you are, just tell me and we can take things slow."

"Uh, yeah. Yes." He nodded enthusiastically. "Definitely. I'm that."

"You're lying."

He sighed. "Fine. You want to know the truth?"

"Yes. Have I not made that clear?" *Cockhat.*

"I pissed off some very dangerous people. Us being together would put you in grave danger, and I'm not willing to risk that."

"Aren't you like…a billionaire? Just give them a couple million and tell them to leave you alone."

"These people don't care about money."

"Have you thought about going to the police?"

"The police would be useless. And even if they could help, it's out of their jurisdiction."

I knew what that meant. That it had crossed state lines. Only the FBI could help him, and from what I'd read in countless crime novels…the FBI usually screwed everything up when they got involved. They were basically dumb babies. "Jesus. Did you piss off a Mexican cartel or something?"

"Pretty much."

Pretty much? That was not an actual answer. I could feel my blood boiling again. He was clearly lying to me. I was going to keep arguing with him, but then I remembered Frankie's advice. *Men want what they can't have.* I needed to keep playing hard to get. "So you're trying to purge me from your life because you're worried your enemies will see us together and kidnap me to hurt you?"

"More or less."

More or less my ass. "Well, you have nothing to worry about then. Because I'm not interested in you. So sign the BIMG contract and withdraw your rape accusation. From now on, our relationship is strictly business. Good day, sir." I spun dramatically on my heel and walked out of his office.

Chapter 30
TANNER'S SECRET
Friday

When I left Tanner's office I had a text message from Chastity: "Mason sent us home early. Meet at your place?"

Ten minutes later, I found Chastity sitting in the hallway outside my apartment.

"So did you get him to sign?" she asked as I unlocked the door.

"Yeah."

"Yeah?" She jumped up. "So it's a done deal?"

"Well, kinda." I almost screamed when I saw all the boxes that still filled my apartment. I kind of thought they had just been part of some weird dream. I tossed my purse on the floor and kicked my heels off. "Actually, now that I think about it, he never said he would sign with us."

"You're gonna have to give me more than that."

"I stormed into his office. I found the Society app on his phone. We hooked up on his desk. He pulled back, pretended to be a born-again virgin, and then told me a Mexican cartel would kill me if we were together."

"Whoa, what?"

"And then I told him I wasn't interested in him and demanded he sign with BIMG."

Chastity stared at me like I was crazy. "And then…?"

"Oh, then I stormed out. It was epic. I even tossed a case of cupcakes into the trash on my way out." Remembering the satisfying *squish* of the cupcakes going into the trash made me smile.

"Wow, that's…a lot."

"It was awesome."

Chastity plopped down in the one chair in my apartment not buried under a stack of FedEx boxes. This was an interesting test to see which she liked more: Odegaards or juicy gossip. So far, juicy gossip was winning. "So just to clarify…he banged you on his desk?"

"What? No. We just kissed. And why are you focused on that instead of the Mexican cartel that wants to dissolve my body in a vat of acid? #AcidDeath."

"No. You're still using hashtags wrong. Don't use them for morbid things like that. They're supposed to be fun. Like #JustBangedMyBoss."

Damn it, I'd been using them in my head so well recently! Why did I always mess them up when I said them out loud?

"And I thought they just wanted to kill you normally?" added Chastity.

"Well Tanner didn't specify the exact method of murder. But I'm just assuming they'd be professional about it."

"Why doesn't he just pay them to go away?" asked Chastity.

"I asked that too. He said that they don't care about money."

"A Mexican cartel that doesn't care about money? And they weren't even going to dissolve you in acid? That hardly sounds like a cartel."

I nodded and gently moved a few boxes off the couch. "Yeah, you're right. I should have known he was still lying. Where is Madison? I could really use some of her anti-man rhetoric right now. They're such lying asshatteries."

Chastity raised an eyebrow.

"You know. Like…a shop where ass hats are sold. It's a few degrees worse than being an ass hat."

"Oh."

"It's a devastating insult. Tanner was devastated when I called him that." Fine, I didn't actually call him that. But if I had, he would have been destroyed.

Chastity nodded. Clearly she wasn't getting it.

"Imagine a hat store, but all the hats are made of asses… You know what? Forget it. Did you see all these Odegaards?!" I gestured to all the FedEx boxes. The ones Tanner had sent me as an apology for running away during make-out sesh. Or for getting me kicked out of the Society. Or for getting me almost fired from my new job.

"First, this is freaking amazing. I'm supes jeals (super jealous, for those of you that don't speak Chastity). Second, were all these shoes an apology for walking out on your kiss last night, or for ruining our lives today?"

"That is an excellent question." I bit the inside of my lip as I thought about it. "I think both?" Although, he may not have known I'd get almost fired. And he certainly couldn't have known about the Society thing. Unless he'd been the one who reported me…

Chastity picked up a box and cut the tape with her terrifying fake nails. "That's what I'm thinking too. In that case, don't half of them belong to me since he was getting me fired too?"

I stared at her. "Aren't your feet like two sizes bigger than mine?"

"I don't care what size they are." She ever so gently removed a pair of Odegaards from the box and cradled them like a baby. "If I have to cut off my toes to make them fit, I'll do it."

"That's one way to keep the foot freaks away."

"Speaking of foot freaks, have you heard anything new from Dr. Lyons about your date tomorrow night?"

I laughed. "I hate that segue for so many different reasons. But no, I haven't."

"Well, you'll certainly be going in style. Which Odegaards are you gonna wear?" Chastity picked up another shoebox. "Oh my God, did he send you the new Medusas?"

"I dunno. I only got to look at a few pairs before work."

"You mean we're sitting in a room with dozens of mystery Odegaards? The fashion police would stick us in a vat of acid for that." She grabbed a pair of scissors and got to work opening the boxes.

"You're confusing the fashion police with the cartel that wants to kill me."

Chastity shook her head. "I'm calling BS on that cartel story. Give me a sec..." She pulled out her phone and started typing furiously.

"Please tell me you're not texting Tanner."

"Nope. It was Dexter."

"That name means nothing to me."

"He's an IT guy at BIMG. I played D&D with him and some friends after work one day, so he owes me one."

"You played D&D?" I really could not picture that.

"Yeah. It wasn't too bad. Did you know there's a spell that makes your shirt disappear?"

That didn't sound right. "Your character's shirt, or yours?"

"Well, both."

Oh sweet, simple Chastity. "I don't know anything about D&D, but those pervs definitely just wanted to see your boobs."

"I knew it seemed suspicious!" She glanced at her phone. "Dexter says that there's no cartel chatter about Tanner."

"What about the mafia?"

After a few more texts Chastity shook her head. "Nope. Apparently there's no chatter about him at all. Not from the mafia. Not from the Russians. And not from anyone else."

"You trust this Dexter guy?"

"Yup. He wouldn't dare lie to me."

He lied to you about that disappearing shirt spell. "Alright, so let's assume all the usual suspects are out. How else do we explain his weird behavior?" And the more I thought of it, the more I realized just how strange Tanner was. One of the first things he'd ever said to me was something about a bed-chamber. And then all those old movies he referenced. And that thing about the Gestapo.

"I don't know. But I intend to figure it out." Chastity grabbed another box. "But I can't think until I know what Odegaards you have in these boxes."

***

We stepped back and looked at all the shoes. They were magnificent.

"So which are your favorites?" asked Chastity.

"Hmm…maybe the Medusas." They were ridiculous in so many ways - the white and green snakeskin, the thigh-high cut, the ridiculously tall heels - but I kind of loved them. It was a shame I'd never have the confidence to wear them.

"Solid choice. But I thought for sure you were gonna choose these." She pointed to a pair of classy 6" black lace stilettos. "The real question, though, is what the hell is up with those weird elf shoes?"

I picked up one of the white heels with the curly toe. "Yeah, I dunno. Ryder really liked these ones though. They were the first ones he tried to get me to try on at the store." Another weird thing to add to the list of weird things about Tanner.

"Interesting." Chastity stroked her chin. "Very interesting."

"You look like you just figured something out."

She stopped stroking her chin and smiled. "Yup. There's only one explanation. He's an elf."

"Say what now?"

"He's an elf," said Chastity with 100% certainty. "Just hear me out. He must have run away from the North Pole. And now he's being hunted by Santa."

I laughed. Santa would never hunt. He was…Santa.

"I'm serious! Think about it. It all fits. It explains his elf-shoe fetish. And why he can't just pay his enemies off. Everyone knows Santa doesn't take bribes."

"Unless the bribe is milk and cookies." I glanced at the two empty wine bottles on the coffee table. Chastity had insisted that we drink while we opened the rest of the boxes. "How much have you had to drink?"

Chastity took another sip from her wine glass. "Not much. Why? You want more?" She picked up one of the empty bottles and shook it furiously to get every last drop out. Before I could answer, her face lit up again. "Oh! I have an idea. As an elf, Tanner must know that you write letters to Santa every year. What if you write an early letter this year asking for an engagement ring from Tanner. Then he'd propose, and his cover would be blown. We'd know he's..."

She's so drunk. And then I remembered something. "I actually did tell him about my letters to Santa." *Didn't I?* I thought I had, but we'd talked about so much that first night that the whole conversation was kind of a blur.

"And who brought up letters to Santa first?"

"I think I did. Maybe he did. Gah! I can't remember." I took another sip of wine to try to clear my head. Was it really possible that he was a runaway Christmas elf? Of course it wasn't! That would be crazy. Then again, I had thought the same thing about my invitation to the Society, but that had turned out to be quite real. And I was kind of dating a billionaire. *Since when did my life get so crazy?*

"Well there you go." Chastity tipped the now empty bottle of wine towards me. "He's a Christmas elf. It's settled."

"It's a fun idea, but you're crazy. He's probably just in the mafia or something. Or pissed off the mafia. The police can't help him because the mob paid them off. And it would explain why he can't buy his way out of trouble. If he crossed them, they'd have to retaliate to send a message. Otherwise they'd look weak."

"Oh!" said Chastity, totally ignoring my very logical argument. "I've got it. He's a vampire!"

"Darn. I was hoping he was a werewolf. After all, I always was #TeamJacob." *Not.*

Chastity stroked her imaginary beard. "I hadn't considered that angle... We better consult the literature." She grabbed my copy of *Twilight* and started reading aloud.

That was about the time that the night really got away from us. First we speed-read the entire Twilight saga, and then we went into a paranormal rabbit hole. I thought we were just going to find more books about vampires, but no - it doesn't stop there. We found books about dragon shifters, and other shifters. Really just about every type of shifter you can imagine. Then we dove deeper and found one series about a BBW (big beautiful woman) witch who fell in love with an alien werewolf dude and encountered some gnomes that lived on giant mushrooms or something. I don't know. That description doesn't do justice to how weird it was. But the weirdest of all…that award definitely went to the bigfoot erotica.

I fell asleep dreaming of bigfoot and when I woke up in the morning, we got right back to our research. Before I knew it, it was nighttime again. And my phone alarm going off told me it was time to start getting ready for my date with Dr. Lyons.

My armpits were immediately drenched in sweat just from the thought of it. I couldn't go on a date with Dr. Lyons. I was in love with my stalker. Well, not in love in love. He was the crazy one, not me. I just had a mega crush on him and I needed to do more research tonight to figure out if he was a vampire or not. He was definitely hiding something. And I had a feeling that the vampire thing might be it. Which led to a whole assortment of other issues. But I'd get to that later. *Please don't suck my blood, Tanner.* I shivered just thinking about it.

"Can you please come too?" I asked Chastity.

She shook her head. "As much as I'd love to date Dr. Lyons, you found him first."

"He's yours. You can have him."

Chastity laughed. "Nope. You need this. It'll be good for you."

"I can't."

"Why not?"

"I'm…sick." I faked a cough. It was entirely unconvincing. "It's probably the flu."

Chastity put her hand on her hip. "Ash. I don't care if you're nervous. Or if you don't like Dr. Lyons. This is the *perfect* opportunity to make Tanner jealous. And let me remind you. He's a billionaire. With a B."

Darn it. She was right. "Fine. Maybe you're right. But if I went, what would I wear?"

"Uh…" Chastity gestured around the room to the Odegaard bags and shoeboxes. "You basically live in an Odegaard boutique now. Pick anything."

"But these are all from Tanner. That would feel so…wrong."

"But oh so right?" asked Chastity hopefully.

"Nope, just wrong."

"But it'll make him so jealous. Didn't you watch any of that hotwife porn I sent you? Where the girls say things to their husbands like, 'Thanks for the lingerie, honey. I bet your best friend will love it on me.' "

"That sounds pretty wild."

"Don't pretend like you didn't watch them."

I rolled my eyes. "Maybe I watched one." I'd actually watched all of them. Was hotwifing now one of my fantasies? Maybe... But no guy in their right mind would put up with that. I knew what it felt like to get cheated on. And it was the opposite of hot. "Why do they even make porn like that? Just so scorned women can watch it and imagine getting revenge on their husbands?"

"Psssh, they don't make porn for women. The only explanation for its existence is that guys love feeling jealous. Which is exactly how Tanner is gonna feel when you Instagram a picture of yourself on a date wearing one of the dresses he gave you."

"I don't know…" I said. But Chastity had a point. And Frankie had given me the same advice. *Make him jealous.* It had seemed to work at the boutique. "Fine. But only if you come and sit nearby. Or even better, we can find a way for you to listen in and tell me exactly what to say. There's gotta be an app for that by now, right? I hereby invoke Single Girl Rule #34: First dates are meant to be spied on by your friends."

"Touché. I love that you're on board with all the Single Girl Rules all of a sudden. But what are you so nervous about?" asked Chastity.

"I mean…I went on a date two nights ago and it didn't exactly go as planned. What if I kiss Dr. Lyons and then he runs away and never speaks to me again?" *Or I try to rape him again.* "And we don't need to speak about *the incident*."

"Oh my God. Just bang Matthew Caldwell already and get it over with."

"He's married."

"Whatever. It doesn't matter. You're not going to light anyone on fire this time. Plus, you have your new fire extinguisher now."

That I did. It was safely in my purse and I couldn't be happier.

"And anyway," said Chastity, "that was like a million years ago."

"Six months ago."

She waved her hand through the air. "Besides, your last date was with a…vampire? Or werewolf. Or maybe a Martian. I'm still not sure, but you're still alive. And following Single Girl Rule #34, I'll tag along just to make sure nothing terrible happens. Plus, I can keep reading the literature while I spy on you."

Now that was a solid plan.

Chapter 31
THE FOURTH INCIDENT
Saturday

Dr. Lyons was waiting for me outside the restaurant. He looked great in crisp blue slacks and a white button-down.

He took my hand to help me out of the Uber. *What a gentleman.* Also, it was good that Chastity had taken a separate Uber so that she could pick up Madison on the way. Otherwise we would have been caught red-handed with her spying. Which would have been awkward. And I was going to try really hard not to be awkward on this date. The last thing I needed was to repeat incidents #1-3. Specifically incident #2 because that involved both Dr. Lyons and rape. I tried not to visibly shudder.

"You look stunning," he said.

I better in this $2000 dress. "And you look quite handsome."

"Shall we?" He put his hand on the small of my back and led me into the restaurant.

The hostess seated us at a cute little table next to a fish tank. We both immediately buried our heads in our menus. An awkward silence took hold of our table. And as much as I wanted it to release its grip, I was unable to speak. *Oh God, oh God.* This was my worst nightmare. Were we just going to sit in silence the whole night? I had to say something. I'd just promised myself I wouldn't be awkward. *Think.*

"Nice place," I said. My voice cracked halfway through.

Dr. Lyons looked up from his menu. "Yeah."

Really? That's all you have to say?

He cleared his throat. "One of my friends recommended it. And I saw on yelp that they said it was nice and spacious. I hate when you go somewhere and end up bumping elbows with the couple next to you."

"I know! That's the worst." I saw Chastity and Madison walk into the restaurant. Madison saluted me and then they somehow convinced the hostess to give them the table right next to ours, which was way too close! What were they doing? Were they trying to get caught spying on my date? "Chastity," I hissed in my head. Except Dr. Lyons lowered his eyebrows, so maybe I'd accidentally said it out loud.

"Who?"

I cleared my throat to stall as I gave my friends a death glare. "My friend Chastity. She knows all about sitting too close." Hopefully she'd heard that and would move. I couldn't have a normal date with them sitting literally right next to me. "We…er…went to this cute little French café a few weeks ago and the tables were so close that we could hear every word the couple next to us was saying. We didn't talk the whole time. We just listened to the couple talk about how much they hated their youngest child. Her name was Mia and they called her Meatball because she was so chunky. I could tell you her entire life story. Although she was only two months old, so it's not a very long story."

Dr. Lyons laughed. "So you like eavesdropping on people, huh?"

"It can be fun." I tried to keep my eyes trained on him even though I could just barely hear Chastity and Madison discussing Twilight. God, that meant that they could hear me. And they were going to critique me later. Just the thought made me want to end the date right now. Where was a candle when a girl needed one?

"What do you think that couple's saying?" Dr. Lyons pointed to an older couple - probably in their 70s.

At least Dr. Lyons was good at distracting me. I watched the couple for a second to get a feel for their conversation. "The lady just said that they should order dessert to go so that he can lick it off her body."

"Right? I had a feeling that's what they were talking about."

I laughed. "Your turn." I pointed to another couple.

"I think he just told his wife how fortunate the gentleman by the fish tank is to be on a date with such a beautiful redhead."

I looked to either side of us. "There's another redhead here?" I was used to being the only one around.

A smile stretched across his handsome face. "No. At least, not any real ones like you."

Blood rushed to my face. Half because of his compliment, half because he understood the difference between real and fake red hair, and half because I had been too dense to realize what he'd been saying. And yes, I know that's three halves. "You know, you're supposed to butter the rolls, not your girlfriend." *Girlfriend?!*

Chastity yelped, like that could somehow undo what I'd just done.

What kind of crazy girl refers to herself as someone's girlfriend five minutes into the first date? I coughed and took a sip of water.

Dr. Lyons laughed and nodded toward Chastity and Madison's table. "What about them? Wait, isn't that the girl that was at your apartment the other night?"

"What? No." *Don't look at them!* "I've never seen those people before in my life. And they're clearly a lesbian couple debating the existence of vampires."

He laughed and looked back at his menu. "So what are you gonna order?"

I took the moment to shoo Chastity and Madison away.

"We're helping," Chastity mouthed silently at me.

"Go away," I mouthed back.

She gave me her sassiest expression.

Get out of here, you psychos. I knew Single Girl Rule #34 dictated that they had the right to be here, but they were too freaking close. They were supposed to spy on me from across the restaurant. This wasn't spying. This was an invasion of privacy.

"Ash?" Dr. Lyons said.

"Hm?"

"I asked what you were ordering."

"Oh. Probably the petite filet Oscar. With a side of lobster mashed potatoes. And a bottle of the 1986 Pinot Noir."

Dr. Lyons' eyes got big. "Sounds delicious."

"I'm just joking. I'm not going to get a $120 dinner and a $600 bottle of wine. I'd only do that on our second date."

"Oh thank God." He wiped a bead of sweat from his forehead. "I want to show you a good time, but I do still have to pay my rent."

"I'm actually just going to get the shrimp and grits. You?"

"Probably the chicken tagine."

"Exotic."

I heard Chastity laugh, but I didn't acknowledge her presence. *Chicken tagine is exotic, Chastity. #Exotic. Boom, nailed the hashtag thing again.*

"I got a taste for it during my tour in the Middle East."

"The Middle East? Were you there for Doctors Without Borders or something?"

He fidgeted with his water glass and looked down at it. "No. I was in the army."

"Wait, so let me get this straight. You're a pediatrician *and* a veteran? Do you also feed homeless children and sing to the elderly?"

He smiled and looked up from his glass. "Only on weekends. Although with my voice, that would probably be considered elder abuse."

The waiter appeared and rattled off the specials. I couldn't really focus though. All I could think about was how this date had really turned around. The conversation felt natural. He laughed at my dumb jokes. He was possibly a real-life superhero. Who knew dating would be so easy? I was hardly even sweating anymore. Which was really saying something, because soon I'd have to talk to the waiter to give him my order, a thing I'd hated ever since I was a child.

You can't tell someone not to speak to strangers and then throw out the rules when a stranger shows up at your table with an apron. Just thinking about it made me start sweating again.

But then something wonderful happened.

"I think we're ready to order," said Dr. Lyons. "Ash will have the shrimp and grits and a glass of Sauvignon Blanc."

Oh my God. Did he really just order for me? That was like…a dream come true. Best. Date. Ever.

"Ow ow," said Chastity. She knew how much I hated ordering.

I tried to give her a subtle thumbs up. But I got distracted by the fact that her copy of Twilight was upside down in her hands. She was being so obvious. *Scram!*

"That was what you wanted, right?" asked Dr. Lyons when the waiter walked away.

"Uh, yes. Hell, you could have ordered me anything and I would have eaten it. I freaking hate ordering. Wait…how'd you know to do that?"

Dr. Lyons looked down and straightened his placemat, a hint of red coming to his cheeks. "Lucky guess?" He was definitely lying.

"Oh my God! You Facebook stalked me."

He scrunched up his face. "Maybe?"

"You totally did. You must have seen my post about Chastity ordering for me at Wendy's."

"So what's your favorite color?" he asked.

"Nope. You're not changing the topic on me. Out with it. Admit you stalked me." Since when did so many hot guys stalk me?

He mumbled something.

"Say it."

"I stalked you." He did his best ashamed face. "Please don't be mad."

"Mad? Quite the opposite. I'm honored that you took the time to stalk me. In fact, I feel a little bad that I didn't return the favor."

Out of the corner of my eye I saw Chastity trying to get my attention.

Girl, can't you see that I'm nailing this date?

The conversation continued from there. I learned all about how he had grown up in a military family. His dad was the stereotypical gruff drill sergeant, while his mom was sweet and gentle. The yin to his dad's yang.

"I also had a little brother," he said.

Had? I couldn't think of the right words to ask if his little brother was dead, so I just stayed silent and let him continue.

"Mikey left us when he was five. Leukemia." He looked away and blinked, almost like he was holding back tears. "He was the reason why I decided to become a pediatrician."

"Dr. Lyons," I said. "I'm so sorry." Tears filled my eyes as I pictured Rosalie. And I could feel my throat getting tight as I tried not to cry. I knew all too well what it was like to lose a sibling.

He suddenly laughed. "Did you just call me Dr. Lyons?"

"Uh…yes?"

"Do you not know my first name?"

"What? Don't be crazy. It's…" I searched my brain for what his first name was. But there was nothing. "Gr…"

Dr. Lyons raised an eyebrow.

"Ro…"

He shook his head.

"Phi…"

"Nope."

"Gah! Fine. I don't know your name. Is that so wrong?"

"Anthony," he said. "Anthony Lyons."

"Right. That was my next guess."

He cracked a smile. "Sure it was."

Chastity slammed her hand down on the table as she tried to get my attention again.

Nope. I didn't need her whispered advice right now. I was doing fine all on my own. Couldn't she tell? "I think

Mikey would be very proud of you. Especially since you're totally slaying this date."

"Really?" He looked so happy.

"Yes."

"What about you?" he asked. "Any siblings?"

"Three. Lauren, Kyle, and Rosalie. Rosalie uh…" I took a sip of water to try to prevent myself from tearing up again. It didn't work. "She actually disappeared a few years ago. I feel like I'm the only one that believes she's still out there somewhere. Everyone else gave up hope."

"That's horrible." He reached across the table and grabbed my hand. "I'm so sorry."

"I miss her."

"I miss Mikey, too. I wish I could tell you that time will make it better, but it doesn't really. I still miss him just as much as I did the day it happened. Maybe more."

I wiped the tears from my eyes. We sat in silence for a few moments. But this time it wasn't awkward. It was more therapeutic. A moment of silence for our lost siblings.

The spell was broken by the waiter bringing our food. And after that I promised myself I'd be more upbeat the rest of the date. No more crying.

"These shrimp are amazing," I said.

"Wanna try some tagine?"

"No thanks." I never tried anyone's food. Sharing all those germs was the most disgusting thing in the world. And yet…I kind of did want to try it. Something about *his* germs didn't seem that repulsive. I still didn't change my answer, though. *Maybe next date.*

"Ash," Chastity hissed at me.

Stop. It. Geez, it was like Chastity was trying to turn my perfectly nice date into a train wreck. Couldn't I just do one thing one time that wasn't an epic fail?

"Are you sure you don't know that lesbian couple?" he asked.

"Nope. Never seen them before."

We kept talking while we ate. He told me all about the different places he'd lived - San Diego, Germany, South Korea - and I tried to make Delaware sound just as interesting. He agreed to visit Rehoboth beach sometime, although I couldn't tell if we were seriously planning a vacation or if he was just humoring me. I kept trying to find an opening to bring up what had happened during my doctor's appointment with him, but I could never seem to find the perfect segue. Which was probably for the best. No need to talk about incident #2 ever again. Instead we went back to playing the lip-reading game.

I pretended like a young couple was hoping to swing with the 70-year-olds from earlier, and then Dr. Lyons...er...Anthony, acted like a very overweight couple was going to go streaking after dinner.

"How about that couple?" he asked, pointing behind me.

I turned around. And OH MY GOD. Joe was there. Joe as in my ex. Joe as in the person on the top of my most hated list. I immediately snapped my head around in hopes that he hadn't seen me.

"Is everything okay?" asked Anthony. "You must have just lip-read something truly awful."

Shit shit shit! This date had been going so well. I glanced at Chastity.

"I was trying to warn you," she hissed.

Damn it. Now that I knew that was what she'd been doing, her actions made a lot more sense. Why hadn't I just looked at her? *What do I do now?* Could I just pretend like Joe wasn't there? He didn't matter. I was so over him. But...who had he been with? It was definitely a date. Had she had stupid fake red hair like Sierra? "That's my ex," I said.

"Boyfriend?"

"Husband." The word felt gross on my tongue. "We just finalized our divorce a couple weeks ago." My stomach turned over. I felt like I was going to be sick.

"Eek. Wanna leave? I'll get the check and we can go grab some dessert. Have you been to the Midtown Pudding Place? It's amazing."

As good as that sounded, I didn't want to leave in the middle of our meal. That would feel like I was letting Joe win. "No, let's stay. He's dead to me."

Dr. Lyons smiled.

We changed the topic, but I couldn't focus. I had to know who Joe was with. I dropped my napkin on the floor so I could sneak a peek.

But as soon as I got down on my hands and knees, I heard Madison trying to get my attention.

She was under their table too, waving at me. "Joe's here," she whisper yelled.

Yeah, I got that.

"How's the date going?" she asked.

I don't have time for this nonsense. I turned to see Joe. Sure enough, he was with Sierra. And he was getting on one knee.

No. Freaking. Way. I tried to turn away from them. To pretend it wasn't happening. But my eyes stayed glued to Joe's table.

He clinked his knife against a champagne flute. But it felt like the knife went straight through my heart.

"Excuse me," said Joe. "If I could just have your attention for one moment."

The restaurant went silent and everyone turned their attention to the happy couple. .

"What are you doing?" whispered Sierra. But she looked so excited. She was already running her hands through her hair and smoothing her sparkly dress to make sure she'd look perfect for the proposal.

"Four years ago, I met the most amazing woman," began Joe.

Four years?! My heart stopped beating. *Four? Fucking four? What the hell?*

Chasity got down on the floor too. "I think he's proposing," she whispered.

Kill me now. My stomach felt like it rolled over.

Joe smiled at Sierra. "I saw her across the room, and my whole life changed. It was love at first sight. Until then I had just been coasting through life. But Sierra gave me a purpose."

Are you fucking kidding me? Yeah, I was definitely gonna be sick. I stood up, tossed my napkin on the table, and ran towards the exit.

I gasped for fresh air, but the warm, stale city air did nothing for me. *Four years? Four freaking years?!* I had thought it was a one-time thing. But instead he'd been lying to my face for years. God, I was such a fool. How had I not seen it? The tears I had barely managed to hold back earlier streamed down my face. *Four. Years.* I could barely breathe. The number just kept rolling around in my head. How many nights had he come home to me after being with her?

I clutched my stomach. This was too much. I was gasping for air.

Dr. Lyons burst out of the restaurant. "Ash." He put his hand on my shoulder and turned me towards him. Just as I threw up my grits. All over his shirt. And pants. And shoes.

Fuck my life! I didn't look at his reaction. I couldn't. I could never see him again. Not after I'd just incident #4'd all over him. I turned and ran away.

Chapter 32

AN UNEXPECTED GUEST

Saturday

It was official. I was never leaving the house again. No matter what I did, tears were still slowly falling down my face. I tried to brush them away to no avail.

And it wasn't about Joe. Yes, that four years shit stung really badly. But I already hated him. I was crying because I was a menace to society, and society was a menace to me. It was better if we were kept apart.

All I needed was pajamas, ice cream, and TV. And a thorough mouth cleaning to get rid of the taste of vomit. If only I could clean my mind too. I searched Google Maps for elective lobotomy clinics, but there were none nearby. *Come on, New York. 8.6 million people, and not a single one was licensed to stick a metal rod in my brain to destroy all my awful memories? Lame.*

I pulled on my snuggliest pajamas and opened the fridge, but I was fresh out of ice cream.

Are you freaking kidding me, Universe? I wanted to scream. This was officially the worst day of my life.

Sure, Chastity would happily bring me ice cream if I called her, but then she'd want to know what had happened after I ran out of the restaurant. And I wasn't ready to relive it yet. Telling someone about it would make it too real. None of it mattered anyway. I'd dehydrate myself soon with all my crying. And then I could just die in a puddle of my own tears. Only an ironic death made sense for a fool like me.

My bottom lip started trembling.

God! Stop!

I tried to take a deep breath. No, I didn't need Chastity. Or ice cream. All I needed was to curl up with an episode of my newest obsession: Gossip Girl. I just HAD to know who Gossip Girl was. Was it Serena? Or Blair? Pssh, no. Those were too obvious. It was definitely Chuck.

But tonight, not even Gossip Girl could distract me from the horrors I'd endured. I just sat there staring at the TV screen. I couldn't pay attention. My mind just kept playing reruns of Joe's proposal and my subsequent barf explosion.

I wonder if they announced their engagement on Instagram yet. I knew I shouldn't look. But I was too curious. I resisted for a full half-episode, but eventually I lost control and opened Sierra's Instagram. There was a new picture from 58 minutes ago. Sierra and Joe were sitting in the restaurant, happy as can be, with Sierra showing off her engagement ring. Which was FREAKING HUGE. I didn't know much about diamonds, but that thing had to be like two carats. Maybe 3. It wouldn't have been out of place on a Kardashian's finger. Which made it about 1,000 times bigger than the ring Joe had given me.

What really pissed me off, though, was that I knew he had bought it with the money that I had helped him make. The money he had stolen from me in the divorce.

Scrolling through the comments didn't make me feel any better.

"You look stunning!"

"Luckiest man alive."

"THAT RING!"

"Congrats to the happy couple! Wishing you two so much happiness."

The compliments went on and on. All 1046 of her comments said something nice, although half of them were just creepy dudes complimenting her tits or sending eggplant emojis.

Why did none of those people comment on the fact that Joe had been married just a couple weeks ago and basically admitted during his proposal that he'd been a dirty cheater for four freaking years?

My phone started ringing and Chastity's name flashed across the screen.

"What?" I croaked.

"Girl, are you okay? You sprinted out of there so fast. I was going to run after you but Madison picked up a butter knife and was threatening to cut of Joe's dick. I had to stop her."

Wow. That was…a lot. "Did she succeed?"

Chastity laughed. "No. But you should have seen it. I almost had to tackle her."

I would have laughed if I didn't feel like dying.

"Do you want me to come over?" she asked.

This was my opportunity for ice cream. But I needed to be in solitude for a while. Back to my vow of reclusivity. It was for the best. "No. I'm just going to head to bed early."

"Okay, Ash. If you're sure."

We both knew I rarely slept anymore. But thankfully she was being merciful.

"And just for the record. Before Joe proposed to Sierra, you were slaying that date."

I really had been.

"But don't ever say I'm Madison's gay date ever again. Gag. I don't want to give her any ideas."

I laughed. "I promise I won't. I'm going to go…to bed now."

"Alright. Love you!"

"Love you too." I hung up the phone and pulled my fuzzy blanket up to my chin. *Woe is me.*

I was just starting to reread all the Instagram comments when someone knocked on my door.

What now? Chastity probably knew I was out of ice cream. It was sweet of her to stop by. But I really wasn't in any place to break my vow of reclusivity. I'd proven to everyone that I couldn't be trusted in the wild. I'd just yell at her to go away through the door. I tossed my phone on the coffee table and walked over to check the peephole.

And I almost screamed. It was Dr. Lyons. Normally I would have thought about hurling myself out of the window. But he didn't look upset. He was just standing there balancing a bouquet of spring flowers and a to-go bag from the Midtown Pudding Place.

I couldn't help but smile. After all that had happened tonight - after I barfed on him and ran away - he still wanted to see me? I didn't deserve him. And I almost didn't open the door. But that bag of dessert…I needed it. I needed it more than life itself. My dessert cravings outweighed my shame. Just barely.

I begrudgingly opened the door.

"I brought dessert," he said, holding up the bag. Even through the bag I could smell the sweet sweet aroma of freshly baked bread pudding. "Oh, and these are for you." He handed me the bouquet.

I didn't know what to say. No words could describe my weird mix of emotions. I was so angry at Joe. So embarrassed about incident #4. And somehow so thankful for this wonderful man in front of me. But most of all, I was just confused about why Dr. Lyons was still pursuing me. He'd already seen so many things he couldn't un-see. Yet, here he was. I thought about all the times Tanner had pushed me away. And here was a guy that just kept showing up? Screw Tanner. Screw Joe. Screw all other men. Dr. Lyons trumped them all.

"Sorry it took me so long," he said. "There was a long line at the Pudding Place. And I had to run home to change."

"You really didn't have to do this. Especially after…well, you know." The projectile vomit thing. God, it was possible that incident #4 was the worst yet. *No.* No, nothing beat the original incident.

"There was no way I was going to let our first date end like that. Honestly, I was happy to leave. That restaurant was a little stuffy for my taste." He pulled out two containers of bread pudding and put them on the coffee table. "Gossip Girl and dessert is so much better."

I laughed. "You watch Gossip Girl, huh?"

"I mean…not anymore. I already binged the entire thing."

"I feel like that's not something a guy should admit."

"Hey, I like what I like." He sat down and took a big bite of his raspberry bread pudding. "I can't exactly watch manly shows, anyway."

I laughed again. "Are you mocking me?" I sat down next to him.

"No, I'm serious." He looked a little embarrassed. "Anything with gunshots or violence is out unless you want to see me scream like a schoolgirl and hide under a couch for thirty minutes. I have the army to thank for that."

Oh. "PTSD?"

He scratched the back of his neck like even hearing the term made him nervous. "Yeah. Being triggered by gunshots isn't so bad, though. I'm just thankful they never threw pudding bombs at us. Then my life really would have been ruined." He took another big bite.

"I want to make a joke about me having PTSD from barfing on you, but I kind of feel like that would be in poor taste."

"Not at all. I probably will too. I'm not sure I'll ever look at grits the same again."

I hid behind my hands. "Oh God. Can we please never speak of that?"

Dr. Lyons laughed. "It's really fine. I totally get it. I don't want to offend you, but…that ex of yours seems like a total douche. I mean…his proposal was somehow so overdone and so lame all at the same time. If someone proposed to me like that, I'd throw a glass of champagne in their face and tell them to try again."

I smiled. "Really?"

"Yeah. And don't get me started on that ring. He must have the tiniest little baby penis."

I nodded. "I know, right?" Dr. Lyons totally got me.

"You're better off without him. But I understand that it still hurts seeing him be happy. You wanna know what the best medicine is, though?"

"What?"

"This bread pudding. I should warn you though…if you don't start eating it soon, I'm gonna eat it for you."

"Don't you dare." I ate a huge forkful and let out an orgasmic moan. *Awkward.* But when I stole a sideways glance at him, he wasn't looking at me like he thought the noise was awkward. He was staring at me like he wanted me to do it again. I tried to hide my smile.

"So what episode are we on?" he asked.

"Uh…the one where Chuck is with the prostitutes."

"That literally gives me no information. That's pretty much every episode."

I laughed. "I know. And before we watch, you have to promise you won't tell me who Gossip Girl is."

"It's all over the internet…"

"I've been avoiding spoilers. Promise you won't tell."

He smiled at me. "I promise."

Something about the way he said it made me believe I could trust him with anything. Which made sense. He was a doctor. I could already trust him with my life.

We watched the rest of the episode and finished our dessert. And then we watched another. And another. Into the wee hours of the morning. Somewhere along the way his arm had wrapped around my shoulders. I had no real desire to move. Ever.

"Well, I should probably get going," he finally said.

The clock read 3:53. In the morning. *Geez.* "You can crash on the couch if you want." I tried not to wince at my own words. I should have been sexier. Like…*come to my bed you sexy man-beast. Gross.* I was bad at being sexy.

He shook his head. "I don't want to impose. I've probably already overstayed my welcome."

"Not at all. This was perfect."

"I had fun too. Maybe we can do it again sometime?"

"Going on a date…or watching Gossip Girl?"

"I was talking about the date," he said. "But I'd be down for more Gossip Girl too. My schedule is a little crazy this week, but how about I text you?"

I couldn't hide the huge smile on my face even if I'd tried. "Sure." We exchanged numbers and then I walked him to the door. There was an awkward pause as he stood in the open door. *Do we hug? Or kiss? Or shake hands?*

He locked eyes with me and leaned in. *He's going to kiss me!* I closed my eyes and let it happen. It was everything I'd needed. He gave me a few pecks and then nipped at my lower lip. I moaned and flicked my tongue against his lips. They tasted like his raspberry bread pudding. *Yum.*

The sound of footsteps ended our kiss far too soon. I pulled back and opened my eyes. Homeless Rutherford was sashaying down the hallway without a care in the world. *Stupid cockblocker!*

Dr. Lyons looked amused by his presence. He gave me a look that said *who the hell is that weirdo?*

"I'll explain later," I said with a laugh.

"Deal. Thanks again, Ash. Tonight was really great." He gave me one more peck and then turned to go.

"Until next time," I said. And then I winked and aimed some finger guns at him. *What in the ever-living hell is wrong with me?* I slammed the door so I couldn't see his reaction. But I'm pretty sure I heard him laugh. Which left such a big smile on my face too.

Chapter 33

SUPER SEXY LUNCH DATE

Sunday

I wish I could tell you that I spent the day after my date floating around on cloud nine. A super hot soldier turned doctor who might also be a superhero had spent all night cuddling me and watching Gossip Girl. Gossip Girl! That was like…every girl's dream. And yet, all I could think about all day was Joe and Sierra.

Even thinking about their names made me feel sick to my stomach. *Four years?* I hated them. And I hated that I was even upset about it. But every good memory I had of Joe during that time had just been destroyed. That vacation we took to Vegas after selling a million dollars' worth of cupcakes? Trash. The time we'd rented a hotel room just for the hell of it and had wild sex… *Oh God.* A horrible thought occurred to me. He had been banging Sierra that whole time. And she definitely had all sorts of horrible STDs. I could tell just by looking at her. Which meant I did too now.

AIDS, chlamydia, gonorrhea. I probably had all of it.

I texted Chastity the bad news and then started searching WebMD for STD symptoms.

Did I have lower belly pain? *Sometimes.*

Sore throat? *Now that I'm thinking about it…I could use a cough drop.*

Pus or a watery/milky discharge from my penis? *No, but only because I don't have one. Oh no…am I going to grow one? Is that possible?*

I was spiraling. I knew it, but I couldn't help myself. I kept reading symptoms. And I literally had all of them.

Chastity called me just in time to stop a total mental breakdown.

"I have all the STDs. I'm dying," I said into the phone.

"Whoa, slow down," said Chastity. "Did you bang Dr. Lyons?"

"What? No. Why would you think that?"

"Well you were just on a date. And I got there late, so you might have hooked up in the bathroom before I arrived. What other conclusion should I have come to?"

"Joe's been fucking Sierra for four years."

"Oh. That. Yeah…that's gross. Let me quote Madison from last night to make you smile: 'I'm going to fucking kill that asshole and shove his dick down his throat.' It was kind of epic."

"I definitely have all the STDs, right?" I asked.

"That would have been my first thought too. But weren't you tested just a few days ago at your spa appointments?"

"Oh my God! Yes!" I gasped for air, finally able to breathe again, and did a little happy dance. I was STD-free! For the first time, I was grateful for my weird Society spa appointments.

"Now that we've cleared that up," said Chastity, "I need to know… Did you or did you not bang Dr. Lyons before I arrived at the restaurant?"

"We did something way better." The relief of not having STDs actually made me sigh.

"Anal?!"

"What? No. He came over last night after you called me. He brought me bread pudding and we watched Gossip Girl all night."

"Hmm…well, let's pretend like you did bang. That'll make Tanner more jealous."

Tanner. My stomach flipped over. Going on a date with Dr. Lyons was supposed to make Tanner jealous. But I'd forgotten all about that because I'd ended up having a really great time with Dr. Lyons. Really, really great. My stomach flipped again. "What do you want me to do? Email Tanner about it?" Would that make him jealous? Did I even want him to be jealous anymore? I bit the inside of my lip.

"Oh, right, you don't know."

"Know what?"

"Bee called me a few minutes ago. Tanner signed the contract."

He'd signed the contract? I pulled out my phone to see if I'd been unterminated from the Society too. And sure enough…the Tax Codes app was working properly again. *Huh.* Storming into his office had actually worked. Somehow.

"And to make it easier to get things up and running, you and I will be working at his office starting Monday."

"For how long?" I asked. "And what about Madison?"

"She was assigned somewhere else. And I guess we'll work there until someone tells us otherwise. So pick out your hottest work clothes and get ready to make Tanner jealous. We're gonna bag you a billionaire vampire werewolf sex god."

***

I almost threw up three times on the way to Tanner's offices. It was like the first day of high school…if you had made out with the principal the week before. Oh, and also pissed off the secretary and thrown everyone's cupcakes in the trash.

Despite that, I was still giddy to see Tanner. How would he act around me? Would he be distant? Would he flirt with me? Would he ask if I was stalking him in that deep sexy voice of his?

Come to think of it, I wasn't even sure he'd be there. He was a freaking billionaire. He had places to be and things to do. Why would he stay in his fancy corner office in NYC when he could be off sipping martinis on a private island in the Caribbean?

The thought of him not being there calmed my nerves. But that was no fun. He needed to be there so I could follow Chastity's advice and ignore him and make him jealous of Dr. Lyons.

And it was my lucky day. Because Tanner was there. He even greeted us at the door.

"Good morning, ladies," he said. He looked so dumb and ugly with his tailored suit and perfect 5 o'clock shadow.

Chastity shook his hand.

No! Don't touch him, you whore! Okay…so maybe he looked good in his suit. And maybe I definitely did still have feelings for him after my date with Dr. Lyons. Was I a glutton for punishment?

"Thank you so much for this opportunity, Mr. Rhodes," said Chastity.

"You're quite welcome. Everything you need is on your desks." He gestured to a little cubicle that we'd be sharing. "If you need anything, my door is always open." A second later he was gone.

"Why didn't you talk to him?" whispered Chastity.

"Did I not?"

"Nope. You just stared at him like a crazy person. You're supposed to be making him jealous, not scared."

"Damn it. I really thought I talked." This was not going the way I had pictured. We needed a new plan. "Keep an eye on him. If you see him coming, kick me and I'll start talking about Dr. Lyons."

An hour later, Chastity kicked me.

"Ow!" I kicked her back.

"What the hell?" she hissed. "You're supposed to talk about…"

"Everything okay?" asked Tanner. He'd stopped outside our cubicle and his arms were folded across his chest. I remembered the feeling of those muscles beneath my hands…

"Yup," I said way louder than I meant to.

"Actually," said Chastity. "We need to know what our hours are. And how long can we take for lunch? Because Ash has a lunch date with her new doctor boyfriend."

Tanner raised an eyebrow. "A lunch date? Sounds…romantic."

I shrugged. "We'll see. I'm a little intimidated by how tall he is." *What else would make Dr. Lyons sound amazing?* "And he loves kids a little *too* much." I heard it the second the words left my mouth, but by then it was too late. Rather than make him jealous, I'd just confirmed what Tanner already thought: I was dating a 10-foot-tall pedophile.

"Take as long as you want for lunch. I only care that the work gets done. It doesn't much matter to me if you finish at 10 am or 10 pm. But uh…be careful. That guy sounds like kind of a creep."

"She'll be fine," said Chastity. "They had an awesome date on Saturday. He took her to Barracuda."

Tanner nodded. "Great place. Did you try the grits?"

Grits. Did he know? *Oh God.* Someone had probably filmed me barfing all over Dr. Lyons and made a meme out of it. My life was officially ruined. I tried to play it cool. "Sure did. He even paid for them."

"Well I'd hope so," said Tanner. "Anyway, glad to hear he's a stand-up guy. Have fun at lunch." He tapped the top of our cubicle and returned to his office.

"Well that went great," I said.

"No it didn't," said Chastity. "It was a train wreck. He didn't seem jealous at all."

Oh, brain fart. I got really distracted when Tanner was talking. "Well…that's because you made it a lunch date. Why'd you pick the lamest of meals?"

"I don't know! I panicked. I thought you were gonna do the jealous-ing."

"Well now we have to go to lunch for hours."

Chastity nodded. "And you have to come back with your skirt inside-out to make it look like you had a double helping of afternoon delight."

"I'm not doing that."

"Suit yourself. But don't come crying to me when you're old and single and penniless." Chastity spun around in her chair and started working again.

"Wait, why is this my only chance to avoid being broke and single for the rest of my life?" *It's not, is it?*

***

Just before noon Chastity and I got up to go to my fake lunch date, but it was hard to get out of the office due to the three tables of food semi-blocking the entrance. No, not just any food. Gochujang Palace. My favorite.

"Going to lunch?" asked Tanner, popping some spicy Korean nuggets in his mouth.

"What's all this?" I asked.

"Oh, you know. Various people like to send us food. Today it looks like they sent…" He picked up a bag and made a show of looking at the label. "Gochujang Palace. Ever had it?"

"Yeah," I said. "It's my freaking favorite!"

"Grab a plate. These nuggets are amazing." He ate another one.

"We'll have to take a raincheck," said Chastity.

But…Korean nuggets!

"Ash has a lunch date," continued Chastity. "Remember?" She elbowed me in the ribs.

Tanner made a clicking noise. "Ah, damn. Forgot about that. You're welcome to invite him here if you want? We have plenty."

"Maybe some other time," said Chastity, pulling me towards the elevator.

I watched the Korean food longingly as the elevator doors slid shut. "Damn it! We just failed so hard. He totally called our bluff."

"Did he?" asked Chastity. "Because I'm pretty sure he just bought $500 worth of your favorite food in a lame attempt to prevent you from going on a date with Dr. Lyons. #JealousAF."

"No he didn't…" My voice trailed off. "Wait. Did he?"

Chastity nodded. "It's too much of a coincidence. You must have told him you love Gochujang Palace at some point."

Had I? I thought back to our first date. *Yup.* I'd ranted about it for like twenty minutes just before we fell asleep. "I may have mentioned it at some point."

"Then there you have it. Phase one accomplished."

"Phase one? What's phase two?"

Chastity pulled a copy of *Twilight* out of her bottomless purse. "We have to figure out his secret."

"And how are we going to do that?"

"You'll see."

Chapter 34
GARLIC AND HOLY WATER
Tuesday

The next few weeks were a blur of work, dates, and spa visits.

Spa visits were the smallest portion of my time, but the time I spent worrying about them was significant. I still wasn't used to lying there completely naked while Moroccan women did weird things to my lady bits. And by that, I mean waxing. Not like…molesting me. *Ew.* The only inappropriate touching going on at the Shifting Sands Spa was happening between Chastity and Hassan the handsy masseur.

Then there was the work, or, as I liked to call it: Tanner Time. At first I came in every day hoping that I'd succeed in making him jealous enough to sneakily deliver me a Society date card. Or, if he was really feeling crazy, maybe he'd just ask me out on a for-realsies date. Alas, the date cards never arrived.

Which brings me to the third and final way I spent my time: dates. Not Society dates. I hadn't been invited to one since the app magically fixed itself on my phone. These were just normal dates. Three in total, all with Dr. Lyons. One was to a Broadway performance of *Playing a Player*. The other two were just dinner dates. It was always tempting to invite him back to my apartment for more Gossip Girl binging, but I always chickened out. As crazy as it sounds, I was too worried about the sex. Yes, I know I almost raped him within 10 minutes of meeting him. But that was spur of the moment. When I had time to anticipate it, I would always get all sweaty and gassy. Which were not the best two ingredients for sexy time. Normally I would have asked my doctor why that happened to me when I thought about sex. But he was my doctor. So I couldn't even get medical help. Also, it was possible that I was maybe subconsciously holding out for Tanner.

I would always make a point to gush about my dates (both real and fictional) in front of Tanner, but he never cracked. Chastity thought that he was passive-aggressively giving us extra work on date nights and trying to bribe us to stay at the office with food. Maybe she was right. Or maybe it was a coincidence. I wasn't sure which.

All I knew was that I wasn't getting invited to any Society events. And to me, that meant he wasn't interested. Or maybe he was playing hard to get when I was supposed to be the one playing hard to get. Or maybe he was just respecting my assertion that I was 100% not interested in him.

No. That wasn't it. He had made it very clear that he believed me being with him would put me in danger. I just didn't understand how. I mean…no mobsters had shown up at the office and tried to break any kneecaps. In fact, no one had even had a heated argument with him. At least not that I had seen. And I definitely didn't watch him through his office windows all day or anything like that…

Okay, fine! I watched him all the time. But it was strictly for security reasons.

"Pssst…look at this," whispered Chastity. I stopped staring at Tanner and spun my chair around to see what Chastity wanted to show me. She was holding her phone out. The gallery app was open.

"Uh, why are you showing me thirty really poor-quality photos of Tanner?" I asked.

"They're not poor quality," said Chastity.

"Really? Because they're blurrier than every photo my mom has ever taken with a camera phone. What's so hard about it? You just point it at the person, tap their face, and then take the picture."

"I know how to take a picture. I'm not a 60-year-old woman."

I pointed to her gallery of blurry pictures. "Not based on that evidence."

"Then you try."

"Fine." I pulled out my phone and discreetly snapped a picture of Tanner in his office. "See…easy."

"Then why's his face blurry?"

"What?" I looked down at the photo. Sure enough, everything was perfectly in focus except for Tanner's face. "Let me try again." I snapped another. Same blurry garbage. And my third photo, taken in professional mode with all the settings perfectly dialed in by hand, turned out just as bad. Or worse, if that was possible.

"See," said Chastity. "I knew he was a vampire!"

"Since when is poor picture quality a sign of vampirism? I thought they just didn't have reflections in mirrors?"

Chastity held up her copy of Twilight. "The literature is inconclusive."

I rolled my eyes. "It seems more likely that one of his companies developed some privacy tech that automatically blurs pictures of him."

"That sounds just as farfetched as my vampire idea. Dude is hiding something. And it's not a mafia connection or a Christmas elf situation here. I swear he's a vampire. Can we puh-leasssse just run a few tests on him?"

That was the third time this week that Chastity asked. Which meant I was literally incapable of denying her. Besides, I really did want to figure out why Tanner kept pushing me away. "Fine."

Chastity gave me a shopping list, and an hour later we reconvened on the sidewalk outside the office. My feet ached from running all over the city finding all the random crap on the list.

"Find everything?" she asked.

I nodded and showed her the very strange contents of my purse. "You?"

"I had to flash a random Papa John's delivery boy, but yes."

"Why didn't you just go to the store? The garlic sauce only costs like 55 cents."

Chastity shrugged. "The girls needed some fresh air. Anyway, get your game face on. It's time to learn all Tanner's deepest, darkest secrets."

Or get fired.

I got more nervous with every number that ticked by on the elevator ride up to Tanner's office. This plan was completely ridiculous. But now that we'd bought the stuff, I felt committed to it. And there was no way in hell Chastity would let me back out. So instead of going to my desk, I went straight to Tanner's office.

"Top of the morning to you," he said.

I stared at him. *Oh my God, he's my soulmate.* I thought I was the only person awkward enough to say something so strange!

He cleared his throat. "I mean, can I help you?" he asked. His dark eyes bore into me from behind his glasses, just like they always had back when he was stalking me. We no longer did that anymore. I mean…I still happened to take that route on my way to spin class, but Tanner was never there. And yes, I totally get how it might seem like I was stalking him because I was the one still showing up and he wasn't. But whatever. Sue me.

"Hey," I said, trying to pretend like I hadn't just been starting at him for a solid 5 seconds. "I was hoping you could look through some of these graphics I've been working on for the winery."

"Sure." He walked around his desk and pulled a chair out for me. The scent of blueberries wafted over me. It made me want to lick him from his head to his toes. Scratch that. Feet were dirty. But his cologne was divine.

We went through a couple of the logos that I'd mocked up for the rebranding of Mills Winery. Their new name was Wineflix and Chill. Which I thought was the most clever name ever. I was super excited to see what Tanner thought of the logos. But I had to play along with Chastity's stupid game. I made a show of squinting to look at them. "Is it just me, or is it really dark in here?"

He gave me a funny look. "It's just you. Do you feel okay?"

"Do you mind if I open the blinds?"

"Be my guest."

"You're sure?" *You're not going to melt in the sunlight, Mr. Vampire?*

"I think? Now that you're being weird about it, I'm kind of wondering if it's some sort of trap. Did Chastity pay the window washer to work nude today or something?"

I winked at him. "Open it and find out."

"No thanks. Anyway, I absolutely love these logos. Especially this one." He pointed to his favorite. "Although I think the text should be pink instead of red."

Hmm. Vampire test #1: inconclusive. Maybe Chastity's crazy theory wasn't that crazy after all. I agreed with him about the text color and then turned to the next page, purposefully running my hand across the edge of the thick paper. I cringed as it sliced into my hand.

"Ouch!" I yelled.

"What happened?" he asked.

I held up my hand. "Papercut. Your damn paper is so thick that it could practically be considered a deadly weapon."

"Those are the worst. Need a Band-Aid?"

"Papercuts don't need Band-Aids," I said. "Everyone knows that the only way to make a papercut feel better is to suck on it."

He narrowed his eyes. "Really? Huh. I must have missed whenever it was announced that there was an updated treatment."

"Yeah. But everyone also knows that lip-gloss stings like a bitch when you get it on a cut. So I'm in quite a predicament."

"Are you trying to get me to suck on your finger?" His eyes dropped to the blood and I swore he licked his lips.

Vampire! "Ew, no. Don't be a freak." I eyed him suspiciously. That was the second vampire test that kind of pointed to him actually being a vampire. I needed to discuss this development with Chastity immediately. Especially because if he actually was a vampire…he might decide to kill me. "Excuse me for a sec."

"So?" asked Chastity as I approached her desk.

"I think he's a vampire," I whisper-yelled. My heart was racing. God, what do I do now? The guy that I was in love with was a vampire? *In love? Stop it, psycho.*

"Uh, duh. I tried to tell you."

"What if he tries to bite my neck?"

"He won't do it in front of all these people. He'd lure you somewhere more private. And I won't let that happen. Besides, we're not sure yet. We have to narrow down the possibilities. It's time for test #3."

"But…his office is kind of private. He could just close the blinds and have his way with me."

"I hope he does. In the sexy way. Not the murder way. But right now you need to focus, you scoundrel." She tossed me a takeout bag. "And don't forget about the werewolf test."

I took a deep breath. I could do this. "Got it." I returned to Tanner's office. "Sorry about that. You hungry?"

"I already had lunch…" he started.

I ignored him and dumped the food on his desk. "Let's see…we've got *garlic* fried-rice. *Garlic* bread. Oh, and that Papa John's dipping sauce. You know, the *garlic* butter stuff."

"I'm seeing a theme here," he said with a smile.

"What's that? All the best foods in the world?"

"No. Garlic."

"Huh, what a weird coincidence. Is garlic a problem for you?" I unwrapped the food and slid it across his desk. The smell of garlic was practically unbearable, even for my non-vampire self. I could hardly imagine how he felt. He was probably moments away from melting.

"Nope, no problem." He grabbed the bread and took a big bite. And then he scooped up some of the rice.

Very interesting. So he wasn't afraid of garlic. But all of it was cooked garlic. Maybe vampires were only allergic to raw garlic? I'd have to consult the literature after work. But in the meantime, I had a few other tests to run.

I loosened one of my earrings and then shook my head to make it fall out. But it didn't work, so I shook harder.

"Are you having a seizure?" he asked.

"No. I'm just…damn! My earring fell out." I fumbled with it to try to get it back in but purposefully failed. "Would you mind?" I held the earring out for him.

"Sure."

"These *silver* earrings are great, but they're so loose." I stared at him hard as I said the word silver. If he was a werewolf, touching silver would be like putting his hand on a hot stove. Or something like that. *Burn, baby, burn.*

He didn't flinch, though. He just grabbed the earring and walked over behind my chair. A chill ran down my spine as he gently pushed my hair out of the way. For a moment I forgot the fact that I was supposed to be figuring out his secret. All I wanted was for him to keep his hands on me. But as soon as I thought it, they fell away.

Maybe I had it all wrong. Maybe he was just a mind reader. Or maybe he kept backing away from me because it was hard to control himself around the sweet scent of my blood. I swallowed hard.

"You're a lifesaver," I said. "By the way, do you want some water?" I took a bottle out of my purse and set it on his desk. "I have the best trick. Rather than paying for stupid bottled water, I always just fill it up at the church on the way to work. They have this pool of free water that they say has been blessed. How cool is that?" *And this holy water is going to disintegrate you, foul demon.*

"You know people put their hands in that, right?"

I shrugged. But really I was dying inside. Even going near the holy water had given me the willies. SO. MANY.

GERMS. I was fully prepared to toss my bottle in the trash as soon as this test was over. "Is that why it tastes so flavorful?" *Barf.*

"I'm not going to drink that. But you can pour it on me if you're worried that I'm an evil demon."

"Say what now?" I pretended to be shocked by his accusation.

"You really think I don't know what you're doing?"

"Before you say anything else ridiculous, I have a present for you." I pulled a wrapped package out of my purse and tossed it to him.

He caught it. "I'm somewhat terrified to see what's in here."

I forced a laugh. "Don't be. It's totally normal. Don't people always bring you presents after you sign with their firm?"

"No. Because that borders on bribery."

"What?" *Is it?* "Ha. No. It only would have been bribery if I'd given you this *before* you signed. Just open it."

He ripped the paper and immediately looked bewildered. "What am I looking at here?"

"Socks."

"Socks?" His bottom lip quivered. "I never thought anyone would set me free..."

"Really?" I had to pick my jaw up off the floor.

"No, I'm not a house elf. And I'm not a vampire or a werewolf or a demon. But if you promise not to tell a soul, I'll tell you my real secret."

"Sure." *Is he really going to tell me?!* I was cautiously optimistic.

"I mean it. Do I have your word?" He seemed strangely serious. His acting skills combined with my gullibility was a dangerous combination for my sanity.

"Fine. I won't tell a soul."

He hesitated for a moment, like he was wondering if he could trust me. But then he leaned in and whispered, "I'm a genie."

I laughed. How stupid did he think I was? "Touché. I deserved that."

"I'm serious." Tanner walked over and shut his office door. "That's why we can't be together." He sighed as he sat back down, as if his confession was a weight off his shoulders.

Fine. I'll play along. "Oh of course. And let me guess - your previous master wished for you to torture me?"

"No. Ava wouldn't have been that wasteful with her wishes."

"Well, Mr. Genie, can I have three wishes?"

"Yes." He leaned back in his chair with his hands behind his head as if this were the most normal, casual conversation in the world.

"Okay then. I'd like a magic carpet ride." *Let's see you act your way through this one, genie boy.*

Tanner nearly fell out of his chair as he sprung forward. His eyes narrowed. "Dear Lord, why would you wish for that? Magic carpet rides are freaking terrifying. Imagine flying around thousands of feet above the ground on a floppy piece of fabric. With nothing to hold on to."

I didn't know what to say. I felt like I should laugh or have something witty to add, but I had nothing.

"When I got caught being unfaithful to the evil Princess Karima," he continued, "the sultan almost sentenced me to death by magic carpet ride. But then he reconsidered and sentenced me to an even worse fate: eternal life as a genie."

Sultan? Evil Princess? What? "Well that's a convenient story to avoid granting my wish." *Definitely a demon.*

He laughed.

And suddenly the tension that had been like a wall between us the past few weeks started to dissipate. The tests hadn't revealed anything about his secret, but his willingness to joke about genies put me completely at ease around him. So at ease that I felt comfortable asking, "So why does being a genie prevent us from being together?"

"A lot of reasons. Are you familiar with the brown recluse spider?"

"A little." *A lot.* I had been bitten by a spider a few years ago. The little bastard had gotten away, so I was left to look up symptoms online. That led me to a Google image search of brown recluse bites…

"So you've seen the pictures of how their bites eat away at your skin cells?"

I nodded. The images of the zombie-like bites were permanently seared in my brain.

"That's what would happen to you if you ever were to come in contact with uh…me." He glanced down at his crotch. "The technical term is *alqadib almushtaeilat aljaniyu*, which roughly translates to flaming genie penis."

I burst out laughing. *Now he's making up words?* I had to hand it to him, he was really committing to this lie.

"It's really not funny," he said. "You try going 300 years without having sex."

"Well, let me be the first to tell you that you've aged magnificently. You don't look a day over 30."

"I appreciate that. Now, do you have any more questions about my true form, or shall we get back to these graphics? I may not be able to die, but my businesses sure as hell can."

I almost pushed him to tell me more. I was sure that if I asked enough questions his silly story would fall apart. Just like it had when I'd figured out he was part of the Society. But questioning him further would most likely ruin whatever weird understanding we'd come to. Besides, all of it was moot. Because we'd grinded pretty hard at Odegaard. And I'd felt no burning sensation on my crotch. He was just a dirty liar. Just like he'd lied about the FBI being after him.

It was pretty clear he didn't want to discuss his actual secret. But I was 97.5% positive that he was a demon. Why did I always have to fall for the bad boys?

Chapter 35

MY SECOND WISH

Tuesday

"I can't believe we didn't think of that sooner!" said Chastity. "*Of course* he's a genie. That's why the Society's logo is a genie lamp. And the whole three wish thing."

I laughed. "He's not a genie, Chastity. And whether he is or not has nothing to do with the Society anyway. It's not like he owns the whole operation. He's just a member. He was definitely just messing with me. But on the bright side, he liked all of our graphics." I opened my laptop to get back to work. That lasted for about three minutes.

Chastity spun my chair around to face her, not caring at all that I was in the middle of typing. "I've got it."

"Got what?"

"Your first genie wish. He said you could have three, right?'

"Society wishes?" I asked. "Or personal genie wishes from Tanner?"

"From Tanner. Did you ever finalize your wish for the magic carpet ride?"

I kind of wanted to get back to work, but my curiosity got the best of me. "Nope. And yes, he said I have three wishes."

"And are there any rules? Like about not killing people? Or not being able to make people fall in love?"

"We didn't get that far." And then something clicked. *Rules. Wishes.* "Holy shit, Chastity! You're a genius!"

"I am? But I didn't even tell you my idea yet."

I got up and ran to Tanner's office. Evie had long since stopped trying to prevent me from going into his office whenever I pleased. Tanner looked up as I stormed in.

"Are you stalking me?" he asked.

I was beaming. He was back to messing with me. "Yup." I closed the door and sat down. "I know what I want for my next wish."

"Your next wish? I never granted the magic carpet ride, so technically you still have three."

"Not your fake genie wishes. I mean my Society wishes. I've only used one. How do I use another?"

Tanner lowered his eyebrows. "On the app."

I pulled out my phone and opened the app. "Where do I click?"

"The genie lamp logo, of course."

"Ah. They really should make that more clear." I clicked the logo and a new screen popped up:

You have three wishes. What is your second wish?

I typed in my wish and hit submit.

"So what'd you wish for?" asked Tanner.

"None of your business. But if you must know, I wished to learn all of Ryder Storm's secrets."

Tanner had no response. He just stared at me as I turned and walked triumphantly out of his office.

Gotcha bitch.

An hour later when I looked up from my computer to stretch, I noticed a little black envelope sitting on my desk. *Where did that come from!?* The obvious answer was Tanner. But how had he put it there without me knowing? He was so damn sneaky.

For once it was my turn to interrupt Chastity in the middle of work. I spun her chair around. She jumped and almost tossed her laptop on the floor.

"What the..." She squealed with excitement the second she saw the envelope. "Open it!"

I slowly broke the gold wax seal and pulled out the thick white parchment. I cleared my throat and read: "Raven Black, it would be my pleasure to escort you to an exclusive exhibition at the Metropolitan Museum of Art this evening at 8:30. Signed, Ryder Storm."

YES! But what did this have to do with his secrets? Was he a world-class painter? I'd find out soon enough...

***

I had polished off half a bottle of champagne by the time my limo rolled up to the Met. It was the only way to prevent myself from hyperventilating. My mind was running a mile a minute, second-guessing every decision I'd made since I got the date card.

Is this too much cleavage? Yes.

Are these the right Odegaards? Definitely not. Choosing one of 74 pairs had been my worst nightmare. Eventually I had just played *eeny, meeny, miny, moe* and landed on the snake-skin Medusas. So I wore them. *Ha. Yeah right.* I didn't have the confidence to wear those things in public. Instead I just wore some sparkly pumps.

Here goes nothing. I took a deep breath and got ready to step out of the limo. I expected to be attacked by paparazzi as I made my way down the red carpet to the doors of the Met...but there was no red carpet. And no paparazzi. Because this wasn't the Met Gala. It was just the Met on a random Tuesday. *Duh.* The only person who even looked at me was a hotdog vendor, and that was just to tell me that I looked like I was in the mood for one of his nice juicy wieners.

See? Too much cleavage.

I tugged my top up and rushed up the stairs to the Met. The view inside took my breath away. And I'm not talking about the view of the great hall. I'm talking about the view of Ryder in his maroon and gold suit. He was sexy when he was Tanner, but when he transformed into Ryder, when he showed his confidence with his man bun and wild tuxedos...that was when I really found him irresistible.

I tried to do my sexiest walk towards him, but I only managed to trip and nearly break my ankle. *Fuck!* I threw my hands out to catch myself, but there was no need. Because Ryder caught me in his strong arms.

"Are you stalking me?" he asked, while still balancing me in his arms.

If I hadn't been before, I definitely would have been now. Because this would have been an epic meet-cute. "Technically you're the one that happened to show up when I fell. I believe that means you're stalking me." I patted his chest. All I wanted to do was rip his shirt off.

He smiled as he steadied me back on my feet. "Your dress is stunning."

"You too." *His dress is stunning?* I coughed to try to distract him from my stupid comment. And I shouldn't have said something nice, anyway. I was supposed to be playing hard to get. I took a deep breath and reminded myself of the plan. I wasn't interested in him. We were boss and employee. Nothing more. I tried to think of a way to change my compliment into an insult. I pointed at his tux. "I know this is an art exhibit, but I didn't realize we were supposed to wear the art."

"You look like a work of art as well," he said.

No! I wasn't complimenting you. It was supposed to be a sick burn. Why did he have to be so dense? "Are you stalking me?" I used his own line against him.

But he wasn't fazed at all. He just grabbed my hand and twirled me. The way he looked at me as my dress flared out made me feel like the most beautiful woman in the world. If he had finished it off with a dip, I would have lost all control and made out with him right then and there.

"You're just in time for the tour. Shall we?" He put his hand on the small of my back and led me to one of the smaller rooms of the gallery. A dozen couples were milling around admiring the paintings. Based on their appearances - all super attractive, dressed to the nines, and wearing black wristbands - I assumed they were all Society members.

The docent cleared her throat and asked for our attention. Everyone gathered around and she started describing some ugly Jacques Louis David painting that was apparently worth millions.

"What do you think?" asked Ryder.

"Of the painting? It's fine."

He nodded. "Insightful critique. Want to know what I think of it?"

"Sure."

"I thought you'd be more excited. You wanted to know all my secrets, did you not?"

I just stared at him.

"Unfortunately telling secrets is strictly forbidden by the Society. But you'd be surprised by how much you can learn about a person based on their art critiques."

"Oh yeah? What did my critique reveal about my soul?"

"That you're too shy to say what you really think. That you're scared of embarrassing yourself and saying the wrong thing."

I opened my mouth to protest. Nothing came out. He had gotten me exactly right. I was always worried about saying the wrong thing. So I usually overthought everything and somehow ended up saying something way worse than the original thing in my head.

"See?"

"Okay, Mr. Smarty Pants. What do you think of the painting?"

Ryder ran his fingers along his five o'clock shadow as he stared at the painting. It looked like he was really studying it.

And I was studying him. Because all I wanted was to feel that stubble against my face again. God, why did he had to be so devastatingly handsome? The fact that he'd been an ass for weeks just melted away when I was looking at him. I bit my lip.

"This is actually one of my favorite paintings," he said. "Do you know what it's about?"

"No."

"It depicts the death of Socrates. Politicians accused him of corrupting the youth and gave him the choice of renouncing his beliefs or drinking hemlock. He chose the hemlock."

"Ah, well it's clear what your critique says about you. You're a showoff."

Ryder laughed. "That wasn't even my critique. I was just giving you some context so that you'd understand why the use of negative space in the piece was so bold. And why the harmonious palette is so evocative."

"Yup, you're definitely a showoff. Do you even know what those words mean?"

"No clue. I just heard some douche use them last time I was here."

Now it was my turn to laugh.

"Really though, I think the message behind this painting is so important. Imagine if everyone was so willing to stand up for what they believe in."

"It's not that simple."

"Sure it is. Take my colorful tuxedos." He pulled the jacket open to reveal the gold lining. "Do you know how many insults I've gotten about them?"

"Depends on how long you've been wearing them."

"Doesn't matter how long. Because the answer is zero. Not a single insult. But I've gotten a ton of compliments. And they got you to stalk me, so I'd say that's a win…"

I shoved his arm. "Uh, excuse me. But if I recall, *you* were the one stalking *me*. #StalkerProblems." I almost squealed. I'd used that hashtag perfectly! It was definitely the best I'd ever done. #Ever. Eh, I ruined it. But #StalkerProblems would go down in history as my best use ever.

"If you say so. Speaking of stalking, you're going to need your stalking skills to find our tour group. It appears we've been left behind."

I looked around. Yup, we were alone. How had I not noticed them leave? Was Ryder really that distracting?

A phone ringing startled me.

"Whoops," said Ryder as he fished his phone out of his breast pocket. Then he narrowed his eyes. "I have to take this. I'll be right back. Don't get into too much trouble while I'm gone." He winked at me and walked out of the room.

I took a few minutes to admire some of the other art in the room. But after I had looked at every piece and read all the placards twice, I started to get antsy. Where was he? Did he think I was going to go find the group? For all I knew, Ryder was with the tour group wondering where the heck I had gone.

I decided to go find him. But the room he'd gone into was empty and the lights were off. Same story for the next room. And the next.

A chill ran down my spine. Tanner had warned me that he'd messed with bad people. Had they taken him? Were they coming for me next? I tried to think of an escape plan, which was super easy. I had lots of practice making escape plans. I'd started making them when I was four years old. I saw something on TV about a home invasion and convinced myself that it was 100% going to happen to my family. After that, before bed every night I'd practiced taking the curtain rod down and swinging it around like a spear. I even taught Rosalie to do it when she was old enough. If only I'd taught her a little better, maybe she could have defended herself from whoever took her...

A footstep behind me made me jump.

Shit! I had gotten so distracted thinking about Rosalie that I hadn't gotten close enough to the display of swords in order to protect myself.

"Everything okay, Miss?" asked a gruff voice.

I spun around, looking for anything within reach that might be a suitable weapon. Pushing a solid marble statue onto my attacker's head felt like a decent option... But then I realized that it was just a security guard. And he didn't look very threatening with his cute bald head and bulging waistline.

His eyes wandered down to my black bracelet. "You're with that tour group, right?"

"Yeah. And my very big, strong friend will be back in just a second. He uh…went to the bathroom." *So don't try to murder me.*

He gave me a funny look and then grabbed his radio. "Hey Mike, you seen that tour group?"

A staticky voice replied, "Yup. They're in room 538."

"You hear that? Room 538." He pulled a map out of his waistband and flicked it open.

Okay, so he was definitely just a helpful security guard. Good thing I didn't murder him with a 900-pound statue. And then I had an idea. If he could find the tour group with his fancy little radio, maybe he could find Ryder. "I'm actually looking for Ryder Storm."

"Hmm…doesn't sound familiar." He picked up his radio again. "Mike, it's Steve again. I've got a girl here looking for Ryder Storm?"

"I bet you do," came the reply with a laugh. "Tell her she can find him in that new exhibit…Exhibit Hall D."

Why did he laugh? Was it because Ryder is so sexy? Was some other girl flirting with Ryder in Exhibit Hall D?!

"Ah, of course," said the guard. "That's over in the modern and contemporary section. Room 913." He handed me the map and pointed to my destination with his big, completely unthreatening, sausage finger.

"Thanks." I snatched the map and hurried off. He didn't look like a cartel assassin, but I couldn't be too cautious.

It took me like ten minutes to get all the way to the other side of the Met. In normal heels, my feet would have been aching after such a long trek. But I felt fine in my Odegaards. *Thank you, Ryder.*

A guard was standing outside of the heavy double doors that led to Exhibit Hall D. I thought his biceps might rip right out of his black V-neck as he crossed his arms and stepped to block the door.

"Hey, I'm looking for Ryder Storm."

"May I see your left wrist, please?" he asked. His voice was even more intimidating than his appearance, if that was possible.

I held up my wrist with the black bracelet.

"Thank you." He stepped aside and opened the door in one fluid motion.

I stepped through the heavy wooden doors. The guard closed them behind me, leaving me in a pitch-black room.

And this is where I'm going to die.

Chapter 36

HAZING THE NOOB

Tuesday

My heart was beating out of my chest. I groped at the wall for a light switch. I only knocked one painting off the wall before I found it. The main lights stayed off, but a few spotlights flickered and then fully illuminated some select pieces of art.

There was no sign of Ryder. Or anyone else. Well, unless you counted the statue of David. Or that group of six terracotta army soldiers. *Are those real?* Something seemed…off about them. Then I saw the Andy-Warhol-style 3x3 grid of multicolored dildos next to a nude version of American Gothic, and it suddenly became very clear why this room had been sectioned off. I looked back at the terracotta soldiers, now noticing that they all had erections. Same with the statue of David. Rather than having a little baby flaccid penis, this rendition was extremely well hung and definitely a little excited.

For some reason I couldn't look away. It was like a fake penis emporium. I walked farther into the hallway-like gallery, passing all sorts of penis art. The only piece that was a faithful reproduction was a fresco of Priapus weighing his penis. If you're familiar with that piece, you'll understand why it didn't need to be altered.

Guess I missed Ryder. I started towards the next room, but something caught my eye. *Did that painting just move?* I took a few steps towards it. It was a human-scale reproduction of Da Vinci's *Vitruvian Man.* I'm sure you've seen it. It's that sketch of a nude man inscribed in a circle. His arms and legs are spread, and then another pair of arms and legs are drawn in a slightly different position. It was supposed to show the perfect human proportion or something.

So what about it caught my eye? Was it like the Mona Lisa, with eyes that follow you around the room? Nope. Definitely not. My eyes went right to the crotch of the painting. Someone had added a sculpted penis to give it a 3D element. And it wasn't just any old penis. It was huge. *Or is that just the perfect proportion for a penis?*

I glanced down at the placard describing the piece: HAZING THE NOOB by RYDER STORM.

Ryder designed this? I hadn't realized he was such a talented painter. Or sculptor. Oh, that's why the security guard thought it was funny that I was searching for Ryder Storm. Because this penis sculpture was by Ryder Storm. He thought I was just looking for the dick art. I giggled to myself.

But wow…the penile part really did look lifelike. So lifelike that it seemed to keep moving. It wasn't a lot, but it was enough for me to notice. I looked around to make sure the guard hadn't followed me in. Then I ducked under the velvet rope to get a closer look. And then I poked it.

I had expected it to be hard and ceramic, but instead it felt soft and…flesh-like. It swayed a little bit.

I poked it again a little harder. It swayed more. And then the hips of the painting pivoted and the penis swung towards me.

I let out a squeal and stepped back. I knew I'd had a lot of champagne, but not enough to make me hallucinate nearly being molly-whopped by a fake dong.

I squinted and stared at the painting. *What the hell am I looking at here?* Most of it was in fact a painting, but part of it had been cut away to reveal the naughty bits of a man standing behind the wall.

Oh, duh! I was the noob. And Ryder was hazing me. Which meant I was looking at *his* penis. My heartbeat doubled the second I realized it. I was looking at Ryder's penis!

So this was his secret, huh? That he had a giant penis. I mean, as far as secrets go…it was a pretty good one.

Then a horrible thought washed over me. *What if he was telling the truth about having a flaming genie penis?* I looked down at my finger. It didn't seem like it was decaying, but now that I thought about it, it did tingle a little…

I needed to find a way to know if all my skin was about to melt off. So I grabbed a little rubber statue off a nearby display and lightly whacked it against his penis. If his penis was dangerous, I figured it would melt the statue. Which it didn't. In fact, the only thing that happened was that Ryder started to get erect. And more erect… And more erect.

He wasn't quite as big as the stacked soda cans that Chastity had warned me about, but he was probably a solid nine inches. And thick.

I gave him one more whack, and that was when I realized that the "rubber statue" I was hitting him with was a big floppy dildo. I burst out laughing.

"You like that?" I asked.

He thrusts his hips a little to make his cock bounce up and down in a motion that clearly meant yes.

Poor guy. If only he knew that he was sword fighting a dildo.

I felt like I should make it up to him. Right? I mean, it was only the polite thing to do. I couldn't just get him all aroused and then leave him there. Wouldn't that make his balls turn blue and explode? *Yeah, that sounds right.* And I couldn't walk away, as per Single Girl Rule #24: No blue balls allowed. Finish what you start.

I took a step closer. *What am I thinking? I can't do this in the middle of a museum!* But for some reason, it didn't matter that I told myself no. I wanted to do something crazy. I wasn't Ashley Cooper tonight. I was Raven freaking Black. And Raven Black was sexy and confident. Or at least, I wanted to be. And the other thing I'd wanted? For weeks? Ryder. Blowing him behind a painting wasn't on my list of things to try. But I could always add it later and then cross it off. It was a win-win.

I slowly reached out my hand and ran my thumb along his tip.

And he groaned. *Oh God.* I loved that sound. I wanted to hear it over and over again. And the fact that he groaned because of what I was doing just made it even more exhilarating.

I looked around to make sure we were still alone, and then I did what any reasonable girl would have done: I wrapped my hand around his beautiful shaft and started pumping up and down. He pulsed in my hand.

I looked over my shoulder again to make sure no one was looking. How had Ryder known that almost getting caught was a fantasy of mine?

I kept stroking faster and faster. My arm started to get tired after a minute though. And there was too much friction with my hand. Which left me with only one choice.

Actually, I had two choices. I could have used the lotion in my purse. But I wanted to use my mouth instead. Don't judge me. I hadn't had sex in like a year. And believe me - if you had such a beautiful erection in front of you, you'd want it in your mouth just as badly as I did. Plus it was Ryder. I'd been fantasizing about him for months. *Screw playing hard to get.* Blowing him was a way better option. Chastity always said the best way to a man's heart was to suck his cock. Or something like that. I didn't love giving head. But I loved Ryder. I immediately shook my head. *Liked him. I liked him.* I didn't love him. That would be…crazy. And I wasn't crazy.

I ignored the thoughts racing through my mind as I stared at his cock. I was overthinking this. I'd been wanting to take things further with Ryder for weeks. This was my chance. And if he happened to fall in love with me in the process? Great.

Besides, it wasn't just Single Girl Rule #24 spurring me on. It was also #23: Never back down from a huge cock. #Fearless. And no, I didn't just slay it with that perfectly executed hashtag. #Fearless was part of rule #23. Because of course it was, since I was 85% sure that Chastity had made them all up. And she was the master of hashtags. But…I wasn't a little bitch. And I wasn't going to back down from Ryder's huge cock.

The painting was a few feet off the ground, so his penis was right at mouth level. I didn't have to kneel or anything. I just took a step forward and flicked my tongue ever so gently against his tip. I'd like to pretend that it was a sexy move, but really I was just checking to see if it tasted clean. I wasn't about to shove some dirty cock in my mouth, even if it did belong to Ryder Storm. When my tongue detected freshly cleaned skin - albeit with a hint of salty pre-cum - I moved on to the shaft. I held his cock up as I licked him from his balls all the way to his tip. And then I corralled him with my mouth.

Ryder groaned from behind the wall.

That's right.

I swirled my tongue around as I took him farther in my mouth. And farther…and farther. *God, how big is this thing?* I opened my eyes and, doing my best to ignore the strange painting, looked down at the enormous cock in my mouth. There was still quite a ways for me to go if I was going to get the whole thing in.

Giving blowjobs to Joe had always been so easy and boring. It was like sucking on a little tootsie roll. But blowing Ryder? It was like trying to jam a water bottle down my throat. A warm, meaty, delicious water bottle, but still a water bottle. I gagged and pulled back.

"Damn man, this thing is huge," I muttered. He thrust his hips out to tell me to keep going.

I tried to deepthroat him once more before accepting defeat and focusing more on tongue action. I worked his tip with my tongue while my hands stroked up and down his shaft in a sort of blowjob/handjob hybrid.

He groaned behind the wall. It felt like he was getting even harder.

He definitely wanted me. And I wanted him. God, I wanted him so badly. I was soaking wet. Would this be the day I finally broke my dry spell and had sex with Ryder Storm? It certainly wasn't how I pictured my first time with him, but I was oddly turned on by the whole thing. Not getting to see his face and doing it in public made it so naughty and forbidden. I mean…literally anyone could walk in and see us. It was freaking exhilarating. This was so much better than trying different smoothie flavors. I kept sucking as I looked around for a chair I could stand on to bang him…

And then I felt his warm cum shoot into the back of my mouth. I had not been expecting that…at all. I gagged a little and pulled back. Which meant my mouth wasn't there to contain his next shot. The sticky white liquid shot onto my chest. I looked down in horror.

Not my dress! That thing cost $2000 and now it was ruined with a big cumstain right on my left breast. I pulled on the fabric to see the damage, completely forgetting about Ryder's exploding penis.

I guess I thought he wouldn't keep cumming when I let go. Or maybe I was too distracted by what happened to my dress. Either way, his cock didn't care. Pro tip, ladies (or gentlemen, if you're into this sorta thing) - when you let go of a penis mid-orgasm, the force of the cumshot makes it shoot *way* higher than you'd expect. It's like when a really weak guy tries to use a firehose in a cartoon. I experienced it firsthand as Ryder's unrestrained cock blasted cum all over my chin and up onto my forehead, narrowly missing my eyes.

At that point I should have moved out of the way, but apparently I thought it would be better to catch the rest of it in my mouth. I wasn't fast enough though, so his fourth and final shot mostly went all over my chin and neck.

Fantastic. At least I could take solace in the fact that Ryder hadn't seen me completely botch the end of his blowjob.

Just then I heard the exhibit doors open. The docent's voice filled the room.

Shit, shit, shit! It was fun *almost* getting caught. But I'd literally die from embarrassment if they saw me. It would be worse than incident #2…when I'd raped Dr. Lyons. *Oh God…did I just mouth rape Ryder?* No…he definitely wanted it. And he'd been totally asking for it by putting his cock in that painting. So that knocked this down to somewhere near incident #3 status…the elevator curtsey incident. Nope, it was worse than that. Because I was covered in cum. *Screw my life!* I searched the room for a good hiding spot. But there wasn't much. Unless I wanted to hide amongst the erect terracotta soldiers or duck behind a 6-foot penis sculpture, my only hope was to make a run for the emergency exit. I hiked up the bottom of my dress and sprinted toward the doors.

And I somehow made it out just in time. *I think.* I hadn't heard anyone laughing or anything. But they were members of the Society, so they'd probably seen worse. I looked over my shoulder to make sure they weren't following me for a gangbang. By some miracle, they weren't. And there was a bathroom just around the corner. It was my lucky night. *Or Ryders, if you know what I mean. #HorseFacts. Damn it! I hate hashtags! They're so hard!* But he had been hung like a horse…

My phone buzzed just as I walked into the bathroom.

Ryder: Sorry, had to run. Major crisis at one of my factories. I'll explain tomorrow.

How rude. First he hid behind a painting for our first sexual encounter, and then he left without even saying thank you? Blowing him was supposed to make him fall in love with me, not make him run away. Why did I have to be crushing on the weirdest billionaire in the world?

And more importantly, how awkward was work going to be tomorrow?

Chapter 37

SO MUCH AWKWARD

Wednesday

It was absolutely impossible to focus on work the next morning. Chastity kept trying to get more details about what I had done to Ryder, while all I could think about was *when* Ryder was going to get to work. It was almost noon and there was still no sign of him.

Was he too embarrassed to even be in the same room as me? The thought that the blowjob had been unwanted had definitely crossed my mind. And when I say crossed my mind, I mean it literally kept me up the entire night. My rapey tendencies had been why I'd decided to become a hermit. But then I inexplicably gave up the #HermitLife and left my apartment. And joined a freaking sex club! What was I thinking?!

"#HermitLife!" I yelled. "I did it!"

Chastity didn't even seem phased by my outburst. She finished what she was typing and turned to me. "What? No. There was literally zero context. You can't just yell out weird hashtags and expect them to be a thing."

I know. It made sense in my head. Just like the fact that in my head it seemed like Ryder wanted me to rape him. I mean, not rape him. I meant that it was consensual even though there were no verbal cues. You know what I mean! He seemed into it. Couldn't he have just escaped from the painting if he didn't want it? *Gah!*

"So which one of these is most accurate?" asked Chastity, pointing to a bunch of bottles on her desk. There was a normal water bottle, a little short one, a 2-liter of soda, and one of those super sleek bottles of flavored water.

I raised an eyebrow. "What exactly am I looking at here?"

"You said he was the size of a bottle. Which kind is it?"

I rubbed my face. *I never should have told her that.* "That one," I said, pointing to the 2-liter.

Her eyes got so big. "How did you even…" Then she glared at me. "You're messing with me."

"I would be dead right now if I put something that large in my mouth." I was going to show her the correct answer (the sleek bottle of flavored water) when my phone buzzed.

Please be Tanner. Please be Tanner. I clicked on my messages. *Yes!!!*

Tanner: Sorry I had to leave so early last night.

I had my response locked and loaded. Like I said…I didn't sleep at all last night.

Me: No problem. I ended up finding a painting that I really loved. The artist seemed so…exposed in it. The most interesting part was how it kept growing on me the more time I spent with it. I even got all choked up a few times. In the end it kinda left a bad taste in my mouth, though.

I giggled at my clever innuendo and hit send.

Tanner: Sounds impressive. Maybe you can show it to me once I get back from Mexico.

Is he asking for another blowjob? Or was he just the most dense human in the world? More importantly…what was he doing in Mexico? Images of cartel assassins stuffing me into a vat of acid raced through my mind. Wait…no. He wasn't actually in Mexico. Because he hadn't really left last night. His urgent phone call had just been a cover so he could go hide in his perverted painting.

I was trying to think of a clever response when my phone buzzed again. But it wasn't Tanner. This time it was Dr. Lyons.

"Oh shit," I muttered.

"What?" asked Chastity.

"I cheated on Dr. Lyons." Saying it made me feel filthy. "I mean Anthony." Why couldn't I ever remember to call him by his first name?

"Since when were you two exclusive?"

"We haven't talked about it…"

"And you've gone out with him what…three times? Four? And all you did was give a blowjob to Tanner? Yeah, that's not even close to cheating."

"Are you sure?" Because I wasn't. God, what had I done? I tried to get the image of Tanner's penis out of my mind. But the bottle on my desk that looked like him made it rather difficult.

"Yes, I'm sure," said Chastity.

"Do I need to tell Dr. Lyons what I've done?" I cringed at the thought of having that conversation.

"Uh, no. Unless he's into that. Do you remember Dan? He loved it when I hooked up with other guys and then told him about it. Like I always say - guys love to feel jealous."

I made a face. "Weird."

"It was actually kinda hot."

"I have to break up with him."

"What? Why?" Chastity stared at me like I was completely insane.

"Because. He's a good guy. It wouldn't be fair for me to string him along. Clearly my heart is with Tanner. I've analyzed what happened last night in a thousand different ways, and Dr. Lyons never even crossed my mind." *I'm a monster.* Was that how it was for Joe when he was cheating on me? He didn't even think about me?

"What did his text say?"

"Good question." I looked back at my phone.

Dr. Lyons: We need to talk. Are you free for lunch?

My heart started beating out of my chest. *We need to talk.* The only time anyone ever said that was if you were in big trouble. "Oh God. He knows."

"Knows? Knows what?"

"About…you know." I made a blowjob motion with my hand and mouth. I thought that was somehow more secretive than saying it out loud, but it wasn't. Because the guy in the cubicle next to us was looking right at me when I did it. I tried to salvage the situation by wiping my mouth, but that just made it seem like I'd been miming an extra sloppy blowjob.

"There's no way he knows," said Chastity.

"Then what does he want to talk about?"

"He said you guys *need to talk.*" She just stared at me.

I felt denser than Tanner as I stared back.

"Ash…the talk. He's definitely gonna dump you. Which is perfect, because you were going to screw the whole thing up by telling him about blowing Tanner. This'll save you the trouble."

I thought about it for a second. She was absolutely right. I wasn't sure if I was sad or relieved. He was a great guy. But even a great guy wouldn't want to hear my confession of what I did last night. It would be better if he just broke things off without ever knowing that I'd cheated on him.

I texted him back and asked to meet at my favorite café right after work. The rest of the day I was super unproductive because I was nervous about Tanner and now nervous about my dinner date too. Well, not date. Breakup meeting.

But eventually I was sitting across from Dr. Lyons wolfing down the most delicious platter of garlicky deviled eggs. I'd been craving these things ever since I ordered that garlic feast for Tanner, but I'd been too worried about bad breath to order it. Today though, bad breath was not a concern since we'd be breaking up rather than making out.

"So what's up?" I asked.

"Not much." Dr. Lyons looked everywhere except for my eyes. "Can you believe how hot it is today?"

"It's supposed to get even hotter tomorrow. But there's a rainstorm coming that should cool things down a few degrees before the weekend. Saturday is only gonna have a high of 79."

He gave me a funny look. "I didn't realize you were such a weather enthusiast."

I shrugged. "Always have been. When I was a kid I'd look at the weather on Sunday night and plan out my outfits for the whole week." Also, that way I always had an umbrella when I needed it. Because when I got wet I looked like a drowned mole-rat. In high school, I didn't have the same confidence I did now. So looking like a drowned mole rat back then was not acceptable. Fine, it was never acceptable. That was why I knew what the weather was for this Saturday. "Anyway, what did we need to talk about so urgently?"

He took a bite of his sandwich, clearly stalling for time.

"You're acting weird," I said. "Just get it over with." *Dump my cheating ass.*

"Well…I…" He wiped the sweat off his brow. "Dating you is messing with my head. I'm so out of practice that I have no idea how I'm supposed to act. I never know if it's okay to call you. Or to…"

"Well it's never okay to call anyone unless you're dying."

Dr. Lyons laughed. "Thanks for clearing that up. But seriously…it's all such a mystery to me. How often are we supposed to see each other? Greg says that I'll look desperate if we go out more than once a week. But then Nora tells me that you'll think I don't care if we don't see each other at least twice a week. And should I even be talking to Nora?"

Who the hell is Nora?! "In general I'd say listen to the female for dating advice. Unless you want to have sex with her. In that case, don't listen to her. Or talk to her at all." Fucking Nora. I hated that chick. No, I didn't know her. But I hated her with a fiery passion.

Dr. Lyons laughed again, but it was more of a nervous laugh. Even though we were about to break up, I suddenly wanted to find Nora and murder her in her sleep. I pictured her exactly like Sierra.

After a long pause, Dr. Lyons said, "I don't know how to say this but, uh…"

Here it comes. I grabbed a few napkins and started to pack up my lunch in the to-go container I'd requested with my order. Even though I knew I was about to be dumped and that I fully deserved it, I was worried I'd still get emotional. Getting dumped sucked. And honestly sometimes my eyes liked to cry even though I specifically told them not to. Stupid eyes.

He cleared his throat. "I did something. Last night. I went out with some new friends. And there was this girl there. She was very forward. And one thing led to another…"

I stopped putting deviled eggs in my to-go container. "You kissed someone?" *Asshole!*

"Worse. But it didn't mean anything."

Worse? Than kissing? There were only a few things worse than kissing! I tried to swallow down my disdain like I'd swallowed down Tanner's… Yeah, I was the jerk, not Dr. Lyons. But I was still mad. "Who was it? Was it that slut Nora?"

He shook his head. "Ew, no. No."

"Then who was it?"

He mumbled something.

I held my hand to my ear. "What was that?"

"I didn't get her name." He winced as he said it.

"Ugh, gross." I stuffed the rest of my eggs into the container. I'd heard enough. I'd thought he was a good guy. But he was just like all the rest of 'em. And I didn't care that I was being a hypocrite. At least I knew Tanner's real name and his fake name in the Society before I blew him. I knew double the names!

"Here's the thing, though. I felt terrible immediately after it happened. In a weird way, it made me realize how much I care about you."

"After the more-than-a-kiss? How convenient for you."

"I want to be with you, Ash. I want us to be exclusive. I want you to be my girlfriend."

I gaped at him. This was not how this breakup was supposed to happen. I was so angry with him. But more angry at myself. I was the monster here. Or maybe we both were. Either way, there was no way we could be together now. There was only one option. I had to come clean. "I hooked up with someone else last night too."

He waved it off. "I forgive you."

Wait, what? "You're not mad?"

"Only at myself for being too scared to ask you to be exclusive sooner."

We stared at each other for a long second. I had no idea how to respond to that. Part of me wanted to say yes to him. But there was also a part of me that didn't trust him. And a bigger part of me that didn't trust myself around him. Because he was saying all the right things. And his face was too perfect. *And Tanner.*

Dr. Lyons pulled his phone out of his lab coat pocket. "Sorry, I have to check this. It might be the office..."

I took that opportunity to pull out my phone too. I needed advice from Chastity immediately. But before I made it to my text thread with her, I got sidetracked by a notification from the Society app. I clicked on it and the RATE YOUR SEXUAL ENCOUNTER screen popped up. The picture beneath it looked vaguely familiar, but it was definitely not Ryder. The man had a twirly mustache, short brown hair, and piercing blue eyes. His name was Flint Ironside.

Who the hell is Flint Ironside? And why does the Society think I had sex with him?

Chapter 38

FLINT IRONSIDE

Wednesday

What the hell? I stared at the picture of Flint Ironside. Had I seen him last night at the Met?

"Where were you last night?" asked Dr. Lyons. He stared at me and then squinted and looked down at his phone.

"I was uh… at home," I lied. "Watching *Gossip Girl*. Duh."

"But I thought you said you hooked up with someone?" He was still looking back and forth from me to his phone.

I took a big sip of water to avoid answering.

"Is this you?" he asked, flipping his phone around.

I spit my water all over him when I saw what was on it. It was my Society picture right below the words RATE YOUR SEXUAL ENCOUNTER.

"Are you Raven Black?" he asked.

Oh God no. "Who is that?" I tried to sound clueless, but it came out weird and robotic.

"The girl I was with last night. At the Met. It's definitely you!"

"Don't think so, buddy. Last time I checked I have red hair. That girl's a brunette."

"Right, because that wig is your Society disguise. All I had lying around was a fake mustache from a Halloween costume, but the disguise wasn't really necessary anyway once they hid my upper half behind that painting."

My jaw dropped as I put the pieces together. *Oh. Fuck.* Ryder really had left for an emergency. And then the security guards directed me to the painting with his name on it. *Hazing the Noob*. Only I wasn't the noob being hazed. Dr. Lyons was. And I'd taken it to the next level by mouth raping him while he was trapped in the wall. I was a horrible sexual deviant!

I took a deep breath to calm my nerves, but it didn't work. I was hyperventilating. It kind of felt like I was having a heart attack. Or maybe I was just going to spontaneously combust. *I raped Dr. Lyons. Again.*

"I'm so so sorry," I whispered. God, this was incident #5. Raping someone for the second time? What the actual fuck was wrong with me?! And no one should be able to have this many incidents in such a short amount of time. I wanted to go back in time before I joined the Society when I only had to dwell on *the original incident.* The OG incident. Just the one! Now I had five to keep me up at night!

Dr. Lyons said something, but all I could hear was my heart beating out of my chest. The walls were closing in on me. I grabbed my purse and my deviled eggs and ran out of the restaurant.

***

I'd shot Chastity an SOS text as soon as I got back to my apartment. And then I climbed onto my couch and hid under my fluffiest blanket. I was never leaving the house again. I was about to call the FBI on myself. Just for the protection of others.

Chastity didn't bother to knock, she just let herself in. "Hey," she said and sat down next to me.

I assumed. Because the blanket was over my head.

"That bad?" she asked and pulled the blanket down.

"It wasn't Tanner's penis," I said as I somehow slumped farther down onto my couch. I wanted to sink into it and disappear from the world.

Chastity tossed her purse on the floor. "What?"

"The painting. The man I blew. It wasn't Tanner. It was Dr. Lyons." I showed her the picture of him in the Society app and told her all about my dinner date from hell.

"Well that's amazing," she said. "Now you don't have to break up with him."

"Are you crazy? I can never see him again! I cheated on him with himself and raped him all at the same time. How is that even a thing that's possible?"

"I have to admit, that is a pretty impressive feat. But if you think about it, this is kind of perfect."

"Hold that thought." My whole body was yelling at me. My head hurt. My chest felt tight. And don't get me started about my horribly uncomfortable slacks. Whoever invented pants should be shot. I was going to lose my mind if I didn't get a glass of wine and change into some spandex shorts within the next five seconds. So I did exactly that. Well, kind of. Technically it was an entire bottle of wine. But after the day I'd had, it felt like the right choice. And I wasn't a total monster - I grabbed one for Chastity too.

"What was I saying?" she asked as we clinked bottles.

I took a huge gulp straight from my bottle. "Something about my disaster of a life actually being perfect?"

"Oh, right. I mean, how *isn't* it perfect? Dr. Lyons still wants to be with you. And he has a huge penis. So you can keep dating him and make Tanner super jealous. Win, win, win."

"Blowing Dr. Lyons isn't going to make Tanner jealous. It's going to make him think I'm a disgusting slut." *Because I am. I'm a dirty, rapey, slutbag.* I took another huge swig of wine.

"Tanner can't really be mad. You two aren't dating, it was only a blowjob, and you were trying to blow *him* for God's sake. It was just a classic masquerade ball mix-up."

"A what?"

"You know…when you go to a masquerade ball with your boyfriend and think you're banging him, but really it's some other dude. Technically it's not cheating since you had good intentions."

"Are you sure that's a thing?"

Chastity nodded. "Haven't you read Lulu the Love Doctor's blog? She talks about it all the time."

"All the time? How often could that situation possibly come up?"

"A lot, apparently. At least in the inner circles of the Manhattan elite. You know how rich people love to throw a good masquerade party. Daddy used to throw them all the time. But it doesn't even matter. Tanner's never going to know what you did."

"I have to tell him, don't I?"

"No. What you do with other men before he asks you to be his girlfriend is none of his business. You're a 28-year-old divorcee. I'm sure Tanner doesn't have any illusions about you still being a virgin. Think of it this way: Do *you* want to know *his* sexual history?"

"Not really." Suddenly all I could picture was him hooking up with every girl in the Society. The thought of it made my stomach turn over. Or maybe I just felt sick from downing half a bottle of wine. Either way, I realized that I needed to be more assertive with Tanner. I was done playing games. They just weren't my thing. I wasn't smooth enough to play games. There was only one solution. No more making him jealous. Which meant no more dating Dr. Lyons.

I got the ball rolling by deleting all the texts Dr. Lyons had sent me since I escaped in an Uber. Then I hovered my finger over the BLOCK button. With one click, he'd be gone from my life.

"Are you *sure* you want to get rid of Dr. Lyons?" asked Chastity. "Maybe you should think about it for a little while. I mean…it *is* that time of the year when you start to act strange."

"Are you talking about my period? You know that's a monthly thing, right?" *Or did Chastity get knocked up and not realize it?*

"Yes, I know periods are a monthly thing. I'm talking about the anniversary of Rosalie's disappearance."

"Oh." I bit the inside of my lip. That was indeed coming up. But I'd been trying not to think about it. Although, by actively forcing myself not to think of it…I was pretty sure that meant I was thinking about it. "I don't think that makes me act differently. Yes, I'll be sad on the day of. But other than that…"

"Ash. Last year around this time you followed an elementary school teacher for five blocks and then watched her with a pair of binoculars through the school windows. You almost got arrested for being a pervert."

"Well she looked a lot like Rosalie. And why is everyone so freaked out that I own a pair of binoculars? They're not the creepy kind. They're…"

"The fancy opera watching ones. Yeah, I know, you told me. But the year before that you ordered 50,000 baking cups that had a picture of Rosalie's face on the bottom in hopes that someone would recognize her and give you a call."

"I stand by that tactic. If Joe hadn't canceled the order, it might have worked."

Chastity took a big swig of her wine. "Okay. But you have to admit that your plan to move to Somalia last May wasn't completely rational."

"I think it was the pinnacle of rationality, actually. They have a very favorable tax rate. With how much the cupcake business was pulling in, it just made sense financially."

"Somalia has been in the middle of a civil war for like the last 30 years."

"Well no location is perfect."

"Last May you also tried to convince me that we should shave our heads."

I waved her comment off. These examples were all so random. She was acting like I wasn't weird the other 364 days of the year. Trust me, I was. "That's also unrelated to Rosalie. I just happened to read an article about the horrors of head lice and wanted to be proactive."

"Fair point. Lice are disgusting. But still…my point remains. Your judgment around his time of year is typically a little suspect. I'm just trying to make sure that ditching Dr. Lyons is really what you want. I feel the need to reiterate that he's a war hero doctor with a giant penis. I don't know what more you could want in a man."

I nodded. "You're right. On paper, Dr. Lyons is perfect. But he's not Tanner. And Tanner is what I want."

"Is he? Or does Tanner just feel like the safer option because you know he's unavailable? And since he won't even start a relationship, then he can't break your heart like Joe did."

"That's crazy talk."

"Is it?" She stared at me.

"I'm not crazy."

She just kept staring at me.

"I'm not sabotaging myself. Tanner gives me butterflies. Honestly, him stalking me every Tuesday and Thursday evening was the only thing that got me through the past few months. And now seeing him at work is the reason why I can bear to wake up at 6 a.m. and put on real people pants. I want him. And I'm going to make him want me. His issues be damned." I slammed my empty wine bottle down on my coffee table to accentuate my point.

"Alright," said Chastity. "Then let's figure out what his issue really is."

"So you don't think he's a vampire?"

"I mean…there's like an 80% chance it's that. I double-checked and the garlic really shouldn't have been cooked."

I knew it. Vampire! "And that's why he couldn't come to work today. It was really sunny out."

"Fair point. But we should probably rule out some other possibilities before we make that leap."

"What possibilities?"

"Well…" Chastity pulled a notebook out of her purse. There were tons of notes scribbled on the first page. Most of them were paranormal creatures.

"Those don't seem more reasonable than him being a vampire. He's definitely not an amphibious larva of the Loch Ness monster."

"Right." Chastity flipped to a blank page and clicked a pen open. "Let's start with what we know."

"Okay. He's a dirty stalker."

Chastity nodded and wrote STALKER. And then she added BILLIONAIRE. "Are we still in agreement that the place he took you to at the Caldwell Hotel was just a random rental? Since none of his stuff was there and one of his LLCs owns a place at One57?"

"Yes. He was just being super secretive." *Like always.* "Or the Caldwell Hotel is just his apartment while he's doing wishes for the Society or something." I was still hoping Frankie would text me and say I could move into the Caldwell Hotel. "Either way, he definitely lives in One57. And he's about 28 years old. He owns Rhodes Venture Capital, which owns a number of businesses and shell companies. Oh, and his Society alter-ego is Ryder Storm."

"Got it," said Chastity when she was done writing all those bullet points. "Anything else?"

"He mentioned that he went to high school overseas."

"Anything about his parents? Or siblings?"

"Uh... No. Not really. Come to think of it, he never really talks about himself that much. Even that first night when we talked for hours, he mostly just asked a ton of questions about me."

Chastity wrote FULL OF SECRETS in big bold letters at the top of the page.

"And most importantly, he claims that he can't be with me because he pissed off someone very dangerous. Really, what kind of billionaire can't just pay someone off? It doesn't make any sense."

"I've been thinking a lot about that very question," said Chastity. "It actually reminds me of when Daddy lost everything. One minute we had it all - an NYC penthouse, a mansion in the Hamptons, drivers, maids. Paintings worth a million dollars. And then one day all of it was gone." Chastity sniffled and looked longingly at the boxes of Odegaards stacked around my tiny apartment. "Daddy never talks about it, but from what I've been able to piece together, he was overleveraged and a few investments started to go south. So then he started making increasingly risky investments to cover those losses. One thing led to another, and even though we were living like billionaires, our net worth was actually negative. Eventually it all caught up to him when the IRS showed up to collect unpaid taxes."

"So you think the IRS is after Tanner?"

"Could be. Or it could be someone scary. Or both. Either way...he must not have the money to pay them. That's probably why he hired BIMG. One final hail Mary to try to make his businesses profitable before it all comes crashing down."

"Damn. You really think so? He seems so calm for someone drowning in debt."

Chastity looked off into the distance. "Daddy never freaked out either before his big collapse. He was working late hours, yes, but that was nothing new."

"I don't know. It seems more likely that he's a Russian oligarch who's done something to piss off Putin. Those guys are billionaires, and they can still disappear."

"That does fit with him growing up overseas," agreed Chastity. "But after that it kind of falls apart. He doesn't have a Russian accent. And he's not exactly hiding. If the Russian government was after me I'd go off the grid in North Dakota or something rather than setting up shop as a venture capitalist in the middle of NYC. Anyway...there's only one way to learn all of a man's secrets."

"Which is what?" I asked.

"Sex."

"Well I should have seen that answer coming. So you think he'll tell me everything if I seduce him?"

"That would be the easiest thing, yes."

"But he keeps running away whenever we kiss!"

"Have you tried taking your top off and dropping to your knees? That always works for me."

"I wish he'd let me do that. But I'm not sure I could handle the embarrassment of trying that and getting rejected."

"Well then you're lucky I have a backup plan."

I reached for my wine bottle and was devastated to find that it was already empty. "I'm going to need about three more bottles of wine before I agree to let you seduce him."

"Are you asking me to have a threesome with you and Tanner?" Chastity smiled so hard. "I'm honored!"

"What? No! Who do you think I am? Madison?"

Chastity laughed. "Ew. I don't want to have a threesome with an actual lesbian. It's only good if both girls are straight."

"What?" I shook my head. "Please tell me that's not really your backup plan."

"Nope. But it's actually not a bad idea as a last resort. Single Girl Rule #28: All girls should try at least one threesome. You'll need to try it eventually. But we can talk about that later. My backup plan is to find a way to talk to some more people in the Society. Didn't Frankie mention something about him being a total player?"

"Yes." My stomach did a little backflip at the thought of him with other women.

"Well, then one of the girls he's banged must know his secrets."

"You really think so?"

Chastity nodded. "Yup. Guys talk after sex. Everyone knows that. That's why prostitutes make the best spies."

"I hate this idea."

"Well it's possible we won't have to talk to one of his former lovers. We could always seduce one of his friends. Surely his friends know his secrets."

"But we don't know any of his friends."

"True. Well, then how about some other guy at the Society? They must all be close."

"It's an interesting plan, but it'll never work. Tanner is always with me during my dates."

"Except when you blew Dr. Lyons."

I cringed. "What are the odds of him getting called away for work again during a wish?"

"He's a billionaire with like 30 different businesses, so actually quite high. But I don't think we have to worry about that. Because I've been asking around, and I've found out an interesting little morsel of information."

"Do tell."

Chastity leaned forward and whispered like she was telling me the greatest secret ever. "Apparently the Society isn't all waxings and wishes. In fact, rumor has it that the wishes are just a screening process before you get access to the real thing - a sex club called Club Onyx."

"It didn't say anything about that in the contract." I got out my phone to check the app to see if I'd missed something.

"Of course it didn't. What kind of amateurs do you think they are?"

"Fair point. So where is this Club Onyx located? And how are we going to get in? And what kind of wild stuff goes on there? Is it even crazier than the wishes?!"

"Oh, I have no idea about any of that. I just found the name of it earlier today, so I haven't had time to do much research. But I'll start digging. And we can get Madison and Liz to look into it too. Maybe Madison can like…torture a dude until he tells her or something. And if Club Onyx ever has a furry night, then it's extremely likely that Liz will have all the details."

"Oh God. If Liz has been there for a furry night, then count me out."

"Right. The Liz thing is mainly just to see if the place is a bunch of freaks that we should avoid at all costs."

"Glad we're on the same page." If Club Onyx was too freaky for Chastity, then it would *definitely* be too freaky for me. "So what's my role in all this? Try to slip away from

Tanner during the next wish to ask some people about Club Onyx?"

"If you get the opportunity, yes. But mainly you should keep getting closer to Tanner. If you open up to him more, then maybe he'll let something slip that we can use to figure out his secret. Asking him for the day off on Rosalie's birthday would be a good place to start."

Oh God. "Just being around Tanner makes me nervous. But the thought of telling him all about Rosalie makes me want to crawl into a hole and never come out. There's like a 100% chance that I'll break down crying like a crazy person in the middle of the conversation. Won't it be easier if I just like…don't show up for work that day and pretend like I got hit by a bus or something?"

"No. Come on! This is the perfect opportunity to open up to him. Just ask him tomorrow and get it over with."

"I hate my life." Mainly because I knew she was right. I had to do it. Especially because most places had a policy that required two weeks' notice for paid vacation.

"It won't be as bad as you think. Guys act weird when girls get emotional. Maybe Tanner will panic and take his pants off right then and there to try to make you feel better."

"Is that really a possibility?"

"Eh," said Chastity. "It's possible, but not likely. In my experience it only works like 33% of the time."

What? How often did Chastity cry to seduce random men? There was no time to think about that, though. Because I was already rehearsing in my head how weird it was going to be when I started crying in Tanner's office tomorrow. I tried to focus on just the image in my head of him whipping his giant dick out to comfort me.

Chapter 39

SWIMMING WITH THE SHARKS

Thursday

I gave a little knock on Tanner's open office door. I'd been working up the nerve to come talk to him all day long.

His face lit up when he looked up from his laptop and saw it was me. "Hey."

"Do you have a minute to talk?" I asked as I stepped into his office.

He glanced at his watch. "Actually, I don't. I have an appointment in 5 minutes."

"Oh." *Damn it!* I just wanted to get this over with. "No problem. It can wait until later."

Tanner waved my comment off. "It doesn't have to wait. You should just come with me."

"To your doctor's appointment?"

"Doctor? Who said anything about a doctor?"

Right. Not everyone scheduled as many doctor's appointments as I did. He was probably a normal person who only had quarterly checkups. Or was it annually for regular people? Who knew. It made sense that it was a business meeting instead.

"Shall we?" Tanner shut his laptop and stood up.

"Uh…sure."

I followed Tanner out to the elevator.

"So why'd you think it was a doctor's appointment?" asked Tanner. "Do I look sickly this afternoon?"

"Not at all." I gave him a quick up-down. Usually he wore a full suit at work, but today he'd taken his jacket off and rolled up his sleeves. His strong forearms were spectacular. "If anything, you look like a strapping young lad." *What the fuck did I just say?*

"Well that's awfully sweet of you. You're looking swell yourself." He held the elevator door open for me. "After you, m'lady."

I stepped on and tried to quickly change the subject. "Are you sure I should come? I don't even know who we're meeting."

"Neither do I. Honestly that's half the fun."

What the hell is he talking about? How could he not know who he was meeting? Then it hit me. He was a billionaire investor. Part of his job was to help his businesses grow, but he also heard pitches from new entrepreneurs who were hoping he'd give them an investment. Like on *Shark Tank*. Which meant this was going to be freaking amazing. "You're really going to let me join you?"

"Sure. It's not a big deal."

"Uh…it may not be a big deal to you. But it's a huge deal for me. I always used to dream of getting to do this. Joe kept telling me that one day we'd get to if we could grow the cupcake business big enough."

Tanner gave me a weird look. "What are you most excited about?"

"I don't really know. I've always imagined just sitting there like a total boss. But I think the best part will be closing the deal. Being able to make someone's wildest dreams come true will be such an amazing feeling."

For a second he just looked…really sad. Which made sense. I sure as hell wouldn't want someone to make investments with *my* hard-earned money.

"Wow, I'm a crazy woman making this all about me. I know that I'm just going to be sitting in the background while you do your thing."

He cleared his throat. "Don't be ridiculous. It's adorable how excited you are. I admit, I'm not thrilled by the idea of it. But I've always known this would happen eventually. It's best to just rip the Band-aid off."

I shoved his arm. "Stop. Seriously…I won't say a word. I'll just sit and watch."

"Let's just see what happens."

We stepped off the elevator at the top floor of the building. But instead of walking through a hallway lined with shark-filled tanks, we were greeted by a bubbly blonde wearing what looked like a cross between a maid uniform and very colorful lederhosen.

"Hello again," she said in a weird European accent. "If you need anything, just let me know." She hit a button and two doors slid open to a hallway. Still not lined with shark tanks.

"Thanks, Olga," said Tanner like they were old friends. "Ash here is new to all this, so it might be nice if you can walk her through the etiquette."

"Of course," she said.

"Great!" Tanner turned to me. "I'll see you in a few minutes. Room three." He walked off down the hallway.

Olga walked around the reception desk. "So there are a few things you need to know."

"Okay…"

"First, you must shower before entering the sauna."

"Sauna?"

Olga smiled. "Yes. This is a Finnish sauna. The very best in the city."

"What about the pitch meeting?" *Does Tanner conduct his pitch meetings in a Finnish sauna?* Rich people were so weird.

She ignored my question and led me down the hall to the women's room.

"There are fresh towels there," she said, pointing to a stack of pristine white towels. "Please sit on one in the sauna."

"Quick question. How likely am I to get a horrible butt fungus today?"

Olga looked shocked. "This sauna is a place of health and purity. There is no butt fungus."

"Pinky promise?"

"I do not know what that means. Any other questions?"

"Uh…" I had so many questions. Mainly I was wondering why the hell Tanner conducted his meetings here. But I also wanted to know more about their sanitation methods. I still wasn't convinced about the whole no-butt-fungus thing. I didn't think I was going to get any more out of Olga though. "Nope. I'm all set."

"Excellent. Enjoy your sauna. If you'd like a lemonade or a sausage, just order through the app."

A lemonade or a sausage? What the actual fuck?

Before I could think anymore about that gag-inducing pairing, the water in one of the showers cut off and a girl in a towel stepped out. Then she walked straight out of the bathroom, not bothering to change.

By the time she was gone, I realized that I should have followed her. Because I literally had no idea what the hell I was supposed to be doing. I would have just left, but I was still so jazzed about getting to play *Shark Tank* with Tanner. Even if I had to listen to the pitches while wearing a towel and sweating my ass off. Honestly, I would have been sweating my ass off either way from my nerves, so it probably worked in my favor that now I could blame it on the sauna.

There were still a few showers running, so I stripped out of my work clothes and threw a towel around my naked body. Yeah, I know I was supposed to shower. But I didn't want to mess up my makeup and I didn't want to get foot fungus, so the public shower was a no-go.

I waited patiently for another girl to finish showering, and then I followed her out of the bathroom. She walked down the hall and through a pair of double doors. And then we were freaking outside. On the roof of a skyscraper. In the middle of New York. *Why did no one ever talk about the fact that there were five giant wooden saunas on the roof of this building?* In winter it might have felt like Finland up here. But in late spring, it was already starting to feel a lot like a sauna.

Except for the wind, which nearly tore my towel right off my body. I reached out just in time to avoid giving all the nearby office buildings a great look at my naked body. In retrospect, I really should have kept my underwear on.

Oh well. No going back now.

I found the sauna labeled *three* and walked inside. Within half a second, I was *drenched* in sweat. But for the first time, it wasn't nervous sweat. Well, maybe a little bit. But mostly just good sweat. If that was a thing. It was more humid than Florida in the middle of summer.

My focus quickly shifted from the awful humidity to Tanner. Because he was sitting right by the stove with a towel wrapped around his waist. His skin glistened with sweat, accentuating every muscle. *Damn.* Now I was soaked everywhere, and not just from sweat.

"I was beginning to think you'd chickened out," he said, waving me over.

"No way."

His eyes went to the heels I was still wearing. "Uh, you know you're supposed to go barefoot, right?"

"Where's the fun in that?"

"I have to admit, heels and a towel is a good look for you." He patted the spot next to him. "Take a seat."

I did. And then we sat there in silence for a few minutes. Somehow it was actually really relaxing.

Eventually Tanner turned to me. "So what did you want to talk to me about earlier?"

Oh right. All this sauna nonsense had distracted me from my main mission today. "I was hoping I could have a day off. May 25th."

"Shouldn't you be asking your boss about that? I may be paying for your expertise, but you still work for BIMG."

"Yeah. But I just started a few weeks ago. I don't have any vacation days yet."

"Ah. So you want me to let you play hooky for a day? While still paying your hourly rate?"

I nodded. "Yup."

"And why would I do a thing like that?"

"Because you're such a nice guy? And I need the money."

For a second he frowned. I would have missed it if I hadn't been staring. But then he smiled, put his hands behind his head, and leaned back on the bench. "Hmmm…"

That position could only mean one thing. I could have the day off, but only if I blew him first. "Oh, I see how it is." I started putting my hair up. I couldn't have it getting in the way while I blew him. *Finally!* I couldn't wait to pull his towel down to get a look at what he was packing. And it was a win-win, because I wasn't going to even have to start talking about Rosalie and bawling my eyes out.

I was just about to yank his towel down when he said, "Okay. I'll *consider* letting you take the day off. But only on one condition."

"Anything you want." I glanced down at his crotch.

"You have to tell me why you're taking the day off."

"Oh." *So no blowjob then?* Why did I always think men were asking for it?

"Is that super tall pervert taking you somewhere fancy?"

"No. Dr. Lyons and I aren't friends anymore."

"Well that's an interesting development. What are you doing then?"

"Instead of talking about why I need the day off, I have a better idea…" I traced my finger along his hip towards his towel. This sauna was about to get even hotter.

He grabbed my hand to stop me. "Are you sure you don't want me to put a privacy sign outside?"

And miss the Shark Tank pitches? "No way."

He lowered his eyebrows. He didn't look happy. At all.

I knew a way to fix that. If he'd just let go of my hand so I could grab his penis.

Chapter 40
SAUNA SURPRISE
Thursday

Just before I could get to his towel, the door swung open and a guy walked in.

Damn it!

The newcomer tossed a little water on the stove to get it extra steamy and then dropped his towel and sat down.

I was beginning to think that I had really hit the opposite-lottery with Joe's tiny penis, because like Dr. Lyon, Angel, and Diablo, this guy had an absolute monster dangling between his legs.

"It's rude to stare," whispered Tanner.

"What? I wasn't…" I made a show of turning my head to look in the complete opposite direction of our new friend.

But that tactic quickly failed, because another beautiful man walked in and dropped his towel. He wasn't quite as impressive as our first guest. But he brazenly looked me up and down and gave me a mischievous little grin.

I turned to Tanner. "Are they supposed to be naked?" I whispered.

"Sure. Back when I lived in Finland, I saw naked people every day at the sauna. No one cares about such things there."

"You lived in Finland?"

Tanner coughed a little. "Yup. For a few years. When I was young."

"What were you doing in Finland?"

"Oh, you know. My businesses take me all over. Anyway, you still haven't told me why you want a day off."

So…he was in Finland when he was young? But also when he owned a business? What? I looked at him to try to figure out why he was lying. But the first naked dude was positioned so that his penis was *right* in my vision. "You're lying."

"What?" he asked. He sounded so guilty.

"I don't believe you lived in Finland. Because if you had, you'd be naked right now too." *Gotcha, bitch.*

"Oh." Tanner relaxed a little. "Of course I would be. But I knew you'd be joining me, and since I'm kind of your boss, I didn't want to be inappropriate."

"Are you sure about that?" I bit my lip seductively.

His eyes dropped to my lips, but he quickly looked away. "I'm sure. You made your decision. And it's for the best. We can't be together, nothing's changed."

Um…what? We'd had a good time at the museum before he left. And what was all this about making a decision? Oh God, does he know I blew Dr. Lyons?!

Three more guys walked in and all dropped their towels. Was this place always such a sausage fest? If so, I was beginning to think that maybe Tanner really didn't want to be with me because I didn't have the uh…right equipment for his taste.

"So you've gotten to sit here like a boss," said Tanner. "Which one of these fine suitors are you gonna seal the deal with?"

I stared at him. "Say what now?"

"Based on how you keep staring, my money is on him." He nodded his head towards the first guy who had walked in.

"Um. What are you talking about?"

"You said you've always wanted to surprise a stranger in a sauna. And as much as I hate the idea of it, I can't selfishly keep you all to myself when I know that we can never be together."

"Did Chastity put you up to this?"

He looked genuinely confused. "No. In the elevator like 20 minutes ago…you said you've never been in a sauna, but that you've always wanted to sit there like a total boss and then make someone's wildest dreams come true. I wasn't sure you were serious, but when you walked in here wearing nothing but a towel and heels, I figured it was really happening. But then it seemed like you were hitting on me, so I tried to get you to put up a last-minute privacy sign and you practically yelled 'no way' in my face."

"What?! No! I was talking about investing money *Shark-Tank*-style, not banging some stranger in a sauna!"

All five guys looked at me.

Oh fuck. My face turned a million shades of red. I wanted to crawl under the benches and never show my face in public again.

"The name's Karl," said the guy who had been checking me out. "Now we're not strangers anymore. And it would be my pleasure to make your sauna fantasy come true."

I stared at Tanner, praying he'd save me.

"Back off," growled Tanner. He grabbed my hand and led me away from the five naked perverts.

I couldn't help but laugh when we were safely outside. The stale city air felt so refreshing compared to the germ trap we'd just be bathing in. And once I started laughing, I couldn't stop.

Tanner started laughing too. I didn't know whether it was with me or at me. But we both couldn't stop. This could have easily been incident #6, but the fact that we were both laughing so hard made it not seem nearly as bad. I couldn't believe he thought I wanted some random sauna dude instead of him.

"Sorry about that," said Tanner as he finally composed himself. He looked so...relieved.

I wanted to do a happy dance. He was relieved that I didn't fuck some stranger in a sauna. *Because he loves me and wants me all to himself!*

Tanner smiled. "In my defense, you were *very* unclear about what you wanted."

"*I* was unclear?! You were the one who tricked me into coming to a sex sauna by telling me that I was going to get to be your right-hand man for some investment pitches." It was tempting to rip off his towel to pay him back, but instead I just poked him in his impossibly hard chest. God, I loved his muscles.

"Uh, yeah. I never said that."

"Yes you did."

"I definitely didn't. Because it wouldn't have made any sense. I just said we were going to an appointment. And that I didn't know who we were meeting."

Shit. He was right. That was exactly what he had said. "Then why did you say that not knowing who we're going to meet is half the fun?"

"Because I enjoy chatting in the sauna. It's part of the experience."

"Well damn it. That makes a lot of sense. Just for the record, I really was talking about giving out investments rather than blowjobs. I wouldn't blow someone in the sauna. I mean, other than you." *Shit!* I clapped my hand over my mouth, but I couldn't put the words back in.

Tanner raised an eyebrow. "I did kind of think you were about to blow me back there when you started putting your hair up."

"I guess you'll never know for sure. If only you hadn't been so caught up in trying to pry into my personal life."

"Speaking of which…you still need to tell me why you want that day off."

I let out a long sigh. I guess there was no getting around it. But now that I thought about it…the sauna was the perfect place to tell him. I could just pass my tears off as sweat. "Okay, let's go back in and I'll tell you."

"Uh…are you sure you want to go back in there?"

"Oh God no. Let's try a different one."

We went into sauna #2, but quickly left when we saw a girl bent over one of the benches getting absolutely railed.

"Was that Olga?" I asked.

"I didn't get a great look, but I believe so. When she said to let her know if there was anything we needed, she meant it."

"So the patrons can just ask to fuck her?"

Tanner nodded. "Yup. What else would you expect from a Finnish sauna owned by the Society?"

"This place is owned by the Society?" I asked.

"How was that not obvious?"

"I don't know! I've never been to a Finnish sauna before. I just assumed they were all this freaky."

"Not at all. I mean, yes, it is totally fine to be naked. But to make it sexual…I think most Finns would consider this a horrible desecration of their sacred pastime."

"Does the Society own any other places?" *Like a sex club called Club Onyx?* Chastity was right! "Or do they just randomly own a Finnish spa?"

"That information is highly classified," said Tanner.

Damn it!

"Now…shall we try sauna #1?"

"Only if you go first."

"You got it." Tanner went in and then called for me to come in a second later. Thankfully, we were all alone. "So let's hear it," said Tanner as he sat down on a bench. "What are you doing on your day off?"

I took a deep breath and sat down next to him. "You promise you'll give me the day off if I tell you my reasoning?"

"I promise I'll consider it."

"May 25th is the three-year anniversary of my sister's disappearance."

"Wow, I'm so sorry. I can't believe I forgot about Rosalie."

"It's okay. You…" Then something hit me. "I've never mentioned her before."

"Sure you did."

"When?"

"On our first date?"

"Nope. I definitely didn't. I would know, because saying her name practically brings me to tears. And that was purely a happy night." I stared at him. "Seriously. How do you know her name?" My mind was moving a million miles a second. First I hated that he was lying, and then I went somewhere darker. Had Tanner known her? Or been the one to make her disappear? My mind started spiraling. Had Rosalie gotten caught up in the Society? Was this place about more than just freaky sex stuff? Maybe…sex trafficking? God, his guilt was written all over his perfect face! I dug my nails into the wooden bench so I wouldn't slap him. "If you had something to do with her disappearance…"

"Whoa, what?"

"Don't play dumb with me. You knew her name. I need to know why."

Tanner scrunched his face up like I'd caught him in a terrible lie. "Promise not to hate me if I tell you the truth?"

"That depends on what the truth is." *If you murdered her, I'll take my heels off and gouge your eyes out.*

"I might have had my PI do some digging into your past."

"Excuse me?"

"It's standard procedure for Society recruiting."

"Oh my God!" I couldn't believe what I was hearing. Tanner wasn't a murderer. But he was exactly what I'd known him to be all along…a dirty stalker. "I knew it!"

"Knew what?"

"That you were stalking me."

"I prefer to call it doing my due diligence."

I shook my head. "Call it whatever you want, but the fact remains that you were stalking me."

"You wish."

"I might wish it a little bit." Actually a lot a bit. "But only if you promise you didn't kidnap my sister. Otherwise you're a horrible stalker. I mean…you did get caught, so you're a horrible stalker either way. But if you kidnapped Rosalie then you're a horrible person too."

"Of course I didn't kidnap your sister." His eyes softened. "I'm so sorry that happened. If you don't want to talk about it, I totally understand. But I'm also happy to listen."

I stared at him. Besides yelling at a bunch of useless cops who weren't looking for her hard enough and drunk-crying with Chastity, I'd mostly held all my anger and frustration and sadness inside. And it all kind of wanted to come out. But I couldn't bring myself to do it.

Tanner scooched closer to me and put his sweaty arm around me. I melted into his very naked, very sweaty side. And then I cried. Because talking about her always made me cry. It had nothing to do with how comforting his arms were. *Maybe.*

We stayed that way for who knows how long.

"I just wish she'd left a note," I said eventually. "Or anything to give me some closure. There's nothing worse than it all being a big mystery."

"Do you think you might still be able to find her?" asked Tanner.

I looked up at him. "I doubt it."

"But is it possible?"

"They never found her body. I know it's stupid, but that's why I go to the park on the anniversary of her death. I keep hoping she'll show up."

"That's not stupid at all."

"I don't know. I keep clinging onto hope, but the detective was probably right. When I pestered him about the odds of finding her, he just asked if I believed in magic."

"And do you?" asked Tanner.

"What? Believe in magic? No."

"Well, maybe you should. I certainly do."

I rolled my eyes. "Don't patronize me."

"I'm not. And if you don't believe in magic…at least believe in my PI. He's the best money can buy. And if he's not, I'll buy a better one."

"You'd ask your PI to track down Rosalie?"

"Of course. My whole family has been dead for years. And I've lost more friends than I can count. If there was a chance any of them were still alive, I'd do whatever it took to find them. And I'll do the same for you and your sister."

That was probably the nicest thing anyone had ever offered to do for me. "Thank you." I was stunned by his generosity. But also by what he'd just said. His whole family was dead? And a bunch of his friends? That was terrible. How did they all die?

"Do you want me to come with you on the 25th?" asked Tanner.

I shook my head. "I prefer to do it alone." Yes, it would be amazing to have him there with me. But what if Rosalie was going to finally come back? Seeing a strange man with me might scare her off.

"Just let me know if you change your mind."

"Does this mean I get the day off?"

"Hmmm…" Tanner made a show of thinking hard about his decision. "I guess so."

"It's good to know that you're not a heartless asshole."

"Well, I do have one other condition," said Tanner. "If I give you the day off, you're going to have to work late for the next few weeks. This launch party for Wineflix and Chill isn't going to plan itself."

I slid away from him. "I take it back. Maybe you are a heartless asshole."

"Would it help if I told you that I'll be working late with you?"

Did he just kind of ask me out? For every night of the next few weeks?! I was pretty sure he had. I tried to hide my excitement, but it was probably written all over my tear and sweat covered face.

"It seems like that's a yes."

"Maybe," I replied. But he was right. It was a definite yes. I couldn't freaking wait to spend the next few weeks working late with him. Because if the porn collection Chastity had given me was at all accurate, *working late* was synonymous with him doing filthy things to me all over the conference room table.

Chapter 41
ARCHER, MUSTANG, AND VANDAL
Wednesday, Two Weeks Later

Tanner was right - I did need to work overtime if I was going to get everything in place for the Wineflix and Chill launch party. Although my overtime during the next two weeks wasn't exactly productive. I spent most of my evening hours eating amazing takeout, secretly staring at Tanner while he worked, and asking him to tell me more stories.

Seriously, his stories were insane. He'd spent six months at a Buddhist monastery. Robes, shaved head, meditation for hours on end. The whole thing. He also showed me a scar he had from the time he got kicked by a horse while hanging out with some Brazilian gauchos. I'd yelled #HorseFacts at him and he didn't even think it was that weird. He'd just smiled at me with that perfect smile of his.

Last Friday evening we played a game where I opened up Google Maps, spun the virtual globe, and then he would tell me a story about whatever place we landed on.

Paris? He'd lived there.

Tokyo? Lived there too, and he had a full set of samurai armor to prove it.

We didn't get any work done that night, so he instituted a new rule: I could ask him one personal question each night. But beyond that, we had to focus on our work.

"Pssst," said Chastity, spinning my chair so I was forced to look at some crazy spreadsheet she'd been working on.

"What exactly am I looking at here? I thought that Wineflix and Chill wasn't going international until next year at the earliest?"

Chastity shook her head. "No, look. I've compiled a list of all the places that you've said Tanner lived or visited. And they're color-coded by how old he must have been when they happened. I mean…I'm guessing tween Tanner didn't get offered his choice of virgin while trekking through the Ugandan countryside."

"That seems like a safe assumption."

"Here's the thing…all of this stuff would have been impossible for him to do unless he'd literally been traveling non-stop since his 16th birthday."

"Hmmm…" I scanned her list to check for errors, but her logic was sound. "Well we don't know for sure that he's 28. If he was like 36 then there would have been plenty of time for all this."

"Or maybe he's a vampire like we originally thought. An immortal being would have lots of time for travel."

I sighed. I'd been giving this a lot of thought. Especially after Chastity had made a scene of not inviting Tanner into our cubicle like how you're not supposed to invite vampires into your home. He'd stared at her like she was a crazy person. Which she was. So was I, but I was really beginning to think we were wrong about this. I'd been alone with Tanner a bunch and he hadn't once tried to suck my blood. "I don't know, Chastity. I'm starting to think vampires aren't even real."

"Say what? Or course they're real. Don't you find it odd that they've been mentioned in so many ancient cultures in completely different parts of the world?"

I shook my head. "He's not a vampire. He goes out in the light all the time. And he has a reflection. Are you really going to make me waste my one question tonight to get him to confirm once and for all that he's not a vampire?"

"No. But only because I wouldn't trust his answer."

"Trust what answer?" asked Tanner.

Chastity slammed her laptop shut as we spun around.

"Nothing," we both said at the same time, sounding totally guilty.

"Well," said Tanner, "you might want to spend a little less time trying to figure out my deep dark secret and more time on the Wineflix and Chill web design."

"You wanted it by Friday, right?" I asked.

"Yes. But tomorrow is your day off, and we're not going to get much work done tonight." He locked eyes with me.

"Oh la la," said Chastity. "Why won't you be getting much work done tonight?"

Tanner gave me a mischievous smile. "It's a surprise."

I stared at him. How the hell was I supposed to focus on my work after he dropped that bomb on me?! "What kind of surprise?"

"A good one. No. A *great* one. A total gamechanger." He turned and walked back to his office.

"Oh my God!" squealed Chastity. "Tonight's the night."

"For…?"

"He's finally gonna bend you over his desk."

I laughed. "I don't know about that. I'm pretty sure he just meant he found a good new restaurant to order from."

"That wouldn't be a surprise. He gets you takeout every night."

Hmm. "Good point. And I wouldn't necessarily classify good takeout as a total gamechanger. Unless it's like…*really* good."

"What if he's going to finally ask you out?"

I wish. But I refused to get my hopes up. "He's not going to do that. Because if he does, bad people will kill me. Or something like that."

"Maybe he got rid of them."

"I doubt it. And anyway, I'm not sure he likes me like that. Two weeks ago he took me to a sauna so I could bang some rando named Karl." Kind of. It had been a terrible misunderstanding and I could still picture how upset Tanner looked when he thought I was going to go through with it. Either way, that sauna had haunted my dreams. Although not always in a bad way. Because in my dreams, Karl and his friends all looked like Tanner. And I didn't run away from them. I crossed my legs and tried not to think about it.

"That doesn't mean anything," said Chastity. "He could have just been testing you. Or maybe he's a swinger and he doesn't want to ask you out until he knows you're cool with his lifestyle."

"I guess I'll find out tonight." *Maybe.*

***

"So what's my surprise?" I asked as Tanner and I dug in to our takeout.

"You mean this Michelin-star risotto isn't a good enough surprise? In that case…" He grabbed my bowl and took it away.

"Hey! That's mine!"

"Oh? Because just a second ago you were talking about how it wasn't a worthy surprise."

"No. It was a good surprise." Just not the surprise I had been hoping for. I tried to visualize him getting on one knee and asking me out. Wait, that was how people proposed. Well…that wouldn't be so bad. I'd say yes to that. I cleared my throat when I realized he was staring at me. "But I think that calling it a game-changing surprise was overselling it a bit."

"You're right," said Tanner. "Your real surprise is like…a thousand times better than this."

I couldn't help but smile. "Well can I have it?"

"Let's wait until I'm finished eating all this." He picked up his spoon and acted like he was about to dig into my bowl.

"Don't you dare!" I snatched it back from him just in time. And then I made sure to put it well out of his reach.

"Don't I dare eat your food? Or make you wait for your surprise?"

"Eat my food. Actually, both. You know I hate waiting." *Why do we have to wait until after dinner?* That kind of did make it seem like it was gonna be a sex thing. I gulped and tried to focus on the delicious risotto rather than his delicious cock. God, why was my mind even going there? He wasn't going to ask me out. *Or is he?*

He smiled at me, like he could hear the internal struggle going on in my brain. "Don't you have a question to ask me tonight? Chastity wanted to know if I'm a vampire, yes?"

I laughed. "Nice try, buddy. But I'm not gonna waste my question on that nonsense. Tonight I'm going to get to the heart of your deepest, darkest secret."

"You're welcome to try." His eyes dropped to the side of my neck.

Holy shit. He was just trying to throw me off. *I hope.* I took a long drink of water to give myself time to decide which question I wanted to ask him. I'd narrowed it down to two options. *Where were you born?* Or… "Who was your high school crush?"

He choked on his risotto.

"Yes! I knew this was gonna be a good one."

He took a big swig of water and cleared his throat. "You know you just celebrated me nearly choking to death, right?"

"Well it sounds bad when you put it like that. But you're fine. You're talking. Now spill it. Who was your high school crush?"

"I went to an all-boys school."

"Is that your way of telling me that you experimented in high school?"

He nodded. "We did experiments, yes."

Oh my God. "With like…you and man parts?"

"Cadavers? We only used those once, if I recall correctly. Or maybe twice. It was a really long time ago."

"Ew. What? Really?" *Is he serious?! Cadavers?*

"Yes. Didn't you?"

"No. I'm pretty sure my biology teacher would have ended up in prison if he'd made us dissect a human cadaver. Now quit trying to distract me from the fact that you hooked up with dudes in high school."

Tanner nearly choked again. "Whoa, who said anything about me hooking up with dudes?"

"You did. Literally two seconds ago. I asked if you experimented, and you said yes."

He looked confused. And then something clicked. "Oh…you thought…" he laughed. "Definitely not. Your modern lingo is weird. You really think I would have screwed around with guys in high school? That would have gotten me a date with the executioner."

"That seems extreme."

"It was a different time back then." He coughed. "In the…90s."

"You went to high school in the 90s?" *What the hell? That would make him like 45 years old! Or had he been some weird genius baby?*

"No?" It looked like he was doing fast math in his head. "No. Stop trying to sneak in extra questions. You wanted to know about my high school crush, so I'll tell you about her. Her name was Sapphire. She didn't go to my school, of course, but whenever I got a chance I'd slip away from school to go meet her down by the river. I'd bring her scraps from lunch and teach her how to read."

I laughed. But when I realized that Tanner was totally serious I turned it into a cough. *What kind of backwards place did he grow up?*

"We were going to run away together once I got enough money, but my parents didn't approve."

"So your parents forced you two apart?"

He looked off into the distance, his eyes starting to water a bit. "You could say that."

"I'm sorry." I wanted to reach across his desk and give him a big hug. I'd never seen him look so sad. But he had a bad habit of running away every time I touched him. And the last thing I wanted was for him to leave. If he wanted a hug, he'd come to me. I shifted in my chair to put my hands beneath my thighs, so I wouldn't be tempted.

He forced a smile. "What about you? Who was your boyfriend in high school?"

"Boyfriend? Ha. Good one."

"What do you mean?"

"Let's just say that for my high school superlative, I won quietest."

"You say that like it's a bad thing."

"It's literally the worst superlative. They might as well have voted me biggest nobody. And anyway, I should have won best hair. Some girl with a pixie cut won it instead of me. A pixie cut!"

"Well that's ridiculous. Your hair is amazing. But I don't think being quietest means that you were a nobody. If you were a nobody, no one would have even known your name to vote for you."

Huh. He did kind of have a point. I'd never really thought of it that way. But I still hated it. "I guess."

"So no boyfriends?"

"Nope."

"The boys in your high school must have had exceptionally bad taste."

I could feel my cheeks flushing. "I dunno…you haven't seen any pictures of me in high school."

"Sure I have. My PI was very thorough with his report."

"Oh God. No wonder you made up a mysterious organization who will boil me in a vat of acid if we start dating."

Tanner laughed. "I thought you looked adorable."

"Right." Adorable. Cute. He always said that about me. "Unfortunately for me, adorable was not what Mustang and Vandal were into. They seemed to be more into double-teaming the head cheerleader in the locker room. God, what I would have given to be in her position..." *Please tell me I didn't say that out loud.*

"You wanted to be double-teamed by two dudes with weird names?"

"What? No."

"You just said you did." Tanner looked so amused.

"In my defense, I didn't mean to say that out loud."

He looked more amused than ever. "So those were your crushes? Mustang and Vandal?"

"I don't know if I'd call them crushes. They were just really hot guys that I watched from afar."

"Ah, so your stalkery ways started in high school."

I tossed my napkin at him. "We've already determined that *you're* the stalker. Not me."

"Mhm. Sure. So tell me more about these guys you stalked." He leaned back in his chair, looking absolutely tickled.

"Mustang and Vandal were the class clowns. One time they put…" I started laughing just thinking about it. "They put a horse on the roof of the school. I still have no idea how they did it."

"That must have been a disaster since horses can't climb down stairs very well. #HorseFacts," said Tanner.

Oh my God, I love you. He was just as bad at hashtags as me. I giggled. "Exactly."

"Did you ever talk to them?"

"Nope. But I'm proud to say that I did talk to my ultimate crush, Archer Murphy."

"Oh yeah?"

"Yup," I said with a nod. "He asked to borrow a pen. And I said yes."

"And that was the beginning of a long, unlikely friendship?"

"Not at all. It was the only time I ever talked to him. Other than when he returned the pen. Which was exactly why I liked him so much. Sure, he was the captain of the football team, had ridiculous 8-pack abs, and could make me melt just with his smile. But what really got me was that he was the only person to have the decency to actually return my pen after borrowing it. As far as I was concerned, that was the epitome of sexiness."

"Well, he missed out. And let's be honest...you probably dodged a bullet by not dating him. I'd bet money that he peaked in high school."

"He got a football scholarship to Notre Dame. But sophomore year he busted up his knee and that was the end of that."

"Okay, stalker."

I tossed another napkin at him. "Facebook stalking isn't stalking. And let's not forget - you're the one who hired a PI to stalk me."

"Speaking of my PI...he just texted me and asked if he could swing by to talk to you about Rosalie."

My heart skipped a beat. "Does that mean he found something?! Is this my surprise?!" If it was, I was 100% going to jump over Tanner's desk and make out with him.

He shook his head. "Sorry, I should have been more clear. Marty - my PI - has been looking into her disappearance. As part of that, he wants to come interview you. He thought tonight would be best, because he's found that people can usually recall stuff better near the anniversary of when it happened."

"Oh."

"You up for that?"

I nodded. I didn't love the idea of talking all about it with some stranger. But if there was even half a chance that he might find her, I wasn't going to pass up the opportunity.

"He's the best in the business," said Tanner as he walked around his desk.

I held my breath for a second as he leaned down. Instead of a kiss, he gave me a big hug. It was just as good as I kiss. I felt myself melt into him.

"If anyone can find something, he can," Tanner said.

I breathed in his blueberry scent. It didn't make me forget about Rosalie, but it was a damned good distraction. And so were the muscles in his back. And the realization that I *still* hadn't gotten my surprise.

I looked up at him. "So is it time for my surprise? I could really use the distraction." And I was going to explode from anticipation if he didn't tell me in the next five seconds. Unless the PI coming was the surprise. Just because he hadn't found out anything yet, didn't mean he wouldn't. And now I just looked super ungrateful.

Tanner let go of me and stepped back.

Shit. He thinks I'm a monster.

"Okay, okay. I guess I've tortured you long enough."

Thank God. "And...?"

"Close your eyes."

I did. *Where is he going with this?* It sounded like he was walking behind his desk. Chastity must have gotten in my head, because I was about 80% sure he was gonna climb onto his desk and shove his dick in my mouth. *Finally!* But I totally should have put some Chapstick on. What had I been thinking coming in here with dry lips?!

It took all my self-control not to peek. Because it sounded like he was opening a desk drawer. For a condom, perhaps? Or maybe not. The Society contract made it sound like they were a condom-free organization. My heart started beating faster. What sinful things was he about to do to me?

"Hold out your hands," said Tanner.

So we'll start with a handjob, then. I held out my hands. It wasn't lost on me that he thought I was gonna need to use both hands to corral him.

"Ready?" he asked.

"Yes." I'd been ready for weeks.

"You sure?"

"Yes!"

Something cold and smooth fell into my hands. Definitely not a penis. *Darn.*

"Can I look?"

"Yup. Open your eyes."

Chapter 42

TOP SECRET

Wednesday

I opened my eyes and looked down at my brand new…sunglasses?

"What exactly am I looking at here?" I asked.

"Your surprise."

"So let me get this straight. My game-changing surprise is a brand-new pair of sunglasses?" They weren't even normal sunglasses. They were more like a weird futuristic shield for my eyes.

"Yes." Tanner looked so please with himself.

"Thanks?"

"You're welcome. I figured you'd want to wear them while Spaceboy performs at our launch party."

I blinked and then stared at him. "Don't mess with me like that." A few days ago I'd jokingly suggested that we invite DJ Spaceboy to our party, knowing full well that it would never happen. I figured he was too busy polishing his Grammys or banging groupies in his ten thousand square foot Beverly Hills mansion.

"I'm serious," said Tanner.

What?! "Just so we're on the same page. You're telling me that *the* DJ Spaceboy agreed to come to some random launch party for a virtually unheard-of winery? Will Taylor Swift be attending as well?"

"No. Why would we have two headliners? We aren't throwing a music festival - we're having a launch party."

"Oh my God. You're being serious. You really got DJ Spaceboy?!" I couldn't believe him. He was freaking amazing. I was pretty sure I'd single-handedly paid for his aforementioned Beverly Hills mansion with all the ad revenue he got from me watching his videos non-stop on YouTube.

"I had to call in a favor with an old friend. DJ Spaceboy demanded that we move the party to a yacht, but yes. I got him."

I stood on my tippy-toes and gave Tanner a big kiss. I didn't care that we were supposed to be just friends. It felt like forever ago that I'd told him I wasn't interested. And he must have known I was lying. Because I was. And this wonderful man deserved a kiss. Actually, he deserved a lot more than a kiss. I didn't want to scare him off though. And as a cherry on top of my already perfect surprise, he actually kissed me back.

And kissed me.

And kissed me some more.

I had to step backwards to keep from falling over. Tanner used that momentum to push me back against the wall. I opened my mouth wider, letting him in. *Yes!*

I wanted it to last forever. But a little voice in the back of my head knew that Tanner was going to come to his senses soon and push me away. Just like he always did. And then things would be painfully awkward for the next week or so.

I couldn't let that happen. I bit at his lower lip and then pushed with all my might to force him off of me.

"Excuse me, sir," I said. "I think you were getting dangerously close to doing something inappropriate with your favorite employee."

He raised an eyebrow. "That was nothing more than a congratulatory peck between coworkers."

"Right. A congratulatory peck. Glad we're on the same page." I smoothed my skirt out and fixed my hair. And then I shook his hand. Because that seemed like something colleagues would do whilst congratulating each other on a big win.

Tanner stared at me for a long second and then went to sit behind his desk. Which was probably for the best. Without that space between us, our congratulatory peck easily could have turned into a congratulatory fuck.

I sat across from him. I needed to compose myself and get us back on track. Because that was the only way to keep him from freaking out. And honestly, I was already freaking out enough for the both of us. *He kissed me back!* I cleared my throat. "So the launch party we've been planning for the last two weeks - a laid back sweatpants-party after hours at a furniture store - is now a yacht party headlined by Spaceboy?"

"Correct. Why do you think I told you to get that website finished? We have a crap-ton of work to do if we're gonna pull this off. This is gonna be the party of the century."

We went back to the drawing board with our planning. At first I was a little concerned that getting Spaceboy - as amazing as it was - wasn't going to fit the brand. But Tanner and I put our heads together and came up with a pretty epic plan. It was so tempting to text Chastity to tell her the good news, but it didn't seem like a text could do this justice. And I really wanted to see her face when she found out. She was going to absolutely lose her shit.

I was planning out different epic ways to drop the news to her when Tanner's PI, Marty, walked into the conference room. I was about to have to relive the day Rosalie disappeared. And just like that, all the exciting energy I had immediately switched to nervous energy. Or…actually, I was still kind of excited. Because seeing how closely he resembled Liam Neeson immediately gave me hope that we would find her. And also hope that he would kill everyone involved in a totally epic action sequence and then say some badass line to make the kidnappers look like a bunch of little bitches.

"Pleasure to meet you, Miss Cooper," he said. His voice was even deep and gravelly like Liam's.

"Thanks for coming," I said.

"No problem." He pulled up a chair and got ready to jot some notes down in a folder labeled TOP SECRET. "So here's how this works. I don't know if this case is going to take two days or two years. But I promise you that I will do my very best to find out what happened to your sister. And when I do, I'll send you the report. When I first started, I used to send weekly updates to my clients. But that just wasted my time and got my clients hopes up for no reason. So until you get my report, assume I have no new information. Got it?"

I nodded. It was going to drive me crazy waiting, but I'd have to deal.

"Good. So I've read the police reports and have a general sense of what happened, but I'd love to get your take on that day."

I took a deep breath and closed my eyes. It had been three years, but I could still picture the day perfectly. I opened my eyes and tried to focus on Marty instead of Tanner, who was watching me silently. "Okay. So it was May 25th, 2020. Rosalie's 23rd birthday. I woke up at 5 a.m. sharp, baked Rosalie's birthday cupcakes, and then biked over to Belvedere Lake. Ever since she'd moved to the city, that was where we would meet on her birthday. We'd hang out all day laughing and having fun." *Those were my favorite days.*

"And when did each of you move to the city?" asked Marty.

"Um… Joe and I moved here after I graduated from college. Summer of 2017. Rosalie transferred to NYCU that fall."

Marty made a few notes. "Got it. And what was the significance of Belvedere Lake?"

"It was more about the castle than the lake. God, she loved that castle. She always said that someday she'd live in a castle like that." My voice caught in my throat as I said it. *And now she'll never get the chance.*

Tanner walked over and put his hand on my shoulder. "We'll find her, Ash. And we'll find her a castle to live in."

The thought made me smile. Even if there was no way he'd actually be able to make good on that promise. Well...he could certainly buy her a castle. But the odds of him finding her were slim.

"So you baked your cupcakes and headed to the lake," said Marty. "Then what?"

"I expected to find her sketching Belvedere Castle, but instead, all I found was her half-finished sketch lying in the grass. And Rosalie was nowhere to be seen."

"Half-finished? Can you put that in terms of minutes? And what time did you arrive? If you can give me some estimates, then I can put it all together to determine roughly what time Rosalie disappeared."

Damn. That was smart. I'd never thought to do that, and the cops investigating her case certainly hadn't. But there was just one problem. "I know I got there just before 8 a.m. But Rosalie and punctuality were not friends. She was a free spirit. She'd always make plans with me, but I never knew for sure if she'd show up. And don't get me started about her art... Sometimes she'd work on a piece for twenty minutes and then frame it on her wall. Other times she'd work for days and it would end up in the trash. So I have no idea how long she'd been there."

Marty nodded. "No problem. And do you remember if it was particularly windy?"

"Uh...no. Why?"

He waved it off. "I can check the forecast from that day. If it was windy, then it's unlikely that her drawing would have lingered on the ground for very long. Putting her time of disappearance closer to your arrival."

Another thing I'd never thought of. I closed my eyes and put myself back at the park on that day. "Actually...I do remember. It was a beautiful day. Not a cloud in the sky. And just a slight breeze." Her birthday was always perfect. Just like her.

Marty took more notes. "Got it. Please continue."

I kept my eyes closed and relived the horror of that day. "I texted her. Called her. Waited for her. I wasn't too worried at that point. Like I said…she was kinda flaky. I assumed she'd forgotten something at home or something. After an hour, I got tired of waiting and went by her apartment."

Marty flipped through his notes and asked me to confirm her address and the time that I'd arrived there.

I nodded. "I tried calling her work and her friends. No one had heard from her all day. And no one…" I stopped and brushed a tear off my cheek. "No one ever heard from her again."

Tanner handed me a tissue from his desk.

"The police got involved that night. They brought out sniffing dogs and made a whole scene of searching the entirety of Central Park. The news picked up the story. The whole city was searching for my sweet, beautiful sister. I'd been so hopeful those first few days. With so many people involved, how could we not find her? But as no clues turned up, the public lost interest. And then the police did too. I think the case is technically still open, but I'm pretty sure it's just a file in some database. I doubt any cop has thought about Rosalie in years."

The look on Marty's face told me I was right.

"I haven't forgotten about her, though. And I still go to the lake every year on her birthday. My stupid ex-husband would come too. We'd eat her favorite cupcakes and I'd sit around telling him all my favorite stories about her. Even if she was gone, telling the stories made it feel like a little part of her was still with me. And then when the sun had set and my voice was hoarse from talking so much, we'd leave one cupcake for her and go home."

"Maybe when you go tomorrow she'll be there waiting for you," said Tanner to try to cheer me up. It was a nice thought - and that idea was partially why I went back every year - but nothing was going to stop the tears running down my cheeks. It felt like it had just happened yesterday.

"Do you remember…" started Marty, but Tanner cut him off.

"I think that's enough for today," said Tanner. I'd never heard him sound so stern.

"No," I said, sniffing back the snot threatening to run down my face. "I want to answer all his questions." I needed to be strong for Rosalie. I turned back to Marty. "What do you need to know?"

"Was Rosalie acting strange at all before she disappeared?"

"Not really." I blotted away my tears as quickly as I could. "She'd been distant for a few weeks, but that was nothing out of the ordinary. Depending on how wrapped up in her art she was, I wouldn't hear from her for weeks. And then she'd call me every day for a month."

"Had anyone new come into her life recently?"

"Yes, but I'd be hard-pressed to tell you who. She was always getting new roommates and dating new boys. Every time I talked to her it seemed like she had a new boyfriend."

"From a dating app?"

"Uh. I know she was on Tinder at one point. But then she got tired of that and tried another. And then she claimed to give up dating apps altogether, but her endless stream of suitors continued."

The questions continued like this for at least another hour. I tried to get a read on if my information was helping at all, but Marty was a brick wall. His face betrayed nothing. But his questions gave me hope. There were at least three times when he pulled some obscure detail out of my brain that I had never thought was important.

"I think that's everything I need," said Marty eventually. "As soon as I have conclusive evidence, you'll be the first to know." He grabbed his TOP SECRET folder and left as quickly as he'd come.

I let out a deep sigh. Reliving all that had been so draining.

"I'm so sorry you had to go through all that," said Tanner.

"Marty wasn't *that* bad. I'd go through his questioning a million times over if it will help him find Rosalie."

Tanner laughed. "I meant Rosalie disappearing. But yeah, Marty can definitely be a little insensitive." He handed me another tissue. "Are you sure there's nothing I can do to help make tomorrow a little less painful for you?"

I shook my head. Having him see me ugly-cry for the past hour had been horrifying enough. I couldn't deal with him seeing how much of a mess I'd be tomorrow.

"Okay. Well if you change your mind, just…"

"Actually," I said. "There is one thing you could do."

He raised an eyebrow. "Anything."

All my instincts were telling me not to ask. I'd already pushed my luck enough by making out with him. But he'd offered… "I wouldn't mind going out to dinner tomorrow night."

He stared at me.

Oh shit. Was he about to freak out? I couldn't handle that on top of everything else. "You know…to work on the launch party," I added. "We need to take advantage of every second we can get if we're gonna pull this thing off. And I could use the distraction." *Of you. I could use the distraction of you.*

"You got it," said Tanner. "I'll pick you up at your place at 8?"

"Sure. My address is…"

"I know your address."

"Of course you do. Stalker."

"I mean…what do you expect when I have Marty working for me? He's very thorough."

"I'd like to change my answer. Going to dinner tomorrow will be nice, but it would really cheer me up if you admitted that you were the one stalking me."

"So you want me to lie to you?"

I slapped his arm. "You're ridiculous."

"Maybe. But at least I'm not a stalker."

I laughed. Even though he hadn't admitted his stalkery ways, he'd still managed to cheer me up. And he'd agreed to go on a date! This was freaking huge. It was going to be our first real date outside of the Society.

Tomorrow was going to be rough. But tomorrow night was going to be everything.

Chapter 43

SON OF A DICK

Thursday

This year I didn't bring the cupcakes. But I still went to the lake. The grass was slick with dew so I laid out a beach towel and plopped myself down.

I stared at the castle for a while, thinking about when Rosalie had tried to convince me to sneak in after dark and sleep there as if it were our house. I pulled my knees into my chest. I'd been too lame to do it. Now I really wished I had.

I rested my chin on one of my knees and I blinked, trying not to cry.

I felt like I should be telling a story about her, but there was no one to talk to. So instead I decided to talk to her.

"Hey Ros," I said to the air. "I miss you." I paused, choking back the tears. "I miss you so much."

Stop. I shouldn't cry. As her older sister, it was my job to be her shoulder to cry on. Not the other way around. And with all the boys she always had chasing after her, she frequently needed a shoulder to cry on. *She'd know what to do about my current boy situation.*

"So I need your advice," I said. "I met this amazing guy, but he claims it would be too dangerous for us to be together…"

"Sounds complicated," said someone behind me.

I looked over my shoulder and saw Joe standing there, holding a box of Dickson & Son's Sugarcakes. *What the hell?* He was the last person I wanted to see ever. And today of all days? I was grieving.

"Mind if I sit?" he asked. But he didn't wait for my answer. He just sat down next to me. On *my* beach towel.

"Yes, I do mind if you sit," I snapped, yanking the towel out from under him. I stomped across the clearing and sat down in a new, Joe-free spot. Maybe someone else would find it sweet that he'd remembered how important today was to me. But that someone wasn't me. I hated him. And he had no right to interrupt Rosalie's birthday. I just wanted to be alone.

He followed me. "Ash, don't be like this."

"Go away." I hated that my voice quivered. Because I really could use a hug. *Don't you dare think like that, Ash.*

"No."

"Why are you here, Joe? Would it kill you to not be an asshole for a single day?" He knew what today was. He knew how much I missed my sister. Why the hell did he have to pick today of all days to show up in my life again?

"I know we didn't end on good terms…"

"You think?" I scoffed.

"…but I thought you might need a friend today. Someone to talk to."

"You're not my friend." But there was a small part of my heart that thawed. Just a little.

"Fine. A person."

"You're not a person. You're a monster." Just because a small part of my heart had thawed didn't mean the rest of it didn't hate his guts.

Joe sat down next to me. "I deserve that. Want a cupcake?" He pushed the box toward me.

I shook my head. "You mean a cupcake made with the recipe you stole from me?"

He stayed silent.

"God, I wish I had listened to Rosalie about you. She always knew you were an asshole."

"I thought she liked me?"

"No. She hated you."

"More than Madison hates me?" asked Joe.

"God no. By the way, you should keep an eye out for her. She's been lobbying hard for me to cut your dick off."

"Maybe then she'd like me. You know…since she hates penises."

I laughed. "I'm actually not sure about that. A few weeks ago she got super drunk and admitted to wanting, and I quote, 'The biggest, blackest man.' "

Joe laughed too. "Are you kidding me?"

"I swear." I couldn't help the smile on my face.

"Well I'll be damned." Joe shook his head.

I started to laugh more but it got caught in my throat. What the hell was happening? Was I seriously sitting here with Joe making lesbo jokes about Madison? It felt so natural. I looked down at the grass so I wouldn't be tempted to look at him. "What happened to us?" I asked.

Joe sighed. "I don't know, Ash."

"Was it this?" I asked. "Rosalie going missing? Chastity says I kind of changed after that."

"You want the truth?"

"Yes." I looked back up at him. "God, yes." I needed to know why I hadn't been good enough. Because I wasn't sure how to move on when I felt so…unwanted. I hated that feeling. Of just being stuck. And ever since Chastity had brought it up, a piece of me wondered if that was why I was chasing Tanner. Because he swore he couldn't be in a relationship with me for my own safety. We'd never move forward. We'd always be stuck. I swallowed hard.

"That might have played a small part. But we were doomed before that. I'm not sure we were ever really right for each other."

"Then why'd you propose to me?"

"I think I just got caught up in the moment. I was intrigued by your innocence. And your refusal to have sex until marriage. It made you kind of a forbidden fruit that I just had to pluck."

I gagged a little. "Gross."

"We were in college. We were young. I don't know what to say."

"Apologizing would be a good start."

"I'm sorry. Rosalie was right - I'm an asshole."

I laughed. *Yes, you are.* I considered asking about Sierra. About him cheating on me. But what could I really say? *Do you love her? Were you really fucking her almost our entire marriage?* I knew the answers to both of those. Yes, and yes. Hearing him say it would just make it more real. And I couldn't handle that. Not today.

"Maybe I will take one of those cupcakes after all," I said.

Joe smiled and put the box on my lap. "Be my guest. I even brought you a fork."

I flipped open the lid and stabbed a delicious-looking banana protein cupcake (one of my best recipes, thank you very much). I was about to take a big bite when I noticed a picture taped to the inside of the lid. No, not just any picture. A picture of me. Naked. Touching myself on our bed. It was a screenshot from the sex tape I'd made for him.

"What the fuck?" I said, slamming the lid shut in case any strangers happened to be walking by. My heart was beating so fast that it actually hurt. Or maybe it hurt because for just a second, I had thought Joe wasn't actually the most evil person on the planet.

"What?" asked Joe, acting totally innocent.

"Don't pretend like you don't know what I'm talking about."

"Oh. The picture?"

"Yes."

He opened the lid and looked at it. "It's a great picture. I'm thinking it'll be what I use for the thumbnail when I post your video to Pornhub."

My body felt like it was on fire. "Are you fucking kidding me? I gave you everything you asked for," I hissed.

"You did. But then you stole my credit card and spent…" He pulled a folded piece of paper out of his pocket and scanned down it with his finger. "…$213,436."

"Dude, that wasn't me. It was probably your instawhore."

Joe glared at me. "How dare you talk about Sierra like that?"

"How dare *I*? How dare *you* fuck her for four years behind my back. What'd she spend the money on? Another pair of fake tits? Or maybe more Botox?"

"*You* spent the money on Odegaards. Chastity convinced you to go on a little shopping spree, huh?"

Oh shit. Tanner hadn't used Joe's card when we were together at the boutique. He'd said it was declined. But he'd never given it back to me. Was it possible he used it to buy me all those shoes later? I tried to hide my look of guilt, but it was too late.

"I knew it," said Joe.

"Knew what? I swear it wasn't me." My voice cracked.

Joe laughed. "You've always been such a terrible liar."

Asshole. "You know what I'm not terrible at?"

"What?"

"This." I grabbed my cupcake and smooshed it in his face. God that felt good.

He wiped the icing out of his eye. "Real mature, Ash."

I took another cupcake and did it again.

"You know what? I was going to give you two days to give me a refund, but you just cut that time in half."

"A refund how? You took everything from me in the divorce. I'm barely scraping by."

"If the money isn't in my account by midnight, the sex tape goes live. Enjoy Rosalie's birthday. Thank God she didn't live long enough to see how much of a slut you are." Joe got up and walked away.

For a second I just sat there, completely stunned. Not that anything he'd done was surprising. Joe had just acted completely like…Joe. I tried to yell something mean at him, but my mind was blank. My body shook with a combination of rage and sadness. I buried my face in the towel and sobbed. Big, fat, ugly tears.

I wanted to just crawl into the lake and drown. How could I have fallen for Joe's trick? For a few minutes I had genuinely thought that there was some shred of decency in him…that he had actually come here because he cared about me and didn't want me to be alone. But really he had just come here to shit all over me. And to do it on today of all days? He wasn't just an asshole. He was heartless. He was the devil. How could I have ever fallen for a man like that? What did that say about me?

I could dwell on that later. But for now, I had bigger issues to deal with. Because if I couldn't come up with $200K by midnight, then the most mortifying footage of me was going to be all over the internet. I'd never be able to show my face in public again.

"I'm sorry, Rosalie," I said into the air. "But I have to go take care of this. And next year, after Marty finds you, we can come back here together."

I took one last look at the castle and then typed out a text to Tanner. "Can you be at my place in ten minutes? I need your help."

Chapter 44

REFUND EMERGENCY

Thursday

Tanner was waiting for me outside my apartment building. Concern was etched all over his perfect face.

"Is everything okay?" he asked as I approached. He frowned even harder, presumably because of my puffy eyes and running make-up.

"Not really."

He pulled me into a hug. I felt so safe in his arms. His big, stupid, stealing arms. I pushed him off. "You lied to me."

"About…?"

"Joe's credit card. The shoes. You said the card got declined."

"Oh, right." He looked so pleased with himself. "Yeah, I did lie about that."

What the hell, man? "I need you to undo whatever you did."

"And why would I do that?"

"Because Joe came to the park this morning and threatened…"

Tanner waved it off. "Don't listen to him. The police will laugh him out of the station."

"What?!" I screamed. People were starting to stare at me. "Now I'm gonna get arrested?! Since when is it illegal to make a film of yourself? I was over 21. I can prove it." *Right?* Was there some law I didn't know about when it came to filming solo sex tapes? *Oh God, oh God, oh God.*

Tanner lowered his eyebrows. "Whoa, slow down. Illegal film? What are you talking about?"

"What are *you* talking about?" I asked.

"The credit card. Dumb-Dumb Joe forgot to take your name off the account. So technically all you did was buy $200,000 worth of Odegaards with your own money."

I shook my head. "He's not threatening to have me arrested."

"Oh. Then what's he threatening? What film are you talking about?"

"There's a uh…" I looked around. I really did not want to have this conversation on a public sidewalk. Or with Tanner, really. But I didn't have a choice here. I had no idea how to fix this. And he might. "Can we go up to my place to talk about this?"

"Of course," said Tanner. "Whatever it is, I'm sure we can sort it out."

I was drenched in sweat by the time we reached my apartment door. This was going to be the most awkward conversation of my life.

"Wow. That's a lot of shoes," he said the minute we walked in the door. "I totally did not think about closet space when I sent you all these."

"Damn right it's a lot of shoes," I said. "That's what got us into this mess in the first place. Wouldn't it have been enough to buy like…two pairs? Rather than 70?"

"Do you not like them?"

"Not if they get my sex tape leaked all over the internet!"

Tanner raised both eyebrows. "A sex tape?"

"Yes! Joe has a sex tape of me. He held it over my head to take everything from me in the divorce. That's why I live in this dumb little apartment. And now he's threatening to post the tape on Pornhub unless he gets his 200 grand back before midnight."

"For real? And he hit you with all this on today of all days?" Tanner looked *pissed.* I had never seen him look so upset before. "What an asshole."

"That's not all. He pretended to come in peace. Said he didn't want me to be alone on Rosalie's birthday. And then after we shared what I thought was a genuine, nice moment, he sprung this on me. Oh, and he finished things off nicely by telling me that it was good Rosalie was dead so that she'd never learn how much of a slut I am."

Tanner made a noise, almost like a growl. Dark circles formed around his eyes. His anger was somewhat terrifying. And also kind of sexy. *And vampiric?*

"I'm gonna kill him," he said.

"As much as he definitely does deserve to die, I'd really prefer if we just give him his money back. He's not worth you going to prison for murder." Then I thought about what I had done. I just asked Tanner to give my ex $200,000 like it was nothing. Which it kind of was for Tanner…but still. I couldn't ask him to do that. "I'll find a way to pay you back for the shoes. I'll work overtime until I'm old and gray. Or maybe we can just return them? Do they even have a return policy at fancy places like that? Just please don't let him leak that tape."

"That tape will never see the light of day. I promise."

I let out a sigh of relief. "Thank you."

"And don't worry about the shoes. They were free."

"But someone…"

"Well, they cost a bit to manufacture. But it wasn't close to $200K. Odegaard has pretty healthy profit margins. Compared to some of my other businesses, at least."

What? I gaped at him. "You own Odegaard?"

"Well, technically I *am* Odegaard."

"Didn't that brand start in the late 60s? Mr. Odegaard must be at least 80 years old."

Tanner cleared his throat. "Long story. Anyway, back to that sex tape of yours. What's on it? Is it like a solo deal, or…"

I slapped his arm. "Ugh, stop. Men are disgusting."

He put his hands up. "I was only asking so I'd be sure I get the right tape from Joe. All the copies of it."

"Sure you were," I said, rolling my eyes. "But…you really think you can get him to give you all the copies?"

"Yes."

"And how exactly are you gonna do that? Have Marty burst into his apartment and waterboard him until he hands them over?"

Tanner considered it. "I guess that would work. But I have a better idea."

"Are you sure we can't do the Marty thing?"

"Trust me. I got this." There was no doubt in his voice. And that made me believe him.

"God, I wish I'd never made that tape. I'm such an idiot."

"There's nothing wrong with making a sex tape. Everyone's doing it these days. The Society even has a workshop about it on the first Tuesday of every month. They have some really interesting pointers about lighting and camera angles. But I think they might under-emphasize the important of not sending your sex tape to an asshole." He pulled a little black book out of his jacket and jotted something down. "I guess you're probably not going to be making any more sex tapes after this though, huh?"

"Nope. Now can we please focus?"

"Hmm?" He closed his notebook and looked back up at me. "Oh, right. We need to get your tape back. Just give me one moment…" He opened his computer bag and pulled out a golden genie lamp. "Just rub the lamp and wish for your sex tape back from Joe."

I crossed my arms. Tanner's antics were usually funny, but not at a time like this. "Are you serious right now? You really went out and bought a genie lamp just to mess with me?"

"You mean the way you bought me garlic bread and threatened me with holy water?" he asked, deadpan.

"How many times do I have to apologize for that?"

Tanner tapped his finger against his lips. "Probably about three more times."

"I'm sorry. I'm sorry. And I'm sorry. Now can you please go get my sex tape? This isn't a joke."

"I told you. Rub the lamp..."

You've got to be kidding me. This wasn't the time for jokes. He was seriously bad at reading the room. "Fine. Toss it to me."

He looked horrified. "You want me to toss my lamp? How would *you* feel if someone asked you to throw your most prized possession?"

This was getting ridiculous. No. It was beyond ridiculous. But he clearly wasn't going to do anything until I played his stupid genie lamp game. So I walked over to him and grabbed his stupid lamp. I expected it to look like cheap dollar store plastic, but based on how much it weighed, it might have actually been solid gold. *Of course it is - he's a billionaire.* "How much did this thing cost?"

"It's priceless."

"Mhm." I rubbed the side of the lamp. It made my fingers feel all weird and tingly. Almost like an electric shock, but the jolt didn't hit me all at once. I pulled back. "Happy?"

"You have to make your wish."

"Oh, right. I wish for..."

Tanner put his hand up to stop me before I could finish making my wish. "Be careful with how you word it. I'm not mean-spirited, but as a genie, I do tend to have a bad habit of misconstruing wishes."

I pursed my lips. This whole genie thing stopped being funny about five minutes ago. "I wish for you to get all of the copies of my sex tape from Joe Dickson."

Tanner nodded approvingly. "Well done. Especially for a first wish."

"I'm glad you approve. Now can you *please* go deal with Joe? We only have until midnight!" I was seconds away from having a total meltdown and throwing Tanner's new shiny toy across the room.

"Yup. Just give me one moment here..." He rubbed his hands together and then snapped his fingers.

I glared at him. He really needed to learn when it was appropriate to joke and when he needed to be serious. "Are you done messing around?"

Tanner ignored my question. Instead, he pulled a flash drive out of his jacket pocket and tossed it to me.

"What's this?" I asked.

"Your sex tape. What else would it be?"

I shook my head. "That's not…that's not possible." He hadn't moved.

"Check it."

I pulled out my laptop and plugged in the flash drive. There was a single video file on it. I clicked the file and… *Oh my God!* I slammed my laptop shut before Tanner could see. "How did you get this?"

"Magic," he said with a wink.

I shoved his arm. He was such an idiot. A sexy, wonderful, prankster of a perfect man. "I can't believe you had it this whole time. I was literally dying inside thinking Joe was gonna leak it. Is this the only copy?"

"Nope." Tanner reached into his jacket and pulled out three more flash drives.

"Seriously, how did you get these?"

"I told you. Magic." It looked like he was unsuccessfully trying to hold back a smile.

"You're infuriating." *And amazing.* God, he really had me going. "You're *sure* these are all the copies?"

Tanner nodded.

A wave of relief rushed over me. Finally, after all this time, I was free from the fear that Joe might leak it. And it was all thanks to Tanner. How could I ever repay him? I was free! I was finally fucking free of Joe's threats! Without thinking, I jumped into Tanner's arms and kissed him.

He hadn't been expecting it. He stumbled backwards and fell onto the sofa. I straddled him as I ran my hands through his long hair. With all the stress gone, all I could think about was devouring him.

"Thank you," I muttered between kisses.

His strong hands ran along my rib cage and up to my tits. I thrust my hips against him. I could feel him getting hard. *Yes!* I'd been dreaming of this moment for weeks.

I pushed his jacket off his broad shoulders and ran my hands over his abs. I wanted to explore every inch of him. To feel him inside of me. To taste his cum on my lips.

And I could tell he wanted it too. He squeezed my ass and groaned into my mouth. "Ash…"

I silenced him with a kiss.

It's finally happening! My whole body was alive. The sensation of every touch was magnified by a million. And yet…a little voice in the back of my head was screaming that I should stop. Because right now I was on cloud nine. Everything was perfect. But if we got any further and he rejected me…

Fuck.

I let myself enjoy him for a few more seconds - to taste his lips, feel his abs - and then I pulled back.

He reached for me to bring me back, but I dodged.

Shit! I knew how it felt to be rejected. Was that how I'd just made him feel? This was the second day in a row I'd been the one to put the brakes on our sexy time. Although…he kind of deserved it after that genie nonsense. That had been cruel and unusual to make me squirm like that when he freaking had the flash drives the whole time.

And then I got a wonderful idea. I grabbed his lamp off the table. It was time for a little payback.

"So how many wishes does this thing grant me?"

"Three," he said matter-of-factly.

"Alright then…" What was it that he had said when he'd first joked about being a genie? Something about a flaming genie penis? It was time to throw that nonsense back in his face. "I wish for…"

He held up a hand. "Remember, be careful how you word it."

I sighed. He was insufferable. "I wish for you to no longer have a flaming genie penis," I said as I rubbed his ridiculous lamp.

"Sweet lord, Ash!" He snatched the lamp out of my hand. "I just told you to be careful how you word your wishes. If that wish wasn't disallowed by rule three of the Genie Code of Magic, then you would have just turned me into a eunuch."

I laughed. "Oopsies."

"Oopsies?! I quite like having a penis, thank you very much."

Then maybe you should use it on me.

"Now, if I give this back to you, will you be more careful? And leave my penis out of your wishes?"

"Maybe." I grabbed the lamp from him. It was a shame that I wasn't allowed to make any more wishes about his penis. Because I wanted nothing more than to drop to my knees and taste him. Although, if Dr. Lyons was anything to go by, it wouldn't exactly be the most pleasant taste.

That's it! I had the perfect wish. Or rather, the perfect two wishes. I rubbed his lamp and made my wish: "I wish for cum to taste like cookies."

"Your wish is my command." He snapped his fingers.

I stared at him expectantly. "So it's done?"

"Yup."

"Good. Now I wish to taste some cookies." I put my hand on my hip and stared at him. Daring him to make the move.

"Man, these are some real softball wishes here. Usually people ask for like, a new house. Or for their worst enemy to be attacked by a swarm of locusts." He reached into his computer bag and tossed me a bag of Famous Amos cookies.

Damn it! What were the odds that he'd just had those on hand? "Just one little bag?" I asked. "I'd been hoping for…more." I wasn't shy about staring directly at his crotch.

"Well what did you expect when you didn't bother to rub my lamp? I can't just pull cookies out of thin air without my genie magic being activated first. If I could, I'd probably weigh like 400 pounds. So if you *really* want to taste cookies, then I suggest you rub my lamp and say it like you mean it."

God that was suggestive. And I was happy to oblige. I rubbed his lamp and said, "I wish for you to fill my mouth with your delicious cookies."

"Now that's how to make a wish." Tanner snapped his fingers and stood up.

I put his lamp down as he walked towards me. His eyes were filled with desire. He looked like he was about to fucking devour me. And I was sure as hell about to devour him.

But then he walked right past me. Towards the door.

Shit! Was he seriously leaving? I knew he was gonna pull this shit. That was why I'd stopped making out with him in the first place.

"Wait," I said. "I'm sorry. I shouldn't have wished for that."

He turned around. "Well this is going to be awkward then." He opened the door and I almost screamed. Because in the hallway was a strange little man in a butler uniform holding a platter of cookies. Actually, it wasn't just any strange little man. It was Tanner's driver. Or I guess…assistant? If he was running around the city delivering cookies on short notice he wasn't just a driver.

"Good day, Master Tanner. I have your cookies."

"Thank you, Nigel." Tanner grabbed the tray, turned around, and shoved a cookie in my mouth.

I almost spit it out, but it was so freaking good.

"More?" he asked.

I had no idea how to answer. I had so many questions running through my head. Namely…who the hell exactly was this little man named Nigel and how did he get here so quickly with a platter of cookies? I'd only made my wish like thirty seconds ago. But if you counted from when I'd *first* asked for cookies without rubbing the lamp, then it was a bit longer. All that silliness with the Famous Amos cookies must have been his way of buying time for Nigel to get here.

Tanner pressed another cookie against my lips. "Let me know when your mouth is full."

He said it in a very suggestive way, but the fact that it wasn't his dick was not sexy at all. I swatted his hand away and tried to swallow down the cookie already in my mouth.

"I guess she's finished. Thank you, Nigel. That will be all."

The little man bowed and backed out of the room.

And then I burst out laughing. And so did Tanner.

We laughed and laughed. Even harder than we had after the weird misunderstanding at the sauna. I hadn't laughed this hard in years.

"Who the hell..." I tried to say between laughs. But I couldn't get it out. The relief of finally having my sex tape safely away from Joe and the ridiculousness of Tanner, his lamp, and that odd little butler was too much. I was in tears from laughing so hard.

Between laughs I was finally able to get the whole question out. "Who the hell was that guy? And how did he get here so quickly with those cookies?"

"Don't even pretend you haven't seen him before, stalker. That's Nigel. My houseboy. Was that not clear from his uniform?"

I stared at him in disbelief. Tanner was officially nuts. But I kind of loved it. I might have finally met the one person in the world stranger than myself. "Oh, of course. Silly me."

"You'll have to meet him properly some other day. I would have had him stay, but he's been quite busy recently. Although I'm pretty sure he's just trying to keep his mind off the departure of our recent houseguest."

Recent houseguest? As in...a female? I was trying to figure out how to ask more questions without sounding jealous when Tanner's phone rang.

He checked his text and shook his head. "Damn. Our caterer just said their head chef gets seasick, so they're pulling out of the launch party. I better head over there to see if I can change their mind."

"Okay, let me fix my makeup real quick and then…"

"You don't have to come," said Tanner. "Today's your day off. I got this."

"I really don't mind."

"Nope," said Tanner. "You didn't even want to go with this caterer, but I pushed for them. This is my mess, I'll clean it up. We'll have to reschedule our dinner for another night though." He grabbed a cookie off the platter and headed out the door. But he stopped just before closing it. "Oh, and Ash?"

"Yeah?"

"I felt bad that you wasted your wishes on silly stuff, so I granted you a fourth wish. I think you'll find it's way cooler than a platter of cookies."

A fourth wish? How very un-genie-like of him. He'd been so smooth with his joke up until then. But I wasn't complaining. I loved surprises. "What is it?" I asked.

"I don't want to spoil the surprise. But you're going to want to take a closer look at that bookshelf."

Chapter 45

THE BOOKSHELF

Thursday

What did Tanner do to my bookshelf? That was the question that I couldn't get out of my mind. That was the question that had forced me to call for an emergency girls' night. Because as far as I could tell, there was *nothing* new or different around my bookshelf.

My books were all in the same place.

The photos of me and Chastity and Madison from college hadn't been disturbed.

And my fake flowers were just as I had arranged them.

If I hadn't been so anal about dusting three times a week then there might have been a trail to show what had been disturbed. But alas, I was an anal freak. In like, a clean way. Not the anal sex way. *Gross.*

The more I stared at my shelf, the more I began to think that Tanner had made the comment about my bookshelf just to mess with me.

I was just about to pull every book off the shelf when Chastity, Madison, and Liz barged in carrying a box of wine.

"Girls' night!" they all yelled in unison.

"Wow," I said. "That was quick."

Chastity opened the box of wine. "You said it was an emergency. Want a drink?"

"Of course. But seriously…how did you guys get here so fast? I literally texted you like four minutes ago." How was everyone getting to my apartment so quickly tonight? They'd come almost as fast as Nigel and the cookies. God, was I high right now? I'd accidentally eaten a pot brownie in college once. I'd been tripping balls for days afterwards, despite Chastity's insistence that it had worn off. I didn't remember eating anything weird today though. Actually, I hadn't eaten much all day… I was probably hallucinating or something.

"We were at Panera waiting for your call," said Madison as she plopped down on the couch next to me.

"What? Why? Did you know that Joe was gonna threaten to release my sex tape again?"

"Whoa, what?" asked Chastity. "We just had a feeling you might need us. Because of what today is. But what's this about Joe and your sex tape?"

Madison looked like she was about to break the stem off her wine glass. "I'm gonna kill that bastard."

"No need. Tanner sorted it all out." I held up the flash drives Tanner had given me. I brought them up to speed on Joe being a dick and then Tanner making me wish on his silly genie lamp prop.

"So the drives just magically appeared in his pocket?" asked Liz.

I almost jumped when she talked. I thought she had fallen asleep halfway through my story. "According to him, yes. But I'm pretty sure his PI just found them a few weeks ago when Tanner was stalking me."

Madison made a weird throat noise. "Gross. How many times do you think he masturbated to it before handing it over to you?"

"Umm…" I hadn't thought about that. I'd been horrified at just the thought of him seeing it. But if he'd seen it and *liked* it, then that was a different story.

"Did you use your other two wishes yet?" asked Liz.

Since when is Liz so talkative? "I did." I took a big gulp of wine. "I wished for cum to taste like cookies. And then I wished for cookies."

Chastity nearly jumped out of her chair. "You little slut! I can't believe you finally fucked Tanner!"

I shook my head. "I wish. Instead he just fulfilled my third wish by having his houseboy deliver a platter of cookies. We did kiss again, though…"

"Houseboy?" asked Chastity. "As in...a gay sex slave?"

"What? No. Tanner's not gay." *Is he? Nope.* The way he kissed me was anything but gay.

Chastity grabbed her phone and pulled up a picture of some random dude wearing way too much leather. "Was the houseboy wearing something like this?"

"Dear lord, no. He was dressed more like a butler."

Chastity nodded in approval. "Oh...classy. Once Daddy gets his money back, I'm gonna have him buy me the hottest houseboy."

"To...do gay things in front of you?"

"Uh, no. My houseboy is gonna keep my house spotless. And he's gonna be excellent at full body massages. And when I say full body, I mean *full* body." Chastity pointed to her crotch and wiggled her eyebrows.

"But I thought you said houseboys are gay sex slaves?"

"When they work for a guy, yes."

"I really don't think Tanner has a gay houseboy."

"But he says the gayest things sometimes," Chastity said.

I shook my head. "He just has weird phrases from having been all over the world. His houseboy seemed more like a manservant."

"I'm not so sure," said Madison. "I think he might be gay. Because if he's not, I don't know how he could resist your beautiful body."

Weird.

"Speaking of Tanner's secret," said Chastity. "Did you guys have any luck digging up info about Club Onyx? I still think that's our best shot at figuring out his secrets. For all we know, maybe that's where he found his houseboy."

Madison shook her head. "I tried asking around, but no one had heard of Club Onyx. If it exists, then those perverts do a good job of keeping their rape parties quiet."

"I found a few things," said Liz, who was somehow still awake. She pulled a notebook out of her purse and flipped to a page absolutely *packed* with notes and doodles.

I craned my neck to try to make out some of the words. "Is that all about Club Onyx?"

"Yeah. Last year a senior overheard his dad talking about a pool party orgy at Club Onyx. Ever since then, it's been an awfully hot topic amongst the students at Empire High. I tried to remember everything I've heard them say about it." She scanned down her notes. "Let's see… A few weeks ago a guy wanted to throw a 'Club Onyx Party' where the girls all had to wear lingerie and do *anything* someone asks them to. But then one of the girls shot back and said that she's heard that all the men at Club Onyx wear gray sweatpants. And that there's no sex allowed."

"I liked the sound of it until that last bit," said Chastity. "God, I can't wait for it to be cold again so guys start wearing gray sweat pants." She fanned herself with her hand.

Tanner likes to wear gray sweatpants… He'd worn them that first night after we got fake raided by the FBI. And he'd looked…amazing. He looked amazing in everything he wore. I looked over at my bookshelf, still curious about what the hell he had done to it. If I was lucky, maybe he'd added a framed picture of himself wearing gray sweatpants.

"Hey guys," I said. "I never told you why I really called this emergency girls night. Before Tanner left, he…" A knock on the door interrupted me. *Tanner's back! Maybe?* "Hold that thought." I jumped up and answered the door.

"Delivery for Ashley Cooper," said a delivery guy holding a huge bouquet of red and yellow roses. At least three dozen. "That you?"

"Yup."

He handed me the roses and walked away.

Chastity ran over. "Oooh! Who are those from?"

"Maybe they're apology roses from Homeless Rutherford for always licking our pizza?"

"Huh?" asked Liz.

"Um, nothing." I spun the roses around so I could read the card stuck among them:

Ash,

I know you don't want to hear from me, and I respect that decision. But I also hate to end things on a sour note.

I don't expect any response, but I wanted you to know that I'm so sorry about how things ended between us. I take full responsibility. If I had just asked you out sooner, none of that would have happened.

I promise that this is the last you'll hear from me. But if you ever do decide to reach out, I'll be here.

Yours,

Anthony Lyons

"O.M.G.," said Chastity. "Dr. Lyons is so adorable. Are you *sure* you don't want to keep dating him until you figure things out with Tanner?"

It was a really sweet gesture. But he wasn't Tanner. "I'm sure."

"Alright then. What were you saying about Tanner before we got interrupted?"

"Right." I closed the door and walked back to the couch. "So after I made my three wishes..." Another knock on the door. *Who is it now?* It was probably Tanner coming back from the caterers. I started to walk over to answer the door, but then the roses caught my eye. "Shit," I whispered. "What if it's Tanner? And he sees my roses?"

"Good call," said Chastity. She plucked the note out of the roses and tucked it into her bra. "Okay, you're good. Now they'll just make him jealous."

Chastity really did not understand that I didn't want to make Tanner jealous anymore. I just wanted to figure out a way to help him through his secret problem and then start a real relationship.

Before I could fully explain that to her, she ran over and opened the door. A single black envelope - much bigger than the usual ones - had been propped against the door. No delivery man in sight.

She picked it up. "Looks like a special delivery from the Society."

"Why's it so big?" I asked.

"Hopefully that's the exact question you'll be asking later tonight," said Chastity.

Madison made her trademark disgusted throat noise.

"Now let's see what they have in store for us." Chastity broke the seal and pulled out a thick stack of papers. She read the top sheet. "Good evening, Raven. It was brought to our attention that your second wish - to learn all of Ryder Storm's secrets - was not completed to your satisfaction. We hope that in the attached documents you will find whatever secrets you seek. Signed, The Society." She flipped to the next page and her eyes got big.

"What is it?" I asked.

She tossed the stack of papers on the coffee table so we could all see what she was seeing. The top photo was of Ryder entering One57 with two gorgeous blondes, their arms linked with his. The next photo was of him at a bar with a brunette. Then another blonde at a restaurant. On and on it went.

The knot in my stomach got bigger with each photo.

"Well, I think that proves he's not gay," said Chastity.

I tossed the photos aside and let the couch swallow me up in its big cushions. "What was I thinking? I should have known better than to go after a billionaire. Especially one who's in a sex club. He's so far out of my league."

"Hold on," said Liz. "These are all from years ago." She pointed to the time stamp on the back of one of the pictures.

I sat up. "Really?"

"What does that matter?" asked Madison. "He's a womanizer. It's irrelevant if it occurred a year ago or last week."

"What's wrong with being a womanizer?" asked Chastity.

"Everything."

Chastity shook her head. "Imagine you hired a plumber to come unclog your sink. If he came and said that he had zero experience with sinks but that he was super eager to give it a shot, would you be very happy?"

"No."

"Then why would you want some inexperienced loser poking around your lady pipes?"

Madison had no response.

"Guys," I said. "Can we focus on the photos? We need to figure out if Tanner has taken any women back to his apartment since the start of April." It was probably dumb of me to dream, but a little part of me dared to hope that meeting me had made him halt his endless carousel of random hookups.

We flipped all the photos over and started tallying the dates. It went surprisingly quickly with the four of us all working on it.

I held my breath when Chastity was about to reveal the results. "There are 150 photos in total, spanning the past 5 years."

Damn.

"But none in the past 6 months."

What?! "Really?" I couldn't believe it. Not only had he not taken a woman home since we first met…he hadn't taken a woman home since he first began stalking me.

"Really," said Chastity. "I dunno what kind of looks you've been giving him as you pass him on the sidewalk for the past six months, but you're gonna have to teach me your ways."

I couldn't contain my smile. Not only was Tanner totally smitten with me, but *Chastity* was complimenting *my* seduction abilities. I never thought such a thing was possible.

But then a horrible thought occurred to me. *What looks have I been giving him?* Did I bite my lip? Open my mouth? Press my tongue against the top of my mouth? I moved my mouth around, but nothing felt right. *What if I can never replicate my sexy look? And why does my mouth feel so weird? Am I supposed to be clenching my teeth? Should my tongue be touching my front teeth?*

"You okay, Ash?" asked Chastity.

"Uh, yeah. I was just thinking about..." *How can I tell them that I forgot how mouths work?* "About what Tanner told me before he left. He said that since I wasted my first three wishes, he had granted me a fourth. Then he told me to check my bookshelf."

"That one?" asked Chastity, pointing at the only bookshelf in my apartment.

"That's the one."

"What did he do to it?"

I shrugged. "No idea. That's why I called for an emergency girls' night. It's driving me crazy that I can't figure it out."

"It looks normal to me," said Chastity. "Are you sure he's not just messing with you?"

"Damn it. Do you really think that's what's happening here?" Because that was definitely plausible. It seemed like everything Tanner said was either a lie or something to mess with me.

"Definitely," said Madison, grabbing the remote off the coffee table. "Let's just forget about it and watch the Yankees."

Chastity snatched it out of her hand. "How could you watch the Yankees at a time like this? We just found out that Tanner is madly in love with Ash. *And* we now have a treasure trove of photos from the Society. There's gotta be some hints in there somewhere about where we can find Club Onyx."

Yes! Was Tanner really madly in love with me? It kind of felt like he was. Maybe he'd tucked a love letter into one of my books while I'd been distracted by his houseboy and the cookies.

The only thing standing between me and my happily ever after with Tanner was figuring out his secret. Whatever it was, I was sure we could overcome it together.

I grabbed a stack of photos and started looking for hints. Someone had painstakingly blurred the background of all the photos. Or...*almost* all of the photos.

"You guys! Look at this!" I put the unblurred photo on the table. It was Tanner and some supermodel walking up the stairs. But I was more focused on the CLUB ONYX sign in the background.

"It exists!" yelled Chastity. "I knew it. God, we're so close I can practically taste it."

"I'm more interested in what the hell is going on back there," said Madison, pointing to the corner of the photo.

I squinted to try to make it out. "It kinda looks like a big helmet?"

"An elephant mask," said Liz.

"Are you sure?" I tilted my head, but there was no way to tell if it was an elephant or not. He was so far in the background that his head was like the size of my pinky nail.

Liz pulled up a picture on her phone of an unzipped backpack on a linoleum floor. Inside was a big elephant head mask made up of little triangular mirrors. "One of my students was showing this to all his friends. He claimed that this is what all the members wear at Club Onyx during some weird sex ritual."

I eyed her suspiciously. That felt more like one of her furry fantasies than something they'd do at Club Onyx, but the mask did look pretty fancy.

"What else have you heard?" I asked.

"Oh, all sorts of stuff." She flipped through her notebook. "I'm pretty sure most of it's nonsense, but there are a few recurring themes."

"We need to hear all of it," said Chastity. "The littlest thing might give us the hint we need to find it."

"Well, there's of course the claim that Club Onyx is an elephant-worshiping cult. I don't buy it, though. If they were furries, I definitely would have heard more about it."

"Okay," I said. "What else?"

Liz looked back at her notes and started reading. "Club Onyx is an illegal casino. A man in a minotaur mask chases women through a hedge maze, and if he catches them, then they become his sex slave. They host water balloon fights. One of the members is a man who never cums so he can just bang you for hours."

Chastity bit her lip. "How likely is that one to be true?"

"Pretty likely. I've heard quite a few stories about him."

"Yeah, we definitely need to find this place. Sorry…please continue."

"There's a rumor that James Hunter is the founder, but I'm not sure I buy that."

"I would die if James Hunter was a member," said Chastity. "One time he came to visit Mason at the office and my ovaries nearly exploded just from being in the same room as him."

"And his wife is so beautiful," I said. Penny Hunter was basically my idol. She'd grown up in Delaware and had red hair. *Real* red hair. Not that fake red hair like stupid Sierra. And she'd bagged herself one of the hottest men in New York.

I'd almost gotten to meet her once. Last year, right before the OG incident happened…I'd found out that the whole time I thought I was talking to Matt on the dating app, I'd actually been talking to Penny. She had been trying to set him up on a blind date. She kinda catfished me, but in the sweetest way possible. I shook my head. No, it wasn't sweet. Because that had been one of the worst days of my life. All of my incidents were bad. But *the incident*? I'd kill myself if I ever saw Matthew Caldwell again.

"There's no way James is a member," I said. "He and Penny are the perfect couple. They wouldn't join a sex club."

"Unless they have an open relationship." Chastity sighed. "A girl can dream. And…I don't know why I didn't think about this before! You can just text Penny and ask her about the Society."

"I don't have her number."

"Of course you do. You talked to her for a few days before your date with Matt."

"Only through the app. Which I immediately deleted after that."

"Why'd you do that?!"

"Because I couldn't show my face on there ever again after I literally lit a man on fire!" Why did this topic keep being brought up? I never wanted to think about it again. For the first time in my life, I turned to Liz to save me. "Was there anything else?" I asked.

"Yup. Two more common rumors. The first is that Club Onyx hosts epic games of Capture the Flag. And the other is that they have an Odegaard boutique on-site."

Chastity scrunched her face to the side. "Very interesting. I always pictured Club Onyx as some underground club in the city, but now it's sounding like it's some estate in the Hamptons or something. The hedge maze, the pool party, the water balloon fights...those all require land."

I nodded in agreement. "I think you're right. The only problem is that Tanner leaves his apartment at 8 every Tuesday and Thursday. And Society events start at 8:30. He'd never make it to Club Onyx in time. That's like a 90-minute drive."

"That's only a problem if you assume that Club Onyx operates under the same rules as your Society dates," Chastity said. "And remember how I said that the wishes might be some sort of try-out for your real membership to Club Onyx? Maybe real events for the Society are just...all the time in the Hamptons." There was a gleeful look in her eyes.

"Rich people do love to hang out at the Hamptons," I conceded.

"Exactly." Chastity turned to Liz. "Does that ring any bells? Maybe those crazy rich kids talk about their parents going to the Hamptons several nights a week?"

Liz shrugged. "All the time. But like half of them have a second home there, so that doesn't tell us much."

"Can I see your notes again?" asked Chastity.

"Sure." Liz tossed her the notebook.

Chastity started scanning through the notes. "Wait a second! You know how in Twilight all of the vampires have special powers? Like telepathy and the ability to see the future?"

"Yes…" I said.

"Well what if Liz's story about the man who can't cum is about Tanner? That's his vampire superpower!"

Could that really be it? Tanner had stared at my neck the other night in his office. And he'd looked very hungry while doing it. "But he overheard our conversation the other night about that being his secret. If it was true…don't you think he would have just finished us off?"

"No, because he loves you. He wouldn't suck your blood now."

That was a valid point.

"And when he confronted you about our suspicions, did he deny it?"

I tried to think back to the conversation. I'd ended up asking him a different question. But I couldn't remember why. Had he deflected it?! "No, he didn't deny it."

"Well…there you have it. And this new information about his vampire ability is a game-changer. I think we need to consult the literature." She walked over and grabbed *Twilight* off the shelf. Or she tried to. "What the hell?" she said as she tugged on the spine. "Did you glue *Twilight* to your shelf to prevent me from reading it?"

"No…"

She pulled a little harder. The book tilted towards her, but before she could fully pull it out, the entire bookshelf swung backwards into the wall. "Uh, Ash. Did you know that this bookshelf is a secret door?"

What the actual hell?

Chapter 46

THE SECRET DOOR

Thursday

I jumped up and stared into the gaping hole in my wall where my bookshelf used to be. All I could see was darkness. What the hell was in there? I had a terrible feeling in the pit of my stomach. Had the previous owner of this apartment had a secret room for his murder victims? Or a creepy way to spy on the neighbors?

"Did you seriously get a secret bookshelf door and not tell me about it?" asked Madison. "I thought we'd promised each other that if we ever got one, we'd both install them at the same time."

"I didn't know I had a secret bookshelf door until about three seconds ago," I said. *Oh. It's new! Of course!* I took a deep breath. This had to be Tanner's doing. There weren't going to be any bodies cut up in little pieces in there. *Hopefully.*

Madison eyed me suspiciously. "If there's a Hogwarts-themed reading nook on the other side of that door I'm gonna lose my shit."

"If there is, then we have Tanner to thank for it. This must be the surprise he mentioned earlier." I peered into the dark space. "The only question is…what kind of surprise?"

"Probably your neighbor's apartment" suggested Liz. "You know…because that's how walls and apartment buildings work."

Fuck you, Liz. "Yeah, that's probably it. And since you solved the mystery, you get to go in first."

Liz gave me a look. "Thanks, but I'd rather not go into the dark scary room. This is a classic sloshing-lure if I've ever seen one."

"Sloshing-lure?" I regretted asking as soon as the words were out of my mouth.

"You know," said Liz. "When your neighbor keeps trying to get you to watch them going at each other on top of baked goods - cakes, puddings…the sloshier the better - and you keep saying no. So they find a way to lure you over, and the second you step foot in their depraved sex dungeon… BOOM. The lights go on and you see them naked and covered in food."

What the hell? "Is that seriously a thing?"

"Walk through the door and find out."

"Uh, no thanks."

"I'll go in," said Chastity.

"Really?" I asked.

"Sure. I mean…so far Tanner has given you two big surprises. First he took you to a museum where you got to suck on Dr. Lyons' beautiful cock. And then he took you to a Finnish sauna and offered you up to all sorts of Nordic hotties. If those are any indication, then I'd guess that this surprise is going to involve dicks. Lots and lots of dicks. I think it's going to be a first-come-first-served situation."

"I'm leaving," said Madison.

"Wait!" I said. "How about we all go in together. The four of us could totally fight off a bunch of naked dudes."

Madison pulled some pepper spray out of her purse. "Let's do this."

We counted to three and then all charged in. The lights flicked on as soon as we stepped over the threshold.

"Holy shit," I muttered. It was like I'd stepped into an Odegaard boutique. There were mirrors and mannequins and racks of clothes everywhere. And shoes. So. Many. Shoes.

"This is the coolest closet I've ever seen in my life," said Chastity.

"You call this a closet?" I asked. "I'm pretty sure it's like twice as big as my apartment."

"And it's two stories," added Madison, pointing to a spiral staircase.

I pinched my arm. Was this real life? "How did Tanner do this?" I asked.

"Probably hired some contractors," said Liz.

"Right. I know he didn't do it all by himself. I was more talking about how he did this without me noticing. You'd think I would have heard or seen the construction people. Especially when they cut a hole in my wall to make the secret entrance."

No one responded. They'd all gotten distracted.

Chastity was holding up clothes and desperately trying to fit her feet into some of the shoes.

Liz was getting ready for a nap on one of the plush blue couches.

And Madison was jumping around corners getting ready to pepper spray hidden sexual predators. She didn't find any.

"I'm always excited about Single Girl Rules," said Chastity. "But I've never been more excited to quote Single Girl Rule #18: Clothes are shared amongst friends. Owner gets first choice." She lifted up a very skimpy dress. "You lucky bitch."

I laughed.

"Hey," said Chastity, abandoning the dress. "There's a note over here." She waved a piece of paper around.

"What does it say?" I asked.

"I figured you needed a little extra room for your Odegaards," she read. "Hope you like it." She tossed me the note and shook her head. "Does Tanner have a brother? Please tell me he does. I would do anything to get a closet like this."

"Tanner really is the best. First Spaceboy, and now this." *How did I get so lucky?* Seriously. I knew he was a billionaire. But it still took a ton of thought and planning to surprise me with the coolest freaking closet in the history of closets. The fact that the entrance was a secret bookshelf just made it all that much better.

"Spaceboy?" asked Chastity.

"Yeah. At the launch party."

"WHAT?!"

"Oh my God! I can't believe I forgot to tell you. I was going to, but I wanted to do it in person. And then the whole thing with Joe happened. And then this closet…"

"Wait. Hold everything. Are you seriously telling me that Tanner got Spaceboy to play at our launch party for Wineflix and Chill?"

"Yup."

"OH MY GOD!!!!" yelled Chastity. I had never seen her so excited. "I'm gonna get to bang Spaceboy!"

"DJ Spaceboy?" I asked. "Or his dancers too?"

"Um, all three of them can do whatever they want to me."

"Ew," said Madison. She'd apparently completed her perimeter check for perverts. "They probably have AIDS, you know. By the way, this closet is even bigger than we thought. There's actually *three* stories."

"Three? Are you serious?"

"Yup. Did you really not see anyone build this place? That seems almost impossible."

"Vampire magic!" said Chastity. "I just wish we could have caught it on tape. Wait…did you ever set up that webcam I sent you when I was trying to convince you to be a camgirl a few months ago?"

"I did not."

"Damn." Chastity plopped down on one of the many couches. "We were so close to learning all his secrets."

"Were we?" I asked. "Because I'm pretty sure all the video would have showed us was what construction company he'd hired. What we really need is a camera in *his* apartment. Or his office."

"Ash! You're a genius!"

"I am?"

"Yeah. Bugging his office is brilliant. Best case scenario he'll just let his secret slip during a private phone call. Worst case scenario, he'll give us enough hints to find Club Onyx, and then we go there and learn all his secrets the old-fashioned way."

I laughed. *Or he gets us fired.* "Of course. How did we not think of that sooner? Especially since bugging an office is so easy. Let me just call my contact at the CIA and get a few pointers."

Chastity rolled her eyes. "I'm serious. It's not that hard to bug an office. I know Dexter has some equipment we could use."

"The IT guy that tricked you into getting naked during a game of D&D?"

"That's the one." She pulled out her phone and texted him. He responded almost immediately. "Okay, he's in."

"Just like that?"

"Yeah. I knew he wouldn't be able to resist a good blowjob."

"You really don't have to do that."

"I don't mind," said Chastity. "He actually has a pretty nice dick. And I don't know what his secret is, but his cum makes my skin so soft. Anyway…my job is easy. You're gonna be the one doing all the hard work tomorrow."

I had a lot of questions about that cum comment. But I was a little more preoccupied with what she was going to make me do. And whether or not my skin was about to be soft too. "All the hard work?" I asked. "What exactly is your plan here?"

"I'm not sure yet. Depends on the tech Dexter has available. But I do know one thing…"

"Which is?"

"One sec." Chastity disappeared among the racks of clothes. When she reemerged, she was holding surprisingly classy work clothes. "You'll need to wear this tomorrow."

"Okay…"

"And this underneath." She let the work clothes slide off her arms to reveal a hanger with some strappy blue lingerie.

"Why exactly will I need to wear that?"

"You'll see."

***

"Did you get the tech?" I asked as Chastity and I walked into Tanner's office building on Monday morning.

"I did. Dexter was happy to help."

"I bet he was."

"Are you wearing what I told you to?" Chastity pulled on my blouse to look down my shirt. "What the hell? Where's the blue lingerie I picked out?" The other people waiting for the elevator pretended not to hear that.

"I thought you were joking." I didn't really. But I wasn't prepared to seduce Tanner in the middle of the office. Or to do a striptease in the middle of our cubicles. Or whatever crazy thing Chastity had planned.

"Eh, no big deal. The plan might work better without it." She stepped onto the elevator.

"Really?"

"Yeah."

I didn't believe her. But I didn't press for details until we were safely at our cubicle.

Chastity pulled a tiny little USB drive out of her purse and put it on our desk. "So this is the bug."

"Is it a microphone? Or camera?" I turned it over in my hands. "Are you sure Dexter didn't just give you the USB for a wireless mouse?"

"Dexter wouldn't dare screw me over. Especially after the things I did to him last night."

"Please don't elaborate."

"Wanna see?"

"No. I don't need to see what you two did behind closed doors."

She stared at me for a second and then laughed. "Wow, not at all what I was offering. Although I'm happy to give you tips any time. All I'm going to say about last night is that he successfully invoked Single Girl Rule #27: If he makes you come, he can cum anywhere he wants." She winked at me. "But really I was asking if you wanted to see how the tech works?"

Where had he cum on her? And I thought it was just a blowjob? What had she been up to? I just nodded.

Chastity took her phone out and put it on the desk a few inches away from the bug. At first, nothing happened. Then part of the bug started unfolding until it had 8 little legs. It scurried over to her phone and attached itself to the charger plug at the bottom.

"Jesus!" I said, nearly falling out of my chair. "What the hell is this creepy thing?"

"What did you expect from something called a bug?"

"I don't know. Like a little microphone that just sticks to the bottom of a desk. Or a camera that you put in a stuffed bear."

"That's a nanny cam. Why would I blow Dexter to get one of those when I could just order it on Amazon?"

"Because you love sucking dick?" And it really seemed like they'd done more than that…

"Hmm…fair point. Anyway, this tech is a million times better than a microphone or a nanny cam. Because not only will we be able to hear Tanner's conversation in his office, we'll be able to hear them everywhere. And track his movement. And see all of the files on his phone."

"Are you serious?"

"Mhm." She slipped me a piece of paper with a URL, username, and password.

I followed the instructions on my laptop. Sure enough, an interface popped up that showed the home screen of a phone. I clicked on the gallery to make sure it was Chastity's. Which was a mistake, because about 75% of her photos were naked mirror selfies. I quickly exed out.

"Pretty impressive, huh?" asked Chastity.

"I mean…it's nothing I haven't seen before. But yeah, you keep it tight."

"Thank you. But I was talking about the tech."

"Oh right." *Awkward.* "Yeah, it's amazing. So it's just gonna scurry in there and hook up to Tanner's phone and then we're all set?"

"Kinda. Dexter is working on a remote-controlled one that could do that, but for now, this one can only locate and run to a signal that's within like 6 inches. Then it connects, uploads the malware, and runs away."

Sure enough, the bug had disengaged from Chastity's phone and returned to its original position. I still had access to her phone on my computer, though. "I admit, this is cooler than I thought it would be. But should we really hack Tanner's phone like this? He just made me the coolest closet ever. And got us freaking Spaceboy for the launch party. This feels like a betrayal."

"What's a betrayal is that he keeps teasing you and then pulling away. If he would just man up and ask you out, then we wouldn't have to do any of this. But noooo… Mr. Vampire boy has to be all secretive. And it's not like we're gonna sell his data to terrorists or something. We're just going to track his every move and listen to all his conversations. And look through all his files. And his search history. No big deal."

"That feels like a pretty big deal."

"Yeah, you're right," said Chastity, putting the bug back in her purse. "It's better for you to just keep blindly pursuing him and then end up being melted in a vat of acid by the cartel he pissed off. Or if you're worried about that, you could just stop hanging out with him. He's not that great, anyway. Who needs private Spaceboy concerts and giant secret closets?"

"Fine! I'll do it."

"Good." Chastity pulled some red lingerie out of her purse and tossed it at me. "Now go put this on under your clothes and we can get started."

I hid the lingerie under the table to try to avoid our coworkers seeing it. "Where did you get this?!"

"I took it from your closet because I knew you'd be lame and not wear what I told you to."

"Is it *really* necessary?"

"Yup. We need to get the bug close enough to his phone for it to latch on. And there's only one way I see that happening." She told me the plan. And as much as I hated it…she was right. The lingerie was necessary.

Chapter 47

BUGGIN' OUT

Monday

I slipped the bug into my bra and made sure I still had easy access to it. "Wish me luck." *And pray I don't make a total fool of myself.*

"You got this," said Chastity.

I nodded and stood up. The plan was simple. Tanner always kept his phone in his jacket pocket whenever he went anywhere, so all I had to do was get the bug into that pocket. The tricky part was that I didn't know exactly where his jacket would be. Generally, he either draped it over his chair or hung it up on his coat rack in the corner. Both of those scenarios would require a slightly different course of action. And since his blinds were pulled shut, I had no idea which scenario I was walking into.

I hurried towards Tanner's office. It was best to just get it over with before I was *entirely* drenched in nervous sweat. Evie tried to stop me, but I ignored her and barged right in.

Tanner was talking to someone on speakerphone, but he stopped mid-sentence and stared at me as I pulled the door shut behind me.

"Ash," he said. "How can I help you?"

"Thanks for the closet full of clothes, big boy." *Big boy? What the hell is wrong with me? And where is his jacket?* It wasn't on his chair. So that meant it was hanging up in the corner. "I thought you'd wanna see how they looked."

"The blouse fits you perfectly," he said. "By the way, have you met…"

"Shhhh," I said, putting a finger to my lips. *What am I doing?* "Just watch." I unbuttoned the blouse, tore it off, and chucked it into the corner, hoping to hook it on the coat rack with his jacket. Then I unzipped my skirt and did the same thing. Two shots at the coat rack were better than one. "So what do you think?" I asked, giving him a little shimmy for added effect.

"I think you look stunning." His eyes wandered to my breasts. "But I also think that you may have slightly misjudged this situation."

I gave him a funny look. "What do you mean?" As I said it, I caught a glimpse of movement in the corner. *Fuck my life.* "We're not alone, are we?"

"Nope."

I turned towards the corner. My aim had been spot on. Unfortunately, a man had been standing directly between me and the coat rack. He pulled my blouse and skirt off his head and looked at me like I was a crazy person.

"Hi there," I said. "Could you just put those on the coat rack for me? Also, please don't look at me. And forget this ever happened." God, the longer I stared at him, the more familiar he looked. Did I know him? I could feel my face turning red as I debated hurling myself out the window. But I didn't want to ruin my new lingerie.

He looked like he really wanted to hand them back to me instead, but didn't want to engage with my craziness. So he hung my clothes up and then turned back around. He drew his eyebrows together, clearly perplexed by what the hell was happening.

"I'm Ash, by the way." I stuck my hand out for him. It seemed like the best course of action to pretend like I hadn't just stripped down to my very revealing lingerie. And the fact that I hadn't put my clothes back on once I realized he was there. But I weirdly felt confident in my outfit. I mean…Tanner said I looked stunning. I was practically beaming through my embarrassed red cheeks.

"James. James Hunter." He shook my hand but was very respectful about not staring at my body.

"James Hunter?! I knew you looked familiar. Oh my God. I freaking love your wife. I mean, I don't know her.

But I've been watching her. In the tabloids. Not with binoculars. I'm not stalking her or anything." I laughed nervously. James was even more handsome in real life than in pictures. I always hoped to meet him someday. I just thought I'd be wearing more clothes. Or less, depending on which of my daydreams we're talking about...

James cleared his throat. "Speaking of my wife, I'm not sure she'd be too thrilled about all this." He put his hand in front of his face, trying to block me from his sight. "So I should probably get going."

"Why? I said I'm not a stalker."

"I was more concerned about the surprise striptease."

"Oh, right. Well if it makes her feel any better, it wasn't meant for you. I can make sure you don't get in trouble if you wanna just call her real quick. You could put her on speakerphone. I'll explain everything. She'll be cool with it. We texted once. I mean, kind of." This didn't feel like a great time to bring up the fact that I'd gone on a date with one of James' best friends because his wife kind of catfished me. That catfishing had been one of the best moments of my life. The actual date had been hell.

"Yeah...I'm not going to do that."

Tanner cleared his throat.

"You know what?" I said. "I should probably get back to work. It was rude of me to interrupt your meeting. Just let me grab my clothes real quick..." I brushed past James and grabbed my clothes off the rack. I was waiting for the perfect opportunity to pull the bug out of my bra and slip it in Tanner's jacket, but it was almost impossible to do with both of them watching me. "Ahem," I said. "Can't a girl have a little privacy while she dresses? Perverts..."

Both of them turned away.

Score! I had been worried that James being here had ruined everything, but really his presence had made my job easy. The original plan had just been to do a little striptease for Tanner and then hope that he'd be so transfixed staring at my ass that he wouldn't notice me slipping the bug into his jacket. There was still a chance he would have spotted what I was doing. But with both their backs turned? No risk. I deposited the bug into Tanner's jacket pocket and finished getting dressed.

"It was so nice to meet you, James," I said and then slipped out the door before the encounter could get any more awkward.

"Well?" asked Chastity when I got back to our cubicle.

"I just stripped in front of James Hunter. But mission accomplished."

"James Hunter?" asked Chastity. "As in…the billionaire who's married to your idol? No way. You're lying."

"Unfortunately I'm not lying."

"Well what happened? Did you blow both of them? Oh my God. I'm so freaking jealous right now!"

"How many times do I have to tell you that a blowjob was completely unnecessary for this mission?"

"And how many times do I have to tell you that you're being silly, because you literally should use sex in this scenario. Single Girl Rule #25: Don't be ashamed to use sex to get what you want."

"I didn't use sex."

"Wait, so James Hunter was offering to let you suck his dick and you said *no?*"

"No!"

"So you *did* blow him?" She looked completely baffled. "You're being very confusing right now."

"Chastity. There were no blowjobs. Or offers of blowjobs."

"Suuuure." She winked at me. "But you still delivered the bug?"

"Yup! Now we just have to wait for him to put his phone in his pocket."

It didn't take long. Because ten minutes later, he and James exited his office and headed towards the elevator.

I logged into the tracking website and watched his GPS tracker go from our office to a restaurant a few blocks away.

We were able to listen in on their convo, but it was nothing exciting. Just something about a potential joint venture between Hunter Tech and Rhodes VC.

It was much more entertaining to poke around his phone.

He had SO MANY CONTACTS. Like, thousands of them. Half of them sounded like dumb sluts. There were at least 20 Hannahs and even more Emilys. Unfortunately, he didn't have any contacts called *Club Onyx*. Not that I would have called the number even if he had it. I was willing to do some crazy stuff to figure out Tanner's secret, but I drew the line at cold calling.

"Why did you start looking at his contacts first?" asked Chastity. "What is this, the early 2000s? You'll find so much more by looking at his texts and emails. Oh! And his browsing history. What kind of porn do you think he's been watching?"

"Better yet…how about I just go straight to the Society app?" I clicked on his *Tax Codes* app. A login screen popped up. *Damn it!* My Society app kept me logged in. Tanner must have changed his settings after that time I'd grabbed his phone and gone to the app to prove he was in the Society.

He didn't have any social media apps, so I went to his email next. And his inbox was completely empty.

"What kind of psychopath doesn't have any emails?" I asked.

"You've never heard of the inbox-zero theory to success?" asked Chastity. "Apparently lots of high-performing CEOs keep their inbox empty. It's a thing. Check his sent folder."

Chastity was right - there were plenty of emails in his sent folder. But after about an hour straight of Chastity and I reading all his sent messages, we found that none of them had anything to do with the Society or what his secret might be. Same with his texts. Well…almost. There were a couple noteworthy threads.

The first was his ongoing conversation with Evie. Not because it revealed his secret. But because they hadn't exchanged a single nude photo. It was all business. *Thank God.*

Then there was his conversation with someone named "Best Friend." Again, it didn't reveal his secret. But it was super adorable that he actually called someone his best friend.

"Oh my God," said Chastity. "I bet his best friend is so rich. And he sounds like a total stallion. Do you think Tanner would introduce me?"

"I think you might have missed the texts about the guy always being busy hanging out with his wife."

"Not at all. She sounds like a needy bitch. I bet he's so unhappy in his marriage."

"Yeah. He was definitely overcompensating by referring to the love of his life in every other text and gushing about how he was happier than he'd ever been in his whole life."

"Exactly. Let's keep reading. I need to find out everything I can about my future sugar daddy." Chastity grabbed the mouse and started scrolling through the conversation between Tanner and his best friend. She paused on a line where Tanner addressed him as *Matt.* "Matt," she said. "Not the sexiest name ever, but it'll work."

The name made me cringe. "Does his best friend really have to be named Matt? That's like the worst name ever." I would never get over *the incident.* And therefore anything reminding me of Matthew Caldwell made me want to die. But it was the same date where I'd gotten to text Penny…so…pros and cons. But seriously, if I ever saw that Matt again, I would definitely jump in a dumpster to avoid him. I wouldn't even think twice this time.

"Pssssh. Worst name ever? More like hottest name ever."

I thought you just said it wasn't sexy?

Chastity bit her lip. "I'm gonna call him Matty Daddy."

"Do you have to?"

"Don't be jealous."

"I'm really not. Just pray that your first meeting with this Matt isn't nearly as awkward as my date with Matthew Caldwell was."

"Dude, what if his best friend *is* Matthew Caldwell?"

"No. Nope." I shook my head. "Not possible." *Right?*

"You sure? Because Matthew Caldwell is super rich. And we're only working with Tanner because he has a contract with Matt's brother. So we know that they at least run in the same circles. And he was just hanging out with James in his office. Isn't James friends with Matt? And when we first got told about Tanner coming in, didn't Bee say he was a friend? They all hang out together!"

Oh good God, she was right. "Chastity." I grabbed her hand to make her stop looking at the texts because I'd just remembered something. Something horribly terrible. "When Tanner was joking about being a genie…he said he couldn't be with me because he had a flaming genie penis."

Chastity laughed. "He was just messing with you."

"I know that. But it's not funny. What if…what if he keeps running away from me because he's scared that I'm going to set him on fire? Like I set his best friend Matt on fire. With the flaming penis incident. Because Matt told him all about it. Why else would he say he had a flaming penis? God, he knows about *the incident.*"

Chastity thought it over. "If that was true, he wouldn't still be into you. And he's definitely into you. It's probably a different Matt. I shouldn't have even said anything. Think of all the Matts there are in the world."

"But you just said James, Bee, and Mason are friends with him. Of course Matt is too."

"Surely. But that doesn't mean it's his best friend. Think about all the Hannahs he had in his phone. Matt is just as common of a name as Hannah."

True.

"Besides, his best friend Matt is going to be a hot single rich guy. I'm visualizing it, so it's gotta happen. Ohh! Look.

Tanner just got a text from Nigel the houseboy. Five dollars says it's a dick pic."

Well, if that wasn't a good distraction from the Matt question, I didn't know what was. "You're on. I'm telling you, Tanner's not gay." I opened the conversation. I was happy to see that it was just a text confirming that he'd booked a yacht for the launch party. "I win."

"You got lucky. Scroll back and I bet you'll find the good stuff." She grabbed my mouse and started looking through the rest of the conversation. It was all pretty boring and decidedly unsexy. Except for one text…

"Wait," I said. "What's that?" I pointed at a text from a few weeks ago:

Nigel: Good news, Master. The island is fully stocked with everything you might need in case you have to make a quick getaway.

"What do you think it means?" I asked.

"I guess he owns a private island," said Chastity. "Man, I still can't believe you somehow called dibs on him before me. Do you think Matt owns a private island too? I bet he does. Imagine the things you could do to a beautiful man on a private island…"

"I was more focused on the bit about Tanner needing to make a quick getaway. Now we have concrete evidence that he does in fact have someone that he's scared of." I'd never been so happy to know that someone was in grave danger. Because for a while I'd been thinking that he just kept pulling away during our kisses because he found me repulsive. And now my most recent fear: that he knew about *the incident*. But this kinda proved that he didn't. *Hopefully*.

We kept searching for more clues in the thread, but hours of work turned up nothing. I stood up and stretched my back out. "This is insane. How does he not have more stuff on his phone?"

"I dunno. He must really believe in inbox-zero, because he's basically applied it to his entire digital life. I'm pretty sure my grandparents use their phones more than he does, despite their complete disregard for internet etiquette. Apparently forwards have migrated from AOL to Facebook messenger."

I shut my laptop and put it in my bag. "Oh well. Even if he doesn't use his phone much, he still has it with him all the time. He's bound to let something slip when he thinks no one is listening. And if not, then the GPS will lead us right to Club Onyx."

"You know what that means, right?" Chastity looked so excited, which made me incredibly nervous. Recently all of her ideas seemed to be geared around embarrassing me as much as possible.

"Um...do I have to send Tanner some naked photos or something?"

"Ohhh, you little slut! I bet you want to send him some nudies. But no, why would that be my plan? My plan is to have a stakeout! Only instead of sitting in an unmarked van eating donuts and drinking coffee, we get to go back to your place and eat pizza. And try on every Odegaard dress in your new closet. Best. Stakeout. Ever!!!"

"I actually kind of love that idea."

"Of course you do. It's an objectively good idea."

It was. Except for one little detail. Chastity ordered the pizza before we were home. And we couldn't get a taxi to save our lives. So the pizza arrived before we did.

"Stop right there, Rutherford!" I yelled as we exited the stairwell. He was *just* about to open the pizza box sitting outside my apartment door.

"Stop what?" he asked. "I just saw your pizza sitting here and I wanted to make sure no hoodlums stole it."

"There's only one hoodlum in this building."

"Nathan from 3B? I couldn't agree more. What a little asshole."

"Nathan is an infant. I was talking about you. I know that you always lick my pizzas."

"Who, moi?!" said Homeless Rutherford in the most overdramatic way possible.

"Yes, yoi," I said, trying to be clever. It did not sound clever. It just sounded like I forgot how to speak.

"Well now I regret keeping your pizza safe. I wasn't even going to charge you for my services. But now…"

"How many times do I have to tell you that I do not have any spare money to pay you for your services."

"Is he a prostitute?" whispered Chastity very loudly.

"I beg your pardon," said Rutherford. "I'm not a prostitute. I'm a hardworking citizen who happened to come across some hard times. But if you have any honest work, I'm more than happy to help."

"Just hand over the pizza," I said. But then an even better idea came to me. "Actually, I'll give you that entire pizza. You can lick it to your heart's content. But there is one condition."

Chapter 48

MY THIRD WISH

Tuesday

"Name your price," said Rutherford with a little lick of his lips. I'd never seen someone so eager to lick a pizza.

How can I word this? I wanted to give him as little information as possible. I knew he licked pizzas, but it was entirely possible he'd love to lick all of my shiny new clothes too if he knew they existed. "I need to know if you've seen any construction workers in this building recently. Specifically on my floor and the floor above us. And the one above that." I still couldn't believe my closet had three stories.

He furrowed his brow, almost enough to knock his busted glasses right off his face. "Let's see…there were those guys repairing the pothole on the corner. I'm glad they're done. Those perverts kept wolf-whistling at me whenever I opened the door for a beautiful woman. Apparently seeing a gentleman in action really revved their engines, if you know what I mean."

"Are you sure they were whistling at you?" I asked. *Pretty sure it was probably more about the women…*

Rutherford nodded. "Um, have you *seen* this new pair of skinny jeans that I found on 5th Avenue a month ago?"

"I have." *But I wish I hadn't.* You can never unsee something like that.

"We're getting a little off topic here," said Chastity. "Listen, Rutherford. Ash's smoking hot billionaire boyfriend turned her neighbor's apartment into a three-story closet filled with millions of dollars' worth of designer clothes, and we need to know how he did it. So did you see any construction workers in the building or not?"

No! Bad Chastity! Don't tell him all that!

Rutherford stared at her. "Billionaire boyfriend? Three-story closet? Hasn't anyone ever told you that it's insensitive to brag about such things to someone who lives in a cardboard box?"

I forced a laugh. "Chastity just has a weird sense of humor. I don't actually have a three-story closet. But someone did do some unexpected construction work in my apartment without me knowing."

"Mhm. Sure." Rutherford did not sound convinced. "I'm afraid I can't be much help, though. Because I didn't see any construction workers in the building recently."

"Are you sure?" I asked. "How is that possible?"

He shrugged. "It's not like I keep a constant watch. I'm a homeless man, not a security guard."

"What about last Thursday?"

"Let me check my planner." Rutherford pulled out a very worn-looking Playboy magazine and leafed to a random page. "Last Thursday I was dumpster diving at the Gochujang Palace, of course. Everyone knows that's the day they throw out all their unused shrimp." He put his fingers to his lips and gave a chef's kiss. "Delizioso!"

I suppressed a gag. "Dude, Thursday is exactly the day I was wondering about. Give me my pizza back!"

"That wasn't part of the deal." He opened up the pizza box and licked *all* of it. Every inch. Then he sashayed away down the hall. "Ciao!"

"Damn it. Rutherford is the worst. And when did he get so Italian?"

"No idea," said Chastity. "I know he said he isn't here all the time, but he's here an awful lot. What are the odds of Tanner being able to build such a massive closet without Rutherford or either of us seeing any construction workers? Or for that matter…how did we not hear them? They were doing renovations four floors above me a few months ago and it was the most annoying freaking thing in the world."

"Yeah, it just doesn't make any sense." I walked into my apartment and flopped down on the couch.

"I told you it was vampire magic!"

"Since when can vampires silently construct the world's biggest closet? That was nowhere in the literature."

"Do you have a better explanation?" Chastity's phone buzzed before I could answer. "Oh! Tanner has an incoming call." She hit a few buttons and then Tanner's phone call was playing through her speakers.

"We've got a problem," said a deadpan voice. Marty the PI. I'd recognize his voice anywhere.

"Talk to me," said Tanner.

"Your email has been compromised."

"Impossible."

"Then how do you explain your email being accessed by two different IP addresses this morning?"

"Maybe I left it open on my laptop?"

"Nope. The second IP was masked with some pretty sophisticated code. It was definitely malicious."

"Shit. Do you think it's dodo?" Tanner suddenly sounded *very* nervous. I'd never heard him like that before.

Dodo?

"Could be. Either way, you need to trash your phone and laptop ASAP. And any other device you've used to access your email in the last 24 hours."

"Got it. Thanks for the heads up." Tanner's words were followed by a splash, a loud cracking noise, and then silence.

"Did he just throw his phone in a puddle and stomp on it?" I asked.

Chastity turned her phone towards me. Dexter's app displayed a big error message: CONNECTION LOST. "Yup."

"Well...at least we got a name of who he's afraid of. Dodo."

"Like the extinct bird? Or like...two female deer?"

"He said it like it was all one word. Let's assume for a moment that he doesn't have an irrational fear of extinct birds. That means dodo must be...an organization? Or an acronym?" I opened Google and searched for dodo. The first result was TheDodo.com. From what I could tell it featured a bunch of cute animals and encouraged pet adoptions.

"Aw, they're so cute. I've always wanted to get a little dog that I could carry around in my purse. Wouldn't that be perfect for me?"

"Only if you want your entire apartment to be covered in hair. #SatanStalin." I shuddered.

"Um…what did you just say?" asked Chastity.

"#SatanStalin. Because dogs are the offspring of Satan and Stalin."

"No they aren't. They're poofy little adorable things."

"Agree to disagree. Because I'm right and you're a fascist." *Or a communist?* I really needed to brush up on my World War 2 history. "Anyway, let's try to stay focused. Is Tanner scared of the people who own this site?" A video of a kitten drinking from a baby bottle popped up on the homepage. "I'm not really getting murderous cartel vibes here."

"I don't know," said Chastity. "Animal rights people can get nasty. Maybe Tanner got caught wearing fur? Ohhh! Or maybe he's a big game hunter."

"Those are definitely weird rich person things to do. But I don't think that's it. That wouldn't create an unpayable debt. He could make those people happy by giving PETA a big donation. Or by posing nude for one of their ad campaigns." A wonderful image popped into my head. I shook my head and tried to focus.

"I agree. I don't think animal activists are the ones he's afraid of. And Tanner doesn't seem like a hunter. The only big game I could see him hunting is cougars. Winky face." Chastity laughed at her own joke.

What the hell? Really…what did she mean by that? Had she seen Tanner hanging out with a bunch of old ladies recently or something? Before I could ask, Chastity composed herself and started talking again.

"What else comes up for dodo? Maybe it's an acronym?"

"Let's see…" I added *acronym* to my search and three possibilities came up. "Dealer Owned Dealer Operated. Apparently referring specifically to the petroleum industry?"

"Nope. Next."

"Director of Digital Operations."

Chastity shook her head.

"And finally, Dad of Daughters Only."

"That's it?"

"Yup. I kind of like that last one. The idea of Tanner pissing off a girl-dad is kind of hilarious."

"Wait…what if that's it?!"

I laughed. But Chastity didn't. "Wait, are you serious?" I asked.

"Yes. Think about it. Tanner is part of a sex club. What if he fucked some dude's daughter? Or *all* of his daughters. Maybe even all at the same time. That could potentially piss a guy off enough for them to accept nothing less than revenge."

"Holy shit. I think you're right!" *That little man-slut!*

"The best part is that this is so easy to fix. Once we find out whose daughter he banged, you can just pretend to be Tanner's daughter and let the guy revenge-bang you. And then you and Tanner can live happily ever after."

"Oh right. Since Tanner would totally be cool with me banging someone else."

"Did you learn nothing from those videos I gave you?"

"The porn?"

"Yes! Specifically the ones where the wives paid off their husbands' gambling debts by fucking on camera? The husbands were always so appreciative."

"Now I have to film it too?!" *This plan just keeps getting worse and worse.* "I just got rid of one sex tape. I'm not going to make another!"

"That part is probably negotiable," said Chastity. "I guess it really depends on if Tanner made a sex tape with the dude's daughter…"

A knock at the door interrupted our conversation.

"You expecting company?" asked Chastity.

"Nope."

"Oh! It's probably a date card!" Chastity ran to the door.

I was right behind her. *Society date tonight with Tanner?! Yes!*

Chastity squealed with excitement. "It's an envelope!"

It was. But it was blue rather than black. And it was a little bigger than the Society invitations usually were.

Chastity tore into it and pulled out another envelope. This one had a message scrawled on the front:

Ash,
If I disappear, open this envelope.
-Tanner

He'd sent me a just-in-case note? I blinked fast to make sure I wouldn't start crying. I'd told him how much I wished Rosalie had left a note behind. *And he remembered.*

"Wow," said Chastity. "The idea of dodo tapping Tanner's phone really has him shook."

"Yeah, good thing it was just us though. So he has nothing to worry about. Either way…this is like, the cutest thing ever."

"Him being afraid is cute?"

"No. Him giving me this note is cute. The other day I told him that I always wished Rosalie would have left me a note. So when he thought he might be in danger…he sent me a note."

"You're right. That's adorable. And depending on what it says inside, it might be even more adorable." Chastity ripped the second envelope open and pulled out the note.

"What are you doing?! We weren't supposed to open it unless he disappears."

"So?"

"So now if he disappears I'll think it's our fault! It's like we're telling the universe we *want* him to disappear."

Chastity scrunched her face up. "Uh, yeah. I don't think that's how anything works. I bet he's gonna tell you he loves you."

"Really?!" I grabbed it out of her hands and started reading.

Ash,

If you're reading this, then things have gotten too dangerous for me to stay in New York. I can't tell you where I'm going. Or when I'll be back. But I promise that I'm safe.

Yours,

-Tanner

P.S. Go to Club Onyx. That's where you'll find what you're looking for.

I stared at the note. "I'm confused. Is this just a really silly way of telling me that if he has to hide, he's gonna hide at Club Onyx?"

"It would appear so. Or at least someone at Club Onyx will know where he is. Which means I was right all along about being able to find his secrets there!"

"I have to admit, I was skeptical. But you were right all along."

"Yeah I was! Ah! We're so close to cracking this whole mystery wide open! I can practically taste it. Although I am slightly disappointed that this wasn't a Society date card. I was so curious to see what they'd come up with next."

"Speaking of the Society… I still have one more wish."

"Well I know what we have to wish for."

"Yup. Glad we're on the same page." This was a no-brainer. The Society needed to step in and fix whatever problems Tanner had caused by banging some dude's daughter. I opened the Society app and clicked on the genie lamp logo. A prompt appeared:

You have three wishes. What is your third wish?

"How should I word this?"

"Hmm…" Chastity tapped her finger against her lips. "You know, I always think better with wine."

"Good idea." I jumped up and went to grab some wine out of my fridge. "Here's to the two best detectives in town," I said. Chastity and I clanked glasses.

"And to us *finally* getting into Club Onyx." She took a giant gulp.

"Hear, hear! So how should we word this?"

"I think I have an idea. Can I take a stab at it?"

"Do it." I handed her my phone and downed some wine.

She tapped out a wish with her thumbs. I gave her a second and then got up so I could read over her shoulder. But all I could see was a message saying *Thank you for submitting your wish.*

"You hit submit already?!"

"Yeah. You told me to do it."

"To draft it! Not submit it."

"Oh. Well lucky for you, I worded it perfectly."

"Are you sure?" I was borderline freaking out. Genie wishes were notorious for getting twisted in horrible ways. Combine that with the Society being a sex club, and there was a high likelihood that a poorly worded wish would lead to a gangbang or something. "What exactly did you type?"

"I wish for me and my best friend, Chastity Morgan, to have access to Club Onyx," recited Chastity.

I stared at her. "Very funny. What did you really type?"

"That was it. Shit. Should I have switched the order that I listed us? I know it's not technically correct to say *me and*, but the other way just felt a little clunky."

"Chastity. What the actual hell?! Why would you wish for that?"

"Uh…what else would I have wished for? All of Tanner's secrets are at Club Onyx. Thus, we need access. You even said we were on the same page."

"Because I thought we were! Clearly we needed to wish for Tanner to be safe." *Damn it, Chastity!*

"Huh, I never thought of that." She cringed a little. "That's my bad."

"You're damn right it's your bad! If something happens to Tanner now…"

"For what it's worth, I actually do think this is a better wish. Tanner is part of the Society. If they could solve his problems, he would have wished for their help already."

Huh. I hadn't thought of that. "You have a point. But I'm still mad at you. From now on, no more submitting wishes for me. Got it?"

"Yeah. I promise, I'll do whatever I can to help keep Tanner safe."

"Does that mean you'll let Tanner's former lover's dad revenge-bang you instead of me?"

"Absolutely. I bet he's quite the silver fox."

Thank God. I didn't know when we'd get access to Club Onyx, but in the meantime I could try to get Tanner to spill the beans about whose daughter he'd banged.

There was only one problem: Tanner didn't show up for work the next morning.

Chapter 49

DODO

Wednesday

"Where is he?" I whispered to Chastity for about the 20th time. It was 10 o'clock and there was still no sign of him. He was never this late to work. Something was definitely wrong. It took every ounce of my restraint to keep my butt parked in my chair so I wouldn't start pacing.

"He'll be here," she said.

"But what if dodo got him!"

"Ash. *We* were the ones who bugged his phone. Not dodo. He's not in any danger."

Right. I kept forgetting about that. Or maybe it was just easier to be worried about him disappearing than to focus on the fact that he couldn't be with me because of some other girl he'd been with. I hated her and her stupid dad. If that was even what was happening. It was just a theory - albeit a more realistic theory than Tanner being a vampire.

And then there was still the mystery of how he made my secret closet. Chastity and I had inspected it more thoroughly last night. Or at least we'd tried to. It had quickly devolved into Chastity wanting to try on more of the clothes. She'd somehow convinced me that I should wear lingerie under my clothes at all times in case I needed to perform an impromptu seduction. Luckily Odegaard lingerie was super comfortable. Despite all the lace and straps, it was basically like walking around in athleisurewear. And it made me feel sexy as hell.

Except when my man was missing! *Gah! Where is he?!*

"Take a deep breath," said Chastity. "And maybe try texting him?"

"And say what? 'Did dodo murder you?' " *I never should have hacked his phone.* I was no good at keeping secrets. I was seconds away from confessing everything.

"Uh, no. Just ask him something about work. Literally anything except for what you just said."

"Oh, right." *Duh.* I got out my phone and typed out a text:

Me: Should I bring anything special to our meeting at the Manhattan Menagerie?

It was kind of a dumb question, but it wasn't the worst. I hit send.

No reply. No reply. No reply. "Oh my God he's definitely dead," I said.

"You sent the text four seconds ago. Take a deep breath."

For some reason I did the opposite and started holding my breath. At least ten more excruciating seconds passed. And then my phone dinged. *Ahhhh!*

Tanner: Nope.

Nope? That's ALL he has to say?

Me: Nope?! That's all you can say? I've thought you were dead all morning!

I was about to hit send when another message came.

Tanner: Actually, on second thought...maybe bring an umbrella. I've heard you can have a pretty shitty time in the aviary if you forget one.

Tanner: To clarify, I meant that the birds are gonna shit on us.

Me: Wow, nice dad joke.

Me: Speaking of dads...I bet dads hate you.

I immediately regretted hitting send on that last one. In my head it felt like the perfect opportunity to try to find out if he'd pissed off some girl's dad. But in reality it was an absolutely terrible segue. And honestly, I bet most dads loved him. He was a very charming guy.

Tanner: They do hate me. But only because I steal their jokes.

Me: And their daughters?

Tanner: What? Is your dad mad that you work for me? I know he would have preferred you go into accounting, but that wouldn't have been a good fit. You were born for marketing. Anyway, gotta go. I'll have a car pick you up at 5 for our meeting at the menagerie.

He was definitely pretending to be innocent with the whole daughter's thing. But there was no time to dwell on that. I'd been neglecting my work all morning, and there was SO MUCH to do. Once Spaceboy signed on, we'd been getting a ton of invitation requests from influencers. Which was exactly what we wanted. But it was too many. So I had to go through and vet each one. Less than 100K followers? *Better luck next time.* Stupid name? *No invite for you.* Ugly pictures? *Byyyye.*

More importantly, though...we still didn't have a caterer. Well...kind of. Tanner had found a replacement caterer for hors d'oeuvres, but apparently their desserts tasted like sand. So we were still in need of a good pastry chef.

No pastry chef worth our time would deign to return one of my calls, but they would likely reply to Tanner. So my job was to make a list of my top 3, and then he'd make the calls.

It took me all of ten seconds to make my list. At the very top was Chef Santiago. He had a restaurant in the city, but he also ran one of the most successful YouTube cooking channels. Without Chef Santiago's videos, I never would have been able to help Joe save his family's sugarcakes business. He was my cooking idol.

"Do you really think I should put Santiago's on the list?" I asked Chastity. "I feel like Tanner wanted a list of bakeries rather than restaurants with 3 freaking Michelin stars. What are the odds that he'd be able to fit us in so late? Even just for dessert?"

"Almost zero," replied Chastity. "But those were also our odds of getting Spaceboy to play at the party, and Tanner made that happen. So I say go for it. You need to get used to Tanner making all of your wildest dreams come true."

"Yeah. When he's not too busy banging people's daughters."

"Would you prefer he bang people's sons?"

"No!" *Gross!*

"Then he doesn't really have many options…"

"Sure he does. He could bang me."

"You're a daughter."

"Yeah, but as long he doesn't break my heart or hump and dump, I'm sure my dad wouldn't mind." *Ew.* I hated everything about that. Why had I said that?

"I don't know. I could see your dad getting jealous when you start calling Tanner Daddy."

"Oh God. I'm gonna be sick." I pretended to throw up in a trashcan.

Then I spent the rest of my day vetting influencers. I kept hoping that Sierra would be one of the applicants. It would have been so satisfying to send her an invitation to get her all excited and then tell her we sent it to her by mistake. Or maybe I could invite her and then push her overboard… Or better yet, we could rent a lion from the menagerie and then accidentally let it free on board. The real trick of it would be convincing her to wear a necklace made of meat.

Alas, she hadn't applied yet. So there would be no rejection and no maritime murder. But I could still try to rent a lion. Just in case. *Will the menagerie even have a lion?* I wasn't sure. But it was time to find out.

The car picked me up at 5 o'clock sharp and took me a few short blocks to an old abandoned-looking warehouse. I was worried it wasn't the right place until Tanner walked out the front door accompanied by a man in a ridiculous circus outfit and the twirliest mustache east of the Mississippi.

"Ash, it's my pleasure to introduce you to Claude. He's been my animal guy for years."

Claude bowed deeply as if he'd just made an elephant jump through a flaming hoop or something.

"Animal guy? How often do you need animals?"

"You'd be surprised. Like I always say - it's not a party unless something ends up a leash."

"A truer saying has never been said," agreed Claude. "If you two will just follow me, we can get started. What kind of animals are you looking for?"

"The bigger the better," I said as we walked inside. Or…outside? Yup. We were definitely outside. It wasn't a warehouse at all. It was like we'd gone into a little zoo. There were a few fences to separate the different enclosures, but no cages.

"Bigger the better, eh?" asked Claude. "Well, I'm afraid that Little Lucy here is already reserved for this Saturday."

"Little Lucy?" I asked.

Claude whistled and an absolutely *massive* bear lumbered towards us.

I let out a little scream and Tanner stepped in front of me. Was he planning on fighting the bear for me? It sure seemed like it. My heart did a little flip.

"Aw, don't be scared," said Claude. "Little Lucy won't hurt 'ya. He's a good boy. Aren't you, Lucy?"

"Good…*boy*?"

"Yup. Little Lucy here is six hundred pounds of pure Grizzly bear muscle. One of our most popular attractions." Claude pulled a fish out of his pocket and tossed it to Little Lucy.

"How about something less likely to tear the face off of one of our guests?" suggested Tanner. "I was thinking we could get a few zebras and paint their white stripes to be fluorescent. Like DJ Spaceboy's visor."

"Heavens, boy," said Claude. "You can't paint a zebra! PETA would string me up by my nuts and get my merchandise sent to the zoo faster than you can say flaming lion manes."

So maybe it is TheDodo.com that hates Tanner. They certainly wouldn't appreciate him painting zebras. But again…that wasn't an unforgivable act. Just an easily fixable faux pas. It had to be the daughter thing. And anyway…I was more fixated on the fact that Claude had just mentioned lions.

"Let's pass on the zebras then," I said. "They're basically just striped horses anyway. #HorseFacts." I lifted my hand for Claude to high-five me.

He did not.

I cleared my throat as Tanner tried to stifle a laugh. I didn't know why I kept thinking everyone would understand my hashtags. Only Tanner did. "Do you have lions?" I asked.

"We do indeed."

"On a scale of one to ten, how likely are they to maul someone wearing a meat necklace?"

"Eleven." Claude's eyes went to my chest.

"Hey. Eyes up here, buddy."

"I wasn't looking at your udders. I was checking to make sure you weren't wearing a meat necklace. I'm one mauling away from getting shut down for good."

Did he just refer to my breasts as udders?

"On that note," said Tanner. "Let's go ahead and rule out anything that's likely to maul someone. Putting a lion on a yacht surrounded by plates of New York's finest wagyu sliders is not a good idea."

"What about a giraffe?" I suggested.

"On a yacht?" asked Tanner. "Please tell me you've seen *The Hangover Part III.*"

"Ah, right. Maybe a giraffe is a bad idea. I'm not sure Wineflix and Chill would be very happy if they were forever remembered as the idiots who decapitated a giraffe with the Brooklyn Bridge."

I thought Tanner would laugh, but he was just staring off into the distance.

"Tanner?" I asked.

No response.

I pulled on his jacket. "Hey, Tanner. You okay?"

He jumped a little. "What? Oh. Yeah. I'm fine. I just thought I saw a uh…ostrich."

"Where?" I looked where he was looking. There was definitely no ostrich.

"It must have flown away."

"Mhm. Right. Except that's not how ostriches work. Wanna tell me what's really on your mind?"

"Just business stuff. I'll handle it."

"Anything I can help with?" asked Claude. "I know you're here about your yacht party, but I can help with all your exotic animal needs. Nothing helps seal a big deal quite like the sight of a panda sitting in the corner of your conference room chewing on bamboo."

"I'll keep that in mind," said Tanner. "But let's get back to the yacht party. We need something exotic but not too dangerous… And bonus points if there's a clever tie-in to Spaceboy's performance."

"How about a dodo?" I suggested.

Tanner flinched at the word dodo. But he recovered quickly. "That would be quite the spectacle. But I haven't seen one of those in like 200 years."

"*You* haven't seen one in 200 years? Ah yes, I forgot about your time spent sailing the east African coast back in the 17th century."

Tanner laughed. "You know what I meant. They've been extinct for years. Now, how about Komodo dragons? Those are exotic."

"I really like the idea of *dodos*," I said. "Are you sure you don't know where to find any *dodos?*" I kept putting more and more emphasis on the word each time I said it.

"Nope. If Claude here doesn't have them, then no one does."

"What about some other type of dodo? Like a dad who only has daughters?"

"What are you talking about?"

I couldn't hold it in any longer. "I know about the daughters, you pervert!"

Tanner looked at me like I was crazy. "What daughters? I'm so confused right now."

"The ones you slept with."

"Is she accusing you of sleeping with young girls?" asked Claude. "If so, then I'm afraid I won't be able to lend you any animals this weekend."

"Will you give us a moment please?" Tanner grabbed my arm and pulled me away from Claude. "What the hell are you talking about?"

"I know all about DODO. An acronym for Dad of Daughters Only. So tell me what daughters you banged to get into so much trouble."

"Wow. WOW." Tanner took a deep breath. "I don't even know where to start."

"Maybe start by telling me how many it was. It was three daughters, wasn't it? Triplets, maybe? God, why are guys so obsessed with banging triplets?"

Tanner leaned in and lowered his voice. "Ash… I don't know where you heard that word, but DODO doesn't have anything to do with dads or daughters."

"Then what is it?"

"You really want to know?"

"Yes!"

"Okay, okay. But you have to lower your voice."

"Why? Worried Little Lucy is going to hear about your perverted ways?"

"No. I'm worried that Claude is a DODO agent. Jesus, I'm worried *everyone* is a DODO agent. I even thought you were for a while there. Back when you were stalking me. And maybe a little after we first actually met."

"You were stalking me!"

"Hmm…no. You were definitely stalking me. Anyway, back to DODO. Everything I'm about to say never leaves this menagerie, okay?"

"Of course."

"Okay, so DODO…" started Tanner.

"Actually, I can't *quite* promise that. I'd like to think I can keep it a secret, but I'm 100% going to tell Chastity everything. She's already in too deep. It's better to read her in than to have her keep investigating."

"Okay, fine. But no one else. Not even your parents. Deal?"

I nodded.

Tanner pulled me farther away from Claude, deep into some sort of tunnel. "DODO is an ancient organization with the power to make me disappear in the blink of an eye. I've been running from them for years, but they're always out there. Watching. Waiting for me to slip up."

"So…DODO is the cartel that's after you? Were cartels ancient organizations?"

"Not exactly, no. It's not a cartel per se. It's worse."

Worse than a cartel? How many daughters had he banged? I shook away the thought. He'd told me that wasn't what was happening right now. Hadn't he? I needed to clarify this. "Wait, so you didn't bang any daughters? Not even those hot triplets?"

"Really? That's what you're going to focus on? And what hot triplets are you talking about?"

"I don't know! The ones you banged."

"I didn't bang any triplets." He paused. "Well, actually, I kind of have. It really depends on your definition of bang."

I stared at him.

"But that has nothing to do with DODO," he added.

"So banging someone's daughter isn't what upset DO-DO?"

"No!" He paused again. Just like he had with the triplet question. "Well, actually…in a funny way, it kind of is. But not at all in the way you think."

"Aha! So you did bang a daughter." *Gotcha, bitch!*

"Literally every female is a daughter. Can we please stop wording it that way?"

"Maybe." I stared at him some more, hoping he'd spill the rest of his secrets. I was so close to learning everything.

"Wait…" he frowned as he stared at me. "How do you know about DODO?"

Oh shit.

Chapter 50

MATTHEW FREAKING CALDWELL

Wednesday

I tried my best to stall. I looked around the dark tunnel he'd pulled me into. But there was nothing to throw or anything. The fire extinguisher in my purse was calling to me. I could just grab it and spray it everywhere as a diversion... "Ash, how do you know about DODO?" he asked again.

Fuck everything. The lie was tearing me up inside. And making my outside sweat profusely. I couldn't hold it in any longer! "Because I was the one who tapped your phone. It was all me. And I'd do it again because clearly I've lost my mind and your stalkery ways have rubbed off on me. I saw everything. I heard everything. Including your call with Marty."

"Are you serious!?" said Tanner. He was practically screaming. But not in an angry way. He kind of seemed overjoyed.

"Yes?" This felt like a trap.

He grabbed my face and kissed me. God, I loved the taste of his lips on mine. And it was refreshing to smell his blueberry skin rather than the pungent stench of the Manhattan Menagerie.

"Jesus, Ash. Next time you want to betray my trust and rifle through all of my personal documents, just ask. Do you have any idea how freaked out I've been since I got that phone call from Marty? I couldn't sleep at all last night. And I've been looking over my shoulder all day expecting someone to pop out of a van and shove a bag over my head. That was how it happened with old Herbert. Those bastards nabbed him right outside of his Upper East Side apartment just last year."

"Is he okay?"

"No he's not okay! No one has seen or heard from him since."

"I'm so sorry."

"It's okay. He was more of an acquaintance, really. But knowing that they grabbed him so close to here definitely made me nervous."

"I still don't understand why you can't just pay them off. And what does DODO even stand for?"

"The less you know, the safer you are. I've already told you too much. Just know that I'm doing everything in my power to get them off my back."

"But…"

"Do you trust me?"

I wanted to. But I barely knew anything about him. I searched his eyes. He looked so sincere. "Maybe." Probably. *Yes.* It was stupid, but I did. Tanner had done nothing but lie to me ever since I'd met him. And yet…he also protected me and did a bunch of sweet stuff too. Clearly he was actually in danger. I'd almost given him a heart attack by making him think I was a DODO agent.

"Well you should. Because these monkeys would be *perfect* for the party."

Wait, what?

He pointed to the monkeys that had stealthily surrounded us while we'd been talking. They were each like three feet tall and absolutely adorable. But they had nothing to do with DODO. Was Tanner high?

"Huh?" I asked.

Tanner nodded his head towards Claude approaching.

Ah, gotcha. "Okay, I trust you," I said. Hopefully I played along quick enough so that Claude didn't realize we had been talking about something else. *Is Claude really a DODO agent?* And just like that, Tanner had added another fear to my list. I just had to decide if I was more scared of being nabbed by DODO or having a centipede crawl up my leg. "I'll agree to get the monkeys on one condition," I added to really sell our change of topic.

"Name it," said Tanner.

"We have to get at least two dozen of them. And they have to all wear little space helmets." The image just popped into my head. And as soon as it did, I knew it had to happen. It was so perfect. If this party didn't go viral, I'd willingly turn myself over to DODO and let them melt me in a vat of acid.

"Did you just come up with that right now?" asked Tanner.

"Yup."

"Wow, you're a genius. That's why I'm paying you the big bucks."

"BIMG actually takes most of my billable hours for themselves. But I appreciate the compliment."

Tanner turned to Claude. "Do you have two dozen of these little guys?"

"I actually have three dozen."

"Don't be ridiculous," said Tanner. "Can you imagine *three dozen* monkeys dancing around the yacht? This is going to be a classy event, not some seedy backroom freak show."

"Of course," said Claude. "My mistake. I take it you'll supply the cages?"

Tanner threw his arm around Claude and pulled him into a hug. "Ah, Claude. You know me too well. *Of course* I'll supply the cages."

Why does Tanner have so many cages? Is it a sex thing? It sure seemed like it was.

"Should I draw up the paperwork?" asked Claude.

"Yes please," said Tanner. "Ash, why don't you go ahead and take the rest of the night off? You've earned it with this monkey idea."

"You sure?"

"Yeah. I'll finish up here. You can go tell Chastity all about the monkeys before she does something she shouldn't."

"Huh? Oh, right. Gotcha." Monkeys was code for DODO. Yeah, it was probably a good idea to call her off before she tried to blow someone for information or something.

"Want me to call Nigel to take you home?"

It was tempting, but I just couldn't accept. When my apartment was only a few blocks away it felt wrong to call Nigel. Surely the little man had better things to do on a Wednesday evening. Although…he had shown up at my apartment at a moment's notice with cookies just because Tanner asked him to. That was a little too eager to serve if you asked me. Nigel was up to something shady. I'd walk, thank you very much.

Besides, a short walk would help me process all this new information. Especially the bit about DODO making people disappear. Just like Rosalie had.

Was it possible that it had been them who took her?

While I walked home, I tried to replay every conversation I'd had with her in the weeks and months leading up to her disappearance. Had she ever mentioned DODO? I really didn't think she had. But then again…neither had Tanner until I bugged his phone and forced him to spill the beans.

I'd only made it about half a block before my chest tightened with this intense feeling of dread. My blouse was drench in sweat almost immediately. It was the kind of feeling you'd get when you're walking down a dark alley and see a bunch of dudes with baseball bats and switchblades approaching. Or when you're about to get bagged by DODO?!

Nope. Neither of those things was happening. It was something much worse.

Matthew Caldwell was approaching.

Yes, *the* Matthew Caldwell. The one that I'd met during the blind date from hell. The one I'd rather die than ever have to see again.

Had he seen me yet? There were two things working in my favor. First, it was twilight, so my bright red hair might not be quite as obvious as it would have been in broad daylight. Secondly, and more importantly, Matt was playing on his phone. So there was still time to avoid an awkward encounter. I just needed to act fast.

I frantically searched for a hiding spot. There were two options: a dumpster, or a bush. *Thank God.* I'd dumpster dive to avoid Matt any day, but today I didn't have to. I ran for the bush. But just as I got there, my heel caught between two bricks and sent me tumbling into the bush headfirst.

Ow. It wasn't the most graceful entry, but it was effective. I moved a few branches around to make sure that I was well hidden.

He was *almost* past me when he stopped and looked directly at me. No…not *directly* at me. Just in my general direction. I followed his gaze and realized that my Odegaard had gotten stuck in the sidewalk when I'd tripped.

Damn it!

Matt cocked his head and squinted at my shoe.

Please keep walking. Please keep walking. I will literally die if you find me.

Then he walked towards my shoe.

No! Bad Matt! Abort! Abort! Where was a lake when I needed it? Why did I think a bush could conceal me? There'd been a perfectly good dumpster right there and I'd passed on it. What was wrong with me? I'd been in a dumpster before and it was awful, yes. I'd had nightmares about it ever since. But sitting in a dumpster was not as awful as Matt spotting me. This is what I got for taking the easy way out. *Keep walking, Matt! For the love of God keep going!*

"Ash?" he said to the bush as he grabbed my shoe. "Is that you?"

I stayed silent. Why would he assume it was me? That was a crazy assumption to make. It could literally be any shoeless woman. *Go away!*

"Come on, Ash. I saw you jump into the bush."

"No you didn't. You were playing on your phone. And who's Arsh?" God, that name switch was so silky smooth. He would definitely start walking away now. *Shoo.*

"Arsh isn't a name. I said *Ash.* Because that's your name. And I know you're hiding in the bush."

"You're mistaken, sir. You don't know me. And I certainly don't know you."

"Interesting." He looked down at my beautiful Odegaard in his hand and carelessly tossed it in the air a few times. "So this isn't your shoe? You wouldn't care if I just tossed it across the street?"

He had me right where he wanted me. I stuck my arm out of the bush. "Shoe please."

"Here you go."

I snatched it from him. "Thank you, stranger."

"Any time, Ash. You really don't have to hide from me. Our date happened ages ago."

It didn't feel like ages to me. It felt like it just happened. That fire I started… I cleared my throat. "I'm so sorry, but I have no idea who you're referring to. *The incident* never happened."

"Did you just whisper *the incident* in a really weird way?"

"No."

"Is the incident you're referring to the one where you tried to set my dick on fire?"

"Absolutely not."

He laughed. "Ash, I'm fine. If you hadn't run away right after it happened, you would have seen that you only scorched my pants."

I didn't respond. I was glad his penis was okay. But it didn't undo what I'd done. "I don't know what you're even referring to. Because I'm not this Ash person you speak of. But she sounds terrible. Now please be gone."

He sighed. "Alright. But you're not terrible, Ash. I hope you know that. And you don't need to jump in lakes and bushes when you see me."

The dumpster it is then.

He shoved his hands into his pockets. "Okay. I'll leave you alone. I hope you have a good rest of your day."

"You too."

"See you around." He smiled and walked away.

"Please don't!" I called after him and peered out of the bush to make sure he was leaving.

He chuckled on his way down the sidewalk but didn't look back.

Phew. That had been a close call of awkwardness. But I felt good about how I handled it. I gave myself a solid 8/10 for creativity and execution. Passing him face to face and having to say hi would have been unbearable. Would we have shaken hands? Hugged? Bowed? Or the worst of all - made fake plans to get coffee and "catch up" some time. Just the thought of it gave me chills.

When the coast was clear I crawled out, pulled a few branches out of my hair, and put my Odegaard on. But not in that order. Because obviously I had to put my shoe on first in order to avoid getting sidewalk foot fungus.

I took a deep breath. I was ready to continue my walk home. And I'd already passed Matt, so nothing else bad could happen. I was basically invincible.

I took two steps before someone ran up behind me and pulled a burlap sack over my head.

Chapter 51

TAKEN

Wednesday

"Matt!" I screamed. "What the fuck! This isn't funny!"

He didn't say anything. He just picked me up in his big football player arms and tossed me into a van like I weighed nothing.

Oh God, was this revenge for the fire I'd set on our date? It had been an accident, I swear. Why was he doing this? He'd just acted so cool about the whole thing. "Matt, I'm sorry. I never meant to set your dick on fire! But you just told me your penis was fine!" Had he lied? Was his penis burnt and mangled? Could it even get hard anymore? *He's going to murder me for maiming his member.* Of course this was the way I was going to die. And I deserved it for penis mutilation.

"Go, go, go!" he yelled as the door slammed shut. Someone else hogtied my hands behind my back as the getaway driver hit the gas.

That was when it hit me. It wasn't Matt kidnapping me. It was DODO. I'd just been bagged. And I was never going to be seen again.

I started hyperventilating. For the first time ever, I wished it was Matt. And that was really saying something, because I hated seeing him. But I wished he was here with me right now. Kidnapping me or something. Because him kidnapping somehow seemed better than DODO kidnapping me. Matt wouldn't actually hurt me. But these guys?

"Am I going to die? Please don't kill me. I don't know anything."

Silence.

"Okay, I know a little bit. Or maybe a lotta bit. It depends on how you look at it. But I promise I haven't told anyone. Except my friend Chastity. Er…I mean Charity. Or maybe she's Charmander. Yup, that's her name. It's definitely not Chastity. Ha, I can't believe I forgot my best friend's name." *Oh no! Now they're going to kill Chastity too!*

I kept rambling like that for a good ten minutes. Which was really bad, because I should have been paying attention to all the turns we were making. Now if I escaped I wouldn't even be able to find my way back home. *Does that make sense? I don't think it does.* Why did people in movies always try to remember the turns when people kidnapped them? *Oh, duh.* It was so that they could sneak away and call the police and lead them right to them. That made a lot more sense. But it was too late. I'd already lost track. It was over for me. I was done. Dead.

"Are you sure this isn't Matt? Matthew Caldwell?" Oh God, why'd I just say his whole name? Now they'd go after him next. "Just kidding. That's just some person I read about in the tabloids. Please leave him alone." Just imagine if I set the man's dick on fire and got him murdered. I was the worst.

Nothing I said got any reaction from my kidnappers. So I stayed silent for the next ten minutes, praying that it actually was Matt and trying to remember our route.

Left. Right. Right. Right. Right. Right. Right.

Why are we taking so many right turns?

Right. U-turn. Left. Left. Right.

Then we stopped.

The DODO agent tossed me over his shoulder and carried me like a sack of potatoes up some stairs and onto an elevator. It went up a lot of floors. At least like 30. Or maybe 40?

The adventure ended with him putting me on a very comfortable sofa. It almost felt like leather.

"Where are we?" I demanded. "Let me go!"

He didn't respond. But he did pull the bag off my head. The room was dim. *Very* dim. But I'd just been sitting in pure darkness for like 30 minutes, so my eyes were very well adjusted. Which was unfortunate, because what I saw was absolutely terrifying. It looked like I was in the prop room at an old abandoned theater. I'd never seen so many creepy mannequins. Or were they mummies?

Oh my God. They're going to murder me and turn me into a mummy mannequin! Tanner *had* said that DODO was an ancient organization. It made sense that mummification was their primary means of making people disappear.

I squirmed against my restraints.

"Why are you doing this?" I asked as my hooded captor walked to the door. It didn't seem like it was Matt. His shoulders weren't broad enough. So that meant…this wasn't some kind of revenge thing like I'd hoped. My heart sunk. *I'm going to die here.* "Please don't make me into a mummy!"

He stopped and looked at me. "That's up to whoever buys you." And then he left, slamming the door behind him.

Whoever buys me?! What the hell is happening?! I rolled off the sofa and got to my feet. There had to be a sharp object around here that I could use to cut this rope off my wrists…

I froze when the door opened. Someone flicked the lights on. It was blinding after being in the darkness for so long.

"I'm sorry!" I yelled. "I promise I wasn't trying to escape! Don't mummify me!"

Someone laughed. The DODO agent suddenly sounded strangely feminine. Or maybe it wasn't the DODO agent at all.

"Who are you?" I asked. "Did you buy me?" I squinted and tried to see the person through the blinding light. The only features I could see at first were her two bubblegum-colored buns and her huge tits. As more of her came into focus - lingerie and heels that matched her hair - it became clear that I'd been purchased by a stripper. Or maybe a madame.

Yup. That was it. I wasn't going to be mummified. I was being sold into prostitution.

"Ash," said my new master. "It's me."

Huh? Wait a second. I blinked a few times and my eyes finally adjusted to the light. "Chastity?! Oh God. No! I didn't mean to tell them your name. It just slipped out. Did they hurt you?"

Chastity laughed. "What are you talking about? And why are you all tied up? Were you doing some kinky roleplay with the chauffeur?" She wiggled her eyebrows.

"Chauffeur?! Those fuckers bagged me and tossed me into an unmarked van."

"Weird. For me a couple of handsome men pulled up in a limo and asked me to get in. Then they handed me a blindfold so that I wouldn't see where were going. For security reasons."

"Are you kidding me?! I thought I was going to be raped and mummified. And meanwhile you were sipping mimosas in a limo?"

Chastity shrugged. "I guess they did their research and knew that I'd be more likely than you to get into a limo with some hunky men. Anyway, we should hurry. We only have ten minutes until the auction starts. We need to get you ready."

"Auction? So we really are being sold into prostitution?"

"I hardly think that a sex club auction is the same as prostitution."

"Sex club?"

Chastity blinked a few times. "Uh…yes. Did you really not put it together that we're at Club Onyx right now? For your third wish?"

"No! How would I have put that together? I wished to get invited to Club Onyx. Not be kidnapped by a bunch of perverts."

Chastity pointed to a giant neon CLUB ONYX sign on the wall above her. "That probably should have been your first clue."

"Well in my defense, I didn't see that. I was too distracted by your bubblegum hair. Is that a wig?"

"Yeah! Isn't it awesome?"

"It actually is." Then again, Chastity could make any hair color look amazing. And it looked like they'd given her blue colored contacts to make her eyes match.

"By the way, why are your clothes so dirty?" she asked. "You look like you walked into a bush."

"Technically I dove into a bush. Matthew Caldwell was coming. It was the only choice."

"Got it." Chastity grabbed some bright pink lingerie off a mannequin and tossed it to me.

"No, wait, don't…"

She laughed as it hit me in the face. "Sorry. Forgot your hands were still tied behind your back."

I turned around so she could undo the rope around my wrists. Then I shook out my arms.

"Man, being tied up is the worst."

"Well don't get too used to being free. Based on my conversation in the limo, I'd say we have pretty good odds of getting tied up again in a few minutes." Chastity smacked my ass with the rope.

"Hey!"

"Sorry. Just giving you a taste of what's to come."

"Oh God."

"Don't worry. I'm sure Tanner will buy you at the auction. And if he doesn't…oh well. Tonight is the perfect opportunity to make him jealous."

"But I don't want to make him jealous." *How many times do I have to tell Chastity I don't want to play games with Tanner?* "Everything is going so well. I finally got him to… Oh my God! I haven't told you yet."

"He asked you out?!"

"Oh. No. But he did tell me about…" I lowered my voice to a whisper. "DODO."

"Really?"

"Yup. I confronted him about it at the menagerie."

"So what daughters did he bang? Was it triplets? I bet it was triplets."

"Nope. No triplets. Or daughters at all! Turns out DO-DO doesn't stand for Dads of Daughters Only."

"Then what does it stand for?" asked Chastity as she tried on a statement necklace from one of the mannequins.

"Uh…he didn't say. But he told me it's an ancient organization."

"That does what exactly?"

"Makes people disappear."

"So he told you…no new information."

"No, he…" *Shit!* "That sneaky little bastard! It felt like he was telling me so much. But now that I think about it, you're right. He told me nothing. Just that they're dangerous and he's working on it."

"It's awesome that he's a billionaire and everything, but I'm getting really tired of him treating you like shit."

"He doesn't treat me like shit. He orders me dinner every night. And saves me from having my sex tape released to the world. And surprises me with the world's coolest closet."

"And strings you along as his not-quite-girlfriend, refusing to bang you because of some mysterious organization. Oh my God…" She snapped her fingers. "That's it. I can't believe I didn't see it sooner. He's totally wifey-zoning you."

"Wifey-zoning? What is that?"

"You know. Like hubby-zoning, only reversed."

"So like…marrying someone?"

"No! Hubby-zoning. It's when you find a great guy who is husband material. But you still wanna keep fucking around with other people for a bit. So you string him along - lots of quality time, gifts, and a little bit of fooling around - but don't give it all up. Just enough to keep them hanging around. Meanwhile you're getting absolutely railed by 10s every weekend. But since you aren't technically dating the hubby-zoned guy, it's not cheating."

"I don't think that's a thing."

"Sure it is. I'm doing it with like…three different guys right now." She looked so pleased with herself.

"Wait, so you're hubby-zoning three different guys? Or banging three different guys on the side?"

She shrugged. "Actually both."

What? "You can't hubby-zone three people. You can only have one husband. And you definitely shouldn't bang three people at the same time." That sounded worse than I meant for it to…

Chastity laughed. "Do you see a ring on my finger?"

I was pretty sure Chastity was doing life wrong. But damnit, what if she was right?

"You really think that's what Tanner's doing to me?" I asked.

"Yes. I've got it all figured out. His whole deal is that he invites random girls to join the Society. He uses their first wish to help them get comfortable, and then on their second wish he has them fulfill whatever sex fetish he's into that night. Then he ghosts them. But since they're now members of a sex club with tons of other hot dudes, he doesn't have to worry about clingers. It's really quite brilliant."

"But he never tried to bang me."

"Right. There are two reasons for that. First, you're the coolest girl ever, so of course he had an amazing time with you on your first date. You guys stayed up and talked for hours, right?"

"Yeah. I fell asleep in his arms." The memory made me smile.

"Well that's adorable. So that might have been enough for him to consider wifey-zoning you, but your accidental meeting the next day at BIMG was the final nail in your coffin. Because now you knew him outside of the Society."

"Damn. I thought your theory was going to be whack, but that actually makes a ton of sense. Is it weird that I can't decide if I'm devastated or excited? Because I hate that he's sleeping around. But I love the idea that he wants to marry me."

"You just have to un-wifey-zone yourself."

"How? And don't tell me to seduce him - my ego can't handle another failed seduction."

"You know how." She waggled her eyebrows at me.

I didn't want to know…but I'm pretty sure I did. *Shit, shit, shit. Triple shit!* "You're going to make me bang so many people, aren't you?"

She didn't respond. She just threw the pink lingerie at me again.

Chapter 52
THE SEX AUCTION
Wednesday

I dodged her lingerie toss. I wasn't putting any of this on. I didn't want to bang any randos. I only wanted to bang Tanner. "I take it back. I'll just seduce Tanner, thank you very much. Now where's the exit?"

"You don't need to seduce him. You need to seduce someone else. Give him a taste of the jealousy that's coursing through your blood right now. He likes to fuck girls at Club Onyx? Well two can play that game."

"Ew. I don't want to fuck any girls here. Or anywhere, for that matter."

Chastity rolled her eyes. "I didn't mean that. I meant that you can let the guys at Club Onyx fuck you."

"Guys plural? As in…more than one guy?"

"Maybe. Get ready for the sexiest night of your life." She bit her lip. I don't think I'd ever seen her this excited before.

"But I'm so awkward. I can't just strut out into Club Onyx and seduce some rando."

"Yeah, I know you can't. But Raven Black can." Chastity grabbed a black wig off a mannequin and handed it to me. She helped me put it on and then I changed into the pink lingerie as I continued to look for an exit sign. Yes, Raven Black could seduce a rando. But…did she want to? It depended on one thing - Was that really the only way for Tanner to commit to me? Because I'd tried a lot of things. And the wifey-zone thing made sense. Maybe I could just let a guy like…touch my boob or something. That seemed innocent enough but might still make Tanner jealous.

Gah! I needed more time to think it through. "So what dresses are we gonna wear?" I asked. "We probably need something with a thick fabric or all the lace from these bras will show."

Chastity laughed. "Do you see any dresses on these mannequins?"

"No. They're probably in the other room."

"Ash, this is a sex club. Honestly we're probably wearing too much already."

"But this is a thong!" I ran over to a mirror. "My ass is literally everywhere."

"Exactly. You look hot."

The door opened and two shirtless men walked in. I didn't even think to cover myself - I was too distracted by their leather masks, leather pants, and the heavy chains criss-crossed over their absolutely jacked chests. One had a full leather mask, complete with a little zipper over his mouth. The other's mask was more strappy. Both were terrifying.

"Hands behind your backs," demanded the one without his mouth covered.

"Ah!" Chastity did a cute little jump. "This is so fun!" She turned around and let Zipper-mouth cuff her.

Strappy-mask turned to me. "You too."

"Why are you wearing so much leather?" I asked.

"This isn't just any old leather. It's *Scottish* leather."

"Okay?" *Is that supposed to mean something to me?*

He held up a pair of thick leather cuffs. "Turn around and put your hands behind your back."

"What if I don't want to be cuffed?"

"Are you disobeying my orders?" asked Strappy-mask.

I didn't know what would happen if I disobeyed, but I was pretty sure it involved his penis. I suddenly regretted sassing him. "Nope. No, sir." I put my hands behind my back like a good little girl. The cuffs were surprisingly comfortable. But that wasn't the point. It was still rude to barge in on some half-naked girls and cuff them without their consent! Although technically that Society contract I'd signed was my consent. *Why the hell did I join a sex club?!*

The men led us down a hallway and into a dimly lit room with about 10 other women. All in lingerie, and all handcuffed. And there was definitely no exit sign in here. Strappy-mask pulled the chain off his shoulder and used it to connect my cuffs to a thick metal ring on the floor.

"What the hell is happening?" I whispered to Chastity as soon as he was out of earshot.

"I don't know," she replied. "But I love it! Can we please come here every night?"

"Are you serious?! This is insane. They're treating us like cattle."

"Right? It's so hot."

"No it isn't!" *Fine. It's a little hot.* But it was so weird! And being chained up with no possibility of escape made me have to pee so badly. "How long do you think they're gonna keep us here?"

"I don't think it'll be long."

A guy in a suit and a cowboy hat walked to the podium at the front of the room and cleared his throat. "In a few minutes, each of you will be sold to the highest bidder. From that moment until 2 a.m., you are their date." He was talking so fast that it was hard to keep up. "You have two options for the kind of date you are. If you'd like to be auctioned as a girlfriend - loyal, but not submissive - tap the purple square on the floor in front of you. If you want to be a sex slave to your owner, tap the red square."

I looked down at the floor. There were indeed two LED-lit tiles in front of me. One purple, one red. I hit the purple one. *Easy choice.*

The floor squares dimmed and one of the walls lit up. It was covered floor to ceiling in masks. Lace masks, bunny masks, leather masks…even scary masks like the ones they wore in *The Purge.* There was a three-digit number displayed next to each one.

"During the bidding you will each wear a mask," said Cowboy Hat. "You may dance to entice bidders, but do not, under any circumstances, remove your mask. Beef and Biff will be walking around to take your mask orders." Strappy-mask, who was apparently named Beef, started approaching girls to take orders while Biff got the masks off the wall. Once a mask was selected, that part of the wall would dim.

Cowboy Hat kept talking. "Once you're all masked, the auction will begin. Just a few rule reminders…" He started rattling off rules faster than I could follow.

"Which mask?" asked Beef.

"Uh…" I saw that Chastity had just selected a nice pink lace masquerade mask to match her hair. They didn't have any more like that, but they did have a similar blue one. "Number 084, please."

Biff walked over and grabbed my mask. My hands were still cuffed, so he put it on me.

"…and just to reiterate one more time - you can always use the safe word." The auctioneer ended his speech.

"Did you hear the safe word?" I whispered to Chastity.

She shrugged. "My safe word is *harder, Daddy*."

"Is that *the* safe word. Or is that just what you say? Because there's a huge difference there."

"I dunno. I wasn't paying attention. Hey, wanna bet on which girl will sell for the most?"

"No." *I want to know the safe word!*

"I'm guessing her." She nodded towards a girl in a leather bunny mask and lingerie made only of leather straps. Something told me she had definitely hit the red button. It was going to be a real downer when I sold for like 1/100 of what she sold for. Or what if I didn't sell at all? Just no bids. Crickets. I'd never be able to show my face in Club Onyx again.

"Everyone ready?" Cowboy Hat didn't wait for an answer. "Great. Let's begin. You're up first." He pointed to a girl in the front row. "Name please?"

"Giovanna," she said with a super cool accent.

Beef unchained her from the floor and guided her up to a platform at the front of the room. Then he pulled a lever and the platform took both of them up through a hole in the ceiling.

Cowboy Hat grabbed a microphone. "Ladies and Gentlemen, it is my pleasure to welcome you to this evening's auction. Our first offering is an evening with the lovely Giovanna. We'll start the bidding at 10,000. Do I hear 10,000? I do. Current bid 10,000. Will you give me 15,000?"

The winning bid turned out to be 30,000 for Giovanna. The platform came back down a second later with only Beef remaining.

"Damn," I whispered to Chastity. "Did he really just say 30,000? As in…dollars?"

"Yeah. But it was probably just monopoly money. Remember clause 24.1? If the Member makes payments to other members during wishes, she will do so using Society-issued credit cards or monopoly money."

It still freaked me out and impressed me that Chastity had the entire Society contract memorized. "Right. Forgot about that."

"Yeah, but I wish it was real money. That would be so much sexier."

"Wouldn't that just make us prostitutes?" I asked.

"Huh. Never thought of it that way. I just like the idea of a guy thinking that one night with me is worth as much as a car. It wouldn't be sexy if he was only willing to pay like…twenty bucks."

She had a fair point.

The next girls all sold for between 20 and 30 grand. Except for the girl in the strappy leather. I was correct that she was selling herself as a sex slave. She went for 50 grand.

And then the auctioneer pointed at Chastity.

"Ahhh! I can't believe this is happening!" she whispered.

Beef unchained her and took her to the platform.

Wait! No! I'd been so distracted by all this craziness that I hadn't anticipated being separated from Chastity. Having her by my side was the only thing keeping me from totally freaking out.

Beef was about to pull the lever when I yelled, "Wait!"

Everyone looked at me.

"We come as a pair."

"Oh really?" asked the auctioneer.

"Yup," said Chastity.

"I like it. Name?"

"Raven Black," I said.

Biff unchained me and took me to the platform with Chastity.

I thought being next to Chastity would make me feel better. But then there was the fact that I was handcuffed in heels and lingerie and about to be auctioned off. Stage fright immediately started to kick in. Was this platform taking us to a stage in front of hundreds of people? For all I knew it could have been taking us straight into the middle of Madison Square Garden. Or into an orgy.

"Bold move," said Chastity as the platform continued to rise. "I never would have guessed that you'd want to have a threesome with me."

"What?! Who said anything about…" Then it hit me. Two girls being auctioned off together at a sex club. Yeah, some pervert was definitely gonna buy us for a threesome. "Shit! I'm not a lesbian!"

Chastity laughed. "Single Girl Rule #30: Girl on girl action is only gay if no guys are watching."

"Wait, that's actually one of the Single Girl Rules? I always thought you just made that one up."

"Nope. It's real. Don't worry - threesomes can be really fun. There's nothing more satisfying than jerking a guy off onto a girl's face. And kissing a girl with a mouth full of cum is super hot."

I scrunched up my face. *Oh God. What have I gotten myself into?!*

The platform came to a smooth stop in the auction room. I'd expected to be standing at the front of a room looking out at lots of rich dudes holding little numbered paddles. But instead we were in a circular room surrounded by black glass.

"Ladies and gentlemen," boomed the auctioneer's voice through a speaker system. "Next up is a special treat. We'll start the bidding at 10,000 for the privilege of having Chastity and Raven as your sex slaves for the evening." He whistled softly. "I envy whatever man wins this one."

"Whoa, hold everything," I said.

Beef looked at me. His face was covered, but the way he had his arms crossed and his air of no-nonsense told me he didn't want me to be talking.

"I selected the purple square. Girlfriend experience. I don't want to be someone's sex slave!"

"Which did you select?" he asked Chastity.

"Sex slave, duh."

Chastity! Why?!

"Well there you have it," said Beef. "You joined her auction, so you go by her terms."

"But…"

"Do I hear 10,000?" asked the auctioneer through the speakers. If he was here I would have tried to argue with him more, but he conducted all the auctions from downstairs.

An LED above one of the windows lit up with 10,000.

"I have 10,000. Will you give me 20,000? 20,000?"

Another window lit up with 20. Then another with 30. The bids were flying in.

I stood there completely frozen, but Chastity was loving it. Each time a window lit up she'd blow them a kiss and give them a little shimmy.

"Will you give me 50,000?"

The window directly in front of us lit up with 250,000. I blinked a few times to make sure I was seeing it right.

The auctioneer sounded just as surprised as I felt. "I have 250. Wow. Will you give me 260? 260 anyone?"

A quarter of a million dollars?! Shit! Chastity was right. There was something really sexy about a man being willing to pay a lot of money for your body. And that was a whole lot of freaking money. Was a threesome with me and Chastity really worth that much? If so, we were wasting our time at BIMG. I'd have to ask her if we could shake Dexter down for a $250K threesome once or twice a year. Hell, I'd even take $100K.

"250 going once. Going twice… Sold!"

The winning bid turned red and a panel of the wall slid away.

Beef uncuffed us and walked us towards the room. "Wow," he said. "$250K sex slaves? The only other time I've seen a bid even close to that was when a bunch of guys all chipped in to get some girls for their buddy's bachelor party. I hope you two are ready to get *fucked.*"

Chapter 53

THE ONYXIES

Wednesday

"Can you tell me the safe word?" I asked Beef as we got closer to the door.

"No," he replied.

"Please?!"

"No," he said again.

Damn you, Beef! What had I ever done to make him hate me so? I'd only sassed him a little bit when we first met.

I slowed my pace even more.

Being a stripper at an anything-goes bachelor party was *not* how I had been planning to make Tanner jealous. I wondered if the groomsmen would be okay with just touching my boobs once. Twice at the most. That was where I drew the line. But I kind of knew they were going to insist on getting their money's worth. My tits were nice and all…but they'd paid a whole lot. And how was this party even gonna work? Would they have me and Chastity go off into private rooms one at a time? Or would they just tear our clothes off and gangbang us? *Hopefully they'll at least all be handsome…*

Then something hit me. Someone had just paid $250K for the night with us. A quarter of a million dollars. I knew it cost a lot to get into the Society, but that much money for one night was on a different level. I only knew two people who had that kind of money - Tanner and James Hunter. And James definitely had not seemed interested in my little striptease the other day.

Was Tanner the one who bought us?! And more importantly…if it was him, was he going to take advantage of us being his sex slaves? Hopefully he'd only take advantage of it with me, because I'd have to murder him if he tried to have a threesome with us.

Beef gave us one final little shove as we walked through the door to meet our owner for the evening.

Please be Tanner. Please be Tanner.

My heart leapt when I saw the back of his bright pink suit.

But then it sunk when he turned around.

Because it wasn't Tanner. It was that probably-gay guy that I'd met during my apartment hunting date. *Pink Ocelot.* His hair was somehow even bigger and more gelled than I remembered.

Why would he want us for a bachelor party? I would have thought that getting a few male strippers would have been more his speed.

"Ah, ladies!" he said. "Sorry about the unorthodox bidding. But time is of the essence here." His phone buzzed. "One moment please." He held up a finger and typed something frantically on his phone. I'd never seen someone's thumbs move so fast. Then he left. And then he came back a second later. "Sorry, I'm all over the place. This is a disaster. A DISASTER! But you two are perfect. Seriously, you both look *divine.*"

Chastity and I looked at each other. I could tell she was thinking the same thing I was: *What the actual hell is happening right now?*

"Uh…are you okay?" I asked him.

"Am I okay?! No I'm not okay. The show starts in 20 minutes and you two aren't even in your dresses yet. What are my 400 guests going to think if that curtain opens and it's just me on stage?"

I blinked. "Did you say *400* guests? And that you'll be on stage with us?" Then it hit me. It was probably a strip show. And he was going to be stripping with us. That made sense. He'd totally be into stripping for a bunch of dudes. But FOUR HUNDRED PEOPLE?! I was thinking it would be like…5 dudes max. But what if it was something other than a strip show? What if Pink Ocelot was about to rail me on stage?

"Yes. It's our biggest turnout ever. And everything is going wrong." He looked like he was about to cry.

I kind of felt the same way. I'd never been so nervous in my life. I had to know what was about to happen to me. "So uh…what exactly are you gonna make us do?"

"I'll explain while we walk." He waved for us to follow him out of the room. He was walking so fast that it was hard to keep up in my heels. "Were either of you here for the Onyxies last year?"

"Uh…no?" *What the hell are the Onyxies?*

He stopped and really looked at us for the first time. "Ah, I'm sorry I didn't recognize you at first. You're the girl who wished for access to Club Onyx tonight, yes? And you're her friend?"

"Yeah."

"Well you're in for a real treat later tonight then." For just a moment, his nerves seemed to be replaced by sheer excitement. "But first we have to get through this award ceremony." We rounded the corner and he nearly ran into a blonde. "Oh, Frankie! Thank God. Can you get these two prepped? I still have to do my vocal exercises and style my hair."

Ah! Yay! Frankie's here! But more importantly…was Ocelot implying that he *hadn't* styled his hair yet? Because it looked like he had spent hours on it.

"Prepped for what?" asked Frankie. She gave me a wave and mouthed, "Hi, Raven!"

"They're taking over for Kristen and Isadora."

"For real? They can't make it?"

"No. Their plane *still* hasn't even landed."

"Damn, okay." She put her hands on Ocelot's shoulders. "Take a deep breath. You're going to kill it tonight. I promise I've got everything all set just the way you want it."

He exhaled slowly and turned to me and Chastity. "Okay, gotta run. I'm so glad both of you are here. You're lifesavers. And to thank you, I have a special treat for you at the end of the show." He winked and sprinted off down the hall.

Special treat?

"Phew, sorry about that," said Frankie. "Ocelot always gets a little uptight on nights like these. Ah! Raven! I'm so excited that you're here at Club Onyx. Who's your friend?"

"Frankie, meet Chastity. You two are gonna love each other." How could they not? They were practically the same person. Tall, beautiful, and super outgoing. They both would have been blonde too if Chastity wasn't wearing that bubblegum wig.

"It's so nice to finally meet you." Chastity gave her a big hug, apparently not feeling at all awkward about the fact that she was only wearing lingerie.

"This is probably a dumb question," I said, "But what are the Onyxies? And how many dudes is Ocelot gonna make us bang tonight?"

Frankie laughed. "Come with me. I'll explain everything." We followed behind her and she kept talking. "The Onyxies are like the Oscars of the Society. We give awards to all of our best members. You know how there are always a few girls in the background who hand the awards out and guide winners to the green room? Yeah, that's what you two will be doing. Ocelot's girlfriend was going to do it, but apparently she and her friend got stuck on a plane. And before that he thought we had lost the Onyxies. Turns out one of the warehouse guys had just confused them for sex toys."

Ocelot has a girlfriend? That didn't seem right. But the rest of the evening was starting to make more sense. Like Ocelot's ridiculous $250K bid. He didn't want to gangbang us - he was just in a hurry and didn't have time for a bidding war.

Now that I knew I was safe, I could only think about one thing: Had Tanner really wifey-zoned me?

"Are you here at Club Onyx very often?" I asked Frankie as we continued down a never-ending hallway.

"Yeah. Ocelot seems to have an endless supply of work for me. There's always some wish to plan or new members to vet or a new room to set up." She pointed to one of the many doors that lined that hallway. Each door was identical - a big heavy slab with a tablet set in the wall next to it.

"What's in these rooms?" asked Chastity.

"It depends. The little symbols on the screens are hints about what you might find inside."

"So what does this one stand for?" Chastity pointed to a door marked with an eggplant emoji.

"Ocelot would kill me if I revealed such a secret." She sounded dead serious.

But there wasn't that much to reveal. Because as we passed it, we could hear loud moaning through the closed door. Someone was definitely getting pounded in there. Sexually. Chastity and I both looked at each other. I'm pretty sure I looked horrified. But there was a look of pure glee on her face. She was probably making a mental note to go back to the eggplant emoji room later tonight.

"Hot damn," she mouthed silently to me.

"Ah, here we are," Frankie said. "But we weren't at a door. It was just a solid wall… Until she pulled on a candlestick and the wall slid away.

Another secret door!

This one didn't lead to a secret closet like my bookshelf. Instead it led to the back of a stage. Stagehands dressed in all black moved walls and taped down wires and wheeled racks of clothes around. Frankie plucked two dresses off a rack and handed them to us. "Let's hope they fit."

I'd had quite enough of prancing around in my lingerie, so I slid into the dress as fast as humanly possible. It fit like a glove. And so did the gloves that matched it. They were so freaking silky. For years I'd been wishing that opera-length gloves would make a comeback. There was nothing better than always having a nice germ barrier on my hands.

Frankie smoothed a few spots on our dresses and then handed us a sheet of paper from her clipboard. "Here are your stage instructions. Nothing too complicated. Any questions before I go?"

"Just one thing. Does Ryder come here often?" I was proud of myself for remembering to use his Society name. I'd meant to ask her about Tanner back in the hallway right after I asked if she was here a lot, but we'd gotten totally sidetracked by all that talk about the secret rooms.

"I meant questions about the instructions. Haven't I told you that I'm not going to dish on Ryder?"

"But we're getting kind of serious…"

"Really?"

She looked so freaking surprised. Which kind of answered my question of whether or not he was still banging tons of girls in the Society. *Fricking frick!* "Yes," I said, trying not to sound deflated.

"Hmm. Okay. Come see me after the show and I'll spill the tea. And believe me…there's *a lot* of tea."

"As in…he's banged a lot of girls?"

Frankie laughed. "After the show. Gotta run!"

"Wait!"

She turned around.

"Can you tell me the safe word?"

"No." She ran off.

"Why won't anyone tell me the safe word?!"

"You're going to be fine," said Chastity. "But I think that pretty much confirms you've been wifey-zoned."

"Hmm…I don't know." I fidgeted with one of my gloves. "What if the hot goss about Tanner is that he's always a perfect gentleman and has never slept with anyone, despite all the girls here throwing themselves at him?"

"Maybe. I'm happy to ask around if you need me to confirm. The way I see it, we have three primary objectives this evening." She held up three fingers. "First, we need to establish that Tanner has in fact wifey-zoned you. Then we need to find a hot guy for you to fuck so that Tanner's head explodes. And finally, we need to get someone to tell us what building we're in right now so that we can find our way back and do it all over again as many times as we need to in order to get you out of the wifey-zone."

"Okay. That's a good list." *Except the part about me fucking a stranger.* "But can I add something?"

"Sure."

I held up the instructions from Frankie. "We have to memorize these immediately." Being on stage was terrifying. But being on stage without knowing what the heck I was supposed to be doing? That was literally the worst thing I could possibly imagine ever happening to me.

We both read through the instructions. Luckily our jobs were nice and simple. The one handing out awards just had to stand there and give an Onyxy to each winner as they came up on stage. The other had to escort the winner to the green room after they gave their acceptance speech.

"Which job do you want?" asked Chastity. "It sounds like the greenroom escort will have the perfect opportunity to flirt with the winners. Could be a great way for you to find a lover."

Lover? Ew. "You can have that job."

"Me fucking a winner won't make Tanner jealous."

"I meant so that you can flirt with the winners and try to get some info out of them. I bet you'll know everything about Tanner and the exact address of this place by the time I hand out the second award."

"Challenge accepted. Eeeep! This is going to be so fun!" She reached out and squeezed both my boobs.

I tried to swat her away. "What the hell are you doing?" If was official. She'd completely lost it.

Chapter 54

GRAY SWEATPANTS GIFS

Wednesday

Chastity reached out again to honk my knockers.

"Would you stop it?" I successfully swatted her away this time. Seriously…what are you doing?

"Single Girl Rule #20: You may squeeze your friend's boobs no more than twice to compliment a good outfit. I was just telling you that you looked amazing. And you barely let me get a honk and a half in. That outfit deserves two full squeezes for sure."

"That's not a rule."

"I told you there were some new ones since you were last single. Did you even bother to read the list I gave you?"

No. I had not. "Why would you add that one?"

"How many times do I have to tell you? I didn't make these rules up. But I'm pretty sure it was added as a precaution since so many people are fluid now or something. It goes against the spirit of the Single Girl Rules for a girl to flirt with a girl who doesn't know the other girl is a lesbian, you know?"

"Sure." I honestly had stopped listening to what she was saying. I was so damned nervous! "I can't believe you think this is going to be fun. I don't think I've ever been this nervous in my life. There's like a 100% chance that I'm going to trip and fall down the stairs while handing out an award."

"You'll be fine. You just have to stand there and look pretty. I'm the one who has to do all the hard work. How do my boobs look?" She reached into her bra and adjusted the girls.

"Amazing as always."

She smiled. "Well good. I wasn't sure because you didn't squeeze them. It makes me feel better that you just didn't know about the new rule. Let's hope the winners agree with you!"

"Places! Places everyone!" yelled Ocelot. "We're on in 60 seconds!"

Everyone scrambled to get in place.

"You got this," said Chastity. "You look totally drool-worthy. Tanner won't be able to take his eyes off of you all night. And then when he sees you with someone else…" She mimed her head exploding.

"Wait, Tanner is gonna be watching?!"

"Of course. I assume anyone who's anyone in the Society will be here tonight. Who knows…he might even be up for an award." She gave me a hug and ran to her side of the stage.

Fantastic. Now I was a billion times more nervous than I had been.

I took a deep breath. *Here we go.*

I walked to my place behind a semi-circular wall just as a stagehand delivered a tray of…giant onyx dildos, complete with thick veins. They were made out of some shiny black metal and each was the size of a Febreze can. No. Bigger. I'd thought Dr. Lyons was big, but these dwarfed him. Hell, these even dwarfed Angel and Diablo.

"Impressive, eh?" said the guy who'd delivered them. "Apparently they were actually cast from one of our members, but I'd have to see it to believe it." He carefully polished each with a cloth and then sped off to his next assignment.

I tried to run through my script again, but one thought kept rolling around in my head. *Was Tanner the model for these awards?*

Because if he was, then it might explain some of his behavior. Maybe he was terrified of tearing me in two. After all, I was only 5'2. I hated to quote Chastity, but she was right. That really would be a lot of meat for such a little girl.

"Ladies and gentleman," boomed the announcer as the stage lit up. "Put your hands together for the imperator of Club Onyx NYC… Pink Ocelot!"

He made his way out onto the stage to thunderous applause.

Wow. Ocelot had said it was 400 people. But it sounded like thousands. There was currently a wall blocking off my part of the stage though, so I couldn't tell for sure.

"Thank you, thank you. Thank you all."

The crowd eventually settled down.

"Wow. What a year," said Ocelot. "I know you're all probably expecting a big dance number or some sort of Broadway reenactment, but this year, I'm just going to keep it simple. And who knows…maybe I have a sexy little surprise waiting for you all at the end. So with absolutely no ado, let's get right to the awards."

The circular wall in front of me rotated to reveal the crowd. *Oh my God, oh my God, oh my God.* It was SO. MANY. PEOPLE. They were all seated around tables like some sort of fancy wedding reception. And all looking at me.

Actually, they were probably looking at the monster dildo trophies behind me. But it still felt like they were staring at me.

I tried to pick out Tanner in the audience, but the lights were blinding. I could only see silhouettes.

"As always," said Ocelot, "we'll begin with the award for Best Ass. The nominees are…" He read a list of 5 girls while their pictures appeared behind him. The only one I recognized was Frankie. "And the winner is…" Ocelot tore into an envelope. "Frankie!"

The crowd cheered while the spotlight searched for her in the audience. Eventually it found her making her way towards the front.

Ah! This is my moment! I ran through the script in my head. Stand and smile. Clap politely. Grab award. Give award to winner and kiss their cheek. Go back to standing and smiling. *Shit! I'm not clapping politely.* I was already failing.

I started clapping way too loud and then dialed it back to an appropriate level.

Then I reached for one of the awards. I tried to wrangle it with one hand right at the base, but it was kind of slippery and so damned heavy that I couldn't get any purchase. My hand just slid right up. I slid it back down to try again…

Someone in the crowd chuckled.

Oh, shit. I was basically jerking off a giant dildo in front of the entire crowd. I awkwardly looked around and then picked it up with both hands.

"You're doing great," whispered Frankie as she took the award from me.

Was I? Because I had definitely forgotten to kiss her cheek. Or more accurately - I'd actively chosen not to. I wasn't a 50-year-old European man or Joe's dad at a Christmas Eve party, so cheek kisses weren't really something I was comfortable with. And actually, Joe's dad was more a fan of mouth kisses. I wasn't into those with creepy old men either.

Frankie got to the podium and looked at the award. "Wow. Wow!"

The crowd cheered.

"Thank you all so much for this honor. I prepared a few words…" She reached into her bra and pulled out a slip of paper. Just as she was about to start reading it slipped out of her hands. "Damn. One sec…" She turned and bent over to get it in like…the most sexual way possible. And then a beat dropped and she started twerking in her evening gown.

That really got the crowd excited. She even got a few whistles.

I had to admit - it was a good move. I mean…how else should a girl accept an award for best ass? Props to Frankie. God knows I wouldn't have had the confidence to do that.

The second award was for Best New Room. Ocelot gave the award to himself for his work on the sky box. Whatever the hell that meant.

Then some guy won best role-player. Chastity kept giving me a look that said, "You gonna fuck him?" I shook my head. Let's just say he was lucky to be good at roleplaying, because his face was kinda busted.

"The next award goes to the member who brought in the most quality members throughout the last year. Four members recruited 100 plus members…but only one can win the award." Frankie was a nominee. So was Ryder Storm. And…Ryder won it. Because of course he did, the little whore.

The spotlight searched the ballroom for him, but it couldn't find him.

Come on, you promiscuous asshole! Show your face and come get your award. I had half a mind to whack him across the face with it. It would serve him right for recruiting over a hundred freaking women. Or maybe I was being too harsh. Maybe he'd just recruited me and a bunch of dudes.

"It appears Ryder couldn't make it tonight," said Ocelot. "But I think we can all agree that he really brought in some top-notch women."

A bunch of guys cheered.

Gross.

I looked over at Chastity. She mouthed, "I'm sorry."

I wanted to have more of a silent conversation about it, but Ocelot was moving on to the fifth award.

"This past year, I challenged all of you to create the best gif of someone wearing gray sweatpants. And let me just say…you all delivered spectacularly. Let's take a look at the five finalists." The wall behind Ocelot turned into a movie screen.

The first gif was a quick clip of two men in gray sweatpants running side by side on treadmills. They might as well have been naked, because their sweatpants did absolutely nothing to hide the outline of their cocks swinging around. And they were *huge*. Like…Angel and Diablo big. Which made sense. Because when I finally bothered to look up at their faces, I realized that the swinging trouser snakes did indeed belong to Angel and Diablo.

Sweet lord. I knew gray sweatpants season was fun, but I'd never seen it like *this.* Their cocks were just as big as I remembered. *Did someone suddenly turn the heat on in here?*

Then an idea hit me: *Maybe I should make Tanner jealous with them… No!* I couldn't. Last time I'd seen them I'd called them rapists and ran away screaming. It would be incredibly awkward to have to hand them one of these trophies. Or would I give them *each* one? *Ahhh!*

The next gif featured a blonde guy who looked vaguely familiar. No, not Dr. Lyons or his alter ego Flint Ironside. But still familiar. Anyway, this gif was just him standing there with a huge erection plastered to his leg in his sweatpants. He gave the camera a little smile and a wink and pulled on his pants to make them even tighter.

First Angel and Diablo and now this blonde dude? *Jesus.* I looked over at Chastity, but she was too mesmerized by the gifs to notice me.

The next gif was a girl in tight gray sweatpants and a sports bra doing a very jiggly dance. *Lame. Next please.*

The final two were thankfully back to being gifs of men.

"And the winner is…" Ocelot opened the envelope. "Gif #2 - Karl!"

Karl! Fucking Karl! The pervy dude from the Finnish spa. *I knew he looked familiar.* But at least I wouldn't have to deal with Angel and Diablo.

The spotlight found Karl and followed him to the stage. I had to admit, he looked good in his tuxedo. And he looked even better when he stopped at the top of the stairs and ripped his pants off. He was, of course, wearing gray sweatpants underneath. And his penis was *very* visible.

It swung a little bit as he walked up the stairs towards me.

Shit! I'd been so mesmerized that I'd forgotten to grab his award. I turned and grabbed one of the big onyx dildos as fast as I could. When I spun back around to give it to him, my hand collided with something hard.

"Hey there," he said. "At least invite me to dinner first."

Did I just touch his penis? I definitely did. *What is wrong with me?!* It had been a few weeks since I'd done something rapey. I'd thought I'd outgrown it for a minute there. But nope…I was still a rapist.

I handed him the award and went in for a hug. At the last second I was like…wtf why am I about to hug him? So I decided to play it by the book and give him the required kiss on the cheek. I'd already botched this handoff enough. It was best to finish strong. But of course I missed and kissed him right on the lips.

Fuck!

Someone in the crowd whistled.

"She likes those sweatpants, Karl!" yelled another.

Kill me now.

He laughed and walked over to give his acceptance speech. I couldn't pay attention to what he was saying. I was too mortified. Not an *incident* level mortification, because I was pretty sure the audience was filled with perverts like me. But it was still pretty bad.

Before I knew it Frankie was coming on stage to collect yet another award - this time for Best Breasts.

Damn. Frankie sure was popular with the guys here. I had no doubt that Chastity would be gunning for some of her awards next year.

Speaking of Chastity…

"Where did Chastity go?" whispered Frankie as I handed her the Onyxy.

Yup, I'd just noticed it too. Chastity was missing from her position. "No idea." Actually, that wasn't true. I did have *some* idea of where she had gone. I bet she was chatting up Karl in the green room.

Frankie gave another acceptance speech, and then Ocelot took over.

"We only have one more award left, but the kitchen just informed me that dinner is hot and ready to be served. So let's take a quick break before we hand out the award you've all been waiting for - Best Member. Oh, and one other quick bit of housekeeping. The theme for this years' gif challenge will be promiscuous girlfriends, also known as hotwives. So grab your girlfriend, find a guy with a big dick, and get the camera rolling."

What the hell kind of theme is that? The sweatpants gif challenge was a million times better.

The other Society members didn't seem to agree with me, though. Especially the women in the crowd. They loudly applauded the announcement as Ocelot walked off stage.

The wall swung back around in front of the awards and I let out the world's biggest sigh of relief. I'd done it! I'd survived most of the award ceremony, and I hadn't fallen on my face. Yes, I'd groped Karl and tried to make out with him. But both those things could have happened to anyone by accident. And now that I thought about it, that was actually kind of a win. Maybe word of that would get back to Tanner and I'd be un-wifey-zoned.

I started towards the green room to find Chastity, but Ocelot stopped me on the way.

Oh shit. Was he gonna reprimand me for ruining the world's easiest job?

"Hey, Raven," he said. "You did *amazing* out there. Did you and Karl plan that penis grab? Or was that just improv? Either way, bravo. You gave tonight's ceremony just the pinch of spice that it needed."

"That was all improv, son. I just saw that big juicy cock and knew I had to touch it." *Why did I say that out loud?*

"I can't blame you," he said. "Anyway, go ahead and grab a quick bite to eat, but don't stray too far. You don't want to miss the special surprise I have for you."

"For me? Or for Chastity?"

"Whichever one of you wants it. But believe me…you're gonna want it. I'd originally planned it for Kristen, but since her flight got delayed, it's your lucky day."

Oh God. I had forgotten about that. But Kristen was supposedly his girlfriend. So if the surprise had originally been planned for her, then it couldn't be too bad… Right?

Chapter 55

THEY'RE BACK

Wednesday

The green room had a nice little spread of appetizers. But no one was in there.

Where the hell did Chastity and all the winners go!?

I couldn't believe she had left me like this. Had she forgotten about Single Girl Rule #11: Only ditch your friends for a hot guy? Wait, that can't be right. I tried to remember. No…that was definitely Rule #11. I guess she did the right thing there then. But damn it, I needed her.

I wanted to find Chastity, but wandering the halls here was a dangerous proposition. Frankie had made it sound like there were all sorts of sexy things going on in those rooms. And I'd *heard* it going down in the eggplant room. Did I really want to risk walking in on an orgy? It seemed much safer to just stay here. And I needed to stick around to hand out the final award or Ocelot would lose his mind. And maybe his surprise would be really great!

So search for Chastity? Or stay here? Gah! I couldn't decide. So instead I made myself a cheese plate. It had been calling to me ever since I'd walked into the green room.

They had all the good stuff. Cheddar, swiss, smoked gouda… And it was all cut into those perfect little cubes that you can stab with a toothpick. No touching required.

I had just popped a cube of gouda into my mouth when Angel and Diablo walked in.

Shit! What are they doing back here? The green room was for winners only!

Maybe they wouldn't recognize me. I mean, I'd only seen them one time. Tons of girls probably yelled rape and ran away from them all the time. Damn it, probably not. No one was as awkward as me. I focused on my cheese and hoped I could avoid another awkward encounter with them.

It didn't work.

They sauntered over to me. Diablo leaned on the buffet table way too close to me. I would have thought I'd have a strong urge to run, but his cologne was kind of amazing.

"Hey Raven," said Angel. "You killed it up there."

"Yeah," agreed Diablo as he rolled up a piece of lunch meat. "But it was bullshit that we didn't win Best Gif. It should have been us up there getting our cocks grabbed by you."

Oh. My.

Angel shook his head. "Ignore him, please. What he meant to say is that he's upset Karl stole our victory dance idea. Well…kind of. He didn't even dance."

"For real?" I asked. "That's messed up. And it's messed up that you guys didn't win. For what it's worth - I thought you should have won. Two is always better than one. Not that I want two cocks. I'm just saying like, in general - two is better than one." I grabbed two cheese cubes and popped them in my mouth to make my point. *What the hell am I doing?* These guys were so distracting I didn't even know what I was doing with my mouth anymore.

"Interesting…" said Diablo, staring directly at my cleavage.

I swallowed hard as I stared at him. The green room suddenly felt stifling.

"Wanna see our victory dance?" asked Angel. "It would be a shame for it to completely go to waste."

"Sure." I pulled my gaze away from Diablo's captivating stare. It was like he could see right through me.

Diablo stood next to Angel, then they counted down from three and ripped their tuxedo pants off. Just like Karl, they were wearing gray sweatpants underneath. My eyes went directly to the outlines of their swinging cocks as they ran in place. *How is it even possible for them to be so big?* And I couldn't help but laugh as they shimmied their hips.

"See?" said Diablo when they were done. "Wasn't that better than Karl's?"

"It was. And you're totally right…he didn't even do a dance after he ripped his pants off. So lame."

"Exactly. Although I feel like something was missing from ours…" Diablo snapped his fingers. "Oh right. Karl got his cock grabbed. I think we need the same treatment."

I nearly choked on a cheese cube. Everything that fell out of Diablo's mouth was shocking and…enticing. And the longer I stood in this room with them, the more I wanted to just say yes to all his propositions.

Angel put his arm around Diablo. "What he meant to say is that we're very sorry for whipping our cocks out while you were touring our apartment. We slightly misread your signals."

That was sweet of him to apologize. I would have thought talking to them would make me want to run away screaming again - especially with what Diablo was saying - but Angel's pale gray eyes were totally captivating. And his apology seemed sincere. He seemed like such a nice guy. Really…why couldn't I stop staring at his eyes?

"Don't worry about it," I said. "I hadn't quite picked up the lingo yet. Technically I did ask you to double team me." I felt my cheeks turning red. I'm pretty sure I was seconds away from asking them to do it again. I'd never felt so sexy and calm at the same time.

"Well, I still feel shitty about it. So we got you a gift."

"Really?" That wasn't necessary at all. But I was dying to know what it was.

"Yup."

I looked down to see if they had a gift for me. But their hands were empty. So I was basically just staring at their junk. *Stop looking at their sweatpants!* I snapped my eyes back to their faces. Diablo raised one eyebrow slightly as if to say, "Like what you see?"

"You used to run Dickson & Son's Sugarcakes, right?" asked Angel.

"Yes…"

"And then your scumbag ex-husband stole it from you in your divorce?"

"How did you know that?"

Diablo cracked his knuckles. "We have our ways."

"Do you have your phone on you?" asked Angel.

"No." In fact, I had no idea where it was. They must have taken my purse when they stuffed me in the van.

Angel typed something on his phone and then handed it to me. It was open to the Google listing for Dickson & Son's Sugarcakes.

"What am I looking at here?" I'd looked at this page a bajillion times trying to get Google to fix various aspects. At one point they'd said we were only open every Tuesday from 2 a.m. to 2:45 a.m. And then after we went on a podcast to promote the brand, they'd decided to label Dickson & Son's Sugarcakes as a musical group.

"Check out the reviews," said Angel. "Their rating plummeted overnight."

"Oops," added Diablo.

I scrolled back to the top. "One star average on 34,000 reviews?! Jesus. How did you get so many?" I'd had to *beg* people to leave reviews, and that had only just gotten us past the 100 review mark. I clicked the link and started reading the one-star reviews:

"The cupcakes are okay, but the owner gives off some serious pedophile vibes."

"Eating these cupcakes made my dick shrink."

And my personal favorite…

"Dickson & Son's Sugarcakes taste like they're made by someone with a small dick."

They went on and on like that. Pages and pages of insults about Joe and his tiny dick. I was nearly crying from laughing so hard. "You guys," I said through my laughter. "This is amazing."

"It was our pleasure," said Angel. "It was actually pretty fun reading tons of bad reviews for other restaurants to get ideas."

"I just wanted to firebomb the place," Diablo said. "But Angel talked me out of it."

I laughed. Because I was pretty sure he was joking. *Maybe?* "Seriously, that's like the sweetest thing anyone's ever done for me. How can I ever thank you guys?"

"You can take that dress off and let us fuck you on the buffet table," said Diablo.

"Excuse me?" *Did he seriously just say that?!* My heart started hammering against my ribcage. Because...I kind of wanted them to do it. I pressed my thighs together and hoped they didn't notice. What was happening to me? Oh right...I'm a sex-starved sexual deviant! God, Tanner needed to ask me out and soon before I gave in to my depraved urges.

Diablo just stared at me. "It's gonna happen sooner or later. No need to delay the inevitable."

"Oh really?"

"Yes." He sounded 100% confident in his answer.

Angel cleared this throat. "What Diablo meant to say was that he thinks you're very beautiful and we'd love to take you out to dinner this weekend. While researching bad reviews we actually came across a few hidden gems that we've never tried before."

I looked back and forth between them. *What is this? Some sort of good cop bad cop routine they use to get girls?* Diablo would say all sorts of filthy stuff, and then Angel would correct him. A devil and an angel. *Weird.* But also kind of effective. Because I was actually considering going out to dinner with them. I still needed to make Tanner jealous, and... My eyes drifted down to their sweatpants. *Seriously, Ash, stop staring at their penises!*

"So what do you say?" asked Angel.

"Based on where she's looking, I'd say it's a yes." Diablo gave a very suggestive thrust.

I snapped my eyes back up. It didn't matter if I wanted to say yes. I couldn't - we had the Wineflix & Chill launch party on Saturday. "I'm actually busy this weekend."

"With Ryder?" asked Diablo.

I nodded.

Diablo laughed. "Well, enjoy that while it lasts. Did he invite you back to his place at One57 yet?"

"No. Why?"

"Because after he does, you're never gonna hear from him again. One and done. That's how Ryder operates."

What the fuck? I suddenly wished I hadn't eaten so much cheese. I felt sick. I'd been dying to know if Tanner was all about one-night stands. And these two had just confirmed my worst fears.

"Here's an idea. How about we have you and Ryder over for dinner. And for dessert you can have two thick cocks while Ryder films it for this year's gif contest. I refuse to lose two years in a row."

Oh my God. Every word out of this man's mouth made me blush. "Ryder would never agree to that," I said.

"You must not know Ryder very well."

"What do you mean by that?" God, I'd already learned too much. But I somehow needed to know even more.

"You'll see." Diablo smiled and grabbed the entire plate of cheese off the table. "See ya around, Raven." He turned and walked out of the green room.

"What did he mean by that?" I asked Angel.

"I don't want to throw Ryder under the bus, but there's a reason why he won Best Recruiter for the third year in a row. He's good with women."

He didn't need to say anymore. I got the hint. I was just his latest recruit. He'd have his way with me and then move on to the next. And Diablo had taken all the cheese so I couldn't stress eat. *Damn it!*

Angel gave my shoulder a gentle squeeze. "Maybe he'll be different with you. And if he's not…" He scribbled his number on the back of a napkin and left it on the table for me as he followed Diablo out of the green room.

Well fuck.

But wait! Maybe this was actually good news. It was exactly like Chastity had said - Tanner was a manwhore who had put me squarely in the wifey-zone. Which was why I had to make him jealous.

I stared at the napkin with Angel's number. Then I folded it up and tucked it into my bra.

I wasn't necessarily going to call them. But if I had to choose someone to make Tanner jealous with…why not go big?

I giggled at my pun.

"Raven! There you are!" said a frantic voice.

I looked over. Ocelot had just burst into the green room.

"Time to hand out the award for Best Member?" I asked.

"Almost. But first you have to choose the winner."

"It sounded like you said *I* have to choose the winner."

"Yeah."

"Aren't I like…the least qualified person in the world to do that? I mean, this is literally my first night at Club Onyx. I know nothing about 99% of the members."

Ocelot shook his head. "Not at all. You'll be perfect."

Chapter 56

BEST MEMBER

Wednesday

I hurried to keep up with Ocelot as he speed-walked out of the green room.

"After tallying thousands of votes," said Ocelot as we walked, "our five nominees for Best Member all ended up being within 10 votes of each other. So I had an idea… Why not let one lucky lady break the tie? That one simple question was really the start of my entire plan for the evening."

"Okay…"

Ocelot pushed a curtain aside and led me out onto the stage next to the one remaining award. The wall was still there, so this area was currently blocked off from the audience. When it was time for the award show to start again, the wall would move and everyone would be able to see me.

"Am I going to be choosing live on stage?" I asked. "That's a lot of pressure."

"Not quite." Ocelot whistled and four men joined us behind the wall. Or at least…I assumed they were men based on their height. I couldn't really tell for sure, because all five of them were wearing elephant masks made of tons of little triangular mirrors - just like the one Liz had described seeing at school - and floor-length black robes. They all stood in a line.

Umm…

Tim stared at them. He did not look happy. He pulled a walkie-talkie out of his pocket and hit the call button. "Frankie - why am I only looking at four men here?"

Static, and then she replied: "No one can find Karl."

Karl's missing, eh? I didn't know *where* he was. But I had a sneaking suspicion about *who* he was with. It wasn't hard to put two and two together. Chastity had literally been drooling over his gif. And then she'd led him off stage and neither one had been seen since.

Yeah, they were definitely banging.

"The show must go on," muttered Ocelot to himself. Then he regained his composure and turned to me. "Raven. It is my distinct pleasure to present to you this year's nominees for Best Member." He nodded at the four men as they let their robes drop to the floor.

I gasped. I shouldn't have been surprised, but… "Dude! They're naked!" I put my hand up to block out their junk. These guys were lucky that the audience couldn't see them right now because that would have been embarrassing for them.

Ocelot smiled. "Of course they are. How else would you choose the Best Member?"

"Uhh…maybe by seeing their faces? Or chatting with them for a few minutes? Or just hearing a simple list of names and accomplishments?"

"That all seems rather unnecessary."

"Does it? Because unless I'm supposed to be judging who has the nicest cock, then this line-up is pretty useless."

Ocelot stared at me.

Oh. Oh! Duh. Best…Member. This award wasn't for who had contributed the most to Club Onyx. It was an award for the best *member*. As in…penis. That made sense, given that two of the other awards had been Best Breasts and Best Ass.

I took a deep breath and dropped my hand.

Holy shit.

I recognized two of the men immediately. The tan skin, excessive tattoos, and huge cocks were unmistakable. Angel and Diablo.

I didn't recognize the other two, but they were similarly well endowed.

I knew that these were probably some of the biggest cocks at Club Onyx, but still… I couldn't believe how small

Joe was in comparison. What would it be like to ride one of these monsters?

I pressed my thighs together and tried to focus. Angel and Diablo had left me feeling a certain kind of way and now I'd completely lost my mind.

"Impressive, huh?" asked Ocelot. He sounded so proud of himself. "Although something feels missing… Gentlemen, if you would be so kind, please picture Raven on her knees. Imagine her soft lips wrapping around your thick cock as she strokes her wet pussy."

All four men started to get hard. At the thought of me blowing them. *Oh my God.*

But seriously, *OH MY GOD.* If they were big earlier, now they were *huge.*

"Ah, much better," said Ocelot. "Now, Raven…if you would be so kind, please announce your choice for Best Member. We don't want to leave our audience waiting any longer."

I looked back and forth between all the men just to be sure of my decision. Or maybe I just wanted to stare at them a bit more. Can you really blame me? Not only were they hung, but they also all had ridiculous muscles. I counted their abs. Yup. All of them had eight-packs. Eight-packs! How was that even possible?

I don't care how much fun Chastity was having with Karl - she was going to lose her shit when I told her about this.

But enough staring - I had to make a decision.

Easy choice. I pointed to the one I thought was Angel. "Him." Despite his brother being a scoundrel, Angel was a total sweetheart. And that kind of behavior should be rewarded.

"Are you sure?" asked Ocelot.

I nodded, but then I noticed a pitchfork tattooed on the chest of the guy I'd chosen. *Shit!* "Wait! No. I pick him." I pointed to the other tan guy with tattoos.

Ocelot looked at me. "Final answer?"

Yes? Maybe? I don't know! I should have paid more attention to their tattoos. "Can I just choose both?"

"Oh you naughty girl!" Ocelot shoved my arm playfully. "I like the way you think. This is going to make *quite* the spectacle." He dismissed the two I hadn't chosen. They both covered their junk and walked away very dejectedly. Then he beckoned Angel and Diablo over.

"Congratulations, gentlemen. You both just won Best Member." He glanced down at their erections. "Well deserved, I must say."

Weird. This Ocelot guy was so confusing. One minute he was talking about his girlfriend, and the next minute he was complimenting two dudes' dicks.

Ocelot turned to me. "Are you ready for the real surprise?" He sounded so excited.

"Maybe?"

"Okay. Here's what's gonna happen." He rubbed his hands together. "Tonight is no ordinary night. Tonight is my secret sex party." He said it as if it was this huge reveal, but I had no idea what the hell he was talking about.

Angel and Diablo gave each other a fist pump.

Ocelot looked at me expectantly. Then he shook his head. "Oh, right. This is your first night. Okay. So… Usually here at Club Onyx we have pretty strict rules to make sure everyone is comfortable. Some clothing required. No sex unless you're in a designated area. That sort of thing. But every now and then, we throw all those rules out the window. And to kick things off, I always surprise everyone with a public display of debauchery."

I had a general sense of where this was headed. And I didn't like it one bit. Well…maybe one bit. But not a lot of bits.

"So here's what we're gonna do. I'm going to reopen the show with a montage of the five nominees for Best Members. Then I'll read out the winners, but the spotlight won't be able to find you. That's when this wall will slide back to reveal you double-teaming Raven on the trophy table."

"What?!" I yelled.

"You heard me right, you lucky little girl. You get *both* of these lovely cocks just like you requested. Kristen is going to be so jealous that she missed out."

"I didn't request this!"

"Masks on or off?" asked one of the guys. It sounded more like Diablo.

"Hmmm…which would be more dramatic?" asked Ocelot.

"What if we keep our masks on the whole time we're fucking her, and then after we cum on her face, we rip off our masks and all yell, 'Welcome to the secret sex party!' "

Yup, that was definitely Diablo talking.

"Oh my God," said Ocelot. "I just got chills." He pushed his sleeve up to show off the goosebumps on his arm. "Pure perfection. This will definitely go down in history as the best Onyxies ever."

What the actual fuck is happening right now? In theory, getting fucked by Angel and Diablo would be spectacularly hot. But the thought of it actually happening was terrifying. Especially in front of thousands of people! Or hundreds. Or however many horned-up people were in the audience.

Although it would definitely make Tanner jealous…

Nope. No way. Not in a million years. I wasn't going to have sex with two strangers in front of an audience just to make Tanner jealous. I just wanted Tanner. *How do I get out of this?! Think!*

"Oh shoot," I said, pretending to check an imaginary watch on my wrist. "I just saw the time. I have to get going or I'm gonna be late for my thing."

"What thing?" asked Ocelot. "Ah, say no more. Stage fright? I totally get it. And I have the perfect antidote." He walked around me and unzipped my dress.

What is he doing?! I put my hand up at the last second to stop the top of my dress from falling down.

"I was going to have you wait until the montage started, but nothing kills stage fright better than taking a big cock. Just promise me you'll take it easy on them so that they don't cum before the big reveal." Ocelot gave me a saucy little wink.

Angel and Diablo both stroked themselves as they walked to either side of me.

Oh God, oh God, oh God.

Was this seriously happening?

"Raven?!" yelled Tanner. He'd just burst through the curtains.

Tanner! I was saved!

"Ah, Ryder," said Ocelot. "I'll be with you in just a second. First we have to get Raven situated here. Don't tell anyone, but tonight is my secret sex party. And she's going to be the opening act."

Tanner looked at Ocelot. Then me. Then the two erections. "Not happening. Let's go, Raven." He waved me towards him.

I almost ran into his arms. But I didn't. Not yet, at least. Because this was the perfect opportunity to make him jealous as hell.

"No thanks," I said.

"What?"

Shit! What do I say now? I tried to channel my inner-Chastity. "Don't get me wrong. I'd love to come hang out with you. But that would be violating Single Girl Rule #8."

He looked so pissed. "Which is what exactly?"

This one was Chastity's favorite. I'd heard her quote it more times than I could count. "Rule #8: If a man has 8 abs and 8 inches, he may not be refused. And well…" I stared at Tanner as I reached out to either side of me and ran my hands down Angel and Diablo's abs. I meant to stop there, but I accidentally went too low and touched their cocks. And at that point it just felt right to give them each a stroke. At the end I booped each one on the tip and said, "Boop!"

Oh my God what is wrong with me?! I just took that way too far! I'd only meant to molest their abs. Not give them handjobs and dirty boops!

Tanner narrowed his eyes at me. His irises almost looked…stormy. God, I loved when he looked all mad like that. It was so hot.

Mission accomplished.

And then a horrible realization came over me. What if I had miscalculated everything? Tanner was part of this crazy sex club. And Diablo had said that I didn't know Tanner very well if I thought he wouldn't be down for a swingers' dinner. If that was true, then Tanner would happily sit back and watch me get fucked. Hell, he'd probably be thrilled that one of his recruits was the opening act for this weird secret sex party thing that Ocelot kept talking about.

For a second no one moved.

Then Diablo reached for my breasts and Tanner growled, "Stop." His voice was laced with danger. Diablo froze in his tracks.

Damn that was sexy. I needed to make Tanner jealous more often.

Tanner opened his tuxedo jacket. At first I thought he was gonna flash a gun holstered under his arm. But he didn't have any weapons. Instead he just had a black onyx medallion in the shape of the Society logo dangling from his inside pocket on a thick black chain.

"Raven's mine. Step away from her," he demanded. "Now."

Angel and Diablo each took a few steps back.

Then he walked over, lifted me over his shoulder, and carried me off the stage like a caveman. I'd never been so turned on in my life.

"Wait," said Ocelot.

Tanner spun around. "What?!" he growled.

"You know I'm in love with you, Ryder, but this is highly irregular."

Did Ocelot just say he's in love with Tanner? This night just kept getting weirder and weirder.

"You took an oath when you received that medallion," continued Ocelot. "To cockblock two of your fellow members is a sick perversion of that sacred oath."

"Report me to the council if you must, but I'm leaving here with Raven. Goodnight, gentlemen." He put his hand firmly on my ass as he carried me the rest of the way off stage. If that wasn't a show of staking his claim, then I didn't know what was. And he didn't put me down until we were back in the hallway with all the secret doors.

"What the hell are you doing at Club Onyx, Ash?" he asked. He put his hand on the center of my chest and pushed me backward until my back collided with the wall. He was caging me in. And staring at me with his stormy eyes. And I was loving every second of it.

All I wanted to do was jump on him and kiss him all over for saving me, but I couldn't ruin my momentum. I had to keep up this slutty charade until I was safely out of the wifey-zone. Because it was working. Chastity was a freaking genius.

"What do you mean what am I doing? Chastity and I got invited..." *Kidnapped...* "And then Ocelot bought us as sex slaves at the auction."

"Sex slaves?! At the auction? Why the hell were you there? That is for experienced members only. There's no way you were ready for that." Then his eyes got big. "Please tell me you didn't go to the sky box."

That place that won best new room? "Nope." I didn't know what the hell the sky box room was, but if I ever needed to *really* make Tanner jealous, it sounded like that was the place to go. "We went straight to the auction room. When someone paid $250K for us I thought for sure we were gonna get gangbanged at a bachelor party, but it turned out that Ocelot needed us to help him present the Onyxies since his girlfriend's plane got delayed."

"And that presentation involved getting double-teamed?" He pulled his hand away from me. It looked like he wanted to start pacing but instead he just ran his hand down his face like the idea literally pained him.

"Yup. Actually, no. I was just supposed to choose one guy. But I got a little greedy. And really, I had no choice. You know… Single Girl Rule #8."

"That's not a thing."

"It absolutely is. And if I'm not mistaken, both Angel and Diablo fit that criteria. Unless they have a fat day or something, then my body is at their mercy."

"Even in front of that entire auditorium of people?"

"Rule 8 isn't shy."

"Why would that be part of girl code?"

"It's not girl code. That's for old ladies and tweens. These are the Single Girl Rules. They're far superior. And of course Rule #8 is a part of them. Didn't your parents ever tell you to eat all your food because there were starving children in Africa?"

"No. That would have been awfully strange of them to say..."

"They seriously never said that? Oh well. It doesn't matter. The concept is the same. It's wrong to waste food because it's a valuable commodity that some people would kill for. The same goes for a man with an 8 pack and a huge cock. To refuse him would be an insult to women everywhere who can't find themselves such a fine specimen."

"I thought the rules were like: If you arrive together, leave together. And friends don't let friends go to the bathroom alone. Things like that."

"Never let a friend go into the bathroom alone is Rule #3. But the rest of what you said is just classic girl code. Which I just told you is for basic bitches. Single Girl Rules are more sophisticated. You're probably thinking of Rule #11. But you got it all wrong. It's really: Only ditch your friends for a hot guy."

Tanner stared at me. "There's no way that's right."

"Sure it is. Anyway, where was I? Oh, right. So Ocelot would only let me choose two. But the others were all double 8s as well, so before they left, I told them they could come take a turn on me once Angel and Diablo were done." *Was that too much?* That felt like way too much. Although if my goal had been to channel my inner-Chastity, then I'd totally nailed it.

"You're a terrible liar, you know," said Tanner.

"What makes you think I'm lying?"

"It's pretty obvious."

"You're mistaken, sir. As a card-carrying member of the Single Girl Rules, I had no choice but to let Angel and Diablo have their way with me. It would have been a totally different story if I had a boyfriend, though." *Boom!* That was it. I'd made my case: Un-wifey-zone me, or I'm gonna whore it up. And that was a promise.

Now the ball was in Tanner's court.

"We're leaving," he said.

Yes, take me home with you!

"It's late and there's still lots to do to get ready for this launch party. You said Chastity was here too?"

"Yeah." I'm not sure why he wanted Chastity to come home with him too. And why we were going to be 'working.' "I'm pretty sure she ran off with Karl after he won Best Gif."

"Any idea where?"

I shook my head.

"Damn, okay."

"Should we split up?" I asked.

"Not a chance."

"But there are like…a bajillion rooms in this place." I gestured to a nearby door labeled with a handcuff symbol.

"If tonight is Ocelot's secret sex party, then all these rooms will be locked until the party begins. That leaves only a few places where they could be."

Tanner grabbed my hand and guided me out of the never-ending hallway and into a ridiculously fancy foyer. Two stories. Double staircase. A chandelier the size of a car. It was insane. There were so many things to explore. Tanner picked up his pace.

We were going to go search one of the lounges, whatever that meant, but on our way down the grand staircase, we heard loud moans coming from the men's locker room.

"Sounds like Chastity took Karl to a bathroom stall," I said.

The moans got louder as we approached. And then I nearly slipped on her dress crumpled in a pile at the locker room entrance.

We walked in and…

"Ahhh!" I tried to hide my eyes. Because Chastity hadn't taken him into a stall. She had just bent over and let him fuck her from behind right in the middle of the bathroom. But the really shocking part was that she was simultaneously giving head to some other guy.

Damn, girl! I'd walked in on Chastity plenty of times in college, but never with two guys.

The guys looked over but didn't stop.

Tanner pulled out the same symbol he'd shown to Ocelot. "That's enough, guys. Party's over."

The guy getting head pulled back immediately and ran away with his junk in his hands. Karl started to pull out too, but Chastity reached back and grabbed his ass.

"Wait," she said. "Don't stop."

"Nope," said Tanner. "It's time to go." He sounded so calm, like the scene in front of us was totally normal.

"Can't he at least finish?" asked Chastity. "I don't want to leave him with blue balls. It goes against Single Girl Rule 24: No blue balls allowed. Finish what you start."

"Fucking Single Girl Rules," Tanner mumbled under his breath.

"Yeah man," said Karl. "Just give me one more minute."

"Out. Now," growled Tanner.

Karl frowned and gave Chastity one more good thrust before pulling out.

"Boo," said Chastity. "Why are you ruining all my fun?"

Tanner grabbed her dress off the floor and tossed it to her. "You shouldn't be here."

"They didn't seem to mind that I was in the men's room…"

"I meant at Club Onyx."

"Who even was that second guy?" I asked.

"No idea. But he walked in on us and asked to join. He didn't quite have 8 abs and 8 inches, but it was close enough."

"See?" I said to Tanner. "I told you Rule #8 was a thing!"

Tanner shook his head. "It all makes sense now. You didn't tell me that Chastity was the one who made the rules up."

"Made it up?" asked Chastity as she put her lingerie back on. "I beg your pardon. The Single Girl Rules are a time-honored tradition among single women all over the world that aren't basic."

I'd described them just right. I gave myself a mental high-five. #NailedIt. *Yas queen!* I'd used a hashtag right!

"We can talk more about this later," Tanner said. "But right now we're leaving."

I zipped Chastity into her dress. I was so excited to be finally going home with Tanner.

"Do we have to?" she asked.

"Yes." Tanner snapped his fingers. Two men appeared, seemingly out of thin air, and bagged me and Chastity.

Chapter 57

HOUSE(BOY) ARREST

Wednesday

"Tanner," I said into the thick fabric of the bag. I couldn't see a thing. And my hands had been tied again. Now we were in the back of a car. "Tanner?" The car made a quick turn and I slid slightly in my seat.

Chastity yelped as she slammed into me. "Ow."

You'd think that Tanner's minions would have been a little more careful with the goods. "Tanner," I hissed. He wouldn't just leave us alone with strangers, would he? But I guess whoever bagged us weren't strangers to him.

I felt a hand on my thigh.

"Don't go to Club Onyx again without me," he whispered.

I'd recognize Tanner's voice anywhere.

"You need a proper guide to..." his voice trailed off. "Just...promise me you won't. Please, Ash."

But he'd sent me the letter saying to go there if he disappeared. Maybe that was the whole problem though. He hadn't disappeared and I'd gone anyway. And I'd taken everything too far. Way too far. God, I'd touched two penises for Christ's sake! My stomach was twisted in knots. "I promise."

His hand fell off my thigh as the car came to a stop.

Someone lifted me over their shoulder again.

"Tanner?"

But there was no response.

"Stop touching my ass!" Chastity yelled. It sounded like she was right next to me. Whoever was carrying her was definitely carrying me too. A huge bodyguard probably, because he was able to carry us both up a flight of stairs.

"I need to talk to Tanner," I said.

No response. He continued climbing up and up and up. We were either going to a penthouse or some cheap ass apartment with no elevator.

We came to a stop and I heard a door open.

"Let us go," I said and tried to wriggle my way out of his grip, but the man's hand was super firm around the backs of my knees.

But he answered my pleas. Because he dumped us unceremoniously on something soft and tore the bag off my head. We were sitting on…my couch? In my apartment? *Not a penthouse then.* Where the hell was Tanner? I'd thought he was taking me back to his place… *Damn it he tricked me!* Although, I guess he'd never actually said we were going back to his place. I just assumed because of all the sexual tension in the air that he wanted to be alone with me to ravish me. But instead he'd just dropped me off at my place. *Wait…what the actual hell? How did he get in without a key?*

"How did you get in here…" I demanded, but my voice trailed off. Because the man standing in front of us looked nothing like I'd expected. He was on the shorter side and decked out in lederhosen. And the strangest part…he looked vaguely familiar. I shook the thought away. There was seriously no way such a petite man could have fireman-carried us up to my apartment. Unless he was magical or something. I just stared at his tiny little arms.

"You're both in timeout," he said. "Until you can learn to behave yourselves. Master is very upset with you."

His British accent finally helped me place him. "Nigel?" I asked. Why was he wearing lederhosen?

"The houseboy?" Chastity's muffled voice sounded underneath the bag on her head.

Nigel looked like he'd been caught in a lie. Which was weird because he hadn't been.

"Yes," he said. "I'm Nigel. A normal boy. Now shut your whore mouths!"

"Nigel!" I said. "You can't talk to women like that."

"Oh." He wrung his hands together. "I'm sorry…I heard Master say it once. I thought it was some of the new lingo he always makes me study. But I'm behind on my lessons. I'm very busy."

What the what?

"Who did Tanner say the whore mouth thing about?" Chastity asked. "Was there a whore at his apartment?"

Nigel took a step away from us like he was scared we might bite.

And I got a fantastic idea. Nigel had all the answers we needed. "Scratch that question." There were a million reasons why Tanner would tell someone to shut their whore mouths. They were either a whore or saying something saucy. I wasn't concerned about that. Honestly, I wanted to start saying that more often. Just like I'd recently started trying to add *yas queen* into my vocabulary. "Nigel, we need your help."

He perked up. "I'm ready to serve."

Weird. "First, can you please take the bag off Chastity's head?"

"Who?"

Who else could I possibly be talking about? I nodded to Chastity on the couch next to me. "My friend over there."

"Oh. Yes, for you, of course." He hurried over and unbagged Chastity. He turned to me like he was waiting for his next order.

Chastity blew her bubblegum-colored bangs out of her eyes. And then she just stared at Nigel like he was an alien. It was probably the lederhosen throwing her off.

"Back to the help I need," I said. "It's about Tanner's secret closet." I could finally get the answers about how he'd made it.

Nigel's eyes grew round. "No. You can't go in there!" He shook his head back and forth.

"What, why?" I asked.

"Not unless you want to get burned."

"What?" Chastity said. "I've been in there dozens of times already."

Nigel gasped. "But you can't. He'll...it'll..." He put his hand over his mouth.

"Are you scared of normal clothing or something?" I asked.

Nigel looked so confused. He looked down at his outfit and then back at me. "No?" He smoothed down his suspenders. "I like lederhosen. They're very comfortable. You got a problem with that?"

"Not at all. You look quite dapper."

He smiled to himself.

"Please just tell us how Tanner made that closet." I nodded over to the bookcase that doubled as a secret entrance to my new closet.

"Oh." He put his hand to his chest. "*That* closet. I thought you meant his..." his eyes grew round again. "Stop talking. Both of you. Timeout! Those are the rules."

"We're grown women, Nigel." Chastity batted her eyelashes at him. "You can't put us in timeout. Now can you please untie us?"

It looked like Nigel was blushing. But then he frantically shook his head. "No."

"Please?" she shimmied a little.

Nigel glanced down at her cleavage and then back at her face. "Never. I love to serve. But I only serve two men."

I glanced at Chastity and then back to Nigel. "Two men? Who's the other man besides Tanner?"

Nigel lit up at the mention of this other man. "Tanner's best friend. I love serving him. Very much so."

"Ah, Matt?" asked Chastity. "We've heard all about Tanner's secret best friend. I've actually been dying to know more about him. Surely you can give us all the details about him."

Nigel squinted at her. "Never."

"But...can't you tell us anything about him? Is he tall? Muscular? Handsome?"

Nigel squinted at her even more. It was a full-on glare now. "He's all of the above. Not that it's any of your concern, whoever you are."

"Is his last name Caldwell?" she asked.

Please, God, no! If Tanner was best friends with Matthew Caldwell, I'd never be able to date him. It would just be way too freaking awkward. But I was dying to know the answer...

Nigel just glared at her.

Was that a 'no' or a 'yes,' Nigel? What did his glare mean?!

"Is he wealthy?" Chastity asked. "I bet he's so wealthy. Nigel, please tell me everything about him. Maybe give us his address?"

Nigel slapped her across the face. "No! He's mine!"

Chastity gaped at him.

"Nigel!" I said. "What has gotten into you?" I didn't really know him that well. But he'd seemed so docile when he'd delivered the cookies.

Nigel pulled his hand back. "I mean...he's...no. Don't talk about Master Matthew. He's not for you. I already have to share enough." He took a step away from us, probably so he wouldn't slap Chastity again. "Excuse me for a moment. I need to use the outhouse." He scurried off.

"Outhouse?" I whispered. "What is up with him?"

"He clearly has a crush on Matt," Chastity said.

I couldn't help but laugh. "I was talking about the outhouse thing. But yeah, his reaction to Matt was a little strong too." I tried to wriggle out of my restraints. "Please tell me you found something out when you were with Karl."

"No, I was going to learn all Tanner's dirty little secrets after Karl was happily banged. That's how that works. But Tanner rudely interrupted us. Like he knew what I was planning all along."

"But you were with him for like...half an hour. How did you not find out anything?"

"I was building a rapport. But I did ask him the most important question of all. Single Girl Rule #22: Always make sure he's 18."

Damn it! I didn't care if Karl was 18 or not. Well…actually I did. I didn't want Chastity to go to jail. But the Tanner questions were equally important!

Nigel walked back into the room. He looked more composed now. "I'm sorry about earlier. I wasn't ready to converse because I wasn't sure it was allowed. But I just received more thorough instructions via my cellular device. Let's start over more formally. Master Tanner had to leave on important business, but he wanted me to watch you both so you didn't do anything else naughty this evening. So…timeout. No more talking."

He crossed his arms in front of his suspenders and leaned against the wall. I was pretty sure it was supposed to be intimidating. But…it certainly was not. He looked ridiculous.

"Nigel, I'm not going to do anything else crazy," I said.

"Shh."

"I swear. Please just untie us."

"No can do. I'm following orders."

"Come on, Nigel. At least come sit down and make yourself comfortable." Despite what he said, his outfit looked wildly uncomfortable. Maybe it was just comfortable in comparison to his butler uniform. Either way, he should at least take a seat.

He slowly approached us. "You're a very kind mistress."

"Mistress? Is that what Tanner calls me?"

"Um…no. He calls you…babe? Sidepiece?"

What?!

He shook his head. "Baby Momma? No…girl." He sighed. "I don't know the words you people use. But I know that Master Tanner is very fond of you. And I can't let anything happen to you."

"Aww, that's so sweet," said Chastity.

He put his finger to her lips. "Hush, child. I don't know who you are."

She licked his finger.

He yelped.

Stop it, Chastity. Couldn't she see that her flirtations weren't working with this guy? "I have one more question. And then I swear we'll both be quiet."

"Splendid," Nigel said. "What is it?"

"What's Tanner's secret?" Honestly he probably had too many secrets to count. But I was hoping Nigel would just spill the biggest. The vampire one. Because I'd had a lot of time to think this over on the ride back here with a bag on my head. Angel had implied that Tanner was a one-night stand kind of guy. And I was thinking that Tanner definitely had tons of one-night stands because that was all that was possible…since he killed all the women he slept with right after he came. It was genius really. Everyone loved a good snack after sex. I preferred ice cream, but Tanner clearly preferred blood. Sometimes I wanted something salty like cheese. But never blood. Not even once. *Vampire!*

"Secretses?" Nigel shook his head. "No, we have none of those. We're very normal boys."

The fact that he'd just said that wasn't normal.

"How about I draw the two of you a bath to help you calm down?"

Chastity laughed. "You want me and Ash to hook up in front of you, you little perv?"

"No. Baths are for relaxation purposes only. They're not sexual. They're soothing. Let me draw you one so you can see. And I'll stay with you the whole time to make sure the temperature of the water stays consistent."

That sounded very sexual to me. He wanted me and Chastity to bathe together? And he wanted to watch the whole time? "That's okay, Nigel," I said. "We don't need to bathe."

He shrugged. "Millennials."

Really, a millennial dig? He looked the same age as us. What was his deal?

"How about some green juice then?" he asked. "I make a juice that will fix all your ailments. It should calm you both down. Maybe even put you to sleep."

I was actually quite calm despite being tied up. A little less so now that it seemed like he wanted to drug us.

"We don't have any ailments," Chastity said. "Just questions."

Nigel pretended to zip up his lips and then swallow the key. Which made no sense. None of what he did made any freaking sense.

But that was a good thing. Nigel was all over the place. And maybe if I started asking questions about something besides Tanner I could slowly trick him into giving us more information. "Do you know Ocelot?"

Nigel just stared at me.

"He was at Club Onyx tonight. Big hair. Kind of a diva vibe. Anyway, it seemed like he had a crush on Tanner. He even said he was in love with him."

"He did?" asked Chastity.

I nodded and turned back to Nigel. "Is Ocelot in love with Tanner?"

Nigel rolled his little eyes. "Nonsensical. Ocelot is an odd little boy. He does not know the difference between love and in love with. Like…I love baths. I'm not in love with baths. Ocelot doesn't understand the distinction. Although he does look like he appreciates a good bath."

Okay. "So he isn't in love with Tanner?"

"No. Ocelot is straight."

"What? How is that possible? And why does everyone keep telling me that?"

Nigel ignored me.

Ocelot was the least of my concerns. "So Tanner isn't dating Ocelot. Does Tanner have a bunch of women over to his apartment?"

No response.

"Do you ever see the same woman twice?" This response would surely confirm whether my vampire suspicions were accurate. Would Nigel even tell me though? Because if Tanner was a vampire…Nigel might be too. He did carry us both up all those stairs to my apartment. If that wasn't super vampire strength, I didn't know what was.

"You wouldn't understand," said Nigel.

Answer my question, damn it! "Please." I was desperate for information. And I could tell by Nigel's guilty face that he had all the juicy gossip. Hmm. Was he a little gossipy? That could help. "Give me the deets you little slut." Wow, that came out harsher than it sounded in my head.

Nigel stared at me.

"That juicy goss."

Nigel frowned. "What is that?"

"Like…gossip. All the hot goss. A girl's chat."

"Oh." He looked sad. "I can't. I want to. But I can't. I love the juicy goss. But you're both supposed to be in timeout! Now you can both shut your whore mouths. And don't you ever say Matthew's name again." Nigel put the bags back over our heads.

A few seconds later it sounded like the bath turned on. And I was terrified that he was either bathing in my tub or he was about to bathe me. *Holy hell, who is this strange man?*

Chapter 58

THEY'RE BACK AGAIN!

Thursday

I'd barely slept at all, thanks to the itchy canvas bag over my head. I was completely exhausted. But when I woke up on the couch, the bag was gone and my hands weren't tied anymore. I looked over at Chastity. She was still hogtied and bagged.

Damn, Nigel really hates her.

The smell of bacon and eggs filled my nose. My eyes snapped to the kitchen, but Nigel was nowhere in sight. There was just some delicious looking food on the stove and a note sitting on the counter. I got up and read it.

Mistress Ash,

My apologies for having to bag you again. But in my defense…you were very naughty. And you were in timeout.

If there is anything you ever need from me, please don't hesitate to ask. My number is below. I am at your service, Mistress.

Have a good and prosperous day at work. And remember, you have a cake tasting with Master Tanner this evening. He does not appreciate tardiness.

Yours,

-Nigel

XOXO

P.S. I made you breakfast. Only you. Not the stranger on your couch.

I looked over at Chastity and then back at the delicious looking food. Nigel said the breakfast was only for me. And

I didn't want to get on his bad side like Chastity was. I'd unbag her right after breakfast.

***

Tonight was the night. Tanner was finally going to ask me to be his girlfriend.

Or at least…that was what Chastity thought. She kept saying it all day at work. And after work in my closet while she helped me get ready.

I wasn't as convinced. But maybe I was still just disoriented from having a canvas bag on my head all of last night. That weird little Nigel man was literally the worst. I tried to focus on Chastity. Just thinking about Nigel was getting me all hot and bothered. In a rage way. Not in a sexual way. I got zero sexual vibes from Nigel at all. And I still had no idea what he'd done in my bathtub. I had a feeling I needed to stop by the store and buy some bleach. I was 99 percent sure he'd bathed in my tub. No, 100 percent sure. *Damn it, Nigel!* Who does that in a stranger's tub?

At least he was an amazing cook. Those scrambled eggs this morning almost made up for all the weirdness. *Almost. My poor tub!*

I shook away the thought as Chastity zipped up my little red cocktail dress. "How can you be so sure Tanner's going to ask me out?" I asked.

"I just know these things. And with you wearing that?" She whistled. "He's done."

I looked in the mirror and spun around with a huge grin on my face. I wasn't sure I'd ever looked this good before. I felt like freaking Cinderella. But in a slutty little dress rather than a ballgown. *It's finally going to happen. Tanner's going to ask me out!*

"Just make sure you don't let up until the moment he asks you out. You're so close to getting un-wifey-zoned. But one misstep and you'll be right back where you started."

"What constitutes not letting up?"

"Just little things. Text me a few times to make sure you aren't giving Tanner too much attention. Make a comment about one of the waiters being hot. Or better yet, flirt with a waiter! And no matter what, do not, under any circumstances, recant your actions at Club Onyx last night. As far as Tanner is concerned, you whole-heartedly believe in Rule #8 and would have gladly let Angel and Diablo go to town on you."

Hopefully that won't come up. "Are you sure he doesn't just hate me?" He'd been out inspecting the yacht so I hadn't seen him all day. And Chastity had forbidden me from texting him so that I wouldn't seem desperate. But I was desperate. I liked him so much my chest actually hurt. *Oh, God, am I having a heart attack?!*

Chastity grabbed my shoulders and turned me toward her. "There's no way he hates you. I could feel the jealousy radiating off of him last night when he dragged us out of Club Onyx. And then he had Nigel babysit us to make sure we didn't go back. That was when I knew for sure he was about to make things official. If he hated you, he wouldn't have done all that. Now put these Odegaards on and go get your man." She handed me a pair of strappy red heels with the signature blue bottoms.

"I think I'm having a heart attack."

She shook her head. "Cut it out and put on the shoes. You're fine."

She never believed me. One day, when I actually was super sick, she'd be sorry. Especially if my greatest fear actually happened and I punctured my liver real good. I'd talked about that so much that she'd never believe me if it actually happened. Which just made the fear of it happening that much worse. I took a deep breath and tried to shake away the thought. *You will not puncture your liver tonight!*

I put the heels on and did a final outfit check in the mirror. *Hopefully sexy is the right vibe this evening...*

Chastity put a few finishing touches on my makeup and then I went downstairs to catch the ride Tanner had sent for me.

Nigel was in a full chauffeur outfit leaning against a limo. When he saw me, he scurried over.

Oh God, please no! Why Nigel again? I wanted to run the other way.

"Good evening, Mistress," said Nigel with a little bow. "Did you enjoy the breakfast I prepared for you?"

I pictured the bacon, sausage, and scrambled eggs from this morning. It was some of the most delicious food I'd ever eaten. But I'd had to scarf it down so that Chastity didn't know she'd been left out. Sure…I could have saved some for her. But even though I was slightly annoyed with Nigel, I still wanted him to like me. Because I wanted everyone to like me. Being unliked sucked. That was why people hating me was #7 on my list of greatest fears. Worse than my fear of going to jail. I cleared my throat. "It was lovely."

"Excellent!" He opened the limo door for me.

What were the odds of me being bagged again if I climbed inside? But Nigel wasn't staring at me like he was about to attack. He just looked very, very friendly. Overly friendly? He was probably going to murder me or something. Or suck my blood…

I awkwardly peered inside without getting too close to Nigel. Tanner unfortunately wasn't inside, but there was at least a glass of champagne waiting for me. And champagne was just what I needed to calm my nerves. I climbed inside. Tanner sending a limo felt like a good sign for tonight. *Maybe he really will ask me out!* My stomach did a little flip. Tanner Rhodes was going to be my boyfriend! How was this real life? I started playing out different scenarios in my head as Nigel crawled into the front and hit the gas.

Would the cake tasting actually be a romantic dinner for two? I could totally see him doing a big romantic gesture and renting out the entire restaurant so that it's just the two of us.

Or maybe he'll put a ring in one of the cake samples…

Okay not that. Who would be crazy enough to propose without even being exclusive first? But Tanner was kinda crazy, just like me. And I'd totally say yes. I mean…it was Tanner Rhodes. My stalker. And I'd been in love with him since the first moment I saw him step out of One57. For the first time I didn't chastise myself for thinking it was love. And I didn't even care how stalkery that was. Because it was true. Tanner was everything I'd ever wanted, wrapped up in a fancy suit.

And he was about to be either my boyfriend or freaking fiancé. I was sure of it. And I had no idea how I'd gotten so lucky.

Or maybe I did. I thought about my list of new things to try.

Try new smoothie flavors.

Go for a run.

Get blackout drunk.

I smiled to myself. It was a dumb list. And it only had three items, one of which I'd definitely not accomplished. Well, technically I had gone on a run…if running away from fake FBI agents counted. But it wasn't about the individual items. It was about the spirit of the list. Because I sure as hell had tried a lot of new things over the past month.

I'd joined a sex club.

I'd blown a guy in the middle of a museum.

I'd auctioned off my body to the highest bidder.

I'd presented foot-long dick trophies in front of hundreds of people.

And most importantly, I'd fallen in love.

All because I'd decided to stop being afraid and start trying new things. Okay, fine. I'd been terrified the entire time. But it had so been worth it. As long as Tanner didn't break my heart.

Was Diablo telling the truth about all those women? I was terrified that he was. Because this wasn't just run-of-the-mill ordinary love. This was the real kind of love. Not whatever

Joe and I had. Because that didn't compare at all. And that meant this could hurt so much worse than when Joe cheated on me. This would…this would destroy me.

"Nigel?" I asked.

He adjusted the mirror to look at me. "Yes, Mistress?"

I had to be careful with my wording. Last time I'd asked him about Tanner's other women, he'd totally shut me down. "It seems like you and Tanner are pretty close, huh?"

"He is an excellent master."

"Do you guys ever just hang out?"

"I occasionally indulge in leisure time, yes."

"With other people?"

Nigel got a big grin on his face. "Sometimes Master Matthew joins us."

So. Freaking. Weird. "Anyone else?"

His grin vanished as quickly as it had come. "Yes."

"A girl?"

"Pardon me, Mistress, but I must focus on my driving." He started to raise the partition.

"Wait!"

The partition paused.

"I'm sorry. I know you don't like when I ask about that. I just need to know…" I took a deep breath. "Is Tanner going to break my heart?"

"Master Tanner will stop at nothing to make your heart whole." He gave me a small smile and then closed the partition completely.

What does that mean? And what was that smile all about? It almost looked like he pitied me. Or was happy for me? I had no freaking clue. His expressions were crazy.

I leaned my head against the window and watched the buildings zip by.

Maybe I was overthinking it. Nigel had a weird way of speaking. I shouldn't read into it. I should just take it at face value. He'd basically told me that Tanner was in love with me!

My heart skipped a beat. God, my emotions were all over the place tonight. Ridiculously excited. Nervous. Terrified. Exhausted.

In just a few minutes, my life could change forever.

I did some breathing exercises to try to calm myself.

It took nearly 45 minutes, but eventually the limo came to a stop. I looked out the window and couldn't believe my eyes.

Santiago's! We were having a cake tasting at freaking Santiago's! First Spaceboy, and now this? Tanner was incredible.

Nigel opened the door for me. Tanner was waiting by the entrance, looking amazing as ever in an impeccably tailored suit. Usually he would have been wearing a colorful tuxedo at this time on a Thursday, but tonight he was just Tanner.

I felt like I was going to barf. Not because of his outfit. He looked amazing. But I was so freaking nervous. Was he going to grill me about last night at Club Onyx? I didn't want to have to lie to him. But Chastity's plan had been working…

Nigel opened the door for me.

"Are you stalking me?" Tanner asked in that sexy way of his.

God, that smirk of his made my knees feel weak.

He didn't wait for a response. He just helped me out of the limo. "Wow." He put his hand up so I could do a little twirl. "You look stunning in this dress."

I couldn't help the blush creeping along my cheeks. I wanted to tell him that he looked amazing in his suit. And that I was so sorry for all the craziness last night. And that I wanted to be his girlfriend more than anything in the world. But then I heard Chastity's voice in the back of my head. *No! Play hard-to-get!* "I hope I'm not overdressed," I said. "Chastity wanted to go dancing afterwards and I didn't think I'd have time to change." Total lie. I was absolutely not going dancing with Chastity tonight. I'd be too busy banging my new boyfriend in his penthouse.

Tanner's eyes darkened. "We'll see about that. These cake tastings sometimes go longer than you think."

"I wouldn't know. Joe thought buying a wedding cake was a waste of money when we ran our own bakery. So for our cake tasting, he bought me a bunch of flour, sugar, and let me loose in our kitchen." There had been so many signs that he wasn't a catch. What had I been thinking? And why the hell was I talking about Joe right now?

Tanner drew his eyebrows together. "Seriously?"

"Yup."

"Wow. Then I guess tonight I have to work twice as hard to show you a good time. And even if I fail, I have a feeling we'll be attending lots more of these."

Like…for our wedding?! Oh my God, is he actually going to propose?

Tanner opened the door for me. "After you, m'lady."

I loved when he said romantic stuff like that. I stepped in and had a total fangirl moment. Because standing at the hostess stand was Chef Santiago. And the entire restaurant was empty.

He seriously rented out the whole place?! Yeah, he was definitely going to ask me out. I was so close to getting out of the wifey-zone!

"Good evening my friend," said Santiago to Tanner.

"The pleasure is all mine," said Tanner. "I can't thank you enough for fitting us in on such short notice."

"Anything for you." They kissed on the cheek.

How very European of them. Or gay? Maybe he wasn't going to ask me out after all. I tried to take a deep breath and clear my thoughts. I needed to just enjoy this moment.

"And you must be the lovely Miss Cooper?" asked Santiago. He took my hand and kissed it.

"I am. And I take it you're the lovely Chef Santiago?" *Fuck. Why? Why did I just call my chef-idol lovely?* I wanted to hide under a table. And there were so many to choose from…. *Stop it! Stop being weird for one second of your life!*

Tanner laughed and squeezed my hand. "I told Santiago all about how you taught yourself to bake by watching his videos."

"I did. But how'd you know that?"

"Chastity made a note of it on our list. Among other things."

Other things? What kind of other things did Chastity tell Tanner?!

Chef Santiago took us to a table at the center of the restaurant. There were lots of plates and forks, but no cake yet.

"The cake will be ready in just a moment," said Santiago. "I just need to add a few finishing touches. Please, make yourselves comfortable. Can I get you anything to drink?"

Tanner pulled out a chair for me. "Just water, please."

I could have used some wine to calm my nerves, but Tanner was probably right to order water so that nothing competed with the flavor of the cakes.

"Muy bien." Santiago nodded and retreated to the kitchen.

"What else did Chastity tell you?" I asked.

"Nothing important. Hold that thought. I need to go wash my hands. Claude had me hand-feeling monkeys all afternoon."

What kind of wonderful man washes his hands before a cake tasting? Tanner really was the best. With Joe I'd been lucky if he even washed his hands after using the bathroom.

While Tanner went to wash up, I started texting Chastity to ask her what the hell she'd told Tanner. I assumed it was sexual. Because...Chastity.

The kitchen doors swung open and two waiters walked out with some water. Wait...no. Not just any waiters. They were Angel and Diablo.

Oh God, oh God, oh God. Last night I'd told them they could do whatever they wanted to me because of Rule #8. And then I'd booped their penises. I'd been strongly hoping to never see them again. *Maybe they won't recognize me with my red hair.* They'd only ever seen me in my black wig.

I shifted away from them and buried my face in my phone. *Please don't look at me.*

They put the water on the table. They were about to walk away when Diablo stopped.

"Raven?" he asked. "Is that you?"

"I'm sorry, you must be mistaken. My name is Ash, not Raven. We don't even have the same hair color. And she's much more confident than me." *Crap!* If I wasn't Raven too I wouldn't know all those details about her. *Be cool!* I tucked a loose strand of hair behind my ear in hopes of looking nonchalant and not guilty of a lie. But all I proceeded to do was almost knock over the water on the table. I grabbed the glass right before I sent it crashing to the floor.

"Ah, so that's your real name. I'm digging the red hair, by the way."

"Thanks." *Damn it!* My cover was blown.

"What are you doing here?"

"Having a cake-tasting with my soon-to-be boyfriend. What are *you* doing here?"

Diablo leaned against the table. "We own the place."

"Actually our dad does," added Angel. "But he's going to retire soon, and then it's all ours."

"Your dad is Chef Santiago?"

Angel nodded. "The old man taught us everything we know about baking."

They're bakers? Somehow that made them even more attractive. Not that such things mattered, because I was about to be Tanner's girlfriend.

"So where is this soon-to-be boyfriend of yours?" asked Diablo.

"He went to wash up before the tasting." Because he was amazing.

"Then this is the perfect opportunity to finish what we started last night."

I stared at him in disbelief. How could he be so brazen? "Not gonna happen."

"But what about that Rule #8? You just said Ryder is still your soon-to-be boyfriend. Which means you're still single. Man, I can't wait to see the look on Ryder's face when he walks out of the bathroom and sees you getting fucked on this table. He's such an idiot to not ask you out and then bring you out in public looking like *that.*" Diablo's eyes went right to my cleavage.

Angel put his hand on Diablo's shoulder. "What he meant to say is that you look absolutely stunning in that dress."

"She does," agreed Diablo. "But she'd look even better with her tits out and her lips wrapped around my cock."

Oh my God. I crossed my legs under the table and I looked over at the bathroom door. What would Tanner do if he came back and heard them talking to me like this? He'd freaking lose his mind. I bet his eyes would get all stormy again like they had last night. God, that had been so hot.

Wait a second! I couldn't believe I hadn't thought of it sooner. Angel and Diablo showing up was just what I needed to push Tanner over the edge! I just needed to stick to Chastity's crazy plan.

It was time to flirt back.

"Can I tell you a secret?" I asked.

They nodded.

"I haven't been able to stop thinking about you two since last night. I'd been so close to finally getting to feel your huge cocks inside of me." *Did I seriously just say that? How much champagne did I have in the limo?!* "I want nothing more than to turn this *cake* tasting into a *cock* tasting." *Wow, I was channeling Chastity perfectly.*

Diablo gave me a cocky smile. As if he'd always known that I'd give in.

"There's only one problem," I continued. "Tanner is gonna come back any second. And when he does, he's going to flash that little badge and stop all our fun."

"Then we better get started." Diablo reached back to untie his apron.

Good God, no. Flirting to make Tanner jealous was one thing. Banging two guys was on a whole other level that I was hoping I wouldn't have to get on in order to win Tanner over. "Wait," I said. "I don't want to blue ball you guys. So here's the deal. If you can get Tanner's permission, then you can do anything you want to me." *Smooth.* I'd get them to make Tanner jealous for me. I would have high-fived myself if that was a suitable thing to do in public.

"Anything?"

"Anything." *Except butt stuff.* Not that anything was going to happen anyway. Because there was no way Tanner would give them permission.

"Even filming a gif for next year's Onyxies?"

Nope. No way. I'd learned my lesson about sex tapes after the whole blackmail thing with Joe. But luckily this entire conversation was nonsense. And not only was it fun to see how excited Diablo was, but the more outlandish this got, the more jealous it would make Tanner when they went and asked his permission.

"Of course we can make a gif. You guys got totally robbed this year. We can't let that asshole Karl win again. What would you make the caption be?"

Diablo grabbed a fork and flipped it around while he thought. "There are so many options. How about: She wasn't planning on cheating, but once she saw the waiter's cocks, she couldn't resist."

"That's decent. But it's a little generic. It would be better to really lean into the cake tasting theme. Tanner and I are just tasting cakes for a party, but for a hotwife gif we could pretend like we were at a cake tasting for our wedding."

"We'll workshop it," said Angel. "But we better get back to the kitchen. I think the cake is probably just about ready."

"We'll be back soon," said Diablo with a wink.

I took a huge gulp of water as soon as they were gone. My heart was beating out of my chest and I had gotten so sweaty. Saying all those saucy things had made me so nervous. And a little turned on. I knew that making another sex tape was insane, but I kind of loved that they thought I was hot enough to be a porn star.

None of that really mattered, though. Because Tanner was going to ask me out in a few minutes.

Right? Oh God, why had I just said all that stuff to Angel and Diablo? What if Tanner didn't ask me out…

Chapter 59

ABSOLUTELY DELICIOUS

Thursday

Tanner got back from the bathroom just as Chef Santiago came out of the kitchen. Santiago was flanked by his sons, each carrying two plates of mini-cakes. I made sure to keep my eyes trained on the cakes instead of looking at Angel and Diablo. Which was actually easy because the dessert looked freaking amazing.

They put them down on the table and added labels in front of each.

Tanner narrowed his eyes slightly at Angel and Diablo. *Does he recognize them from last night?*

Santiago gestured to the cake plates. "I have prepared for you the three flavors you requested, along with our house specialty - angel food with my signature frosting."

"These look incredible," I said.

Santiago waved off my comment. "This decoration is nothing compared to what I will do for the final cake."

Nothing? I'd spent years making cakes for Joe's business, and it still would have taken me hours to decorate something *half* as fancy.

"If you are ready to begin, please put this on, Señorita." Santiago pulled out a black satin blindfold and handed it to me. "The most important thing my mentor taught me was *solo un ciego puede ver de verdad.* Only a blind man can truly see. It is nonsense in most cases, but when applied to tasting the beauty of my confectionary creations, it is quite accurate. Cutting off one sense enhances the others."

I thumbed my finger over the silky fabric of the blindfold. I couldn't believe I was about to taste Chef Santiago's cakes. I'd watched hundreds of his YouTube videos, but I'd never imagined I'd actually get to try one of his cakes. Much less *four* of them. This was a freaking dream come true.

"I'm sorry, but I must excuse myself," said Santiago. "I have a cake I must finish for a wedding tomorrow."

"Of course," said Tanner. "Thanks again for fitting us in on such short notice."

"It was my pleasure. Please enjoy. If you have any questions, we will be in the kitchen." Santiago and his sons left us alone to try the cakes.

I breathed a sigh of relief when the door closed behind Angel and Diablo.

Tanner looked at me. "You okay? You seem a little nervous."

Of course I'm nervous! There had been at least a 50% chance that Diablo would come right out and ask Tanner if he and Angel could bang me. But I couldn't tell Tanner that. "Wouldn't you be nervous too if you were meeting your culinary idol?"

"I suppose so. Try to relax and enjoy this." He rubbed his hand on my leg and all my worries melted away.

"I still can't believe you convinced him to do this," I said.

"He owed me one," said Tanner.

"For what?"

"His restaurant was going to go under a few years back. I gave him the cash he needed to keep going."

Wow, I had no idea. Tanner had saved my chef-idol. That made me like him even more.

"Which cake do you want to try first?" asked Tanner.

"How about the triple chocolate?"

"Works for me." He lifted up the blindfold. "Might as well try it the chef's way."

I smiled as Tanner slid the blindfold over my eyes.

I heard a napkin unfold. A clink of silverware. The delicious sound of a fork cutting through cake. Really none of this should have been erotic, but I was a little overheated from my conversation with Angel and Diablo. And the blindfold did actually heighten everything. Especially the smell of Tanner's expensive blueberry cologne.

"Open up," said Tanner.

I parted my lips and *holy shit.* I had been expecting it to taste amazing, but this was next level. Cake had a tendency to be too sweet - sometimes even grainy from all the sugar. But this cake was moist and chocolatey and just the right sweetness. It was heaven.

"That good, huh?" asked Tanner.

"I didn't say anything yet."

"Your orgasmic moans said everything I needed to know."

"I wasn't moaning." *Was I?*

"Yes you were. And now that I'm tasting it too, I can see why." Tanner made an exaggerated moaning noise.

I couldn't help but laugh. If I hadn't been blindfolded, I would have shoved him. Or smooshed some cake in his face. Which gave me an idea… If I could somehow get him to put the blindfold on instead of me, I could really have some fun with him.

"I know you're mocking me," I said. "But if you had tasted it with the blindfold on, you would have moaned too. Chef Santiago was right about it really enhancing your senses. Wanna give it a try?"

"I'll go blindfolded at our next cake tasting."

Another mention of future cake tastings?! Ahhh! I could have squealed with excitement.

"Besides, I prefer you wearing one." He lightly touched the side of my neck.

A shiver ran down my spine. Not because his words were dirty. But because I was almost positive what his secret was now. He had me blindfolded and had just touched my neck in a really seductive way. *I knew it!* He was a freaking vampire! My heart started beating even faster. Oh God, was this how I was going to die? Blindfolded during a cake tasting with a secret vampire? What was my life?

"Ready for another bite?" asked Tanner.

Was he referring to me eating more cake? Or to him biting me? I needed to stall him. "Yeah, but I need a palette cleanser first." I reached out for a water glass and promptly knocked over three glasses. *Oops.* Actually, not oops. Because even though I hadn't meant to knock anything over, this was an even better distraction than just drinking some water for a second.

"Whoa!" I heard Tanner jump back and then lots of rustling of fabric. He was either drying his pants or taking them off. *Or doing whatever vampires do before devouring their prey.*

"Did I just spill that all over you?" I asked.

"Yup."

"Sorry about that," I said with a laugh.

"It's fine. Here." He grabbed my wrist. I almost pulled away, but he quickly guided my hand over to a glass of water without any more accidents. I sipped some down. And then some more. And some more, like I was a freaking horse in a desert. *#HorseFacts.* Wow, I really nailed that one! Maybe I should just start talking about horses to distract him. Or I could keep drinking. That seemed like the more normal thing to do to prevent him from sucking my blood. I gulped more down. I was going to have to pee like a racehorse after this. OMG. #HorseFacts again! Double #Horsefacts!

"You're thirsty," Tanner said.

"Well that's rude. I'm not a thirsty bitch."

"Um…what? I never said anything about you being a bitch."

"You just called me thirsty."

Tanner laughed. "Because you just downed a whole glass of water like you hadn't had anything to drink in a week."

He didn't know what a thirsty bitch was. Because of course he didn't know current slang. He was clearly from another time. A time where vampires were spreading rampant all over America. So like…maybe civil war time? That made sense.

"Open wide," said Tanner.

Shouldn't that be what he was doing? But it seemed better to follow his directions, so I did.

"Wider. I accidentally cut an extra-large piece."

Oh no. Suddenly all my thoughts about vampirism faded away. Because a terrible thought had just occurred to me. Was I going to get food on my face? That was one of my biggest fears. Not top 5 bad. But definitely top 10. And with my blindfold on, I wouldn't even be able to grab a napkin to wipe it off. Why had I not planned for this?! Eating blindfolded was about to be added to my list of fears. Or maybe it was just kind of a sub-fear. Hmm…

I opened as wide as humanly possible. I was sure I looked ridiculous, but hopefully it was wide enough to avoid him making a mess. I'd take looking like a fool over making a mess any day.

Instead of biting my neck, he put a huge piece of cake in my mouth.

Mmm. Somehow, this cake was even better than the first. I let him push the cake further into my mouth before closing my lips around the fork. But my mouth was stopped much sooner than it should have. And instead of meeting metal, my lips were on something soft and…fleshy.

I was like 95% sure there was a dick in my mouth.

I pulled back and yanked my blindfold up. Tanner was standing there completely naked with his cake-covered cock inches away from my mouth.

Holy. Shit. I choked on the cake still in my mouth as I stared at his massive cock. And his abs. And his pecs. And back to his cock… How could a human be so perfect? The answer: they couldn't. Only a vampire could!

"How do you like this one?" he asked.

It took me a moment to recover from my surprise. I always would have thought that I would have been upset if someone blindfolded me and shoved their dick in my mouth, but in this case, I kind of loved it. And I was relieved. He wasn't about to suck my blood. He was about to fuck me. For just a second I glanced from his cock to his eyes. They were doing that stormy thing again. But this time he didn't look angry. He looked like he wanted to devour every inch of me. But he had the wrong idea…because I was about to do that to him. I'd been waiting so long for this moment. He didn't want to kill me. He just wanted…me.

"Absolutely delicious," I said. I had so many questions. What had finally made him decide to take things to the next level with me? Had he taken care of DODO? Or did this red dress just make me too sexy for him to resist? And most importantly…did this mean I was his girlfriend? In most normal situations I would have assumed yes. But Tanner was part of the Society, so who really knew.

Either way, we could discuss that later. Because right now I wanted more uh…cake.

"Better than the first cake?" asked Tanner.

I had Tanner right where I wanted him. Chastity's advice had gotten me here. So I needed to keep playing a little hard to get. Well, as hard to get as I could be with his dick in my mouth. Scratch the hard to get then. I just needed to tease him a little. That totally stayed the course. "I think so. But I should probably take another taste just to be sure." I leaned forward and licked a glob of cake off of him. And this time I was very aware of the moan that escaped my throat.

He gestured to some icing near the base of his penis. "I think you missed some."

"Well I would hate to waste any." I opened wide and took him into my mouth. I made it about halfway down before my gag reflex kicked in.

God he's big. Somehow he was even bigger than Dr. Lyons. But I was determined to get that cake. Wasting it would have been a crime.

I powered through my gag reflex and went even farther. Tanner groaned. God, I loved that sound. And I finally got to the cake. I stayed there for a few seconds, swirling my tongue around to get every last bit, and then pulled back.

"Did I get it?" I asked and batted my eyelashes at him.

"Hmm..." said Tanner. His eyes had gotten even stormier. "I think you missed a spot."

"Really? Because it looks pretty clean to me."

Tanner swiped his finger through the remains of the cake and smeared it on his cock.

I smiled up at him. "Oh, I see it now." I went back to sucking him. But this time I didn't stop once the cake was gone. I just went faster and faster, pulling out all the moves I'd seen the girls do in Chastity's porn collection.

Tanner seemed to especially enjoy when I locked eyes with him and flicked my tongue against his tip.

"Fuck," he groaned and sunk his fingers into my hair. I thought he was gonna guide me back down, but instead he pushed me backwards. "It's my turn to have a taste."

I made a face at him. "Can you really bend far enough to suck yourself off?"

"What? No." He ran his thumb along my lip, removing some of the smeared icing. And then he shoved it in my mouth. "I want to taste *you*."

Chapter 60

BETTER THAN CAKE

Thursday

I could barely focus on his words because I was licking the icing off his thumb. Which I would normally never do because hands were dirty. But fucking hell this was somehow even hotter than when I was sucking his cock. We locked eyes. *Oh God. Wait a second. Did he just say he wanted to taste me?* Was he talking about what I thought he was? Joe never did that for me. But Tanner was nothing like stupid Joe.

Wait. Oh no. Taste me? He wanted to taste my blood. He really was a vampire! God, why did he have to do that right now? Couldn't he tell how much I needed him based on what I was currently doing? I was scared, but I was pretty sure I was more turned on. Maybe him taking one little taste of my blood wouldn't hurt that badly. I honestly had no idea what was happening anymore. "Hm?" I moaned against his thumb.

He groaned. "Jesus, Ash." He pulled me to my feet and his lips crashed against mine as he pushed me back onto the table. One swipe of his arm sent plates and silverware clattering to the floor.

A second later I was flat on my back on the table, one hand in a plate of cake.

"What are you doing?!" I squealed. "They're going to hear us." Part of me wanted them to. They could save me from having my blood sucked. But at the same time…if Tanner was about to do what I actually wanted him to do…I'd die if someone stopped us. I'd just die of horniness. I was pretty sure that was possible.

"I don't care." He pushed the hem of my skirt up until it was bunched around my waist. "Do you have any idea how long I've been waiting to do this? How many times I've jerked off to the thought of you spread out for me just like this?" Then he tore off my thong. And I don't mean he pulled it down my legs in a hurry. I mean he *tore it off of me.* Like, split it in half.

And then he was kneeling in front of me, pushing my legs apart.

He tossed my ruined thong to the side. I thought he was about to devour me, but instead he gently kissed up my inner thigh. He was going so slowly. Torturously slowly. What was he trying to do to me?

"Please," I moaned.

That just made him go even slower. "Your skin is so fucking sweet."

God. Of course! He was excited about sampling my blood. I knew that's what this was. I knew it and yet…God, I couldn't move away. I felt like I was going to explode. I just needed him to touch me where I was dying to be touched. Just once, and then I'd die happy when he killed me. "Please, Tanner. I need you."

He ran his tongue up the inside of my thigh. And instead of biting me, he sucked on my clit. Hard.

I threw my head back, thankfully not into a piece of cake. But honestly…I wouldn't have cared if I had. Because Tanner brushing his tongue against my clit made all my worries about vampires disappear.

Tanner groaned. It was the sexiest sound I'd ever heard in my life. And then he started feasting on me. God, I'd never felt anything like this before. His fingers dug into my hips like he couldn't get close enough to me. His nose brushed against my clit as his tongue explored all my walls. It was like he thought I was more delicious than all the cakes in the restaurant. I'd never felt more desired in my life. And I wanted it to last forever.

I dug my fingers into his hair to keep him from ever leaving.

Every suck, every flick, every time he plunged his tongue deep inside of me… It all brought me closer to the edge. Everything else faded away. The only thing in the world that mattered was Tanner devouring my pussy.

"Oh God," I panted. "More."

He obliged, thrusting his tongue even deeper, circling my wetness. I clamped my thighs around his head and my whole body shook with pleasure.

"Yes!" I screamed. *God! Oh God.* My fingers tightened in his hair.

When my body finally relaxed, Tanner pulled back.

"No," I gasped. "Don't stop." I needed that again. And again and again. I was wrong before. He wasn't the one starving for me. I was literally starving for him. I'd never felt anything like that in my whole life. And I wasn't done yet.

"I have a better idea." He stood up, his hands on my thighs still keeping me spread wide. And his cock was inches away from me.

My eyes got big.

"You're mine," he said. "And I'm going to show you that you're mine."

I nodded. "Did you bring a condom?"

"No. I want to feel you. *Really* feel you. I need you, Ash."

I gulped. *Should I really do this?!* I wanted to. So badly. But I was also kind of terrified. I'd never had unprotected sex before. I'd always been so worried my birth control would fail. It was only like 99% effective. Which meant there was a 1 in 100 chance that he'd get me pregnant! *Ahhh!*

I took a deep breath. At this point, I didn't fucking care about possibly getting pregnant. I just needed to feel him. It was time to stop being afraid and start living. I could deal with the consequences later. Right now…I needed this too. God, I needed him.

"What are you waiting for?" I asked.

He spread my legs farther and guided his thick cock into me.

Oh God. Just like he had with his kisses, he insisted on going torturously slowly. But this time, it served a purpose. Because if he had gone any faster, he probably would have ripped me in half. When he was finally all the way in he looked down at me. "Are you okay?"

"Yes!" I didn't mean to scream it. But I was literally about to explode.

He started moving in and out of me slowly. It felt better than anything I'd ever experienced in my life. I could feel every ridge, every vein. All rubbing me in spots I didn't even know existed.

He kept going slowly, his hands tracing every inch of my body. They landed on my tits. He gently squeezed them.

I loved that he was going slowly and cherishing my body. But I had been horny for far too long to keep up this slow pace. I wanted him to fuck my brains out. No…I *needed* him to fuck my brains out.

"Faster," I panted.

"God, where have you been hiding for the last century?"

The last century? What?

He slammed into me and I forgot what I'd been thinking. He pushed into me. Again. And again. Each time quickening his pace, his fingers digging into my hips until he was fucking me so hard it would have hurt if I wasn't so far gone. *God, yes.*

I was loving every second of it. But my mind was a ridiculous place to be. And as much as I'd tried to push the question out of my mind, I couldn't help but wonder…

"Does this mean I'm your girlfriend now?" I asked.

He thrust into me. "Try more cake."

What? "Now?"

He silenced me by shoving a cake-covered finger into my mouth. God, he could tell how much I'd loved this earlier. And sucking on his finger while he fucked me was somehow even hotter. Especially when it was covered in the most delicious cake I'd ever tasted. Or was this one second best? Hmm… I swirled my tongue around his finger to taste it more.

Tanner groaned.

You like that? The look in his eye told me that he did. So I started sucking on his finger harder, jamming it down my throat like it was a second cock.

"Fuck you're hot," he muttered.

I pulled back from sucking his finger and looked up at him. His abs tensed every time he thrust into me. I couldn't take my eyes off of them. All eight of them.

Was that why he hadn't asked me out yet? Because he had eight abs and eight inches. Which according to Single Girl Rule #8 meant he could do whatever he wanted to me as long as I was single.

Damn it! All that teasing had totally backfired. Kind of… Because even though he hadn't officially asked me out yet, him giving me the best sex of my life wasn't a bad consolation prize.

I propped myself up on my elbows and watched him thrusting into me. I couldn't even believe how lucky I was to be with such a perfect specimen of a man.

He slammed into me harder.

God. I tried to remember every moment of this in case it was a one-time thing. And I wanted to make sure he remembered it too. I ran my index finger through some icing, locked eyes with Tanner, and licked it off as seductively as possible.

"Damn," he groaned as he dug his fingers into my hips. "Do you know what that does to me?"

"Mhm," I said. I lifted up a piece of caked and intentionally let some fall onto my cleavage. "Oops."

"Let me help you with that." He leaned over and licked it off my tits as he slammed into me harder.

Fuck.

He kept his face buried in between my breasts. "You're perfect," he said. Or at least I thought he did. His words were kind of muffled by my breasts.

"You're perfect," I replied. "And good at distracting me. But you can't get out of answering my question forever."

"Sure I can." He pulled out and flipped me around so that I was bent over next to the table. And then he was inside of me again. Like…*really* inside of me. The new angle let him go even deeper than before.

And this time he didn't start slowly. In fact, his thrusts were so forceful that the blindfold slid back down over my eyes.

I reached up to move it, but he grabbed my arms and pinned them behind my back. Chef Santiago had been telling the truth, because being blindfolded did indeed enhance all my other senses. Especially the feeling of getting filled with Tanner's beautiful cock.

"Tanner!" I hissed. "You're being so bad right now! I need you to answer me."

"Or what?"

"Or I'll…make you stop." I didn't really want him to ever stop. But it felt like a good bargaining chip.

"Were you serious about Rule #8?" he asked.

Apparently he'd realized what I had earlier. According to Rule #8, I was at his mercy. And I had to say I was serious about it, or he might put me right back into the wifey-zone. Which I could never go back to now that I knew how amazing he felt inside of me. Damn he was clever! But I could be clever too.

"Of course I'm serious about Rule #8. In fact…you better hope that Angel and Diablo don't catch us. Because if they do, I have a feeling they're going to make me do something that you wouldn't like very much."

Tanner growled and thrust into me harder.

"But you can stop that from happening if you take me off the market. It's up to you. Am I still single and ready to mingle? Or am I your loyal girlfriend?"

"I think I'm ready to tell you my secret."

I didn't even care about the change of topic. "You are?!" *Finally!*

"Yes."

"What is it?"

He paused for a long moment.

This was it. The moment I'd been waiting for. I tried to turn so I could see him ask me out. But he was still pinning my arms down. And I was still wearing the stupid blindfold.

"My secret is…" his voice trailed off.

Say it. Please say it.

"I'm in love with you, Ash. I've been in love with you ever since I first saw you months ago. And yes, I was the one stalking you, not the other way around."

I knew it!

He pulled out of me and flipped me back over. He slowly lowered the blindfold from my eyes. "Look, baby. We have an audience." He grabbed my chin and turned my head toward the kitchen.

I could see Angel and Diablo watching through the window of the swinging door. *Oh fuck*. I tried to push my dress back into place, but Tanner caught my arms.

"I know you've been trying to make me jealous by flirting with them. This is what you wanted, right? For me to claim you?"

God, everything he said somehow made me wetter and wetter. Claim me? Yes, that's exactly what I wanted.

The corner of his mouth rose slightly as he watched me squirm. "And I also know you love the thought of getting caught. That's what the Society is all about. Acting out your wildest fantasies. This is one of them, yes? Having an audience?" He lightly bit my bottom lip.

I yelped.

"Do you want me to keep fucking you right in front of them? To show them what they're missing out on?"

"Tanner…"

He leaned forward and whispered in my ear. "It's not a trick. It's okay, baby. I'll keep you safe. They'll never touch you. This is as close as they'll ever get. I'm going to show them what they're missing out on. Your lips." He kissed me hard. "Your tits." He pinched one of my nipples. "And your sweet pussy." He grabbed my hips and thrust his cock back inside of me.

"Tanner!" My fingers dug into his back.

"You're going to come on my cock. For me. Only for me."

Jesus.

He thrust faster.

"They're watching," he whispered in my ear. "They so desperately want to be me. They saw you taking my cock and sucking my finger at the same time. That's what they wanted to do to you." He ran his finger through some icing again and shoved it into my mouth. "Just like this. Using you for their pleasure. But you're mine, Ash. And you're only going to please me."

Fuck. I sucked on his finger at the same time he was thrusting into me. He was right. About all of it. This was so hot I was about to explode. I knew he felt the same way about me as I did about him. But this? It was like his fantasies aligned perfectly with mine. Because I could feel him getting harder by the second. And I was so close to…

He brushed his fingers against my clit.

And I was coming so hard I think I might have bitten his finger.

He hissed and wrapped his hand around the side of my neck. "Fuck. Ash," he groaned as he rode out my orgasm.

And as soon as I was able to catch my breath, he pulled out of me. "No one will ever make the mistake of flirting with you again. Because you're mine." He started stroking himself. "All mine, Ash. Do you understand me?"

I could barely catch my breath. I just nodded as I watched him stroking himself. I couldn't think straight with my foggy after sex brain and watching him looking like a Greek God in front of me.

"Say it, baby. I need you to say it. Tell me who you belong to."

"You. I'm yours."

As soon as the words left my mouth he exploded. Shot after shot of cum all over my face and my tits. Again and again. I was freaking drowning in his cum. It was like someone had tossed a glass of water in my face. But it tasted like cookies. Man I loved cookies. And cum. And Tanner.

I was completely drenched. God, if this was his way of claiming me, I was here for it.

"All mine," he growled.

I went to wipe the cum out of my eyes so I could open them, but he stopped me.

"But unfortunately no one is ever mine for more than one night."

Wait, what? I felt his lips brush against the side of my neck.

"Because you were right all along, baby. My true secret? You found it in the literature. I'm a vampire. And you're my dessert."

I screamed at the top of my lungs as he bit down on the side of my neck. And suddenly I was drenched in cum and blood. I screamed again and tried to push him off but I couldn't see anything.

"Mistress?!" he yelled. "Mistress! You're awake!"

I threw out a punch where I thought Tanner's blood-sucking vampire throat was.

He wheezed. "Ow," he groaned in a weird British accent.

It was a perfect throat punch. I was finally able to wipe the cum off my eyes lids and open them.

I blinked a few times. *Who the hell is that?!* Because the man next to me was definitely not Tanner.

"Nigel?" I blinked again. I was definitely looking at Nigel, sitting there in his weird little chauffeur uniform. And then I screamed at the top of my lungs. Because that meant…that meant I thought Nigel was Tanner. The weirdest case of mistaken identities ever because they couldn't look more different. *Oh no.* And if I mistook Nigel for Tanner…that meant Nigel had just done two things to me that he shouldn't have. And I think the first one was worse somehow. "Nigel, did you just cum on my face?!"

Chapter 61
DRENCHED
Thursday

Nigel was still holding his throat, but his eyes got big and he stared at me.

Oh my God. What had I done? I'd just had sex with Nigel while Angel and Diablo watched. And it didn't matter that I thought it was Tanner. I'd fucked his houseboy! And his houseboy bit my neck! I reached up to touch my wound, but my neck felt fine. "You tried to suck my blood!"

His eyes grew even rounder. "I'm sorry, Mistress," said Nigel. "I think you were having a naughty little dream. I tried to wake you, but you just kept moaning and wiggling around. I didn't want you to be late for your appointment with Master Tanner, so I had no choice but to splash champagne in your face."

I looked at my hands. Instead of being covered in cum and blood, they were shimmering. And I was no longer at Santiago's. I was in the back of the limo.

"You must have taken a quick snooze, Mistress."

Fuck my life. Nigel was right. I'd dozed off and had the craziest sex dream ever. But I couldn't get my heart rate to slow down. I still felt like I was in danger. Did Nigel look hungry for blood or was it just me?

"I didn't mean to get you so wet," so Nigel. "Here." He pulled out a hanky and started dabbing the champagne off of me.

"Stop. Stop!" I swatted him away. I didn't want anyone to touch me. I just needed a second to calm down.

"Ash?" asked Tanner. He was peering into the limo over Nigel's shoulder.

I screamed at the top of my lungs. *Oh God, why did I just scream?* He wasn't a vampire, it was all just a dream.

"Are you okay?" he asked.

My first reaction was to try to hide. I couldn't face him. Not after screaming in his face like a crazy person. And especially not after that dream. I liked to think it was just a harmless fantasy. But Chastity always said that dreams had meaning. They were a window into my psyche. My very dirty psyche.

So what the hell did this dream mean?

The first part was obvious - I wanted Tanner to tell me he loved me and then fuck the shit out of me.

But the other part? The weird bit with him wanting Angel and Diablo to watch us because he knew I wanted it? God, that was so fucked up. *And hot. I'm so weird!* And it was even weirder that I was obsessing over that instead of the fact that he'd tried to suck my blood!

"One moment, Master," said Nigel. "Mistress Ash was having a naughty..."

I put my hand over his mouth. "He's lying. I didn't have a naughty dream. He's delirious." I gave Nigel what I thought was a pleading stare, begging him with my eyes to keep his little mouth shut.

"Why are you so wet?" asked Tanner.

He was right. My panties were completely soaked after that dream. But how did he know?! "I'm not wet. What makes you think I'm wet?"

"Because Nigel is literally wiping water off your face. And your hair is soaked."

"Oh. Oh! Right. Yeah, your little houseboy hit the brakes too hard and I spilled champagne everywhere. I wish it was water. Freaking maniac!"

"Is that true, Nigel?"

"That most certainly is not true! She was having a naughty dream. Lots of moaning. The only way to rouse her was with a glass of champagne to the face."

"That didn't happen." How could he not read my pleading glare? *Look at me, Nigel! Help me out of this mess!*

"Yes it did!" replied Nigel. He started dabbing at my face again.

I swatted him away. "No it didn't." I was considering grabbing my fire extinguisher and blasting the little man away.

"Yes it did."

"No it didn't."

I slapped his hand away as he tried to blot my face again and we somehow started slapping at each other's hands repeatedly in what I can only describe as…ridiculousness.

Tanner started laughing and grabbed both of our arms. I tried to fight against his grip, but he was too strong.

"I'm sorry, Master," said Nigel. "I shouldn't have hit the mistress. Technically she punched me first. But I am sorry. I was bad. Are you going to have Master Matthew come punish me?"

Oh my. I had never heard someone sound so excited to be punished before.

"No," said Tanner. "But please don't hit her again. Can you give us a moment?"

Nigel bowed and crawled out of the limo.

"So…" said Tanner. "You just had a sex dream?" The smirk on his face made me want to run away and hide again.

"No! Don't listen to Nigel. He's lying."

"Who was in this sex dream?"

"No one. Because there was no sex dream."

"Mhm. Sure." He grabbed Nigel's hanky and dabbed it against my chest. Dangerously close to my cleavage. I flashed back to my dream when he'd licked the cake off my tits. It was so tempting to pull his face down into them. If I did, would he go down on me like he had in my dream? Because I needed that in my life. But he could just as easily bite my neck too.

I needed to distract myself before I did something crazy. I pulled out my phone to see how much Nigel had screwed up my makeup. The answer was…a lot. My mascara was running down my cheeks. And my hair was totally flat. I might as well have had a middle part like some dumb Gen-Z girl. Yeah, it was that bad. And I was horrified that Tanner was seeing me looking like a drowned naked mole-rat.

"Can you just have Nigel take me home? I can't go to a cake tasting like this."

"Like what?" asked Tanner.

"Like *this*." I pulled on a few strands of my soaking wet hair. "I look homeless. And you look all perfect." *And vampirey.*

He moved back a little and gave me the up-down. "I think you look great. But if it will make you feel better…" He grabbed a glass of champagne, shrugged his shoulders, and splashed it in his own face.

I laughed.

And then he tore one of the sleeves off his suit. "How's that?"

I was smiling so hard it hurt. "Perfect." Seriously. That was like…the sweetest thing anyone had ever done for me. That suit must have cost like 10 grand. And he destroyed it just to make me feel more comfortable.

"Shall we?" He held his hand out for me.

I hesitated to take it. Ripping his suit was sweet. *Too sweet.* It was exactly the kind of gesture a vampire would do in order to lure a girl into their lair. "Where are we going?" I asked.

"Inside. To the cake tasting."

"Yeah, but *where*? What restaurant?"

He pointed out the window. I scooched over and looked up. We were at Santiago's. Just like in my dream. *Oh no! It's happening.*

"Can you go grab our table? I promised I'd call Chastity as soon as we got here. To tell her exactly where we are. And who I'm with." I stared at him. Would that be enough to deter him from murdering me? Probably not. He would just go murder her next. "And I should probably call my mom to tell her too. And one other person whose identity shall remain secret."

"You can text them once we're inside. Otherwise we'll be late." He reached for my hand.

That settled it. I didn't want to get eaten by a vampire. But I would rather die than be late for something. Especially when that something was a date with Tanner at the best restaurant in the city.

Please don't eat me. I took Tanner's hand and slid out of the limo.

Just like in my dream, he looked me up and down.

I returned the favor. I was digging his wet-faced, torn-suit look. No one should look that good when they'd splashed champagne in their own face. Yet...Tanner looked like he'd just emerged out of pristine ocean water. He was dripping wet in the sexiest way possible.

"What are you looking at, Stalker?" he asked.

"You're the stalker. It hardly seems like a coincidence that you happened to be here when I arrived."

"We had plans to meet here. That's hardly stalking."

"Yeah, but what about when you hunted me down at Club Onyx last night?

He narrowed his eyes.

Shit! Why had I mentioned Club Onyx? That was the one topic that I had wanted to avoid at all costs.

"You shouldn't have gone to Club Onyx alone," said Tanner. "You aren't ready."

"Ready to learn about your sexcapades with millions of random women, Mr. #1 Recruiter?"

"We really should go inside for the cake tasting." He gestured towards the door. "But if it will help put your mind at ease, you can ask me one yes-or-no question about Club Onyx, and I'll answer 100% truthfully."

"So like the world's worst version of 21 questions?"

"Yup."

Gah! I had so many questions about that place. But mainly I wanted to know if Tanner was a vampire. And if he slept with thousands of women. Or ate them. *Ah! That's it!* I had the perfect question.

"Have you banged and sucked the blood of more than ten women from Club Onyx?"

Tanner laughed. "No."

"So you don't bang them? Or you don't suck their blood?"

"Or maybe I don't do either. But you'll never know thanks to the extremely poor wording of your question. Was this your first time playing 21 questions? You should never go that specific." He looked so happy with himself.

Damn it! It had seemed like the perfect question. But now that I thought about it, it was kind of the worst question ever. It could have only been 9 girls. Or maybe he didn't bang them before he sucked their blood. Or maybe it was more of a drinking action than a sucking action.

"Can I have one more question?" I asked.

"Later." He grabbed my hand and pulled me into Santiago's.

Chef Santiago greeted us at the door.

"Buenos noches mis amigos," said Santiago.

"Buenos noches," replied Tanner in perfect Spanish. Then he said a bunch of other stuff I didn't understand. The only thing I caught was when he said my name and gestured over at me.

Are they making plans about how best to suck my blood? I'd never considered that Santiago might be a vampire too. That would explain why he'd been so willing to clear out his entire restaurant for us on such short notice...

"Ash, it is a pleasure to meet you," said Santiago. He took my hand and pulled it towards his mouth.

Ah! Don't eat me! I yanked my hand back. And when he reached for me again, I slapped his hand away.

Santiago and Tanner stared at me.

"What?" I asked. "Don't you guys know the secret baker's handshake?" I took his hand and recreated the handshake and slap. And then I added all sorts of moves that basically resembled baking a cake. There was a mixing motion, a spin, something that looked like putting a cake in the oven... *What am I doing?!* I felt incredibly awkward. But I was in too deep. I had to keep going. I added like five more moves, and then I was going to finish it off by putting some sprinkles on my imaginary cake. But then I realized that this "handshake" was basically a solo dance, so I brought Santiago back into it by booping him on the nose. *God, why do I keep booping things that don't belong to me?* I was seriously seconds away from going back to my vow of reclusivity.

"Fantástico!" said Santiago. "I can't believe no one ever taught me this before. May I try?"

"Please do."

"I'll do it with you," offered Tanner. "It looks fun."

"*Fun?*" asked Santiago. "The bakers' handshake is not *fun*. It is a sacred tradition stretching back centuries. Right, Ash?"

"Yup. Mhm," I said. "Sure is." I turned to Tanner. "Sorry, bud. This is only for bakers. In fact, please forget everything you've seen." *Seriously. Please forget this weird handshake dance thing.*

Instead, he got to watch me and Santiago practice it four more times. I kept having to correct him. What was so difficult about spinning clockwise four times while waiting for the cake to bake?! Or maybe he was just having trouble because I definitely kept changing the order of things. I couldn't remember the stupid handshake! Especially when I had to keep watching Tanner out of the corner of my eye to make sure he wouldn't pounce on me to suck my blood. And with my other eye I was watching the kitchen in case Angel and Diablo decided to pop out and try to fuck me or something.

Oh God...are they here? Were they even Santiago's sons? Or was that just in my dream? Santiago had their same tanned skin. And he looked about the right age to be their father.

"You can practice more with your sons," I said.

"Sons?" asked Santiago. "I only have three daughters."

He was a Dad of Daughters Only? *Those must be the triplets that Tanner banged!*

"What made you think he had sons?" asked Tanner.

"I didn't mean sons in the biological sense. I meant baking sons. That's how we American bakers refer to our sous chefs." I was so freaking smooth.

Santiago shook his head. "First the handshake and now this? You are making me feel like a true amateur this evening, Señorita Cooper."

"My baking etiquette is impeccable, but I'm sure you could bake the hell out of me." *What the actual fuck did I just say?* It sounded oddly sexual. And maybe kind of violent? I had been trying to concede that he was the superior baker.

Both men stared at me.

"Shall we begin the tasting?" said Tanner.

"Si, si. Please, take a seat and I'll be right out with the cakes." Santiago took us to a table and then disappeared into the kitchen.

"So you want Chef Santiago to bake the hell out of you, huh?" asked Tanner as he hung his torn suit jacket on the back of his chair.

I shook my head. "It's a bakers' phrase. You wouldn't understand."

"I'm sure it is. Just like that magnificent handshake you made up for God knows what reason."

"He was going to kiss my hand! And then I panicked. It seemed like he believed me though."

"I think he actually did. In my experience, Spaniards rarely use sarcasm. Their humor is more based around intense physical danger and sexual innuendo."

Oh, I know. Diablo was the master of sexual innuendo. Actually, maybe he wasn't. His sexy comments were neither funny nor innuendo-y. *Should I tell Tanner that?* It would certainly make him jealous. And I'd kind of loved what had happened in my dream as a result of making Tanner jealous.

I pressed my thighs together and tried to ignore my overwhelming horniness. But the only thing I could focus on was all the things I could do to Tanner if I could convince him to wear a blindfold during the cake tasting.

No! Stop it, Ash! I'd already tried to rape Dr. Lyons. I didn't want it to become a pattern. Besides, I already had to keep track of five incidents. I couldn't imagine having to keep track of any more. I made a mental note to write them all down. Even if they were all nightmarishly unforgettable.

Oh no. Whenever I started thinking about *the incidents*, something terrible usually happened. I swallowed hard. What unspeakable thing was I about to do to Tanner?

Chapter 62

HIGHLIGHT OF MY LIFE

Thursday

I looked around for some candles that might accidentally somehow set him on fire. But there weren't any. Besides, I had my fire extinguishers. I breathed a sigh of relief.

"Have you spent a lot of time in Spain?" I asked to try to distract myself. "Your Spanish was so good."

"Yeah, I spent a few years there. But I actually learned Spanish when I was living in Argentina."

"How many places have you lived?"

"A lot. I lived all over when I was young."

I'd never been able to get a straight answer about his childhood. But by my count he'd mentioned living in at least ten different places. "Was your dad in the military or something?"

"He was."

"What branch?"

"The royal guard." Tanner looked away and straightened his utensils.

"So he was British?"

"Don't insult the British like that. What's taking so long? I better go check to see if Santiago fell asleep back there." He got up and walked over the kitchen.

I tried to think over what I'd just said that agitated Tanner enough to excuse himself from the table. His father was part of the royal guard. But not the British one? I was so confused. What other royal guard was there? Maybe he was just saying his dad was a dick. In which case…what did his dad do to piss him off so much? Maybe he was the one who turned Tanner into a vampire…

Speaking of which, this was the perfect opportunity to text Chastity and tell her where I was. That way they'd at least find my body to give me a proper burial if Tanner decided to suck my blood.

Me: Tanner took me to Santiago's! I think you might be right about him being a vampire. Please call the police if I'm not home by midnight.

Chastity: Did he try to bite you?!

I was about to text her back when Tanner reemerged from the kitchen.

He cleared his throat and sat down next to me. "Santiago will be out in just a moment."

"Can I get one more question?"

He pulled his eyebrows together. "That depends on what you're going to ask."

I smiled. He really didn't like when I asked him personal questions. "Doesn't that kinda defeat the purpose?"

"Fair point." He rubbed the side of his jaw as he stared at me. "Hit me with one more."

I needed to word this one better. And there were even more options now. *Why do you hate your dad? Was he British or not? What other royal guard was there? Are you a vampire?* Screw all the rest of it. The vampire thing was the most important question and I'd flubbed it last time. This time I'd just get proof. "Show me your teeth."

"Excuse me?"

"You heard me, buddy. Let's see those chompers."

He laughed. "That's not a question, Ash."

"Just do it."

He stared at me like I'd lost my mind. "You are probably the weirdest person I've met in my entire life." He said it like it was a compliment. But the actual words weren't that complimentary.

"You're weird." *Smooth.*

He smiled. "I know."

Okay. Why was he smiling at me like that? "Calling someone weird isn't exactly a nice thing."

"But we're both weird," he said. "We can be ourselves around each other. Isn't that refreshing?"

I was literally sitting here drenched in champagne. And he was staring at me like he always did. Like I was the most beautiful girl in the room. Ignoring the fact that I was literally the only woman in this room, it was sweet. "Honestly? Yeah. Who wants to be normal anyway?"

His smile grew. "You're a breath of fresh air, Ash. Truly."

I opened my mouth and then closed it again. I didn't know what to say to that. If he liked being weird with me, if he thought I was a breath of fresh air…why wouldn't he date me? "Can I ask you one more question?"

"Hold that thought," Tanner said as Santiago walked out of the kitchen doors holding a tray of cakes.

Santiago placed down the tray and described the cakes we'd be tasting. They weren't the same flavors from my dream, but I could still picture Tanner licking icing off my nipples perfectly. I crossed my legs under the table and tried my best to pay attention. Santiago excused himself and Tanner turned to me.

He was about to grab the blindfold, but I reached out and snatched it before he could. "Close your eyes and pucker up, big boy."

Tanner laughed.

"I mean like…open your mouth so I can put stuff in it." Yeah, he was right. I was a total weirdo. And he just rolled with it.

"Don't you love this place? I want you to have the full experience." He moved so quickly that I barely even saw him steal the blindfold before my eyes were covered.

Freaking vampire.

Before I could figure out how to trick him into wearing it instead, he was putting cake into my mouth. Not his rock-hard dick. Just delicious cake. Bite after bite. And I was groaning just like in my dream.

Tanner laughed. "I haven't had something this good in years. Marie Antoinette's baker used to make something just like this last one. It's heaven. This brings back so many memories."

Marie Antoinette? *What the what?* But before I could ask him about it, he put a forkful of cake into my mouth. *Mmmm.* It was to die for. I could literally die eating this cake and I'd be happy. When I finally finished moaning around that perfect bite, I threw another question at him. "Have you read a lot about Marie Antoinette?"

"Hm?"

"You said her baker made something just like this."

"Yeah…" his voice trailed off. "I must have heard it in a documentary or something."

But he said it brought back memories. Maybe he used to watch Marie Antoinette documentaries with one of his many hookups before he sucked their blood?

He cleared his throat. "You have a little icing on your chin."

No. Noooo. Food on my face? Kill me now! I reached up to wipe it away.

"A little to the left," he said.

God, it's everywhere?! I moved my hand to the left. This was one of the worst moments of my life. "Did I get it?" I started wiping frantically. *Please for the love of God.*

"Let me," he said. He lightly brushed his thumb beneath my lip.

And all my worries about food on my face and Tanner's vampiric tendencies disappeared. Because it felt like I was back in my dream.

He ran his thumb slowly along my skin. And like the weird person he knew that I was, I licked the pad of his thumb.

For a second, there wasn't a sound in the whole restaurant except for my heart pounding. Why did I lick his thumb? *He's going to think I'm a lunatic.* But I couldn't think of a single thing to do to fix it. And his thumb was still just paused on my lip. So my brain short-circuited and I licked his finger again.

He groaned and shoved his thumb into my mouth.

If this was what being weird together meant, I wanted more of it. I closed my lips around his thumb and sucked hard.

"Fuck," he hissed.

"What's the verdict?" Santiago said.

I jumped and Tanner laughed. Although, I don't know why he was laughing, because I could have easily bit him. He was lucky to still have that finger.

Tanner lowered the blindfold from my face. "What do you say? Which one was your favorite?" He kept his hand on my cheek and stared into my eyes.

All the cakes were astounding. But I knew which one Tanner preferred. "The Marie Antoinette one."

He smiled and turned to Santiago. "Cake #4."

"Perfecto. They shall be delivered to the yacht tomorrow afternoon. It was wonderful meeting you, Ash. I will work on that handshake." He winked at me and then hurried back into the kitchen.

"So that's a wrap." Tanner dropped his hand from my face. "Your work on this party is officially done."

"Kind of. Except for everything tomorrow before the actual party."

Tanner waved off my comment. "Not necessary. You've already done so much. You should just take the weekend off."

What? But... "I can still come to the party though, right?"

"Did you get an invitation?"

"No. Do I need one?"

"Of course."

I stared at him in disbelief. Was he seriously disinviting me to the party that I'd planned?! God, he was doing that thing again. Running because I'd made things sexual. I'd licked his finger one time and now he wanted to avoid me again? It wasn't even his dick. If he knew what he'd done to me in my dreams he'd be in Montana by now.

He stood up. And for a second, I thought he was just going to walk away. But then he put his hand out for me. "Luckily for you, I have a plus one. Would you like to be my date?"

"Your date?"

"If you'll do me the honor." He bowed slightly like he was asking me to dance with him circa 1850.

He always surprised me. "Why, yes, sir. I'd love to accompany you to the ball." I placed my hand in his.

He laughed and helped me out of my chair. "There are two conditions though."

Anything. I just nodded.

"No more of this Rule #8 nonsense. I've never been good at sharing."

It was somehow like my dream but also the opposite. I nodded again.

"And promise me you won't go to Club Onyx again without me. It's something we should really be experiencing together."

I nodded. But…then I started freaking out. His note told me to go to Club Onyx. But it also said not to open it unless he disappeared. *Damn it.* I started to sweat. I needed to tell him everything. I started to hold my breath because I didn't know what else to do.

"Good."

"Good," I said. But then I shook my head. "Wait. Did you just ask me to be your plus one to the party? Or did you just ask me to be your girlfriend?" Because those conditions made it seem like it was more than a one-date kind of thing.

"I've been running from my past for a really long time. I'm so tired of not having roots anywhere."

I was pretty sure he was very well known in NYC. And he had Nigel and his best friend Matt who definitely wasn't Matthew Caldwell…

"I don't want to run anymore. My past is complicated to say the least. And when I thought you were DODO…" he shook his head. "My paranoia has gotten the best of me over the years. I thought I was out of time. And I just kept thinking about…you. Really I think about you constantly."

My heart was racing so fast that it actually hurt.

"I don't want to waste any more of what little time we have together."

Little time? I didn't dwell on it, because I was pretty sure he was asking me something huge. "So that means…"

He smiled. "I have to warn you, I'm not very good at this. I haven't dated in a really long time. But I think we should give it a go. Normally I'd talk to your father about the courting process…but since I've never met the man…let's just go crazy and do it the modern way."

"You mean dating?" Because he'd said a lot of weird shit and I really needed to know this answer.

He reached out and tucked a strand of my matted hair behind my ear. "Be my girlfriend."

It wasn't really a question. More or a statement. A declaration I'd been dying to hear. I squealed and threw my arms around his neck. I was un-wifey-zoned! I'd freaking done it!

"Your skin is so sticky," he said with a laugh.

For a second I thought about the cum all over my face in my dream. But then remembered I'd had champagne thrown in my face. And cake smeared around my mouth. None of that mattered though. We could be weird and sticky together. I kissed him. And then kept kissing him as he carried me out to the limo.

But as soon as he set me down in the limo, I pulled back. I couldn't start a relationship without getting something off my chest. "I have a confession."

"Okay…"

"I do promise I won't go to Club Onyx again without you. But I only wanted to go to Club Onyx in the first place because I was bad and opened your note that I wasn't supposed to open unless you disappeared. But it's too late now, because it's already done. And it said to go to Club Onyx to find what I was looking for. And I was looking for your secrets. That's the only reason I went early. But I promise not to go again now. Please don't break up with me already." I waited for him to curse me out.

Instead he just laughed. "I should have guessed you'd open it right away. Ash, it doesn't matter. And I'm not going to break up with you. Or disappear. I'm not the one going anywhere." He looked sad for a second and I had no idea why. I wasn't going anywhere either.

"You promise?" I asked.

He pulled me onto his lap as the limo sped off. "I promise." And then he kissed me again. And again. He kissed me the whole way back to my apartment.

I stared up at him as he opened up the door to my apartment complex. I didn't want tonight to end. And yet…here we were. I stared up at…*my boyfriend.* I tried not to squeal.

"Until tomorrow."

I felt like I was floating. "Until tomorrow."

He lifted my hand and placed a kiss on my knuckles before walking back to his limo. But before he climbed in, he turned around. "Oh, and Ash?"

"Yes?" My voice came out breathy and weird. This wasn't real life. How had I gone from stalking him to dating him? I mean…him stalking me.

"There's a surprise for you upstairs."

A surprise? I looked over my shoulder expecting to see a FedEx man leaving the building. But of course there was no one there. I turned back around and Nigel was already driving Tanner away. How did he keep getting into my apartment?

Dumb question. It didn't matter. I wanted to go see what my freaking boyfriend was about to surprise me with now.

Chapter 63
THE SPACEBOY COLLECTION
Thursday

This was the best night of my life. I hurried up the stairs to my apartment. Literally nothing could ruin my mood. Not the fact that I was running in heels. Or that I was still sticky from champagne. I couldn't wait to see what Tanner's surprise was.

But when I turned out of the stairwell, my heart sank.

Oh no.

There were seven big boxes stacked by my apartment. And Homeless Rutherford was next to them.

"Hey!" I yelled. "What are you doing? Those are mine!"

He dropped something and then looked over and gave me a saucy little wave. Then he sashayed away down the hall. I'd seen him happy before, but never like this. It was like he was at a pizza buffet and had just gone to town on the whole spread. Except it hadn't been a pizza buffet. It had been my presents from Tanner.

"You better not have licked anything!" I yelled to him. But I knew in my heart that he had.

I scanned the boxes to try to identify what he'd licked. An opened letter sat on top of one of the boxes. That must have been what he'd dropped when I caught him. I wanted so badly to read it, but I had to take proper precautions. So I opened up my apartment to get my rubber gloves.

"Hey," said someone as I walked into my apartment.

"Ah! Rape!" I threw my keys at the rapist.

Chastity just barely dodged them. "It's just me! Calm down!"

"Sweet lord, woman. Why would you scare me like that?"

"Why would *I* scare *you*? You're the one who texted me that Tanner was a vampire and that I needed to call the police if you weren't home by midnight."

"Did I do that?"

"Yes!"

"Well in my defense, I just had the best night ever, and…"

"And is he a vampire or not?"

"I don't know. Maybe." Honestly I didn't even care. If he was a vampire, he hadn't tried to kill me yet. And he was amazing and perfect and beautiful. I couldn't walk away now. I was in too deep.

Someone knocked on my open door. My next-door neighbor. "You okay?" she asked. "I thought I heard you scream something about rape…"

"Yeah," I said. "But it was just Chastity."

She gave Chastity a weird look. "So you're good? Rutherford didn't try to rape you?"

"No. But I think he licked my boxes."

My neighbor laughed. "I don't know why he always licks your stuff. See you later." She walked back toward her apartment.

I frowned and turned to Chastity. "Did she just say Homeless Rutherford only ever licks *my* stuff? What the actual hell? I assumed he licked everyone's everything. Why did he single me out?"

"Maybe he likes you," Chastity said.

"Gross. And speaking of licking things…why didn't you bring those boxes in?"

"What boxes?" asked Chastity.

"All the ones outside my apartment."

"They must have just been delivered. Oooh. What's inside?"

"I don't know yet, but I know they're from Tanner. I need my rubber gloves."

"More Odegaards?!" Chastity was over by the door in a flash. Apparently she didn't care that the boxes might be contaminated, because she lifted up the certainly-licked letter.

I read over her shoulder:

Ash,

I had Odegaard design a special Spaceboy themed collection for the launch party tomorrow. I can't wait to see which outfit you choose.

See you at the pier at 8 pm.

-Tanner

P.S. Chastity can take her pick as well, but I have a feeling I know which outfit she'll want…

"Tanner is officially the most amazing man ever," said Chastity. "He's definitely going to ask you out tomorrow at the party."

"I'm 100% sure that he won't." I tried to act casual. But I was definitely beaming.

"Why? Did something happen at the cake tasting?"

"Not really. Just the usual… Had a wild sex dream on the way there. And then we tried some cake. And then he asked me to be HIS FREAKING GIRLFRIEND!"

"WHAT?! Are you serious?!"

I nodded.

"Ahhh!" She tossed the note aside, bear-hugged me, and then started jumping up and down with me. "We did it!"

"I have to admit, I didn't think that your crazy advice would work. But it totally did. He was so freaking jealous about what happened at Club Onyx that he couldn't even help himself."

"I told you it would work!"

I nodded. "I owe you one."

"I'll be more than happy to take half of these clothes as my payment. But before we get to that, I need to know… Did you two bang it out on the way home? I bet that limo ride was fire emoji fire emoji fire emoji." She fanned herself with her hand. "Oh! And how big is his penis? Eight inches?" She stared at me. "Nine inches? A FOOT?!"

I laughed. "We didn't bang. Just lots of making out."

"For real?"

"Yes."

"Weird."

"Why is that weird? I think he's just like…old-fashioned or something. Maybe he's waiting for us to say the L-word before we bang." He had briefly mentioned courtship. He was just an old soul. And a little weird. *Just like me.*

"Well then why didn't you tell him that you love him?"

I laughed. "Because I don't love him yet." It was a lie and I was pretty sure she knew it.

"Who are you most excited to see every day at work?" asked Chastity.

"You," I lied.

Chastity stared at me. "Really?"

"Fine. Tanner."

"Mhm. And what do you think about at night when you're trying to fall asleep?"

"Whether or not I have to pee again before I fall asleep."

"What else?" she asked.

"Tanner."

"And why do you do your makeup and put on real-girl clothes every day?"

"To look good for Tanner."

"I rest my case. You love Tanner. And really…even if you don't, you should still just say it. Anything to get that D, girl."

I tried to hide my smile. I did pretty much spend every waking moment thinking about him. And seeing him was always the best part of my day… God, I was so in love with him my heart was about to explode! I tried to focus on the boxes he'd sent me. I needed to get all this love talk under control. The last thing I needed was to accidentally tell him I loved him and scare him off. For now, we were boyfriend and girlfriend. That was perfect.

"So are we gonna open these boxes or what?" I asked.

***

"I don't know if you love Tanner or not," said Chastity. "But I love him." She'd said that a lot last night while she'd tried on every outfit he'd sent. And most of this morning. And this afternoon.

"Look at this outfit!" she said. "It's exactly what I envisioned." She turned to check out her ass in one of the dozens of mirrors in my gigantic closet.

"Don't forget these." I handed her some metallic blue thigh-high boots.

"YES." She pulled on the boots and then finished things off with a big space helmet. Just like she wanted, she was a female version of the Spaceboy dancers. I looked away just in time as she unzipped the white bodysuit and shook her tits in the mirror. "I'm totally gonna fuck Spaceboy tonight. And you're gonna fuck Tanner. The only question is…which outfit shall you use to seduce him?"

I stared at the pile of metallic blue and pink clothes and shoes. We'd been in my closet trying them on pretty much all of last night and most of today.

"I don't know," I said. "How about you choose for me?"

"Okay." Chastity picked up the tiniest little bikini that had ever been made. "Wear this."

My eyes got big. "No! I can't wear that in public!"

"You told me to choose…"

"Well choose again. That was a bad choice."

The metallic pink lingerie she chose next was almost somehow worse.

"Nope. No way. This is a classy work party. Not a gentlemen's club."

"It's a Spaceboy concert. Futuristic lingerie is a perfect fit."

We went back and forth like that for another hour or so before finally settling on a blue bikini, thigh-high boots just like the ones Chastity was wearing, and a mesh cover-up. I went to the bathroom and did my makeup before sending a picture to Madison to see what she thought. Her response came a second later:

Madison: You look beautiful. Liz agrees. Btw, do you have an extra ticket for her?

Liz!? No! Why would she tell Liz about the party? Having Liz there would totally ruin the vibe.

Also, Madison thinking I looked beautiful was a bad sign. It probably meant this outfit was way too sexy… Or that I looked butch or something. But there was no time to change. Because Nigel had just appeared out of nowhere.

I almost screamed when I saw his reflection in the bathroom mirror. Where had he come from? "Nigel?"

"Mistress Ash." He was staring at my tub instead of at me. "It's time to go."

"One second." I took a deep breath and put on a second coat of mascara. Chastity had most likely let him in. So it was all fine. As far as I could tell, Nigel was harmless. Unless he'd been instructed to bag me again.

"I think Chastity and I are both ready," I said and turned to him.

He blinked at me. "Chastity?"

"Yeah."

"Who is this person you speak of?"

"My friend. You met her the other night. And she just let you in."

Nigel shrugged. "I don't recall."

What was with him and hating Chastity? "Um. Okay. Well, we're ready."

"I guess there's room in the limo for Chastain."

Chastain? Come on, he'd literally just heard me say her name.

"Bring her if you must, Mistress Ash."

I grabbed my Spaceboy sunglasses and headed out the door. It was party time.

Chapter 64

MONKEY PARTY

Friday

I could hardly believe my eyes as we pulled up to the pier.

"Wow," I said.

"Right?" agreed Chastity. "That's the biggest yacht I've ever seen. It's like a mini cruise ship."

"Huh?" I hadn't even noticed the yacht. I'd been too busy staring at Tanner standing on the pier. The way the lights on the pier reflected on his metallic blue tuxedo was captivating. But I was more intrigued by how much leg he was showing, because the bottom half of his tuxedo ended a few inches above his knees. Tuxedo shorts. Most men couldn't have pulled it off. But he had the confidence to make it work - matching Crocs and all.

Yeah, my boyfriend was hot AF.

I hardly even waited for Nigel to bring the limo to a stop before I jumped out and ran over to Tanner.

He lowered his Spaceboy-style visor and gave me the up-down as I approached.

Guess he likes my outfit as much as I like his.

"Are you stalking me, baby?" he asked as he pulled me into his arms. He didn't wait for a response. He just kissed me like he hadn't seen me in years. He groaned into my mouth.

God, he was so sexy. I wanted him to do that again and again. I buried my fingers in his hair to deepen the kiss.

His hand slid to my ass and squeezed before he pulled back. "Welcome to my yacht," he said, gesturing to the massive boat behind him.

"*Your* yacht?" I asked.

"Who else's yacht would you expect me to use?"

There was no way one person owned such a big yacht. "Stop messing with me."

"I'm not. Come on, I'll give you a tour before everyone else arrives."

Chastity, Nigel, and I followed him around the massive ship. Each room was more impressive than the next. It was like we were in a floating castle. Complete with a two-story foyer, an old-fashioned armory, a great room the size of my secret closet, and lots of caged monkeys in space helmets and…lederhosen?

"Why are the monkeys wearing lederhosen?" I asked.

Tanner tilted his head to the side. He seemed as confused as I was. "Nigel? Could you please explain?"

"Of course, Master," he said with a little bow. "You asked me to get them something spacious."

"No," said Tanner. "I said to get them something *space-y*. As in, pertaining to outer space."

"Well that was very unclear. But I think it's safe to categorize this as a happy accident, because the monkeys look quite dapper. I dare say they'll be the talk of the party. And they'll be comfortable in their spacious outfits."

I'd only ever seen lederhosen on Nigel and the monkeys. And it didn't look all that spacious to me. If anything it looked tight and uncomfortable. If I was one of those monkeys I'd be screaming and getting naked. But they looked happy enough. Maybe Nigel was right.

"As ridiculous as it is, I think this will be good," said Chastity. "People on Twitter won't be able to stop talking about these little cuties. Isn't that right?" She stuck her arm in a cage and petted one of the monkeys. It grabbed her arm and pulled her closer while another one tried to unzip her bodysuit. "Ah! You naughty little monkey!" She got free and swatted his hand away just in time.

"Be careful," said Nigel. "They're a bit handsy."

Chastity shrugged. "Can't blame them for having good taste. Let's hope Spaceboy acts the same way."

"When you say Spaceboy..." said Tanner. "Do you mean the entire band? Or just DJ Spaceboy?"

"Hopefully all of them. But I'd settle for just one if I had to."

"Good luck with that. I tried to get you a backstage pass, but they said they don't do that sorta thing. And I've tried multiple times to get them to join the Society. Apparently they're too focused on their music to have any fun."

Chastity waved his comment away. "Sounds like a fun challenge. Where can I find them?"

"If they didn't show, I'll be happy to fill in," offered Nigel. "I've been working on a new single that is...what are the kids saying these days?" He stroked his wispy mustache. "It's a bop. My bars are straight fire."

I stared at him. Was Nigel an aspiring rapper? If so, I *needed* to hear it.

"I would love that," said Tanner. "But unfortunately Spaceboy is already in the building. The concert will be starting in..." He checked his watch. "Five minutes. Wow, we better get up there or we're gonna miss it." He led us through a twisted maze of magnificent rooms until we came out on the roof deck of his yacht. About a hundred people all dressed in wild metallic outfits were all milling around. The main dance floor was sectioned off by black drapes. We walked over and peered through.

Spaceboy was performing on the other side, but their only audience was a couple in their pajamas snuggled up on a couch. They were some influencers we'd paid to livestream the whole thing.

"How many views do we have so far?" I asked.

Chastity pulled out her phone. "Only about 1K so far. The feed looks good though."

I looked over her shoulder. It did look good. The way they were filming it really made it look like they were in their basement watching Spaceboy on TV.

"I hope this works," I said. In theory, it felt like the perfect plan to get people talking about Wineflix and Chill. But it wasn't a sure thing.

The girl on the couch sat up and turned to her husband. "Want some wine?"

"Sure," he said. "What do we have?"

"How about some Wineflix and Chill?"

"What's that?"

The girl shrugged. "I dunno. The box says something about turning an ordinary night into a party." She poured them each a glass.

Here we go.

The second they took a sip, things went NUTS.

The base dropped. The curtains all disappeared. Fireworks went off. And we all rushed the dance floor. Not just me, Chastity, Tanner, and Nigel. But *everyone*. In the blink of an eye the quiet scene of some couple snuggling in the basement had turned into a wild party. Even the couple tore off their pajamas and started dancing.

The best part, though, was the monkeys. They were all dancing in their cages and swatting at the UFO-style drones flying all around.

"You pulled it off!" yelled Tanner over the music as he spun me around.

"*We* pulled it off," I yelled back.

Dancing always made me feel so self-conscious, but Tanner's gaze on me made all my worries melt away. For once in my life, I didn't care if I looked like a fool. As long as Tanner liked what he saw, I was perfectly happy to dance my heart out. I just mimicked every move he made. Or at least…I tried to. He had a move for everything. And he never seemed to get tired. That was good news for what I suspected we'd be doing later that night…

My favorite dance of the night was when we went over to one of the cages and mimicked what the monkeys were doing.

Actually, that's not true. My *favorite* dance was when Tanner led something called a quadrille. It was like a weird formal square dance sorta deal. It made absolutely no sense to do it to a Spaceboy song, but that just made it even more fun.

Thanks to Chastity, the quadrille quickly devolved into her just grinding on every guy she could find.

I was happy to follow her lead and grind on Tanner. And based on his raging boner, I was pretty sure I was doing a good job.

"I have a surprise for you!" he yelled.

"What is it?" I yelled back. "You gonna cream your shorts?" Just as I said it, the song ended and everything was completely quiet. Except for me. Asking Tanner if he was gonna cream his shorts. *Fuck my life.*

Everyone stared at me.

It felt like the silence lasted a lifetime. But then Chastity yelled, "Hey Spaceboy!" She pointed at one of the dancers, unzipped her suit, and let her tits free.

All the guys on the dance floor cheered for her. And then Spaceboy started playing again.

Bless your slutty soul, Chastity! She was a lifesaver.

I rushed off the dance floor, hoping that if I disappeared quickly enough no one would remember what I had just done.

"Sorry about that," I said.

Tanner laughed. "Sorry for what? Not making me cream my shorts? I admit, you were close. Where'd you learn to dance like that?"

"No idea." That was a lie. I knew exactly where I'd learned to dance like that. I'd never been confident enough to dance in public, but I happened to love jamming out to a Nelly CD I'd pilfered from my older brother. "Where'd *you* learn that weird square dance thing?"

"You learn a lot of different dances when you move all over. Anyway…do you want your surprise?"

"So you do want me to grind on you until you cum?" I spun around and shook my ass for him.

He slapped my ass and then gave me a good squeeze.

God.

"I want that very much, yes. But that's not your surprise. Come with me." He took my hand and led me down some stairs to a lounge area with a bar. We were the only ones there.

I was like 99% sure that his surprise was going to involve cum. But now I was starting to think it was going to end up somewhere other than his shorts.

"So what's my surprise?" I not so subtly pushed my breasts together for him.

"Well aren't you eager. Let's get something to drink first." He opened the fridge. There were tons of beers, a few bottles of liquor, some bottles of water. And then I saw the crown jewel of party drinks.

"Is that Kool-Aid?" I asked.

Tanner grabbed the pitcher of red juice and spun it around to check the handwritten label. It was indeed Kool-Aid. "Looks like it. You want some?"

I nodded and he poured some into a solo cup for me. I'd already had a few glasses of wine upstairs. Which was probably why I'd yelled about him creaming in his shorts. It was best not to drink any more around Tanner. Because drinking made it much more likely that I'd either embarrass myself or try to rape him. And as much as I thought he wanted it, I didn't want to make any more mistakes.

I took a big sip and scooched onto a bar stool. "*Now* can I have my big surprise?" That sounded way more sexual than I'd meant for it to. But really...I wanted my big surprise.

He pointed at my cup. "You're drinking it. I know how much you loved it as a kid."

"Oh..." I tried to hide my disappointment but failed miserably. And how did he know that I loved Kool-Aid as a kid? Was his PI really that good? If so, maybe there was a chance we'd find Rosalie after all. I took a huge sip. It was nothing compared to the sex I'd thought he was gonna surprise me with, but it was still delicious.

"Wow, I didn't think you'd actually fall for that. I swear you get more gullible by the hour."

I glared at him. "I'm going to murder you in your sleep." But the joke was on him. I freaking loved Kool-Aid.

He laughed. "Not after you see my real surprise." He tossed me a small package. About the size of a ring box.

Chapter 65

A KOOL-AID PROPOSAL

Friday

Oh my God. Oh my God! Was he about to propose? If so, it was way too soon. Right? We'd only known each other for like two months. And been dating for 24 hours. Although he had been stalking me for a while before that. Or I'd been stalking him. Or whatever. We never could agree on that.

I laughed nervously and pressed my arms against my body to try to stop myself from sweating. It didn't work. And my throat was suddenly dry because all the liquid in my body was heading straight to my armpits. I downed the rest of my Kool-Aid.

"Open it," he said.

My fingers were shaking as I unwrapped the tiny package. Yup, definitely a ring box. This was insane. *He* was insane. But maybe I was insane too. Because I kind of wanted this. Nope, I *definitely* wanted it. Part of me was terrified about moving too quickly. But the other half of me just knew. Tanner was it for me. He was the one. I could imagine a forever with him so easily. Could he see it too? I expected to look up and find him on one knee. Or for him to at least snatch it from my hand so he could present it properly. But nope. He just stood there, watching me expectantly.

I flipped the lid open and… *Oh.* It wasn't a ring. Which was probably for the best. It was too soon. Way too soon. I swallowed hard and looked back down at the box. Actually, it wasn't jewelry at all. Instead it was a key and a flash drive.

I pushed the key aside and focused on the drive. "Another copy of my sex tape?" I asked. *Oh no. He watched it.* "Did you like what you saw?" *Shit.* Had I just said that out loud? My stupid dry throat was speaking by itself. I slid off the barstool and poured myself more Kool-Aid.

He smiled. "It's not another copy. Your first Society wish was for shoes and revenge on Joe, remember?"

What was with me and terrible wishes? "Right. So you stole his credit card and used it to buy tons of Odegaards. Boom. Done." Revenge was best served with Kool-Aid.

Tanner nodded. "That was the original plan. But after I found out about him blackmailing you, it felt woefully insufficient."

"So…what's this?"

He hit a button and part of the counter flipped up to reveal some sort of built-in computer screen. "See for yourself." He plugged the flash drive into a USB port on the side of the screen. Windows Media Player popped up and video footage of a hotel room started rolling.

Sierra was straddling Joe on the bed, her long (and very fake) red hair falling over some tight workout clothes.

"Okay, two questions," I said. "One, why do you have a creepy surveillance video of Joe and Sierra? And two, why would you think that I'd want to see this?"

"Just keep watching. And make sure the sound is on."

I turned the volume up.

"Are you sure we should be doing this?" asked Sierra. "Didn't you just get engaged?"

Wait, what? I squinted and looked harder at the girl. It looked like Sierra. Long red hair. Impossibly small waist. Huge boobs. But it wasn't her. This girl must have just gone to the same plastic surgeon as her.

"Maybe," replied Joe as he squeezed her ass. "But what my fiancée doesn't know won't hurt her. And anyway…we're not married yet. So it's not technically cheating." He unbuttoned his shirt and threw it on the ground.

"Damn," said the girl, running her hand along his mediocre abs. "Your future wife is one lucky girl."

"Not as lucky as me."

"Because of your engagement? Or because you get to touch these?" She pulled her sports bra over her head.

Joe laughed and squeezed her breasts. "What do you think?"

God, he was disgusting.

The girl slithered down until she was kneeling in front of him. "Ever been blown by a Cali girl before?"

"Nope."

I turned to Tanner. "I really don't want to see this."

"Trust me. You do." He pointed back to the screen.

I reluctantly looked back.

"Then get ready for the best blowjob of your life," the girl said.

"Only a blowjob?" Joe sounded so disappointed.

"Well you just told me you're engaged," said the girl as she put her hair up into a messy bun.

"All the more reason to fuck you. Fucking only one person for the rest of my life is going to be so boring."

I spit out a sip of my Kool-Aid. "Ha! Like he's actually gonna stay faithful to Sierra after the wedding."

"Yeah," agreed Tanner. "That seems unlikely. But keep watching. It gets better."

"You're so bad," said the girl, pushing his thigh playfully. Then she yanked his pants down and laughed.

"What?" asked Joe.

"It's so…cute," said the girl. The camera didn't have a good view of his member, but I'd seen it plenty of times. *Cute* was a generous description. *Disappointing* would have been more appropriate.

"It's normal-sized," snapped Joe. "Big cocks are overrated. It's all about what I can do with it."

"I hope that's true," said the girl. And then she got to sucking.

I was about to turn it off. I didn't need to see Joe bang some random girl. Hearing her insult his penis and then seeing him start to cheat on Sierra was enough. I didn't need to see them get down and dirty.

"Well that was amazing," I said as I put down my Kool-Aid and reached for the mouse. "How'd you get…"

I was interrupted by the girl choking and pulling back, cum dripping from her mouth. "What the fuck?" she said, but it was all garbled. And then she did the most amazing thing ever: she stood up and coughed, spitting his load right in his face. For a second she looked embarrassed. But then she just rolled with it. "Thanks for the warning, asshole," she said sarcastically. She wiped the side of her mouth. "I don't care how many Lakers tickets you can get me, it's not worth dealing with your tiny, overeager dick."

I was speechless. I just sat there, staring at Joe with a face full of his own cum. I couldn't help but laugh. Joe was such a freaking loser. I couldn't believe that I'd let his happiness with Sierra drive me crazy. They weren't happy. They may have looked happy in their Instagram pictures, but their whole relationship was a joke. Kind of like Joe's sexual prowess. Total. Joke.

I couldn't stop laughing. Which made Tanner start laughing too. I clutched my stomach where a cramp was starting to form.

"Has Sierra seen this yet?" I somehow managed to ask through my laughter.

"Nope. This is the only copy. What you do with it is entirely up to you." Tanner popped the flash drive out of the computer and handed it to me.

"How'd you get this footage?"

Tanner smiled. "I have my ways."

I should have asked for more details, but all I could think about was how priceless it would be to see the look on Sierra's face when she saw this. I just needed to figure out the best way to present it to her. Invite her out for a drink? Oh! Or maybe show it to her with Joe in the room too. That way I'd get to see both their faces. Two for the price of one. I started giggling again just thinking about it.

I just wanted to sing and dance and scream. And lie down. My body so badly wanted to plank. Maybe it was because my arms were so heavy. Would Tanner mind if I planked right now on this counter? Probably not… More importantly, why had I never thought to spit Joe's cum in his face? I kind of wanted to watch it again.

"This is so amazing," I said as I looked down at the flash drive. "I can't believe you got this footage for me. I freaking love you." The second I said it, I clapped my hand over my mouth. *Shit!* Why did I say that to him? Yes, it was the truth. But we'd only been dating for 24 hours. I couldn't drop the L-bomb that fast! Only psychos did that! "I mean…I don't love you love you. I love you as in…love ya', bro. Buddy old pal." I lightly punched his arm.

He gave me a funny look.

Oh God. What had I just done? Before he could say anything, I jumped off my chair and ran out of the room. But my brain was so foggy that I forgot we were on a boat. As I flipped over the railing and fell three stories into the Hudson River, I realized that the Kool-Aid had been spiked.

Chapter 66
THE L WORD
Friday

Falling three stories into the river sobered me up *fast.* My initial belly flop probably would have been enough, but then the water was freaking freezing. Worst of all though was the panic of watching the yacht float away.

Was I going to die here? It seemed like a fitting end for me - embarrassing myself beyond belief and then drunkenly throwing myself overboard. Drowning in my awkwardness.

It was official. I'd tried so hard not to do it. But here it was. Incident #6. *Damn it! That's way too many incidents!*

"Help!" I screamed. But no one heard me. *Yup….this is how I'm going to die.* "Help!!!" I screamed again. A guy looked over the side of the yacht and pointed at me. A second later Tanner dove over the railing. *Oh, thank God.*

He wrapped his strong arms around me and pulled me back to the yacht. Nigel lowered a little ladder for us to climb. Tanner let me go up first. A whole crowd had gathered to see the dumb girl who'd fallen overboard. *Great.* My face flushed. Everyone was staring at me. No…not just me. They were staring at my breasts.

Fuck. My. Life. My coverup and bikini top must have caught on the railing as I flipped overboard. Because the only things left on my body were my bikini bottom and boots. Which meant I was flashing everyone. I threw my hands over my breasts. Incident #6 was worse than I'd ever imagined. It just kept piling on. I was still drowning in awkwardness even though I was standing on two shaking legs. I considered jumping overboard again to hide, but the water was too damned cold for that.

Tanner wrapped a towel around me and glared at the crowd. "Show's over," he said, waving everyone away.

"Thank you," I said, my teeth chattering from the cold.

"What the hell were you thinking?" asked Tanner. "And why'd you get naked in the river? That water is freezing. Are you trying to catch a cold?"

I slapped his arm. "I didn't mean to do either! This is all your fault. What did you put in that Kool-Aid? Did you roofie me?!"

A smile tugged on the corner of his mouth. "Ooohhh. It all makes sense now." He laughed. "Sorry about that. I didn't realize it was spiked."

"I'm glad you think my humiliation is so funny." My wet hair dripped onto my shoulders. I pulled the towel tighter around myself.

"I mean…have you ever seen someone run straight into a railing and flop off the side of a yacht?"

I tried to picture it. He was right - it was pretty hilarious. "I think I might need you to reenact it for me," I said.

"Maybe some other time." He wrapped another towel around my shoulders and I finally stopped shivering.

"Well at least be a gentleman and immediately sell all your shares of Wineflix and Chill."

"Why? You worked so hard to make this all possible."

"Um…maybe because everyone in the company just saw my boobs?" *And heard me yell on the dancefloor about making you cream your shorts.*

"They're probably all too drunk to remember. And you shouldn't be too embarrassed. You have lovely boobs." His eyes went to the knot in my towel.

"Oh yeah?" I opened my towel and flashed him. *What am I doing? Oh, right. I'm still kinda drunk.* Not drunk enough to tell him I loved him again, though. God, what had I been thinking? I needed to sober up and fast. I tapped the side of my face like I was trying to slap myself sobber. *Yeah, I'm so drunk.*

"So about what I said earlier..." *Well, this conversation will definitely sober me up.*

An awkward silence filled the air.

Kill me now. "I wasn't trying to say that I *loved* you. I was just so happy that Joe and Sierra's relationship is a total joke. Combine that with the spiked Kool-Aid, and I chose my words poorly."

"I really didn't think anything of it," said Tanner.

"Oh." *Great!* So why was he staring at me like he was thinking about it? His eyebrows lowered as he continued to stare at me. I swallowed hard.

"At least, I didn't until you totally freaked out and jumped overboard. That was my first hint that maybe you had actually meant that you love me."

"What?" I laughed awkwardly. "Ha, no. I wasn't freaking out about saying I loved you. I just wanted to go for a swim."

"You're a terrible liar. And that's just one of the many things that I love about you."

"Don't mock me."

Tanner shook his head. Then he grabbed either side of my face and looked into my eyes. "Ash. From the moment you started stalking me, I knew that you were special. But I didn't know how special you were until you hit me with a door and laughed in my face. Seriously...who does that?"

"I didn't mean to."

"I know." He brushed a strand of wet hair off my face. "And that's another thing I love about you. You never mean to do any of the crazy stuff that you do. It just comes naturally. I'm so sorry I've been pushing you away all this time. I'm just...I'm not used to something like this. Something real. My whole life has just been lies. Running from one city to the next. Waiting for DODO to catch up to me."

I couldn't speak. Or maybe I just didn't want to speak. Or move. I just wanted this very moment to last forever.

"I've had close calls with DODO before. But this time, when you bugged my phone...it was different. Because instead of grabbing my go-bag and running, I grabbed a pen and wrote you a letter. And in that moment, I realized that I cared more about spending one more night with you than I did about DODO bagging me. And I can't run away from something like that. For once in my life I want to have something real, even if it's the last thing I do. You're it for me, Ash. I love you."

I wiped a tear from my cheek. That was the sweetest thing anyone had ever said to me. "Is this real life?" I asked. "Please tell me I'm not having another crazy vampire sex dream?"

He smiled and kissed me. And kissed me. And kissed me some more. Just as I reached for the button on his tuxedo shorts, a horrible whooping sound filled the air. Then people started screaming as glass shattered.

"What the hell is that?" I asked.

One of the Spaceboy drones dropped out of the sky and smashed on the deck a few feet in front of us. It was followed by a lederhosen-clad monkey. He did a little roll and then sprung to his feet. I couldn't see his eyes under his space helmet, but I was pretty sure the little pervert was staring right at my towel.

"The monkeys got free!" yelled a woman running towards us. One monkey jumped on her shoulders while another tore her bikini top off. "Ahhh!"

Another woman befell a similar fate a second later. And someone else jumped into the river to avoid the monkeys.

More crashing and screaming. Everyone started running around. More people jumped into the water. I watched as another monkey lifted up some girl's skirt and slapped her butt. God, those handsy little monkeys were ruining the launch party!

"Do something!" I screamed to Tanner as more people hurled themselves into the freezing water. *Fuck!* This was being live-streamed to people all over the world!

Tanner lowered his eyebrows and just watched the scene unfold.

How was he so calm right now? I watched as one of the monkeys stole some man's toupee and started sashaying around like they were channeling Homeless Rutherford. I wanted to laugh. Or cry. What the hell was happening?

"Tanner!" I screamed as one of the monkeys swung a sword around that he must have stolen from the armory. The little guy started running toward us.

"Enough," said Tanner. Then he snapped his fingers and all the monkeys stopped. It was like they were frozen. They looked so docile and cute after almost destroying the whole boat and sexually assaulting all the guests. The one running toward us dropped his sword and sat down.

"How did you…?"

Tanner smiled at me. His voice must have been so commanding that all the monkeys just obeyed him. He was such a boss. A hot, sexy, total boss.

But then his smile disappeared behind a thick black bag. Someone dressed in all black commando gear pulled him backwards off the side of the boat and into a little dinghy. It was already speeding away by the time I could process what had just happened.

Oh fuck. "Tanner!" I screamed and ran to the railing. *Oh God. No.* "Tanner!" But the boat had disappeared into the darkness faster than I thought possible.

I couldn't care less about the disaster of a party behind me. Tanner had just been taken. By…DODO. *I think.* Or maybe it was Club Onyx? Damn it! I had no idea. But those assholes had just stolen my boyfriend!

Not on my watch. Whoever they were. Whatever they were. They'd messed with the wrong girl. Because I was a great freaking stalker. And they were about to get stalked so good. Tanner had nothing to fear.

I picked up the sword that the pervert monkey had dropped. *I got this.*

What's Next?

So I meant for this to be a standalone, but I couldn't *quite* fit Ash and Tanner's whole story into this beef book. *The Society #StalkerProblems* is 168,000 words. That's twice the girth of a normal book! Maybe epic-romcoms will be a new genre now. So…

Ash and Tanner will be back next year in *The Society Book 2!* Or at least Ash will be back. Who knows if she'll find Tanner…

In the meantime, you can see exactly what Tanner was thinking when he first caught Ash stalking him. And maybe learn his secret?!

To get your free copy of *The Society #Tanner*, go to:

www.ivysmoak.com/tssp-pb

A Note From Ivy

After reading this girthy book, you're probably thinking 3 things right now:

1) Ash is your spirit animal. #HorseFacts

2) You wish you had #StalkerProblems like Ash, because Tanner is amazing.

And most importantly…

3) You need to know Tanner's secret!

Girl, same. I promise you'll find out Tanner's secret soon. And as for wanting some #StalkerProblems of your own? You could make a wish! After all, the Society is all about granting wishes. And no one said the Society was a fictional place. This book is based entirely on facts! #HorseFacts.

Make your wildest dreams come true by placing your wish at www.ivysmoak.com/thesociety2021. (Password: PinkOcelot)

Yes, I officially wrote the craziest book ever. But there was a reason for all these hilarious words! Ash is all of us. Yup. You heard that right! We're all awkward and weird in our own way. And I'm hoping that living in Ash's shoes for a few days made you realize that being weird is actually a great thing. We should all embrace our weirdness. And have fun doing it. Shake off the haters and live your life however the heck you want! Penis booping and all. We've all been there, am I right?

And since you made it this far, you're automatically a card-carrying member of the Single Girl Rules. I don't care if you're single or not. It just happened. Boom! And I'd love to see you bring your favorite #SingleGirlRules to life on TikTok! Channel your inner-Chastity and bring the sass. The sassier the TikToks, the better.

And don't forget the most important Single Girl Rule of all – Rule #1: Boys are replaceable. Friends are forever. So make sure you come meet all your new besties in the Smoaksters Facebook Group! Where we dish about books and all the hot goss.

P.S. I'm sorry about all the #sickburns, Steve Forbes. I have no beef with you. For some reason all the sass just came out naturally once I started talking about you and your dumb site. Probably because you're basic. See – I can't stop! Seriously though, I actually really like looking up random celebrities' net worth on your site. And I'm sure you're not basic at all. <3

Ivy Smoak
Wilmington, DE
www.ivysmoak.com

About the Author

Ivy Smoak is the Wall Street Journal, USA Today, and Amazon #1 bestselling author of *The Hunted Series*. Her books have sold over 2 million copies worldwide.

When she's not writing, you can find Ivy binge watching too many TV shows, taking long walks, playing outside, and generally refusing to act like an adult. She lives with her husband in Delaware.

Facebook: IvySmoakAuthor
Instagram: @IvySmoakAuthor
Goodreads: IvySmoak

Recommend *The Society #StalkerProblems* for your next book club!

Book club questions available at:
www.ivysmoak.com/bookclub